THE
BODY
ON THE
DOORSTEP

THE
BODY
ON THE
DOORSTEP

A. J. MACKENZIE

ZAFFRE

First published in Great Britain in 2016 by

Zaffre Publishing
80–81 Wimpole St, London, W1G 9RE
www.zaffrebooks.co.uk

A CIP catalogue record for this book is available from the British Library.

Hardback ISBN: 978-1-78576-113-3
Ebook ISBN: 978-1-78576-121-8

1 3 5 7 9 10 8 6 4 2

Printed and bound by Clays Ltd, St Ives Plc
Typeset by IDSUK (DataConnection) Ltd

Zaffre Publishing is an imprint of Bonnier Publishing Fiction,
a Bonnier Publishing company
www.bonnierpublishingfiction.co.uk
www.bonnierpublishing.co.uk

To J and KL for their faith that this would happen.

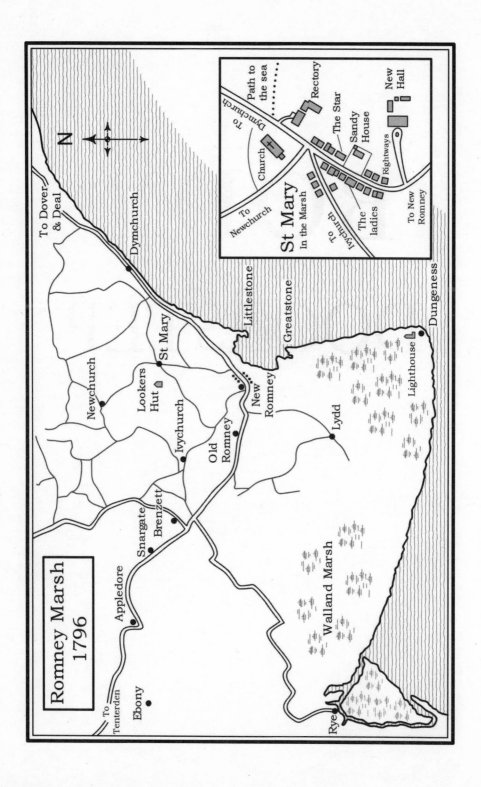

Romney Marsh
1796

N

To Dover
& Deal

Dymchurch

Littlestone

Greatstone

Dungeness

To Tenterden

Ebony

Appledore

Snargate

Brenzett

Newchurch

St Mary

Lookers
Hut

Ivychurch

Old
Romney

New Romney

Lydd

Walland Marsh

Lighthouse

Rye

St Mary
In the Marsh

To Newchurch

To Dymchurch

Church

Path to
the sea

Rectory

The Star

Sandy
House

The
ladies

Rightways

To
Ivychurch

New
Hall

To New
Romney

THE
BODY
ON THE
DOORSTEP

1

Death of a Stranger

THE RECTORY, ST MARY IN THE MARSH, KENT.
6th May, 1796.

To the editor of *The Morning Post*.

Sir,

For the past four years, BRITANNIA has been engaged in a state of continuous warfare against the regicides of the French REPUBLIC and their *blood-stained minions*. During this time, millions in treasure and thousands of men have been committed to expeditions to Corsica, Toulon, Holland, the Indies; expeditions which have resulted in *no other good* than the capture of a few small islands. Meanwhile, the coastline of BRITANNIA itself lies *naked and open* to the enemy . . .

The quill began to splutter. 'Damn!' said the rector. He dipped the pen into the silver inkwell sitting on his desk, and began again.

. . . *naked and open* to the enemy, so close that an *invasion fleet* might well reach the shores of Kent just A FEW HOURS after setting out from French ports. Yet, *not a single shilling* has been spent on the protection of the English coast, which is *completely defenceless*. How long, sir, before His Majesty's government realises the danger that we face? Must we wait until France's *blood-stained sans-culotte hordes* are ~~marching over the fair fields of Kent~~ marching over the fair fields of BRITANNIA ~~itself~~ herself . . .

The fire popped in the grate and a little shower of sparks flew up the chimney. The rector crossed out the entire final sentence and sat back in his chair, muttering to himself. 'Damn, damn, damn. Not right, no, not right at all. Blast and damn!'

He needed inspiration. He dropped the pen, reached for the port bottle that stood beside the inkwell, and upended it. A thin trickle of muddy liquid ran into the bottom of the glass, and stopped.

A sudden rage seized the rector's clouded mind. '*Damn!*' he shouted, and he hurled the bottle into the fireplace. It smashed against the fire-guard, spraying bits of broken glass onto the parquet floor. A few drops of port lay on the polished wood, glinting like blood in the firelight.

'Mrs Kemp!' the rector shouted. 'Mrs Kemp!'

Waiting a few seconds and receiving no answer, still fulminating over the injustice of the empty bottle, the rector bellowed again. There came a sound of shuffling feet in the hall, and the door of the study opened to reveal a grey-haired woman with a downturned mouth, holding a candlestick. At the sight of the rector, the corners of her mouth turned down still further.

'For heaven's sake, will you stop shouting!' the woman scolded. 'Don't you realise it is nearly midnight?' Then she saw the broken glass around the fire, and raised her hands in despair. 'Oh, Reverend!' she said, her own voice rising. 'Reverend *Hard*castle! What have you done *now*?'

The rector stared at her. Nearly midnight? It had just gone nine in the evening when he sat down at his desk to write his latest letter to *The Morning Post*. How could three hours have passed? Then he spotted another empty port bottle, and knew a moment of unease.

He rallied quickly. 'Never mind all that,' he said brusquely. 'You can clear up in the morning. Go to the cellar, and fetch me another bottle.'

'I will do no such thing, Reverend Hardcastle! You have drunk quite enough for one evening!'

'For God's sake, woman, you are my housekeeper, not my wife! Go and fetch a bottle, and have done arguing!'

The housekeeper shuffled towards the cellar door and the rector sat behind his desk, both muttering under their breath. The clock in the hall chimed midnight, confirming the hour. The rector yawned suddenly. He considered going to bed and finishing the letter in the morning . . . but then, the housekeeper had just gone to the cellar. It would be a pity if her errand were wasted.

A thunderous noise interrupted his reverie. It took him a moment to realise that someone was knocking on the rectory's front door; knocking, and with considerable force. He opened his mouth to call Mrs Kemp to answer the door, but remembered she was down in the cellar and would not hear him. Muttering again, he rose to his feet, staggered, recovered, walked steadily to the door, turned into the hallway, over-rotated, bumped into the wall, stopped for the moment to take a deep breath and then walked in a fairly straight line down the hall to the door, weaving just once when he collided with a side table. He reached the door just as the heavy door-knocker thundered again, reverberating in his fume-filled mind like the stroke of doom.

'Wait a blasted moment!' shouted the rector, fumbling with the bolts. 'Look here, whoever you are, don't you know what time it is? It is after midnight!' In answer there came more noises, a sharp crack and almost immediately after the heavy thump of something landing hard on the doorstep. Puzzled, the rector drew the last bolt and opened the oak door.

Outside all was very dark. A brisk offshore wind was blowing, roaring in the invisible trees. He peered into the night, remembering vaguely that it was the new moon. His forehead furrowed and he opened his mouth to shout again, for he could see no sign of the man who had knocked at the door and interrupted his writing.

Then he looked down and saw the body on the doorstep, lying slumped almost at his feet. He saw too the blood, pooling darkly on the stone.

Frowning still, not yet fully comprehending what he was seeing, the rector knelt down for a closer look. That action saved his life. From the corner of his eye he saw a flash of light at the end of the garden, and in the same instant something tore the air just over his head, so close that he could almost feel it in his hair. From behind came the sound of shattering glass.

Instantly, the rector's mind was very clear. Someone had shot at him. He knew he had about thirty seconds before the invisible marksman reloaded and fired again. He seized the body by the shoulders and, with a strength that few would have guessed he possessed, dragged it into the hall, slammed the door shut and bolted it. Panting, he stood leaning against the door, listening for another shot or the sound of an intruder approaching the house. His own pistol was in the desk in his study; he wished he had had the forethought to collect it before answering the door.

The housekeeper stood at the far end of the hall, motionless, mouth wide open, holding a broken bottle. Her apron was covered in blood. No, not blood, port; the shot meant for his heart had instead smashed the bottle she was holding as she returned from the cellar. 'Reverend Hardcastle,' she whispered.

'Hush.' The rector held up a hand, still listening at the door. At first there was silence. Then another shot sounded, then two more in close succession; but these shots were fainter, more distant. The sound seemed to be coming from the east, towards the sea, and he thought at once: *smugglers*. The gunfire popped and crackled uneasily for about thirty seconds, then died away. Once again all was silent, save for the moaning wind.

Now the rector moved swiftly. He pulled the body into the middle of the hall and took down a lamp from the wall so he could see more clearly. The body was that of a man, young, not more than twenty or so. He was well dressed in a dun brown coat and breeches and darker brown waistcoat, the latter stained with the blood that still bubbled brightly from the hole in his chest.

'He breathes,' the housekeeper whispered. She had not moved from where she stood, but she could see the faint rise and fall of the shattered chest in the candlelight.

'Merciful heavens, so he does.' The rector knelt by the young man's head and saw that his eyes were open, and saw too that he was trying to speak. He bent still further, taking the man's hand in his and feeling a light fluttery pulse in his wrist.

'Lie still,' said the rector. 'We will send for help.' But even as he spoke he knew it was too late, the pulse was growing slower and fainter and the blood bubbled faster. There were smears of it on the floor where the body had lain when he first dragged it inside. He doubted if the young man even heard him. It was the latter's last moment of life, and still he strained to speak, yearning to pass a message to the stranger who leaned darkly over him.

'*Tell Peter*,' he breathed, his whispered voice only just audible. '*Tell Peter ... mark ... trace ...*'

The young man exhaled once more and then lay still. His heartbeat flickered to a halt. The rector knelt for a moment longer, then very slowly and with great gentleness and compassion, lifted the man's lifeless hands and crossed them over his chest, hiding the wound that had ended his young life. Then he bowed his head, and, kneeling there on the bloodstained floor with the wind roaring outside, prayed softly for stranger's soul.

2

Spring Morning

'There it is,' said Dr Morley. He held up a pair of forceps, between which a small object glinted dully in the sunlight. 'That is what killed him.'

The rector took the object, which the doctor had just excavated from the dead man's chest. It was silver-grey where it was not covered in red, round with a flat base at one end and a blunt tapered nose at the other. Its sides were marked with narrow grooves. 'Curious thing,' remarked the doctor. 'Not an ordinary musket or pistol ball.'

'It is a rifle bullet,' said the rector. 'See these grooves? Those are made by the riflings in the barrel.'

The doctor raised his eyebrows. 'I've not seen one before.'

There was an unspoken question in his voice, and the rector answered it. 'I've handled rifles a few times. Some of the sporting set bring them over from Germany, where folk use them to shoot deer and boar. They are not common, although I hear talk that the army is thinking of adopting them.'

'Really? Why?'

'Because,' said the rector, 'with a rifle you can kill men at long range. Even a new musket is barely accurate at fifty yards. A rifle can hit a target at three, even four times that distance.'

'Wonderful,' said Dr Morley. He was a clean-shaven, well-dressed man in his early thirties, the normal elegance of his face slightly spoiled by the lines of fatigue around his eyes. 'Just what we need. New and better ways of killing people.'

'Are there any signs of other injuries?' asked the rector.

'A few cuts and bruises. I suspect he might have been in a fight recently, but that is hardly unusual for a man of his age. Otherwise, he was strong and healthy.'

The doctor began to clean his instruments in a pail of water. They had brought the body out to the tack room, the housekeeper having expressed an indignant objection to the carrying out of a post-mortem on her larder table. In the stables beyond they could hear the horse whickering. The rector was reminded that horses did not like the smell of blood. Come to that, neither did he.

He rubbed his eyes. Both he and Morley were tired, the latter with rather better reason. Last night there had been a skirmish out on the Marsh between smugglers and Preventive men, and Morley had been called from his bed just after midnight to attend the wounded. Dawn had been breaking over the English Channel by the time the doctor returned home, and then two hours later the rector's message had arrived, asking him to examine the body of the man who had been shot on his doorstep.

Ordinarily, any instance of violent death would be reported to the parish constable, but St Mary in the Marsh had no constable; the last holder of the post had been dismissed for constant and intemperate drunkenness, and was now in the workhouse at Rye. In the absence of a constable the rector should have contacted Fanscombe, the local justice of the peace, but he had no high regard for Fanscombe's abilities or intelligence. Instead he had sent for Morley, who was also a coroner's deputy and could examine the body in his official capacity.

He had also hoped, he supposed, that Morley might see some clues that he had overlooked, be able to tell him something more about who the man was and why he had died. He himself had gone through the young man's pockets and clothing before the doctor arrived, and had found nothing; his pockets were as empty as if they had been picked, not so much as a farthing or a scrap of paper to be found. A glance at his clothing told him that the London tailors the young man patronised were good but not absolutely of the *ton*. The clothes themselves had a few stains and looked as if they had been slept in, and his black half-boots, also of good make, were newly and heavily scuffed.

Now, Morley had shown him that the man had been shot by a rifle rather than a musket or pistol, which was not really very much help at all.

The rector stood and brooded over the body.

'What is the matter?' asked Morley, wiping his hands on a towel.

'What do you think? As you said, he was a strong and healthy young man. His whole life lay stretched before him, waiting to be lived. Last night, that life was snuffed out in a moment. So much potential, wasted and gone.'

The doctor laughed. 'What, this from a clergyman? No words of religious consolation? The Lord hath called this man unto himself, or some such?'

'The Lord did not call this boy,' said the rector, staring at the doctor. 'It was the hand of man who sent this lad on his final journey. I don't think this is a matter for levity, doctor.'

'That is because you don't see enough dead people, Hardcastle. If you saw more corpses you would realise that, while life is ridiculous, death is more ridiculous still. Be a good fellow and pass me my bag, will you?'

Hardcastle had seen many corpses and did not think there was anything remotely ridiculous about death; indeed, nothing in life was more serious. He passed the medical bag in silence, and Morley began packing his instruments. 'So, who in these parts might have a German *Jäger* rifle?' the doctor wondered.

'No one that I know. You shoot as much as I do; have you ever seen such a thing?'

The doctor shook his head. 'Never. Most folk around here stick to fowling pieces, as I know only too well. I spent half the night picking buck-and-ball out of an Excise man's leg.'

The rector paused. 'Where was this?'

'Up at Dymchurch.'

Dymchurch was on the coast, to the north of St Mary. The rector frowned; something about this did not make sense. 'Why Dymchurch?'

'The Excise men ran into smugglers up there; about halfway between St Mary's Bay and Dymchurch, I think. I wasn't there.' He sounded as though he did not particularly care, either. 'They took three wounded men back to Dymchurch, where I was called to attend them.'

The rector looked up. 'Smugglers, or Preventive men?'

'Preventives, all three. From the Excise service, as I said. Why do you ask?'

'Curiosity, I suppose. I heard the shooting last night, you see. You say it happened up towards Dymchurch?'

'So I was told. As I said, Hardcastle, I wasn't there.'

Another silence fell while the doctor finished packing his bag. He took a pillbox from his pocket and tapped it in his hand until it emitted a small pill, which he popped into his mouth. A faint smell of liquorice reached Hardcastle's nostrils, mingling unpleasantly with the tang of blood.

Morley picked up the bag and straightened, looking at the rector. 'Look here, I'm sorry if I was brusque. Put it down to lack of sleep. This has been a dreadful business for you.'

'Worse for Mrs Kemp,' said the rector, looking down at the body.

'Was he dead when you found him?'

'Oh, yes, quite dead,' said the rector, the words coming easily to his lips. 'I checked at once. He was not breathing and there was no heartbeat. I suppose we can thank our mysterious marksman for one thing. The end must have been very quick.'

'I would imagine so,' said the doctor, nodding. 'I'll send for the undertakers and have the body taken away, and I'll report the death to Fanscombe and the coroner. There will be an inquest, of course, but the coroner may decide that my examination of the body is sufficient. In that case, you can go ahead and bury him.' The doctor paused; the rector watched him with a stony expression. 'And I'll suggest that Fanscombe sends some militia down to patrol the area for the next few nights,' Morley said, 'in case the rifleman returns. We don't want you murdered in your bed.'

'That is good of you,' said the rector reluctantly. In another mood he might have damned the doctor's impudence and stated flatly that he was able to take care of himself, but at the moment he had other things on his mind.

'And, Hardcastle,' said the doctor, turning in the doorway. 'The front hall of your house positively reeks of port. May I suggest that you lay off the drink for a little while? Give your liver a rest. You'll feel better for it.'

This time the rector's temper did flare, and he looked up angrily. 'Thank you, doctor. I shall bear your opinion in mind.'

Morley's face froze for a moment. Then he shrugged and, carrying his bag, walked out through the sunlit yard to the front of the house. Mrs Kemp was down on her knees before the door, scrubbing hard at the bloodstains on the stone step. His own pony and cart stood nearby, and the doctor put his bag in the back and stepped up onto the driver's seat.

'Good day to you, Mrs Kemp,' he said, taking the reins in his hands.

'Good day to you, Dr Morley,' the housekeeper replied without looking up.

The rector remained in the tack room for some time, staring at the body. Then he raised his head, a little like a man waking from a dream, and ran a hand through his sandy, thinning hair before turning and walking out into the sunlight.

It was a glorious morning on Romney Marsh, warm and sweet with the scents of spring. Scattered puffs of cloud drifted across the blue sky on a hurrying wind. Seagulls wailed and squawked in the distance. Hardcastle inhaled deeply, breathing in the fresh air, as questions formed themselves slowly in his mind.

One question that nagged him – and he did not know why it nagged him – concerned the gunfire he had heard last night. Morley had said the skirmish between smugglers and Excise men had been up the coast, half-way to Dymchurch. Therefore, the fighting had taken place well over a mile away to the north-east; indeed, closer to two miles. Surely the south-easterly wind would have blown the sound of any gunfire away from him. Yet he *had* heard shots, quite clearly, and he had been certain they came from the direction of St Mary's Bay to the east and – experience told him – much closer to the village, probably not more than half a mile away.

But . . . he could have been wrong. A fluke of the wind might have carried the sound of more distant gunfire to his ears. Or Morley might have been mistaken about the location; as he said, he was not there.

And, did it matter? The shot that killed the young man had come from close by. A good rifleman could kill a man at two hundred yards, but only in clear light. Last night had been inky black. The killer must have been close when he fired the fatal bullet, probably even inside the grounds of the rectory. He remembered the crack of the rifle as it fired, the sound sharp and distinct. Yes, it had come from near the house. Yet, he could not get the sound of that more distant gunfire out of his head.

The rector frowned, his concentration deepening. Why had he lied to Morley? He had been surprised by his own glibness, by the ease with which the invention came to his lips. He realised that if he and Morley had been more friendly, he would probably have told the truth.

He drew a deep breath. He did not want to think about the doctor. He listened to the distant rasp of the scouring brush as Mrs Kemp scrubbed steadily at the doorstep, and something about the noise brought back to his memory those terrible last breaths of the dying man. What did those breathed last words mean? *Tell Peter . . . mark . . . trace . . .* They must mean something; the boy had clung desperately to the last shreds of his life so as to get those words out, to pass on what he knew to someone, anyone. Why? What was so important about that message?

A long time would pass before he could forget that dying voice.

The rector shook his head. 'Poor lad,' he said softly to himself. 'I can make nothing of it, nothing at all. The fates served you badly indeed, if they chose me to hear your dying words. The doctor, I am sure, would have understood.' But still he did not regret not telling Morley.

Still the questions echoed in his mind. Who was the young man with the good if not entirely fashionable clothes from London? What had brought him to Romney Marsh in the darkness of a new moon? And who was the midnight rifleman who had killed him?

The rector roused from his reverie. Leaving the tack room, he walked back to the house, stepping carefully past the housekeeper, and fetched his hat and coat and walking stick. 'Mrs Kemp,' he said, 'I am going out for a while. I will return in a few hours.'

'I will leave some cold beef out for you,' said Mrs Kemp, still not looking up.

'I am sure that will be capital,' the rector said kindly. He was not certain how badly his housekeeper had been affected by last night's events, and thus his behaviour towards her had an unaccustomed gentleness. Hardcastle had enough self-knowledge to realise that he was not an easy man to live with, and that in Mrs Kemp he had found one of the few people who would put up with him.

Buttoning his coat against a chilly spring breeze, he walked down the drive through the garden. Ahead of him the squat brown tower of St Mary the Virgin lifted over the trees; beyond it he could see the line of low hills above Appledore, where the Marsh ended and the rolling hills of Kent began.

As he reached the gates, Hardcastle turned on impulse and looked back at the rectory. Two big elms flanked the carriage drive. Beyond the right-hand elm lay a thick hedge, about four feet high and rather ragged and in want of a trim, separating the rectory gardens from the road and then the churchyard of St Mary on the far side. An open lawn ran from the trees back to the house.

The grass needed cutting. He spotted a dandelion thrusting its yellow head insolently out of the lawn and lifted his stick to behead it; but halfway through the stroke he paused and then slowly lowered the stick. There had been two shots. The first had killed the boy. The second, fired as he bent over the body, had flown past his head into the hall and narrowly missed the housekeeper standing at the far end.

The voice in his head whispered again. *Tell Peter . . . mark . . . trace . . .* What did it mean? Mark, trace. Trace a mark? There was a mark that must be traced? A mark on something, on a person, on a map? Trace a source, trace a reason, trace a clue?

Tell Peter, tell Peter. Tell Peter.

Suddenly alert, Hardcastle turned and looked at the rectory, a handsomely proportioned building of mellow red brick with a stone portico. The housekeeper had left the door open while she worked, but from this angle he could not see inside the house. He walked swiftly around the left-hand elm, stopped on its far side, and turned to look at the house again. This time he could see through the doorway and straight down the hall.

This, then, was the angle from which the rifleman had fired. He looked down, and saw that the grass around the base of the tree was flattened; someone had been standing here. He saw too a greenish score on the smooth bark of the elm at about shoulder height, showing where something hard had been rested against it; something like the barrel of a rifle, for example, braced against the tree as its owner steadied it for a shot in the dark. A mark, certainly, but not one the dead man could have known about.

He searched around for confirmation of his theory and found it: a fragment of charred cloth lying on the grass six feet away in the direction of the house. Hardcastle recognised it at once: wadding, a patch of cloth that had rested between powder and bullet in the barrel of the rifle, and had been blown out of the barrel when the weapon was fired.

The marks in the grass were few; the rifleman had not been here long. Walking back to the hedge that enclosed the rectory garden, the rector found a few broken twigs on the ground. Someone had come over the hedge in a hurry, either the rifleman or his victim; quite possibly both. He moved swiftly now, walking through the open gates and across the road to the churchyard. Here, under the branches of the great spreading yew tree that grew next to the lychgate, there was soft ground and here he found the definite marks of running booted feet. He traced them across the churchyard between the fading headstones and then over the low stone wall into the fields beyond for about fifty yards, but here the ground grew firmer, and the trail faded.

It did not matter. He knew now that two men had passed through here last night, both running, moving across the churchyard from west to east towards the rectory, the pursuit of hunter and hunted. He paused, turning back towards the rectory with a frown of concentration on his face. Another question occurred; the boy had been shot in the chest, not in the back as one might have expected had he been facing the door. What had happened? Might he have heard some sound behind him, and turned just as the rifleman pulled the trigger?

'I failed him,' the rector said aloud. 'Had I been faster to my feet, had I not fumbled with the bolts, he would have passed safe inside.'

He stood a moment longer, remembering opening the door, the wind and the darkness. He tried to think of anything he might have missed, any slight sound, anything that would give him a clue; but in his memory there was only the wind, and the flash of the shot that nearly killed him, and then the scattering of further gunfire blowing in on the wind from the sea.

Those shots! Why did their memory nag him still? What could *they* possibly have to do with this matter? Frowning, he turned his face into the wind, crossing the road and followed a gently meandering footpath that led past the rectory grounds, then east through pastures full of sheep towards St Mary's Bay and the sea.

It was a truly glorious day. The wind hissed gently through the grass around him. White-faced Romney ewes raised their heads as he approached, bleated once and then went back to eating. Lambs galloped insanely across the path, stopped and stared stiff-legged, then turned and began head-butting each other. A skylark carolled its delight into the spring sky. In the meadows that had not yet been grazed, daisies bloomed in snowy profusion. The rector walked quietly through the profusion of spring life, seeing and hearing very little. His mind still echoed with the sound of the dying voice. *Tell Peter . . .* He wanted – no, he *needed* – to know what had happened last night, and why.

Twenty years ago, someone had said of Hardcastle that he had the finest mind in the Church of England. That mind had become rusty of late – its only intellectual exercise was composing letters to *The Morning Post* – but it still functioned when it needed to. Now, as he walked, the rector began to analyse the problem. Three questions required answers. First, who was the dead man? Second, what did those dying four words mean? Third, what exactly had happened out on the Marsh last night? If he could answer these questions, he should find the way to the truth.

But how in heaven's name was he to answer them?

He reached the dunes at the edge of the sea, their rearward slopes covered in coarse grass, and climbed twenty feet up to their crests without slackening pace. I may be thirty-nine, he thought with satisfaction as he climbed, but I still have it in me . . . Then at the top of the dunes he had to stop and lean on his walking stick, wheezing and recovering his breath. That damned doctor would doubtless say that this was because he drank too much. What nonsense. The rector took his drinking seriously, and regulated it strictly. He rarely drank more than two bottles of port a day, and as a matter of routine limited himself to nothing stronger than small beer before midday. Drink too much? What rubbish.

When he could breathe freely again, he looked around. The seaward face of the dunes glowed pale in the sun, while below them the waves foamed creamy white as they broke and rolled inshore. Out at sea two coasters were making their way north, the wind on their quarter filling their dark red sails as they worked their way inside the Varne Bank on a course for Dover. Further east, shimmering a little in the sea spray, stood a white line of chalk cliffs, the coast of France.

The rector glowered darkly at France, then looked again at the coasters. He was no expert in nautical matters, but he guessed that, running before the wind, they were making six or seven knots towards the English coast. The English Channel was perhaps thirty miles wide at this point. What had he said in his unfinished letter? Given favourable winds, a French invasion fleet could cross the Channel in just a few hours.

'And if the French do land here,' he said aloud, 'there is not a damned thing to stop them.'

3

The Star

'Nothing but you and me,' said a voice in response.

The rector turned. He could see no one at first, and he wondered briefly if he had imagined the voice. Then he looked down at the beach and saw a man standing at the foot of the dune. About twenty, sturdily built with a mop of wind-blown fair hair, he wore duck trousers and a polychrome-stained smock. Hardcastle recognised him at once; his name was Turner, and he had come down from London to stay at St Mary for the spring and summer.

'Mr Turner,' said the rector, still blowing a little. 'You gave me a start.'

'My apologies, sir,' said Turner a little curtly. He was standing in front of an easel, on which a large canvas was anchored securely against the wind. As the rector scrambled down the face of the dune, Turner walked to one side and raised his paintbrush, pointing it at the coasters and squinting along the handle as if he were sighting a rifle. Then he returned to the easel, picking up his palette and making a series of careful strokes on the canvas. The rector climbed down the dune, boots slipping in the soft sand, and came to a halt a couple of yards or so behind the painter's shoulder, watching silently as the other man worked.

'An interesting picture,' he observed when Turner next paused and lowered his brush.

'Oh? What makes it so, do you think?'

The rector paused. 'The quality of light, I expect. You have a way of magnifying the light in your painting. There is a great contrast between light and shadow.'

'I do not magnify anything, sir,' said Turner sharply. 'I paint exactly what I see.'

The rector looked at dunes and sea and ships crisp in the bright clear light, and then at the canvas, where the entire scene seemed to be blurry and shrouded with mist, the outlines of everything vague and out of focus. The light was brighter than in reality, the shadows much darker. No, he thought, this man paints much more than he sees . . .

He changed the subject. 'If you don't mind my asking, Mr Turner, how long have you been here today?'

'About three hours,' said Turner. 'I came to get the morning light. Why do you ask?'

'Mere curiosity. You see, I had a fancy that the smugglers made a run here last night. I wondered if you had seen anything when you arrived, marks in the sand, or other signs of disturbance?'

'Wondering if your brandy had arrived safely, were you? No, I have seen nothing here this morning. But I *heard* plenty, last night.'

The rector's ears began to tingle. 'Oh? When was this?'

'Just on midnight. I was outside, but I heard a clock in the Star toll the hour, and then I heard the gunfire.'

Hardcastle reckoned he owed the younger man one for the crack about the brandy. 'I see. And what was your business outside the Star at midnight?'

'I was waiting for Bessie Luckhurst to open a window and let me in,' said Turner. 'And to save you the trouble of guessing further, it was her bedroom window. While waiting, I heard the shots, quite clearly.'

'Oh? Where would they have come from, would you say?'

'From this direction, from St Mary's Bay. But not as far as the sea; rather further inland, closer to the village.' Turner began to paint once more.

'You are quite certain?' asked the rector.

'I am quite certain,' said Turner. 'I'll tell you what. When I am finished here, I will cast around and see if I can see any sign of where the action took place.'

'Be careful if you do,' said the rector. He looked up at the sun. It was approaching midday, and all this walking and talking had made him thirsty. 'If the free-traders see you, they might think you are spying on them. Watch your step, young fellow.'

'I don't need your advice, granddad,' muttered Turner as the rector turned away, but the latter was labouring to climb back up the dune and did not hear him.

The rector walked back to the village, thinking hard once more. Turner was younger than himself, and his hearing was probably better. If he too had heard gunfire coming from the direction of St Mary's Bay, that was good enough; that was certainly where the fight between smugglers and Excise men had taken place, and never mind what Dr Morley had said.

He might have questioned Turner further about what he had heard, but the young painter was clearly in a prickly mood. He had seen the scowl on the younger man's face as he passed on his well-intentioned warning against taking too close an interest in the smugglers. But the risks were real. Young, excitable people thought there was something romantic about smuggling and went out onto the marshes or the dunes to watch the fun; but smugglers did not like spectators, and sometimes these young excitable people came back with broken limbs and staved-in skulls. He had seen it before.

Many of the shepherds and farmers and fishermen who drank at the Star, St Mary in the Marsh's watering place, also engaged in smuggling. Hardcastle was fairly sure that Luckhurst, the landlord, was involved in the trade too. In fact, it would probably be easier to make a list of his parishioners who were *not* involved in smuggling in some way, than to try to enumerate all those that were.

The rector knew that the smugglers existed; they knew that he knew. Neither side ever spoke of the fact, and a quiet laissez-faire had developed. The smugglers often used the tower of St Mary's church to hide goods run in from the coast before transhipment up to London; at night, when the wind blew from the right direction, he could find his way from the village back to the rectory without a lantern, simply by following the smell of tobacco on the wind. He never reported this; he was a clergyman, not a Preventive man, and he had spent six years earning the respect of his parishioners. He was not about to throw that away over a few bales of run tobacco, or tubs of untaxed gin, or bottles of French scent.

The smugglers appreciated his discretion in these matters, and were willing to pay for it. Early in his tenure as rector, Hardwick had woken the morning after a run to find a tub of gin on his doorstep. That evening in the Star he had remarked casually to his neighbour, a fisherman named Stemp, that he was not fond of gin. By the following morning, the keg had disappeared and a dozen bottles of extremely palatable Hennessey cognac had appeared in its place. These thoughtful little gifts had continued over time.

The rector stopped, gazing unseeing out over a field of sheep. He had advised Turner to be careful. That advice applied equally to himself. The smugglers tolerated him because he was harmless; he was the genial, alcoholic old buffer up at the rectory, easily bought off with a few bottles of brandy. If he started to investigate any business concerning them, he could be putting himself into harm's way. The smugglers referred to themselves ironically as 'the Gentlemen', but there was nothing gentle about their practices. If they thought he was a threat to them, they would stop him. The penalty for smuggling was death by hanging. These men had everything to lose.

'Wool-gathering, Reverend?' asked a woman's voice.

The rector collected himself and turned and bowed to the woman who stood on the footpath ten feet away. She was tall, in her early thirties, wearing a short grey coat. A green and white bonnet covered her dark brown hair and framed a slightly thin face, made pleasing by blue eyes with long delicate lashes and a dimple at the corner of her mouth when she smiled. She was smiling now.

'It was a joke,' she said. She had a light voice and spoke with very little inflection and just the merest hint of a fashionable drawl, which made it hard to tell what she was really thinking. 'You were gazing at the sheep. Gathering wool.'

'I beg your pardon most humbly, Mrs Chaytor,' said the rector. 'My mind was indeed far away. You are going for a walk?'

She wore sturdy brown boots and carried a light blackthorn walking stick in her hand, so this was not a difficult deduction. 'I thought of walking down to the sea,' she said. 'Do I perceive that you have just come from there?' When he looked at her, she added, 'There is sand on the hem of your coat.'

'Oh!' Hardcastle bent automatically to brush it off, collecting his thoughts. He did not know Mrs Chaytor well. She had moved into the village last year, taking a pleasant house and living, so far as anyone knew, a blameless life. She had given out that she was a widow, but said little else about herself. In other villages, a woman of marriageable age living on her own would have been a source of gossip, but most people in St Mary had secrets, and she was allowed to keep hers undisturbed. She did not attend church, but then neither did anyone else in the parish, so the rector bore her no particular animosity on that account.

'Yes,' he said, straightening. 'It seemed a pleasant day for a stroll by the sea.'

'Indeed,' she said, and her smiled faded. 'Reverend Hardcastle, I have heard the news. It must have been a terrible shock for you.'

He looked at her again, and realised she was talking about the death last night. Of course, it would be all over the village by now. Morley's housekeeper must have talked, or perhaps Fanscombe's servants; the justice of the peace's household ran to gossip like dogs run to fleas. 'I fear my housekeeper is suffering the blow most of all,' he said. 'She is a peaceful soul who hates violence. Let us hope things settle down quickly, and we can put this dreadful business behind us.'

It was her turn to look at him; she recognised a platitude when she heard one. 'Is it known who the man was?'

'Not at all. His pockets were entirely empty, and there was no clue about his clothing or his person. We are completely in the dark.'

She arched her eyebrows. 'His pockets were empty? How curious. I wonder who emptied them, and why?'

'A very excellent question,' said the rector, bowing and thinking, *another one*. Mrs Chaytor regarded him, her blue eyes perplexed. 'Why do you suppose he knocked at your door in particular?'

'The lamp was still lit in my study,' said the rector. 'I expect he saw the lighted window, and made for that.' He paused, and then to his own faint surprise added, 'Also, the rectory was the nearest house. I found tracks this morning, indicating that he and his pursuer had both come from the west. They crossed the churchyard and then entered my garden, you see. The poor lad was shot just as he knocked at my door.'

'My goodness . . . When was this?'

'Midnight. Just a minute or so after, to be precise.'

'Why, then it must have happened at about the same time as the shooting down towards the bay.' Her blue eyes regarded him. 'Did you hear it?'

His ears began to tingle again. Not one but two other witnesses had now confirmed that his hearing had not betrayed him. 'I did,' he said. 'I have just come from the bay myself.'

'I see.'

'And you are planning to walk there now?'

'I am.'

There was a wealth of meaning in her short answers. He thought of giving her the same warning he had passed to Turner, then hesitated. She had lived here long enough to know the risks, and in his limited experience of her, she seemed a woman who knew her own mind and would do exactly as she pleased in any case. 'Then I wish you good day,' he said bowing again, and she smiled and moved past him down the path. He gazed after her for a moment, but then remembered his thirst.

The village of St Mary in the Marsh was strung out along the road that ran from New Romney north up to Dymchurch, surrounded by fields full of sheep. The church and the rectory lay on opposite sides of the road, at the north end of the village and a little detached from it. To the south, set back from the road and surrounded by parkland, was New Hall, the home of Fanscombe, the local squire and justice of the peace, and his family. The rest of the village consisted of a series of thatched or tile-roofed cottages, a few pleasant larger houses, one of which belonged to the doctor and one of which, Sandy House, was rented by Mrs Chaytor. There was the usual range of village services: bakery, forge, wash-house and a few shops and workshops. At the centre of the village was a white-washed two-storey structure with a sign creaking on hinges over the main door. The sign showed a rather crudely painted white star on a black background.

The rector ducked through the low doorway of the inn into the common room, and a handful of men sitting and smoking pipes and drinking looked up at him, eyes keen with curiosity. Clearly they too had heard the news. He bowed to them, silently, and they waved their hands and went back to their conversation and pipes. Bessie, the landlord's bright-eyed daughter, came smiling to take his coat and hat. He had always thought of Bessie as a rather sweet girl, but after his conversation with Turner he saw her in a rather different light. 'Are you all right, Reverend?' she asked in a voice of gentle concern. 'That was a dreadful thing that happened.'

'I'll be better still, my dear, once I've a mug of beer in me,' said the rector, shrugging off his coat. Behind the bar her father was already pouring a large tankard of small beer; he slid this over the counter to the rector, who pushed a few coins back.

'Been out for a walk, sir?' asked the landlord.

None of the other customers were in earshot. 'Just down to St Mary's Bay. Saw that painter fellow down there, Turner. Do you know him?'

He had his mug to his lips, and he nearly choked when Bessie thumped him on the back with a broom handle. 'So sorry, Reverend,' the girl said sweetly. 'Could you move along just a little so I can sweep up? There's a good gentleman.'

The rector caught the warning look in her eyes and changed the subject. 'Have you seen his pictures? They're really rather good.'

'I couldn't say,' said Luckhurst. 'Don't know much about painting myself.'

The rector drained the mug and passed it across to be refilled. 'I'm sorry about that business of yours last night,' said Luckhurst, filling the mug from a cask and passing it back. 'That must have been something of a trial for you.'

The rector mumbled a response, face buried in his mug. 'Any idea who he was, sir?' asked Luckhurst, carefully.

'Not at all. He had no papers, nothing to identify him. And he was stone dead by the time I found him, poor fellow, so there was nothing he could tell me.' Each time he repeated it, the lie became easier to tell. The rector wondered if he would soon start to believe it himself.

He decided to chance his arm a little. 'I wondered at first if there was some connection with the run last night,' he said, pushing his mug back for a second refilling. 'You heard about that?'

'I did,' said Luckhurst soberly. 'That was a bad business.' He gestured around the common room. 'Reckon that's why things are a bit quiet today. Folk are keeping their heads down.'

'Oh?' said the rector, raising his eyebrows.

Luckhurst nodded. 'They're saying a Customs man was killed, stone dead. They took his body down to New Romney, and he's lying there now.'

'Customs?' said the rector, blinking. 'I heard it was the Excise that were out last night.'

'No, this was definitely a Customs man. Jack Hoad came up from New Romney this morning with the news. It's a bad business,' the landlord reiterated. 'The government don't mind a few broken bones, but they take it serious when a Preventive man gets killed. This will be reported to the lord-lieutenant, I should think.'

The rector thought about this. The Lord-Lieutenant of Kent, the Duke of Dorset, cared for very little except cricket and women, and was unlikely to stir himself over this matter. In practice, responsibility for any investigation would devolve on his deputy, Lord Clavertye. Hardcastle knew His Lordship well; among other things, Clavertye was patron of the living of St Mary in the Marsh; it was thanks to his influence that the rector held his present post. Clavertye was a bit puffed up with himself, these days, but he had a sharp mind.

'It will depend on what verdict the coroner's inquest brings in,' he said slowly. 'If they find it was unlawful killing, then I expect you are right. Does anyone know how this unfortunate fellow met his end?'

Luckhurst looked around the room. The men, heads over their mugs of beer and cups of gin, looked silently back; they were of course listening to every word. 'Not a blessed thing,' said the landlord. 'He was shot, that's all I've heard. The affray wasn't much to tell about apart from that. The lads got their cargo ashore up towards Dymchurch, and were just about to move off the beach when the Preventives appeared. There were only a few shots fired; the Preventives were outnumbered and gave way. That's about all there is.'

Damn and blast, thought the rector. There it was again; just when he had it settled in his mind that the firing had come from near St Mary's Bay, up popped this rumour of Dymchurch once more. But could it be dismissed as rumour? Luckhurst had probably been out on the run last night, which was why his daughter had felt bold enough to entertain a lover in her bedroom. What he was hearing came from the horse's mouth.

He sat silent over his beer, brooding and trying to make the facts fit with each other. This they resolutely refused to do.

The door of the common room opened and shut and a man moved up to the bar beside the rector; a big man, much more stout than himself, balding with brown hair and red flabby cheeks above his white stock and big, meaty hands. He looked as if he had had a sleepless night; his eyes, small and bright, were rimmed with red.

'Mr Blunt,' said Luckhurst in a carefully neutral voice. 'Always a pleasure to see you, sir. What can I get you?'

'Pale ale,' said the head of the Customs service in Romney Marsh. He had a loud rasping voice which he seldom bothered to moderate. His eyes swept the room. 'Bit quiet today, ain't it, Luckhurst?'

'It's Saturday, sir. A lot of folk are at market in New Romney. Rest are out in the fields, or the boats.'

Blunt grunted and took his drink. Hardcastle noticed that he made no move to pay for it. The other men in the room were talking in low voices, pretending to take no interest but watching the Customs man out of the corners of their eyes.

'Bad business last night, sir,' said Luckhurst, wiping the counter with a cloth. 'I was sorry to hear about that poor fellow of yours. Is it known what happened?'

'Not yet.' He looked at the rector. 'I heard you had a bit of bother too, rector. I trust you came to no harm yourself?'

Hardcastle knew Blunt – everyone on the coast did – and thought him detestable. Blunt was an uncivilised brute, big, boorish and bullying. To save himself from having to reply Hardcastle took a deep drink from his mug, waving his hand as if to signify that the matter was of no account. Blunt at once lost interest in him and turned back to the landlord.

'People are asking questions about last night, sir,' said Luckhurst quietly. 'They're saying a Customs man was killed.'

'Tell them to mind their own god-damned business.'

'That won't do no good, Mr Blunt. Every tongue from here to New Romney is already wagging like a dog's tail,' said the landlord, mixing his metaphors, 'and rumours are flying thick as feathers.'

'Look here, Luckhurst,' snapped the Customs man. 'This is a Customs matter, do you understand me? You and the rest of these god-damned peasants will stay out of it, or else face the consequences. Do I make myself clear?'

'Very clear, sir. But that won't stop the rumours.'

'The rumours are bollocks. Ignore them.'

'Are they? Some of the stories seem pretty believable, Mr Blunt. For example, some folk are saying that the Twelve Apostles are back.'

Blunt had half turned away from the bar, but now he turned back to face the landlord squarely. His beefy face had set hard as stone, and his hands clenched a little. He glanced at Hardcastle, but the rector was nodding over his beer mug, eyes closed. 'Forget about the Twelve Apostles,' the Customs man said in a low voice. 'Don't ever mention that name in public, do you hear? That lot are gone and are never coming back. Savvy?'

'Yes, sir,' said Luckhurst after a long pause.

'Good. Then I'll be on my way.' The door opened and closed once more; outside, they heard the clatter of hooves as the Customs man rode away. Luckhurst muttered under his breath.

'Mr Blunt seemed in a bad temper,' observed the rector in his most neutral voice.

'He's never in any other kind of temper,' Luckhurst grumbled. He shook his head. 'I know what I heard. The Twelve Apostles went away, but that doesn't mean they're not coming back. And I reckon they *are* back.'

'Who might the Twelve Apostles be, Tim?'

'They're a gang that used to operate on this coast. You know. Free-traders.' Luckhurst shot the rector a glance. 'Not from around here, but they operated here. So people said, anyway.'

'I see,' said the rector mildly. 'And Mr Blunt has something against them?'

'Maybe so. Or maybe they have something against him. I've heard it said both ways.' Luckhurst looked up sharply at this point, suddenly aware that he might have said too much. He turned and went down into the cellar, and Bessie tapped the rector on the shoulder.

'Time for your luncheon, Reverend. Unless you want a scolding from Mrs Kemp for arriving late? I thought not. I'll help you with your coat. Stand up, now, there's a good gentleman.'

The rector walked slowly home, where he ate his luncheon of cold beef with a tankard of claret and thought about what he had heard. Dr Morley had been right; there had indeed been a skirmish involving Excise men up towards Dymchurch. However, he, Turner and Mrs Chaytor had also heard firing coming from the direction of St Mary's Bay. Blunt's men had also been out, and had lost a man. Had the Customs men been involved in a second, quite separate incident? One that Blunt was unwilling to talk about?

It was entirely possible. The Preventive men, charged with stopping the smuggling trade, were divided into two separate services: Customs, which collected duties on all imported goods, and Excise, which collected taxes on all goods of certain categories such as liquor and tobacco, regardless of provenance. In theory they worked together against the free-traders. In practice the heads of the two services in the Marsh, Blunt of the Customs and Juddery of the Excise, hated each other passionately and never worked together if they could help it.

If both services had men out on the Marsh last night, they would have been operating independently. It now looked as if, at about the same time, both had run into parties of smugglers and come under fire.

Very well, he thought, where does that get me? He had solved the puzzle of the gunfire, but he was no closer to knowing who the dead man was, or what his dying words meant.

He was tired now, and it was time to stop thinking. The rector rose and went into his study, where a little smile crossed his face. There, sitting on his desk on a silver tray, was an open bottle of port with a napkin around its neck, and a single glass.

'Mrs Kemp,' he said aloud, 'You are a queen among women.'

An hour later the rector lay stretched out on the chaise longue before the study window, bathed in sunshine and surrounded by an aura of port fumes, fast asleep.

4

Unwelcome Visitors

'Behold,' said Lord Clavertye, raising one hand and pointing in dramatic fashion, 'the most advanced system of communication yet devised by man!'

'What about woman?' said Amelia Chaytor, but she said it under her breath and not even Captain Shaw of the militia, her nearest neighbour, heard the words. She stood with her gloved hands clasped together, the wind tugging at her hat and pulling out stray curls of brown hair; every so often she moved impatiently to tuck these back in again. Clavertye prosed on, describing the workings of the semaphore system in exacting, ear-aching detail.

She looked up at the semaphore station, a tower about thirty feet high with a rectangular frame containing six large wooden shutters arranged in two vertical rows. Really, she thought, it is all quite simple. Each shutter can be opened or closed, and each pattern of closed shutters symbolises a word, a letter of the alphabet or a number; not unlike the flag system used by the navy. A man in the distance watches with a telescope, notes down the patterns and decodes them into a message, then uses his own semaphore station to pass the message on. The system could be described completely in about two minutes. Clavertye has been talking for nearly half an hour. The man used to be a barrister, but even so!

'And so,' said the Deputy Lord-Lieutenant of Kent, 'this is the first in a chain of fifteen semaphore stations that will soon connect London directly with the Channel coast. I invite you to consider this. The fastest courier, riding post and changing horses every ten miles, will still take four or five hours to reach London. But with *this* system, should the French attempt a landing in Kent, His Majesty's government in Whitehall will know about it within a mere fifteen minutes!'

'Capital!' said the rector of St Mary in the Marsh, standing a little way to Mrs Chaytor's left. He clapped his hands. 'When the French land on this *undefended* coast, they can take over this station and send a message to London announcing their arrival, without the rest of us having to trouble ourselves.'

'Yes, Hardcastle,' said the deputy lord-lieutenant with an indulgent smile. 'We've all read your letters in *The Morning Post* and we know your feelings on the subject. But believe me, the government does take the French threat seriously. This semaphore system is the first step towards creating an entire system of coast defences. Given time, there will be forts, garrisons, artillery batteries. It will come.'

Yes, thought Mrs Chaytor, *given time*. She looked at the rector, hoping that he would not be such an infernal fool as to pick a quarrel with his own patron, but the rector merely smiled at Lord Clavertye and bowed in response. Hmm, she thought, he appears to be sober this morning.

'And how soon will the rest of the chain be built?' the rector asked.

'Soon, Hardcastle, very soon. I give you my word on it. I have paid for this station out of my own pocket, as you all know, but the government will pay for the rest of the system. It is merely a matter of finding the necessary funds.'

That means in a year's time, thought Mrs Chaytor, or two years, or never. Then Fanscombe, the justice of the peace, asked some technical question and the men were off again, discussing windlasses and springs and paddles with all the air of men who actually knew what they were talking about.

As it was fairly clear that they did not, Mrs Chaytor slipped through the little crowd and walked out towards the crest of the low hill above Appledore. Here she stood for a while, gazing out over the Marsh. The late morning sun was brilliant and blue, the distant sea shining with a white row of surf where it met the dunes. She picked out, without effort, the squat tower of St Mary the Virgin in the far distance, just short of the sea. The distant bleating of sheep came to her ears. Really, she thought, the weather has been very fine.

She was still a little astonished at how quickly she had come to feel at home on the Marsh. It was not always an easy place to live. In winter, storms blew salt spray inland as far as the village, playing havoc with her roses. In summer, mosquitoes whined over the lagoons and stagnant pools, and marsh fever hovered in the background. *Evil in winter, grievous in summer, and never good*, was how folk from up-country in Kent described the desolation of the Marsh. Yet, she had found a measure of peace here.

She raised her eyes and looked across the Channel to the chalk cliffs of Cap Gris Nez, and thought that in this clear air France seemed even closer than usual. She remembered France in better days, the delights of Paris and the happiness she had once known, and sighed.

'Gazing at the enemy, Mrs Chaytor?' the rector's deep voice said beside her.

She turned and dipped a little curtsey as he bowed, and gestured towards the French coast. 'Looking for signs of the invasion,' she said in her light, slightly emotionless voice. 'Nothing visible so far. Did you grow tired of the conversation?'

'Every man present is an engineer, it seems, except for me.' His square face was beginning to develop jowls. Drink will do that, she thought without sympathy.

'I drove up here thinking that the opening of the station might prove diverting,' she said. 'But honestly, I have never seen an occasion so dull. I think I shall return to St Mary.' She glanced at the rector. 'Did you drive, or ride?'

'Neither. It is a pleasant day, and I enjoy walking.'

'You walked from St Mary? Why, it is the better part of ten miles.'

'Not if you know your way through the Marsh. There are paths that shorten the distance.'

She wrinkled her nose. 'Smugglers' paths.'

'It may be that smugglers have used them in the past,' he said gravely. 'If so, I have no knowledge of it.'

She glanced at him. He really *was* sober. 'If you wish to return to St Mary,' she said, 'I would be happy to take you in my gig. And I have something to say to you. Concerning last Friday.'

The rector glanced around. 'It would be a pleasure,' he said, and hesitated. 'I fear driving is not one of my skills that has improved with age.'

'I drive rather well. Can you bear to be seen in public, driven by a woman?'

'I am a clergyman. We are permitted a degree of licence unknown to other men.'

She did indeed drive rather well. She handled the little gig and the smart young horse with neat precision, her gloved hands strong on the reins. They trotted down the ancient highway from Appledore to New Romney, he sitting beside her and watching her driving. She seemed lost in thought; they were past Snargate before she spoke again.

'I found the scene of the fighting the other night,' she said. 'There was a disturbance in the sand at the back of the dunes, where they brought their cargo ashore. Not so much as I might have expected. I don't think there can have been very many of them. The smugglers, I mean. I followed the tracks through the grass where they had dragged the cargo. About half a mile on, the tracks stopped suddenly and there were bootprints in the soft earth all over the meadow. The sheep had spoiled quite a lot of the traces, unfortunately. But I found it at the edge of a drainage ditch. The blood.'

She fell silent again and the rector stirred, wondering what words of consolation he should offer her to ease her shock. But when she spoke again she sounded quite normal. 'The bloodstain was quite large,' she said, 'although most of the blood had already soaked into the ground, of course. I do not believe that the man who bled there could have survived for long. I think that was where the Customs man was killed.'

The rector forgot about consolation and stared straight down the dusty road, thinking hard. 'Did you see any further tracks?' he asked.

'Some. One group of men made off south towards New Romney. I rather think those were the Customs men, don't you?'

'Any others?'

'Nothing. The smugglers might have gone up the ditch, of course, in which case the water would have washed away their footprints.'

The rector conceded that this was likely. The Preventive men sometimes used bloodhounds, and the smugglers used the sewers, as the drainage ditches were known in these parts, to throw the dogs off their scent. However, the main thing was this: the customs officer and the boy at the rectory had been killed at almost the same time, half a mile apart. But . . . did that mean that the deaths were connected in some way?

'Damn,' he said aloud. 'Damn and blast.'

'Language, Reverend,' she said lightly.

'My dear Mrs Chaytor, I do apologise. I am in the habit of talking out loud to myself and I fear that sometimes my language is . . . intemperate.'

'Particularly when you are puzzling over something,' she said. They trotted briskly through Brenzett, and once past the village she whipped up on the long straight to Old Romney. The gig flew down the road, so fast that the rector had to hold on to his hat.

'What puzzles you now?' she called over the noise of iron-shod hooves and iron-rimmed wheels.

'Two men died that night, half a mile apart and within five minutes of each other.'

'I see. You wonder if the two events might be related. Either your killer, or your victim, or both, might have had some connection with the smugglers.'

'What other reason would either have for being out on the Marsh on the night of a new moon?'

'I see your point,' said his companion thoughtfully, shaking the reins and urging the horse to further speed. 'It does not feel like coincidence, does it?'

'Over the years, I have learned to distrust the very idea of coincidence,' said the rector, clutching again at his hat. 'My dear Mrs Chaytor, there is a dray in the road ahead.'

There was indeed a dray in the road ahead, loaded with timber and drawn by two plodding horses. Mrs Chaytor touched the reins to guide the pony and, without slackening speed, pulled around the dray on the outside, one wheel running onto the grass verge, and then swerved back onto the road. The driver of the dray, startled out of his doze, yelled abuse after her. The rector stared at his companion, wondering where she had learned to drive. Thereafter he concentrated on holding his seat as they shot through Old Romney at a speed that left chickens squawking indignantly in the road behind them, and raced on towards the coast. Only on the outskirts of St Mary did she slacken speed, and she trotted the gig sedately up the high street towards the church.

Not until they reached the gates of the rectory itself did he speak again. 'Have you ever heard tell of a group of men called the Twelve Apostles?' he asked. 'Around here, I mean?'

'Never, I am sure. Who are they?'

'I don't know. But some folk around here do. What is more, the name frightens them. If you do hear the name mentioned, will you please tell me?'

'I shall do so.'

He realised belatedly that he had involved her in this matter; he had never meant to do so.

'Mrs Chaytor, it is good of you to tell me what you have learned, and I thank you for it. But . . . the men we are dealing with are dangerous. I beg you to take care, and not expose yourself to danger.'

His only answer was a gentle smile. The gig pulled up outside the rectory and he stepped down a little clumsily, then looked up at her. 'Thank you,' he said simply, and then added on impulse, 'Will you be at the inquest tomorrow?'

'I have already been summoned to give evidence.'

He bowed, hiding his surprise. It was not usual to call women to give evidence. She must have approached Fanscombe with what she knew; or, more likely, Clavertye. 'Then I shall see you there.'

'Indeed you shall. Good day to you, Reverend.' She turned the gig smartly and drove through the rectory gates, turning again towards the village. Extraordinary woman, thought the rector. She seems absolutely nerveless. I wonder what sort of fellow her husband was.

Today was Tuesday, and already the events of last Friday night were beginning to recede, the memories fainter and less distinct, the colours and images in his mind less bright.

Life had resumed its normal rhythms. On Sunday he had preached the usual sermon to the usual empty church; then, suddenly exhausted, he went home to drink a bottle of port and fall asleep. Yesterday morning he had paid a pastoral visit to the Cadman family, who lived on an isolated farm to the north-west of the village. Cadman's father was increasingly unwell, and he had spoken to the old man and offered what comfort he could to the worried son and daughter-in-law.

He had asked, too, if any of the household remembered anything about the events of Friday night. Everyone had been charmingly vague, deeply regretting their inability to remember anything useful.

The coroner had given permission for interment to take place. Hardcastle returned to the village to conduct a brief burial service for the dead stranger, then stood by the grave watching the earth cover his coffin while the dying voice whispered in his ear. This spurred him back to the problem of the last four words. Yesterday afternoon he had sat in his study at the rectory and covered several sheets of paper with scrawls as he concocted various messages: all of them equally possible in theory, all of them equally unlikely in practice.

Tomorrow, Wednesday, the coroner would arrive to conduct inquests into the two deaths. This afternoon Fanscombe, the justice of the peace, was coming to take his statement. Conscious of the time, he ate his luncheon swiftly and then sat sweating in the afternoon heat in his study, listening to his stomach rumble. Half a bottle of claret and a very small glass of port, he decided, were not enough to enable easy digestion.

Preoccupied with his stomach, he did not hear the knock at the front door. He looked up suddenly to see Mrs Kemp standing before his desk. 'Mr Blunt of the Customs to see you, Reverend.'

Blunt? thought the rector. What the devil could *he* want? A remembered smell of tobacco from the church tower wafted guiltily through his mind, and he glanced at the wooden cabinet where he kept his cognac. 'Show him in,' he said slowly.

Blunt strode into the room as Hardcastle rose to his feet, and stopped and gave a stiff half-bow.

'To what do I owe the pleasure, Mr Blunt?' the rector asked.

The Customs man surveyed the room, his eyes resting for a moment on the brandy cabinet, and the rector knew a moment of unease. 'About this business the other night,' Blunt began.

Hardcastle tried not to let his relief show. 'Do you mean the man who was murdered here?'

'Yes, since you put it that way.' The rector wondered how one could put it any other way. 'Did you see anything?' asked Blunt.

The rector stared at him. 'You have the advantage of me,' he said finally.

'It's a simple enough question,' the other man said sharply. 'Did you see what happened?'

'No, I did not. I opened the door and found the body lying on my doorstep. The fatal shot had already been fired.'

'And the man was dead when you found him?'

Unease, of an entirely different sort, grew once more in the rector's mind. 'Mr Blunt, I'll be obliged if you would tell me why you are asking these questions. I would have thought you fully occupied with the death of your own unfortunate officer.' He looked at Blunt and said directly, 'Are the two events connected?'

He saw sweat on Blunt's forehead, sudden beads of it glowing in the afternoon sun. 'I don't need you to tell me my duty, Hardcastle,' he said, blustering. 'I'll ask again. What did you see and hear that night? Did you see anyone else around this house?'

Unease began to turn to anger. 'I don't see how this is any of your business, Blunt.'

'One of my men was killed out there!'

'Correction: *two* men were killed. I will ask again. Are their deaths connected?'

Silence. The rector made a dismissive gesture. 'I'll make my statement in due course to Mr Fanscombe. I am sure that he too will conduct a full investigation.'

'Fanscombe,' snorted Blunt. 'That booby. Man couldn't investigate his own arse. Look here, Hardcastle. I've asked you a question, and I demand an answer! *What did you see?*'

'Blunt,' said the rector, his frangible patience reaching its snapping point, 'what I saw is none of your damned business! Now, kindly remove yourself from my rectory!'

The front door slammed behind the Customs man, and the echo seemed to take a long time to die away. The housekeeper appeared in the doorway once more. 'Whatever was that about?'

'Mrs Kemp,' said the rector heavily, feeling his stomach rumble again, 'I really have no idea. But if Mr Blunt calls in future, I am not at home. Ever.'

The housekeeper clicked her tongue, a sound which she managed to imbue with a singular level of contempt. 'Here comes Mr Fanscombe,' she said, seeing a little party of men riding up the road from the village. 'I'll let him in, shall I?'

Fanscombe was accompanied by Captain Shaw of the militia, a freckled young man in his middle twenties. He was, thought the rector, by far and away the worst turned-out captain in His Majesty's service. His breeches were wrinkled, the buttons on his coat were dark with tarnish, and one cuff was distinctly longer than the other. His sword hilt looked none too clean either, and the scabbard had scuff marks where it had banged into other objects. His hair needed brushing.

'I will not stay long, Reverend,' said the captain, bowing. 'I came down from Appledore to see if you and Mr Fanscombe wanted my men to continue their patrol. Have you had any trouble since Friday night?'

'None at all, captain, thank you very much. All has been very quiet. I am sure your patrols are no longer needed, if Mr Fanscombe agrees?'

Fanscombe nodded. 'Then I'll call my fellows in,' said Shaw. 'But if you feel in future that there is any danger, do be so good as to inform Mr Fanscombe. I am sure he would call us out at once.'

'Oh, aye, certainly, certainly,' said the justice of the peace, nodding again.

'I shall certainly do so,' said the rector. 'And my thanks to you, Captain Shaw, and your men for watching over me. It was very good of you.'

Shaw looked vaguely pleased. He glanced around the room, clearly keen to stay and see what happened next but unable to think of a reason for doing so. 'Then I shall take my leave,' he said, bowing in an angular manner. 'Good afternoon, gentlemen.'

Shaw departed. Fanscombe pulled up a seat before the desk, opening his writing case to set out paper and pen and ink and sand. He was acting as his own clerk; Hardcastle wondered why he had not thought to bring a secretary.

'What did you think of this morning, Hardcastle?' he asked. 'That semaphore system is capital, ain't it? That'll put the wind up the Froggies, to be sure.'

'Oh, indeed,' said the rector, wishing he had a drink. 'No troops will be available to prevent a landing, of course, but once the French are ashore, His Majesty's government will then use the semaphore to send them a series of insulting messages. Half a day of this, and the French will be so offended that they will climb into their boats and row back to France, vowing never to return to this rude country.'

Fanscombe gave a hearty chuckle, and the rector's desire for alcohol intensified. His stomach was churning more than ever. Blunt had called

Fanscombe a booby, and on this point at least the rector conceded that the Customs man was right. Fanscombe looked like what he was: a bluff country squire, a huntin', shootin' and fishin' man who wore his blue riding coat and leather breeches on all but the most formal occasions. His air of manly jocularity almost but not quite concealed the fact that he was savagely henpecked by his rather younger French wife. His hail-fellow-well-met attitude grated on the rector's nerves like glass paper.

'You say there's no troops,' he said, 'but what about young Shaw and his militia?'

'A few hundred farm boys and shopkeepers in red coats are hardly going to stop the French Army of the North.'

'No, I suppose not. Well,' said the justice of the peace, briskly dismissing the prospect of imminent French invasion, 'let's get started, shall we?'

The rector gave his statement, watching Fanscombe's pen scratch unevenly across the paper. His penmanship was terrible, and Hardcastle felt a flash of pity for the coroner who would have to read the statement. 'You say the second shot came from the same rifle as the one that killed the victim?'

'I am certain of it. I dug the second bullet out of the wall at the back of the hall with my penknife. It is identical in every respect, including the rifling marks.'

'Phew, you had a lucky escape there, old fellow. There were no further shots?'

'None nearby. A few moments later I heard more shooting in the distance. I believe that the noise of this frightened off the killer. The following day, I found the spot from where he had fired.' Hardcastle described the evidence, watching the other man write hurriedly. He asked a question of his own. 'Does anyone have any idea as to who the dead man might have been?'

'No, no. No. Complete mystery.' Fanscombe said this with some relief; the fact that the body could not be identified meant that the dead man could be shovelled into the ground and forgotten, with no need for any tiresome investigation. On the heels of the thought the justice of the peace asked, 'Has he been buried?'

The rector's desire for drink was now overwhelming. 'Yes. We buried him yesterday, and I read the service over his grave. He is gone. It is as if he had never existed.'

'Yes, I daresay.' Fanscombe scattered sand on the final page of the deposition and looked up. 'I'll need Mrs Kemp's statement too; just a formality, you know, for the record. Oh, just show me where you found that second bullet, will you? Might be important. Never know.'

Hardcastle stood by while the justice of the peace took down Mrs Kemp's brief statement. She stated without blinking that, so far as she knew, the young man had been dead when the rector brought his body into the house. Following this, after assisting in the – completely pointless – inspection of the damaged wall the rector showed Fanscombe out. He then returned to his study, took out his keys, unlocked the wooden cabinet and took out a bottle of cognac and a glass. He filled one glass and drank it very quickly, then filled another and drained it a little more slowly, feeling the fire burn in his belly and his mind and spirit begin to relax.

He was just about to return the bottle to its place when there came a knock at the door. Mrs Kemp entered the study a moment later, bearing a silver salver with a card.

'Lord Clavertye to see you, Reverend,' she said, looking reproachfully at the brandy.

'Oh, God's truth. Show him in, Mrs Kemp, then bring us some Madeira, if you please.' As soon as the housekeeper was out of sight, the rector poured another glass of brandy, sank it down, then replaced the bottle and glass, locked the cabinet and moved quickly to his desk. He rose again when the deputy lord-lieutenant was shown in.

Clavertye was a man of his own age, tall and immaculately groomed in well-fitted riding coat and boots as shiny as mirrors, dark-haired with an authoritative trace of silver at the temples. His handshake was firm without being overpowering. 'Hardcastle, my dear fellow. How good it is to see you. Do forgive me for calling upon you without notice.'

'You are always welcome here, my lord. Please, do sit. My housekeeper will bring us refreshments in a moment. Will you stay to supper?'

'It is kind of you to offer, but I must be away to Ashford this evening.' They talked about the semaphore system for a few minutes until Mrs Kemp brought the Madeira and withdrew, closing the door behind her. 'Now, to business,' said Clavertye briskly. 'Tell me everything you know about this affair last Friday.'

Sitting up straight behind his desk with his hands clasped before him, Hardcastle told him. He concluded by describing the tracks he had seen in the churchyard the following morning, and his conclusions about the clashes between smugglers and Preventive men. Unlike Fanscombe, whom he dismissed as a fool and a bore, he respected Clavertye's mind. They had known each other for twenty years; they had been at Cambridge together, the one studying divinity and the other reading law. Clavertye had gone on to a highly successful practice as a barrister, until the death of his older brother at Yorktown had unexpectedly handed him a barony and an estate. Now he was a man of substance, a rising star in the Whig faction with high political ambitions of his own.

And it was Clavertye, of course, who had procured for him this living at a time when doors throughout the Church of England were closing against him and he had been contemplating the living death of an army chaplaincy or migration to the colonies. The rector knew that he owed His Lordship a great deal.

So he told the truth; but not quite the whole truth. He did not repeat the dead man's four last words. It was not that he did not trust Clavertye; but if he repeated those words to the deputy lord-lieutenant, the latter would be duty bound to ensure that they were entered into evidence tomorrow. And the rector was not sure that he wanted those words to become public knowledge just yet. They had been uttered to himself alone. That rendered them sacrosanct. When the time came, he would divulge them; but he would decide when that time was.

Clavertye listened intently, making no notes, everything filed invisibly in his barrister's brain. When the rector had finished, the other man rose to his feet and walked to his window, looking out over the sunlit garden. His Lordship studied the scene for a moment, then turned back to look at the rows of leather-bound books that lined the study walls, some old and battered, others in expensive red morocco with gold lettering. There were more books than shelves, and many of the volumes were wedged in wherever space could be found. Most were covered in a fine layer of dust.

'Very well,' he said finally, 'thank you. You have given me a wealth of detail that no one else has yet provided.'

The rector blinked; he did not realise that Clavertye was investigating these events personally, rather than delegating everything to Fanscombe.

He wondered why the deputy lord-lieutenant was taking such trouble, and who else he had interviewed. Mrs Chaytor for one, he thought, remembering their conversation this morning. Did she approach Clavertye, or was it the other way around?

'Your Lordship is taking a keen personal interest in this matter,' he said.

'An officer of the law has died in the performance of his duty, Hardcastle. I take that very seriously, and I am not alone. Did you know that the death of the Customs officer was reported in some of the London papers?'

Well, that explains it, thought the rector. Clavertye wants to get his own name in those papers, by solving the murder.

'I have a question for you,' His Lordship continued. 'In your opinion, is there any connection between the two events? The shooting out on the Marsh, and the murder here?'

'Yes,' said the rector, coming to a decision. 'I am convinced of it.'

'Why?'

'There are several reasons. First, the smugglers who landed at St Mary's Bay were making their way *west* from the beach when they encountered Blunt and the Preventives, while the young man and the other man, his pursuer, were moving *east* towards the beach.'

He recalled his conversation with Mrs Chaytor. 'Of course, this may be coincidence, but I doubt it. I think the man who was killed knew the smugglers were coming, and was moving east deliberately to intercept their path; for what motive, I do not yet know.

'Also, he had been imprisoned somewhere rough and all his belongings taken. His pockets were entirely empty and his clothes were somewhat the worse for wear. I observed that his boots were badly scuffed as if he had been kicking at something; trying to break down a locked door, perhaps. He was also bruised as if from a recent fight. I believed that he escaped from his prison, wherever it was, and was on his way towards the smugglers when he was tracked down and killed.'

'That is conjecture, of course,' said the deputy lord-lieutenant absently.

'Of course.'

'And what of the other smuggling gang? The one that attacked Juddery's men? Do you think that was connected too?'

'I can think of no reason to believe so. But I wondered if our second party, the men that landed at St Mary's Bay, knew the first gang were making a run that night. They may have hoped that the first gang would draw away the Preventives from this part of the coast and allow them a clear run. Which raises the question of how Blunt knew that the second group had landed, and where to find them.'

He looked inquiringly at Clavertye, who looked blandly back. It was clear from His Lordship's expression that he had already spoken to Blunt and heard his version of events, but it was equally clear that he was not going to let anything out before the proper time – in other words, before tomorrow's inquest.

'Very well,' said Clavertye, walking back to the desk and sitting down. 'I will instruct the coroner to consider these two deaths as possibly linked. Given the circumstances, I am quite certain that a verdict of unlawful killing will be returned in both cases. That will allow me to investigate both as a single case. What is it?'

He looked sharply at the rector, who had made a small motion with his hand. 'My lord,' said Hardcastle, 'I will make you a wager. A pound to a shilling says that the verdict on the Customs officer comes back as death by misadventure.'

'What? Of course not. The man was shot!' said Clavertye sharply.

'Nevertheless,' said the rector stonily.

There was a long silence, during which Clavertye's eyes bored into the rector's face. A ghost of their old friendship still existed, but only a ghost; Hardcastle was aware that he had stretched Clavertye's patience in the past, and was in the process of doing so again.

'You know something,' said Clavertye.

'I do not know anything for certain, my lord. But I *think* I know something.'

'Then spit it out, man!'

'I think that Blunt is in league with the free-traders. He stopped on Saturday to have a drink at an inn which is known to be a rendezvous for smugglers, and he did not pay for that drink.'

'That's not enough to damn a man.'

'No. But Blunt also called on me earlier this afternoon. He demanded, in quite a menacing way, that I tell him all that I have told you about the events of last Friday. When I asked why he wanted to know, he refused to answer. I don't believe that he is actively investigating the death of his own officer. Instead, for some reason, he is taking a very close interest in the killing here at the rectory. And there is one other thing.'

'Go on.'

'Blunt is afraid of something, my lord. And I would say that in particular, he is afraid of a group of men known as the Twelve Apostles.'

At the door, hat and coat in hand and his chaise waiting outside, Clavertye turned to Hardcastle. 'I will return tomorrow, but after the inquest I must go at once to London. Important business at the House, I fear; can't wait. While I am away . . .' He paused. 'Should you learn anything further about this affair, I would esteem it a great favour if you would kindly report it to me at once.' He raised a finger. 'But be discreet. Don't draw attention to yourself.'

It had been couched as a request, but the rector knew an order when he heard one. 'I will do my best, my lord. Kindly remember me to Lady Clavertye.'

After the coach had rolled away Hardcastle returned to the study, where he slumped down behind his desk. 'Kindly report it to me at once, kindly report it to me at once,' he muttered. 'Damn the man! I'm a clergyman, not a blasted Bow Street Runner.' He was still grumbling when the housekeeper knocked and entered the room, setting down an open bottle of port and a glass at his elbow. 'Whatever is the matter with you, Reverend Hardcastle?' the latter asked, setting her hands on her hips.

'This whole business, Mrs Kemp. I've had enough of it. Lord Clavertye wants me to report to him if I learn anything further. Well, blast him, I won't do it. I've had enough of the entire affair! I shall give my evidence at the inquest tomorrow, and then it is over. Finished. Done.'

'You are the most perverse man ever born,' the housekeeper commented. 'You've spent most of your waking hours these past days investigating that boy's death, and now, when His Lordship asks you to do what you are already doing, you refuse.'

'What I do is none of his business,' said the rector, pouring a brimming glass, 'and none of yours either, you nosy old baggage.' The atmosphere in the rectory had returned to normal, to the relief of the housekeeper;

she could cope with the rector's temper, but she had found his solicitude unnerving. The rector raised the glass to his lips, and stopped. 'Oh for the love of God, who is it *now*?'

The sound of swift clopping hooves and carriage wheels could be heard again in the driveway. 'If it is Fanscombe again, or that fool Shaw,' he said, 'tell them I am not at home.' The housekeeper gave him a look of contempt and departed to answer the door. In a moment she was back in the study doorway, a look of utter horror on her wrinkled face.

'It is the *dean*,' she whispered, in a tone that suggested that the Four Horsemen of the Apocalypse had tethered their horses on the lawn and were now standing in the hall examining the pictures. 'It is the dean, just driven down from Canterbury and asking to see you at once. Shall I send him in?'

The Very Reverend Folliott Cornewall, Dean of Canterbury Cathedral, was a tall man with a long equine face and fleshy lips. His black eyebrows were perpetually arched, making him look as if he doubted everything that he heard or saw around him. Despite being only forty-two, the same age as Hardcastle, he wore an iron-grey wig that made him look older, perhaps in an attempt to give his face more gravitas.

'Hardcastle. Good evening. Forgive my calling unannounced.'

'Good evening to you, sir,' said Hardcastle standing stolidly in his hall. 'To what do I owe the pleasure?'

Cornewall looked down the very considerable length of his nose at Mrs Kemp. 'Not in front of the servants, if you please.'

'That will be all for the moment, Mrs Kemp,' said the rector to the silently furious housekeeper. He led the way into the study and sat down behind his desk, offering the dean a glass of port. The dean, still carrying his hat and coat, refused in a manner which suggested that an assault had been made upon his chastity. The rector drained his own glass and poured another, then sat staring in silence at his visitor.

Cornewall drew a deep breath. 'I come,' he said, 'with a direct message from the archbishop.'

'Indeed? And how is the butcher's boy?'

Cornewall drew another breath. His Grace the Archbishop of Canterbury had indeed been born plain Master John Moore, the son of a butcher, but only a bounder would mention this. 'He sends you no good wishes,' said Cornewall huffily. 'You are aware of his opinion of you.'

'As indeed I hope he is aware of my opinion of him,' said the rector nodding. 'Given the air of cordial dislike that exists between my spiritual master and I, what message can he possibly wish to send me?'

'His Grace has heard of the unfortunate events that took place here last Friday evening.' Cornewall shuddered, and looked around the room as if he expected the walls to still be dripping blood. 'His Grace is *most desirous* that no scandal attach itself to the Church, either to the See of Canterbury within which this parish lies, or to the chapter. He would like to see this matter kept as quiet as possible, within the law, of course.'

To the chapter. Oh, thought the rector, there it is; I should have seen that coming. Owing to one of the all-too-frequent quirks of the English landholding system, while the living of St Mary's was in the gift of Lord Clavertye, the freehold of most of the parish belonged to the Dean and Chapter of Canterbury and many of his parishioners were the cathedral's tenants. It was not the spiritual implications of the murder that worried the dean, but the commercial ones. Murder was bad for business.

But what business would be affected? The sheep, who were the core of legitimate economic activity in Romney Marsh, would hardly be perturbed. Markets would go on and tolls be levied as before. Tolls . . . He snapped his fingers, and Cornewall looked at him in wide-eyed surprise.

'Let us speak plainly,' said the rector. 'The free-traders are bringing goods ashore and transporting them across lands owned by Canterbury. Along the way, they pay off a good many people to ensure their silence. Some of that money finds itself, by indirect and devious and slippery routes, into Church coffers. Yes?' Cornewall sat motionless, staring at the rector with bulging eyes. 'Am I correct?' snapped the latter. 'Or is His Grace simply concerned that there might be an interruption to his supply of run brandy? If so, permit me to offer him some of my own! I'll have a dozen bottles loaded into your carriage before you depart!'

Cornewall was on his feet, horse's face white with indignation. 'How dare you, sir! How dare you speak of His Grace thus!'

'Damn the butcher's boy, and damn you too, Cornewall, for a blithering idiot!' His rage boiled over; twenty years of resentment and dislike vented themselves in a flood of anger. Cornewall too had been at Cambridge, his bitter rival, resenting the praise that had been heaped on Hardcastle, who had been seen as the golden boy. Now, all the successes that had passed Hardcastle by were within the other man's reach: he would be a bishop soon, perhaps one day an archbishop while Hardcastle remained here, mouldering on the Marsh.

'You dare to walk into my house, insult my housekeeper, then order me about like a servant! A man died, Dean! Does that mean nothing to you? He died, and I said his burial service as we laid him in a nameless grave in the churchyard. He—'

'You buried him in the churchyard?' interrupted Cornewall, his anger changing to horror. 'My God, man, have you lost your mind? We don't know who he is! He could be anyone!'

'No!' roared the rector. 'He was *someone*! He was a man, a young man who should have lived long and died happy and peaceful in his sleep at a ripe old age. And I shall find out who killed him, Dean, by God I shall, no matter how long it takes me!'

'No! I forbid this! You will stay out of this matter! Those are the direct orders of the archbishop!'

He had told Mrs Kemp he intended to wash his hands of the matter. Cornewall was now ordering him to do exactly that. And that was all the impetus he needed to make his final decision.

'I don't give a damn about the archbishop,' he thundered in his pulpit voice, 'and I don't give a damn about you! I will see justice in this matter. Do you understand, sir? Do you understand me?'

'Understand you!' exploded Cornewall. 'Listen to you, man! You are so drunk you can barely understand yourself, and it is not yet gone six in the evening! You are a disgrace to the Church, Hardcastle, and a disgrace to yourself. By God, sir, if you carry on like this very much longer, one fine day you will find yourself out of this living and out on your ear. Do *you* understand *me*?'

The rector took a deep breath and resisted the temptation to plant his fist on the dean's long nose, much as he had done on a memorable occasion at Cambridge twenty years ago. 'You have no authority over me, Cornewall,' he growled. 'My superior is the archdeacon, not you. And the archdeacon cannot remove me from my living, not without Lord Clavertye's consent.'

'The archdeacon will do exactly what His Grace and I tell him to do,' sneered the dean. 'As for Clavertye, don't count on him to protect you for ever. You'll offend him in the end, just as you offend everyone around you. No, don't bother to see me out.' He raised a finger. 'I am warning you, Hardcastle. I will be at the inquest tomorrow, watching you. Stay out of this affair, or I will make it my personal business to see that you are removed from this living and expelled from the clergy!'

In the silence that fell after the dean's carriage had departed, the housekeeper came with her shuffling gait into the study. The rector held up a hand. 'Mrs Kemp, I am sorry. That man had no right to be so rude to you.'

'No, Reverend Hardcastle,' the woman said, her face unchanging. 'That is your prerogative. Shall I go to the cellar and fetch another bottle?'

'If you please,' said the rector heavily.

5

The Inquest

The inquest was held at the Star the following day, starting at eleven in the morning to allow the coroner and his jury time to travel down from Ashford. By the time the rector arrived the common room was already full, much of the population of St Mary in the Marsh having turned out to see the show. In this parish, the death of a Customs officer was a matter for curiosity and, perhaps, secret celebration; but everyone wanted to know what had happened at the rectory. Even decent women who would otherwise never darken the door of a public house were there, thought the rector. He saw Mrs Chaytor talking with Fanscombe's wife, Eugénie, a small sharp-faced Frenchwoman, and bowed to them both. Fanscombe's daughter, Eliza, a well-proportioned young woman in her late teens, was not far away, enjoying the admiration of a group of young men.

He made his way through the press, and people made room for him cheerfully. 'Good day to you, Reverend!' someone called. 'Going to give evidence, are you?'

'I shall do my duty as a citizen,' he answered, smiling a jovial smile. They laughed, and a couple of men slapped him on the back. He was a popular figure in the parish, and not just because he bought them drinks and kept quiet about their nocturnal activities. Everyone tolerated him; many respected him, and some actually quite liked him.

Reaching the bar, he looked across at Bessie Luckhurst, looking very neat with her hair pinned up. Out of the corner of his eye he saw Turner the painter, leaning on the end of the bar.

'What can I fetch you, Reverend?'

'Strong ale,' he said. 'The strongest you have.' The girl raised her eyebrows but said nothing, taking down a mug and filling it.

Walking off his hangover that morning had given the rector time to plan his tactics for today. He had sworn to Cornwall that he would find whoever shot the boy, but he knew also that discretion was in order. Clavertye's warning had been unnecessary. The killer had already taken one shot at him; if he thought that Hardcastle was on his trail, he would strike again. The men of the parish, too, would not take kindly to any intrusion into their own affairs; they respected and tolerated him, yes, but there were limits beyond which he could not go.

He had to pretend, therefore, that he was in no way interested in this affair, while in fact he had to remain very interested indeed. So he sipped his ale – by thunder, this stuff *was* strong – and watched from the corner of his eye as Luckhurst and another man dragged a trestle table to one end of the common room and then placed two chairs, one for the coroner and one for his clerk. The twelve jurors, all Ashford men – no one from the Marsh could be trusted to be impartial where smuggling was concerned – sat silently along one wall, looking apprehensive as the locals stared back at them and murmured behind their hands. Hardcastle thought they looked like castaways who had suddenly found themselves among a tribe of cannibals.

Seated at his table, the coroner began unpacking his case and his notes. Someone else came and bent down beside him, a big man with a beefy face: Blunt. The Customs man talked quietly but urgently, and the coroner listened, eyes still fixed on his papers, nodding from time to time. Fanscombe, the justice of the peace, joined them too, spoke briefly and then withdrew. Turning his head, the rector saw Captain Shaw in his scruffy uniform, standing next to the door and watching this interaction.

On the far side of the room Cornewall sat watching too, his arched eyebrows drawn together a little and his forehead furrowed. He had seen the rector enter the room, but had pointedly ignored him. 'Did the dean stay here last night?' the rector asked Bessie.

'Aye, he did,' said the girl. 'I don't think much of him. He's got a poker stuck up his bum, if you ask me. Why can't all clergymen be like you, Reverend Hardcastle?'

'I don't think that is a thing to be wished for, my dear. Is Lord Clavertye arrived?'

Bessie pointed and the rector looked across the crowded room to see Lord Clavertye leaning against a wall, arms folded across his chest. He too was watching Blunt and the coroner, Hardcastle saw. Fanscombe had joined Dr Morley, both talking quietly; the doctor looked bored. Juddery of the Excise stood alone, conscious of the waves of silent dislike radiating from the villagers around him.

'Ah, good stuff,' said the rector, sighing and holding out his empty mug. 'Another, Bessie, if you will, there's a good lass.'

The coroner was a long thin man with a long thin face and spectacles that kept slipping down his nose and threatening to fall off. He rapped his gavel on the table and declared the inquest in session.

'At the request of the deputy lord-lieutenant,' he said, looking around the room, 'I shall conduct a joint inquest into the deaths of the anonymous man found at the rectory, and of Curtius Miller, Customs officer, who died on the Marsh.'

Curtius Miller, thought the rector. At least one of our dead men has a name ... Blunt was speaking. 'Is this usual practice, sir? I understand joint inquests are held only when the deaths are in some way linked.'

'It is my hope that this inquest will establish whether they *are* linked, Mr Blunt,' said Clavertye, still leaning against the wall.

'Indeed, my lord,' said the coroner, 'though I would remind you that the purpose of this inquest is to establish how these men came by their deaths. It is not for this court to investigate why these men died, or to determine issues of guilt or innocence. That is for a subsequent inquiry to determine,' and he bowed to the deputy lord-lieutenant, who inclined his head in acknowledgement. Hardcastle wondered how the man who had once prosecuted cases before the House of Lords liked being lectured by a county coroner.

'One moment first,' said Clavertye. 'May I ask the court what has become of the bodies of the deceased?'

The coroner consulted his notes. 'The unnamed man has been buried in the churchyard here in St Mary in the Marsh. The body of Mr Miller was reclaimed by his family and taken to Deal, his home. Both bodies were viewed by Dr Morley in his capacity of deputy coroner, and I am satisfied that his examination was complete.'

'Very well, carry on.'

'The court calls Dr Morley.'

Morley, slim and debonair, took the oath and sat down, taking out his pillbox and popping a liquorice pastille into his mouth. The coroner shuffled his notes and adjusted his glasses. 'In your written report to me, you stated that you examined the body of the man found at the rectory. Will you tell the court when you examined the body and what you found?'

'Reverend Hardcastle sent me a message on the morning of the seventh of May, stating that a death had taken place. I attended the body as soon as possible thereafter. I found that the man had been killed by a single gunshot, a rifle bullet, which severed an artery close to his heart. I believe that death was almost instantaneous. This accorded very closely with what Reverend Hardcastle told me.'

'We will hear the rector's testimony shortly, doctor. For the moment, please confine yourself to your own observations.'

'I accept the court's correction most humbly.' Morley bowed. A small, feminine titter ran around the room, and the doctor permitted himself to smile a little. The rector took another gulp of his beer.

'At what time did you estimate death to have taken place?'

'Judging by the appearance of rigor, around midnight.' Morley paused. 'Reverend Hardcastle will doubtless confirm this in his own evidence.'

He really does look bored, thought the rector. He does not care about the dead man. He simply wants to get this over with.

'Were there any other distinguishing features about the body?'

'Apart from a few cuts and bruises, none.'

'And was there any evidence on the body that might confirm his identity?'

'None whatever.'

'Any distinguishing marks?'

'None. Until the time of his death, the man had been healthy and fit.'

'You also examined the body of Curtius Miller, late of His Majesty's Customs. Will you explain the circumstances?'

'Shortly after returning from the rectory,' said Morley, 'as I sat down to a much delayed breakfast, I received another message from Mr Blunt of the Customs. He asked me to attend the body of one of his men then lying at New Romney. I proceeded to New Romney and examined the body.'

'And what did you find?'

'This man too had died of a gunshot wound, this time to the belly. I found that the weapon, a pistol ball, had damaged the abdominal artery. This man would have bled to death quite quickly.'

The rector sat puzzled, his ears ringing a little from the strong ale. Why call Morley all the way to New Romney, two and a half miles away, when the town had a doctor of its own? Dr Mackay was also an assistant coroner, fully qualified to conduct post-mortem examinations. 'And did you estimate the time of death?' asked the coroner.

'Again, very close to midnight. The state of rigor was almost identical to that of the other body.'

Lord Clavertye held up a hand. 'Do you have any idea as to how this wound might have occurred, doctor?'

'I can only observe that the shot had been fired at very close range, my lord. There were powder stains and grains of unburnt powder on the deceased's clothing. Any further observation would be beyond my competence.'

'Thank you. You may stand down, doctor.'

'State your name.'

'Joseph Mallord William Turner.'

'And your profession?'

'I am a painter.'

'A painter of houses?'

'No, a painter of pictures.' Sniggering in the common room.

'You were abroad in the village at midnight on the sixth of May?'

'I was taking the air, yes.'

'According to your statement, you heard shots coming from the direction of St Mary's Bay.'

'I did.'

'Did you hear any noise coming from the direction of the rectory?'

'None whatever.'

'No?' The coroner raised his eyebrows. 'Not the sound of a rifle, perhaps?'

'The rectory was to the north of me, and there was a stiff wind blowing from the east. It would have carried any sound away from me.'

'I see. Now, tell the court about the following morning.'

'I went down to St Mary's Bay to paint, as is my custom. Return-ing from my morning's work, I discovered the place where I believed the free-traders had run their cargo ashore. I followed their track for about half a mile inland, where I found the scene of a skirmish between the free-traders and Preventive men. Searching the area, I saw several traces of burnt wadding from muskets or pistols which had been discharged nearby, and a large bloodstain on the grass next to a ditch. I also spotted the footsteps of men making off to the south towards New Romney. They were in great haste; I would say they were running from the fight.'

'The smugglers?'

'No, from the direction of the footprints I would guess it was the Preventive men.' Someone in the common room started to laugh and then turned it into a fit of coughing. The coroner looked over his glasses at the witness. 'Have you anything further to add, Mr Turner?'

'Yes. I think I may have seen the man who was killed at the rectory, two days before the murder.'

Everyone sat up very straight at this. The silence was broken by the rector, belching.

'Where did you see this man, Mr Turner?'

'Right here, in St Mary. I saw him walking past the entrance to New Hall, Mr Fanscombe's house. He was about my age. He was dressed in a brown coat and breeches and a darker brown waistcoat, with black half-boots. He had a gold watch on a fob. I knew at once that he was not from around here.'

There were murmurs in the audience; it was clear that one or two others remembered seeing him too. 'You have an eye for detail, Mr Turner.'

'I am a trained artist, sir.'

'Have you anything else to add?'

'Yes, sir. It crossed my mind that he was French.'

Another murmur ran around the room. The rector saw Eugénie Fanscombe's eyes flicker. 'Why do you say that?' asked the coroner. 'Did you speak to him?'

'No, I exchanged no words with him, nor did I hear him speak. It was something about his face, the set of his jaw and the cast of his mouth. I cannot explain further.'

'Indeed,' said the coroner drily. 'But that hardly counts as evidence.'

'Nevertheless, the man was French, sir. I am quite certain of it.'

'State your name.'

'Mrs Amelia Chaytor.'

'You are married?'

'I am a widow.' Three years, and the words still hurt.

'Mrs Chaytor, your statement to the justice of the peace accords closely with that of Mr Turner. You found the same marks on the sand, the same scene of the skirmish, the same bloodstain.' The coroner paused. 'Mrs Chaytor, I know this must be very distressing for you, and if you wish to be excused, I would quite understand.'

'I am not remotely distressed,' said the light, softly drawling voice, 'and I do not wish to be excused.'

'Very well. Did you see any sign of a weapon at the scene of the death of Mr Miller?'

'None. I fear that I can add nothing to the account that I gave in my statement to Mr Fanscombe.'

'Then you may step down.'

'A moment, though, if you please. I do have an additional statement to make concerning the young man who died at the rectory.'

A murmur ran around the common room. The coroner, who objected in principle to the idea of women being called as witnesses in court, and had only called this one because Lord Clavertye had insisted, glared at her over his spectacles. 'As you please. Make your statement.'

'Yesterday afternoon, after I had given my statement to Mr Fanscombe, I walked the path from St Mary in the Marsh to Ivychurch. About halfway between the two villages there is a patch of marshland, with a looker's hut on its edge.'

The coroner raised his hand. 'A moment, if you please. What is a looker's hut?'

'The shepherds use looker's huts for watching over their flocks in summer', said Mrs Chaytor. 'I believe this paricular hut is also sometimes used by sportsmen as a blind for shooting duck. I trust the gentlemen in the room will correct me if I am wrong.'

No one corrected her. The rector belched again and asked for his mug to be refilled.

'I cannot say what instinct of curiosity drew me there – perhaps it was woman's intuition?' No one but the rector would have caught the note of irony in her voice. 'But at all events, I went into the hut. The building, as some here would doubtless confirm, is divided into two rooms; the forward room, where the shepherds sit when they watch the sheep, and a second, windowless room at the rear, which I suspect is normally used for storage.'

There was dead silence in the room, and the rector wondered whether Mrs Chaytor knew that some of those who used the looker's hut for 'storage' were the local smugglers. He decided she probably did.

'It was clear that the hut had been recently used,' she continued, 'and further, that one of the rooms, the smaller, had been used as a place of confinement. I saw marks on the door where someone had tried to kick it down. The wood around the hasp was splintered, indicating that he might have succeeded; certainly the door was no longer locked. I also found pieces of rope on the floor.

'In the other room, the front room, there was a table with crusts of bread and other scraps of food, all of which had been much worried by mice. But in a far corner of the room I saw a glint of metal in the shadows, and upon taking a closer look, I found this.'

She reached into her reticule and held up a gold watch on a chain and fob. A buzz of fascinated voices rose, and the coroner banged his gavel on the table for silence. 'I opened the case, and found it to be of French make,' said Amelia Chaytor, looking across at Turner. 'I also found signs of damage, such as might have been caused by recent submersion in water.'

'Are you a watchmaker, madam?' asked the coroner crossly.

'No, sir. It is merely that I too have an eye for detail.'

The court was still laughing when she was dismissed. Clavertye had a slight smile at the corner of his mouth, and the rector realised that he had known in advance about the watch; Mrs Chaytor must have shown it to him yesterday afternoon. He began to appreciate just how much work

Clavertye had already put into this case, confident of the verdicts of the inquest.

'The court calls Joshua Stemp.'

The fisherman, a short dark man with cheeks badly pitted by smallpox, took the oath to tell the truth, the whole truth and nothing but the truth, and then sat back, casually ready to perjure himself whenever required.

'You were at sea on the night of sixth May.'

'Yes, sir. Fishing, I was.'

'Did you see anything of the events that took place on shore?'

'No sir, on account of it being the darks, you see. I saw flashes and heard shouts and shooting up towards Dymchurch way, that's all.'

'You saw nothing at sea? No boats? No men on the beach?'

'Swear on my honour, sir, not a blessed thing. It was too dark, you see.'

The rector surveyed his mug, drained it and handed it across the counter to be refilled; he was by no means drunk enough yet.

'Mr Stemp,' said Lord Clavertye, 'does the name the Twelve Apostles mean anything to you?'

Absolute silence fell in the room. The coroner looked perplexed. Blunt sat up straight, his beefy face turning deep red.

''Fraid not, sir. Never heard of them.'

'Not even the ones in the New Testament, Mr Stemp?' asked Clavertye ironically.

'Oh . . . *them* Apostles, my lord. I recollect them just fine.'

Tension began to ebb out of the room, and there was even a murmur of laughter. 'Mr Stemp,' said Clavertye, 'I put it to you that there were two gangs of smugglers at large on the night of sixth May. You say you saw one group, further north along the beach. You saw no sign of any group landing at St Mary's Bay?'

'Upon my honour, sir, no sign at all.' Well, thought the rector, that was probably true. Stemp himself had almost certainly been on the beach further north, exchanging pot-shots with Juddery's Excise men. He would have been in no position to see anything in St Mary's Bay.

Juddery of the Excise was called, taking the oath without looking at his rival Blunt. He confirmed that his men had engaged a gang of smugglers

about two miles from St Mary in the Marsh and been driven off by superior numbers. None of his men had come near the village, said the Excise
man, so there was no question of them being involved in either incident.
He doubted whether the smugglers would have done so either, as after the
skirmish the gang had made off west across country. Yes, he had attempted
to track them, but in the dark and without bloodhounds he had soon lost
the trail; this was the cue for more sniggering. Stemp sat listening to this
account with his face a picture of innocence.

Captain Shaw of the militia was next. He had been out on patrol on
the night of the two killings, and knew nothing about either incident
until informed by Mr Fanscombe around midday the next day. During
the afternoon of the 7th, Saturday, he had sent two files of men to sweep
the fields around St Mary in the Marsh, but they had found no trace of
any fighting. No, they had not seen any sign of the skirmish described by
Mr Turner and Mrs Chaytor. No, they had not investigated the looker's
hut. Behind the bar, Mr Luckhurst snorted.

'You could run a herd of elephants under the nose of that ragamuffin,
and he wouldn't see or hear a blessed thing. You sure you want another,
Reverend? They'll be calling you in a moment. Well, on your head be it.'

'State your name.'

'Henry Blunt, supervisor of His Majesty's Customs.'

'According to your deposition, Mr Blunt, you were the first man to find
the body of Curtius Miller.'

'Yes, sir.'

'Describe the events of the night of sixth May, if you please.'

'We were on a routine patrol near St Mary's Bay when we came under
fire from a gang of smugglers. We returned fire at once, but my men were
armed only with pistols while the smugglers had muskets. As it was clear
that we were outgunned and outnumbered, I told my men to withdraw
to the south. We withdrew *in good order*,' this with a look at Turner, who
looked impassively back, 'and it was only when we had withdrawn about
half a mile that I found Mr Miller was missing. I was concerned at this, for
he had only lately joined us from the patrol at Deal and does not know the
Marsh. I decided to return to the scene of the fighting to look for him.'

'That was very brave of you, Mr Blunt. The smugglers might still have been there, waiting.'

'It was a chance I had to take, sir. The interests of my men come before my personal safety, always have done and always will.' Was it the rector's imagination, or was there a faint hiss somewhere in the room? 'As I say, I returned and began casting about in the darkness, calling his name. Then, very sadly, I found him lying by the edge of a sewer. I felt for his heartbeat but it was too late. He was already dead.'

'And what time was this, Mr Blunt?'

'About half past midnight.'

'Wait a moment,' interposed Lord Clavertye. 'How could you know what time it was? According to other witnesses, the night was very dark. You could see the face of your watch?'

'No, my lord, not just then. I dragged Mr Miller's body towards the rest of my men, and when I reached them I lit a lantern so that we could check for certain that he was dead. It was then that we saw the full nature of his wound. *Then* I checked my watch by lantern light and found that it was about one in the morning.'

'Half an hour to drag a heavy body that distance seems reasonable,' said Clavertye, nodding. 'Go on.'

'There's little else to tell, sir. We made a litter and carried poor Mr Miller down to New Romney, and there once it was light I sent word for Dr Morley.'

Why Dr Morley, the rector wondered again, and not Dr Mackay in New Romney? However, the coroner did not ask the question. 'Mr Blunt, you said in your written statement that you do not believe the wound received by Mr Miller was caused by fire from the smugglers. Can you explain why?'

The rector watched Blunt from under lowered eyelids. 'I'm not saying it is impossible, sir,' said Blunt. 'But 'tis unlikely. For one thing, the fire aimed at us by the smugglers was wild, and most of it went high. A man would have been unlucky indeed to have taken a hit. For another, as Dr Morley said, the shot was fired at very close range, and I would swear none of the free-traders came within fifty yards of us. I know it was dark, but by the gun flashes I reckon they were at least that far away. And finally, poor Mr Miller was in the habit of carrying a cocked and loaded pistol in the waistband of his trousers. I warned him of the dangers of doing so, more than once, but he insisted this was his habit. He could draw his pistol and return fire more quickly, he said, if we were attacked.'

'You think that this wound might have been caused by an accidental discharge?'

'It's the thing I warned him against, sir. A trip over a tree root, a slip in the mud, and bang.'

'Mr Blunt, when you found Mr Miller's body, was the pistol still in his waistband?'

'It was, sir.'

'And had the pistol been discharged?'

'I very much fear that it had, sir.'

Lord Clavertye interposed again. 'Mr Blunt, how did you come to be near St Mary's Bay, and not further north working with Mr Juddery to intercept the other run, which we now know to have been much larger? Did you have some specific intelligence to indicate that a second run was being made?'

An expression of disgust at the idea of working with Juddery crossed Blunt's beetroot face. 'Absolutely not, my lord. This was merely a routine patrol. I was as surprised as anyone when the smugglers opened fire on us.'

'And prior to their commencing firing, you had no idea they were there?'

'None at all, my lord. I'm afraid they had the drop on us.'

'And have you any idea of the destination of this run?'

'Again, none at all, my lord. To be honest, I am not convinced it was a real run. I think it more likely to have been a flanking party covering the main run to the north, keeping a lookout for more Preventive men and ready to drive us off if we tried to intervene.'

'In that case, they did a good job,' said Clavertye drily. 'One more question, Mr Blunt, before you stand down. What do you know about the Twelve Apostles?'

It was well done, but Blunt was ready for the question. 'Like Stemp, my lord, I've heard of the Apostles in the Bible but no more.' He smiled. 'Perhaps you should ask the reverend.'

*

'State your name.'

'I am the Reverend Marcus Aurelius Hardcastle, rector of St Mary in the Marsh.'

'Do you swear to the tell the truth, the whole truth and nothing but the truth?'

'I do, so help me –' Another thunderous belch escaped into the room. An expression of pain crossed Folliott Cornewall's face. Amelia Chaytor had bowed her head. 'So help me God. I do apologise most profushly,' said the rector gravely.

The coroner peered at him, clearly wondering whether he was sober enough to continue. 'You may sit,' he said. 'I have here your statement as given to the justice of the peace.'

'Fanscombe,' nodded the rector. 'Capital fellow. Is he here? Ah, there he is. How are you, Fanscombe?' and he beamed and gave a cheerful wave.

'There are a few points on which I do need to press you, Reverend Hardcastle. Firstly, you said in your statement that the man was entirely dead when you found him. You are certain of this?'

'Curious how everyone keeps asking that,' said the rector. He swayed a little in his chair and then sat up. 'Quite certain, sir, quite certain. I checked for a pulse as soon as I brought him into the house, and found none. Not surprisin'. I've seen a fair few gunshot wounds, and as soon as I saw this one I knew it was all up. Poor fellow.'

'You have seen gunshot wounds?' said the coroner in surprise.

'A long time ago,' said the rector, not looking at either Clavertye or Cornewall.

The coroner reverted to the matter at hand. 'So there was no question of his being able to speak or pass on a message to you, or anyone else?'

'Well, he *might* have,' conceded the rector, 'but I think if a dead man had sat up and given me a message, I would have remembered it. I might even have thought it important enough to mention to Mr Fanscombe.' There was laughter in the room, and a man's voice called, 'Good old reverend!' The rector watched his audience hazily, the voice whispering in his mind. *Tell Peter . . . mark . . . trace.*

'Be pleased to bear with me,' the coroner said testily. 'We are hoping obviously to establish this man's identity.'

'Are you? I thought the purposh— the purpose of this inquest was to establish how he came by his death.'

More laughter, and the coroner resorted to his gavel again. 'You stated also that you searched the body and found nothing.'

'He bought his clothes in London. That is all that I can tell you. At least, if there was anything else, I don't remember it.'

'Mr Turner has stated that he believes he saw the man several days earlier. Are you certain that you did not see him also?'

The rector paused for a long time. 'I cannot remember, really I cannot. I don't think I have seen him. I might have, and not remembered it. You'll have to forgive me, you see. My powers of observation are occasionally . . . what shall we say . . . impaired.'

Another burst of laughter and the coroner, losing his temper, banged his wooden gavel so hard that the head snapped off and flew onto the floor. The more juvenile members of the audience, including Eliza Fanscombe, crowed with delight. Mrs Fanscombe, her face sharper than ever, turned and shot her stepdaughter a stern look, which was ignored. The rector sat beaming benevolently at them, his eyes watchful. Cornewall's face was full of disgust; Blunt was sneering openly, Morley the same but a little more discreetly. Clavertye watched him with expressionless face; the rector thought that His Lordship, at least, understood the game he was playing.

'Reverend Hardcastle,' said the coroner crossly, 'given your . . . impairment, I am not certain it is worth proceeding with your testimony. You are excused.'

'Thank you, sir. Thank you. May I just add one further thing?'

'If you must.'

'This has been a terrible business.' The rector shook his head. 'Terrible business,' he repeated. 'It has been a great shock to me, to us all. Violence has come amongst us, the peace of our little community has been broken, and now we are frightened and full of sorrow. In this hour we must turn to God, who sees all things and who will comfort and protect us.' He struggled to his feet, 'I should like to lead a prayer now,' he said, 'and ask the Lord to aid us in our time of need. Will you join me, so that He may hear our voices?'

He raised his hands. 'This really is not appropriate,' said the coroner, but the rector ignored him. 'Heavenly Father,' he intoned in his bass voice, 'we beseech you to watch over us. We are poor and humble people, Lord, deserving of your mercy. Shend us your blesshings and help ush to find the path of . . . of . . .'

The rector wavered. He took a step forward to regain his balance, but stumbled in doing so. Arms flailing, he took several more steps and crashed into the table where Stemp and several of his friends were sitting, oversetting several pots of beer and cups of gin. He heard the men's cries of distress as he sank slowly to his knees.

'Amen,' said the rector solemnly, and he slumped under the table.

6

Peering Through the Haze

'I thought I would find you here,' said Amelia Chaytor.

The sound of her light voice roused him from his black stupor. He raised his aching head and looked at her. She seemed to shimmer. Was that blurred vision, or just the effect of the light coming through the stained glass windows on the south side of the nave?

They were in the church, he slumped in a wooden pew, she standing beside it looking down at him. He had made his way here after being carried out of the Star; in the street he had shrugged off his helpers and staggered artistically up the street. Once out of sight of the inn he had carried on with somewhat more composure, though he still weaved from time to time. He had come into the church rather than going home because the church was cool and quiet and peaceful, a place where he could collect his thoughts.

'Why did you think I would be here?' he asked.

She smiled. 'Because it is the one place in St Mary where no one is likely to disturb you.'

That was true enough. 'How did you know that?' he asked.

'I know St Mary folk. They go to church three times, twice in life and once after it. I am not criticising them, you understand. I myself have not darkened the door of a church for many years.'

He gazed at her. 'You're not an atheist.'

'Goodness, no. My late husband was. I used to twit him about it, telling him that atheism was a belief and he was just as deluded as you lot. No, I'm a non-practising agnostic.'

'And what does that mean?'

'It means that I don't know if there is a God, but I really don't feel like making the effort to find out.' She glanced at the altar. 'And if a thunderbolt strikes me down now, so be it. Do you really desire solitude? Or may I sit down?'

He opened the door of the pew while seated, not yet trusting himself to rise, and she sat down, folding her skirts neatly as she did so. There were no thunderbolts. 'Do you want to know the verdict of the inquest?' Mrs Chaytor asked.

'In the case of the anonymous man found dead at the rectory,' he intoned, 'the court returns a verdict of unlawful killing. In the case of Mr Curtius Miller, the court returns a verdict of death by misadventure.'

She opened her fine eyes wide. 'Well, well. How did you guess?'

'It was all in Blunt's testimony. The man was already at serious risk of accident. The shot was fired at close quarters, but the free-traders fired from a distance. Miller's pistol was in his waistband, and had been fired. The poor man clearly tripped or stumbled and the pistol went off.'

'Do you believe this?'

'No. Anyone could have fired that pistol and then replaced it his waistband. Miller himself might have fired it at the smugglers, before being killed by another weapon. Whatever happened, he was shot at close range by one of his own people.'

There was a little pause and she said reflectively, 'So you were paying attention. That was quite a performance, Reverend. You would be a credit to any stage. Do you mind telling me what it was about?'

He knew he should go no further with this conversation; it was unpardonable to involve a woman in an affair where two men had died. He thought of asking her to leave. Instead he said, 'Mrs Chaytor, I am a man playing two different hands in two different games at the same time. My patron, the deputy lord-lieutenant, suspects that all is not as it seems in this matter.'

'As do you. As do I.'

'Indeed. And he has asked me to investigate further. At the same time, the Dean of Canterbury has told me to have nothing further to do with this matter. If I carry on, he has threatened to take action against me. He himself has no official power over me, but he has much influence with the archdeacon and archbishop, who do.'

'They cannot take away your living. That is in the gift of Lord Clavertye.'

'Cornewall will find ways of making trouble for me, believe me. We have a certain . . . history.'

'I see. Who was it that said, no man can serve two masters?'

'It was the Apostle Matthew, and clearly he was never a clergyman in the Church of England.'

'If you continue to investigate you will displease the dean, and if you do nothing, you will displease Lord Clavertye.'

'Quite.'

'So, your solution was to do something while pretending to do nothing. But why pretend to be drunk? Why not just keep your head down and play King Log?'

He thought of telling her that there was not much pretence involved. 'Because,' he said, 'the man – or men – who killed Mr Miller and the boy at the rectory were almost certainly in the room today; or if not, they had agents there. I have been questioned repeatedly about the events of that night, most recently by the coroner. Someone suspects that I know more than I am letting on.'

'Ah,' she said softly. 'Keeping your head down is not enough. You want to convince them that you are harmless.'

'And what can be more harmless than a foolish, forgetful old drunk? It is a role,' he said with sudden bitterness, 'that I was born to play.'

She did not know how to answer this, and they both sat in silence for a moment. The rector's head ached. He wanted a drink, a real drink, not beer.

'Tell me what you have done so far,' she demanded, and he blinked at the sudden authority in her voice. The drawl had gone too.

'Most of it you know already,' he said reluctantly. 'In fact, you and Mr Turner knew more than I did. The man may have been French, and he was a man of enough substance to own a gold watch. And he was held prisoner at the looker's hut; for some time, would you say?'

'Yes,' she said. 'There was a chamber pot in the room where he had been confined. I won't bore you with the details.'

Once again he looked at her in astonishment; she was like no woman he had ever met. Her calm was phenomenal. He paused and gathered the thoughts circling in his cloudy mind.

'The morning after the murder at the rectory,' he said, 'I worked out that there were three ways of trying to solve the puzzle. One was to try to establish the identity of the dead man, which I judged impossible. We know a few more things about him now, but we are still a long way from the truth. Another was to find out exactly what had happened out on the Marsh that night. We have now done that. We know that there were two lots of Preventive men, and two lots of smugglers.'

'And two skirmishes,' she nodded.

'Yes. And we also know that there is a mysterious group called the Twelve Apostles, who may have been present and may be intimately involved in the affair, or alternatively, may have nothing whatsoever to do with it . . . Increasingly, I feel that I have been chasing a red herring. Understanding the events on the Marsh has got me no closer to the truth.'

'Has it not? I would not say so. For one thing, we can now leave aside the affray to the north, the fight between Mr Juddery's men and our near and dear neighbours in this parish. Neither party had anything to do with the events down here. That narrows our field of inquiry. For another, we have a very strong circumstantial link between the second party and our dead Frenchman. When I visited the looker's hut, I also found the trail he took after he escaped, and followed it across the fields. He was heading east, straight for St Mary's Bay, when he was killed. Had he carried on, he would have certainly encountered either Mr Blunt's men, the second band of smugglers, or both.'

'So it would seem.'

'You mentioned three ways of solving the puzzle. What is the third way?'

The time had come, he knew, but his reluctance remained. The last words of the dead man were like a confession, to be kept private and secret. He stared at the altar, asking silently for forgiveness. Then he told her.

'*Tell Peter . . . mark . . . trace*,' she repeated softly. Her voice held some of the same reverence that he felt. The dead man had entrusted them with something precious; they must use this knowledge well, and not let him down.

'He was speaking English? You are quite certain?'

'I am entirely certain. *Tell Peter, mark, trace.*'

'Was there an accent?'

'His voice was nearly gone; there may have been an accent, but I did not detect it. Why?'

'How is your French, Reverend?' He looked at her, and she said softly, half under her breath, '*Trace. Tra-ace. Trahis.*'

Revelation exploded in the rector's mind. He clenched his fist and struck his own forehead, his headache quite forgotten. '*Trahison*! I can hear it clearly now, it wasn't *trace* at all, it was *trahison*! Treason! So Turner was right. He *was* French.'

'But his first words were in English.'

'Poor, poor boy, he was dying; his mind was wandering. Actually, my dear, I don't think he knew where he was, or *what* language he was speaking. He was so desperate, desperate to tell someone, anyone, so that his death would not be in vain ... Mrs Chaytor, may I congratulate you on your splendid reasoning? My tired old brain has been struggling with these four words for days. You have worked them out almost at once.'

'You should have told me sooner,' she said smiling. '*Peter*, of course is a name. Possibly not a real name. The smugglers around here all use nicknames when they are on a run.'

'Yes, of course. Old Fred, Nasty Face, Pinch-Purse, Big Belly, the Clubber, Yorkshire Tom.' He chuckled. 'There've been at least six Yorkshire Toms over the years, and they all have two things in common. None of them is called Tom, and none has ever been to Yorkshire. I think they make up the names to amuse themselves.'

'Boys will be boys,' she said drily.

'Indeed. Now, what do you suppose *mark* might mean? A mark that would indicate treason? An identifying mark, by which the traitor would be known; a scar, a mole, a tattoo? Or a mark indicating a place where they could find the traitor? The looker's hut, perhaps? Or a mark on the door of a house? They used to put secret marks on the door of the church tower to indicate whether a run cargo was stored inside ...'

His voice trailed off. Mrs Chaytor, watching him, thought that some of the colour drained from his face. 'Oh, dear heavens,' he said softly. 'I have indeed been going about this all wrong. Entirely wrong, right from the start.'

'My dear man, whatever do you mean?'

'It is not *a* mark. It is *Mark*, Mark the Evangelist. Tell Peter, Mark, treason. Mrs Chaytor, we have stumbled across the track of the Twelve Apostles.'

*

'I need air,' he said. 'Will you come and walk with me in the churchyard?'

'If someone sees us talking together, might they become suspicious?' she asked as they rose.

'We shall tell them that you are making a donation to repair the church roof,' he said, opening the door of the pew, 'and we are examining the condition of the roof in order to determine the size of the donation.'

'Is the church roof in need of repair?'

'My dear Mrs Chaytor, the first immutable law of the Church of England is that the church roof is usually in need of repair. And when the church is as close to the English Channel as we are, it always is.'

Outside, there was a fresh wind blowing and clouds were building up on the south-western horizon beyond Rye. The rector looked at the sky and wondered if there was rain coming. They walked in silence for a moment, past the yew tree and across the churchyard with its rows of mossy tombstones, and stopped and looked down for a moment at the fresh earth covering the grave of the young man. Mrs Chaytor waited quietly while the rector bowed his head and uttered a short soft prayer.

'It brings it all home,' she said after a while.

'What does?'

'Seeing the grave. I confess I have been rather fixed on poor Mr Miller. I have regarded your man as more of an academic exercise. Standing here now, I am reminded that he too was a real man who lived, and died.'

She looked at him, her blue eyes very clear. 'Let me hazard a guess. We talked earlier about the nicknames used by smugglers. Might the Twelve Apostles be a gang of smugglers, whose members each take the name of one of the twelve?'

'It would seem to fit. It would make them a rather small gang of smugglers by local standards; it is not uncommon for fifty or a hundred men, or even more, to take part in a run. But perhaps these are the core brotherhood, with other men working for them. Or perhaps they are smuggling different goods. Any involvement with smuggling would also explain Blunt's interest.'

'And two men were killed because of some connection with this gang?'

He nodded slowly. 'It is a working hypothesis.'

'One thing bothers me,' she said after a little pause. 'Well. Many things about this affair bother me, but one frets me particularly. Why go to such lengths to stage Miller's death as an accident? Why not simply claim that the smugglers had shot him?'

'Because then the coroner would have returned a verdict of unlawful killing,' said the rector. 'The case would be treated as murder, and Lord Clavertye would be required to investigate it. That is the last thing Blunt wants. It is my belief that Blunt is corrupt, that he is receiving money from at least some of the smugglers, and an investigation might well turn up evidence of this. But if the death is treated as misadventure, the case is closed and Clavertye has no legal reason to investigate. Blunt carries on in perfect security.'

'Ah,' she said gently. 'I should have thought of that. I was sure that Blunt was lying about Miller's death, but I could not understand what he was covering up, or for whom. Now it makes sense.'

'I have never liked Blunt,' said the rector, 'and I now see why. He must know who the killer is, and why Miller was killed, but he will sweep all of that under the carpet. It takes a very special kind of evil to cover up a murder in order to protect oneself.'

'And Blunt did more than lie,' she said. 'I believe he bribed that odious coroner to deliver the verdict he wanted. I watched them together before the inquest opened. I can read lips, a little.'

He blinked at her. 'You can?'

She disregarded this. 'I did not understand everything they said, for they were turned partly away from me. But Blunt repeated the same phrase several times: "as arranged". And each time he did so, the coroner nodded. And he said something else too, about a question. "If the question comes up, you must stop it." That was what he said, I think.'

'Ah. I wonder if that is the question that I kept hoping the coroner would ask?'

'Which was?'

'Why, when Blunt and his men had retreated to New Romney, did they send for Dr Morley from St Mary to attend the body? Why not ask the doctor at New Romney?'

'Perhaps Dr Mackay was out on another call. We could find out, I am certain.'

'Yes. There must be a good reason for his absence. What puzzled me was why the coroner did not ask the question. Of course the issue lies outside the scope of the inquest, which was to determine how the two men came by their deaths. But he asked plenty of other questions that were also outside the scope of the inquest. Surely natural curiosity would have compelled him to ask this question as well?'

'Unless he was told not to ask it; or paid not to ask it. Which might mean that Dr Morley was summoned to New Romney for a particular reason.' Mrs Chaytor gazed out over the fields. 'I don't like Dr Morley very much,' she said.

The rector could guess why; Morley was young, single and handsome, and had something of a reputation as a ladies' man. It would be unsurprising if he had paid court to Mrs Chaytor, and even more unsurprising if she had declined his advances.

He glanced at her, but she had already dismissed Morley from her mind. 'So, Blunt carries on as before,' she said. 'And poor Mr Miller lies up in Deal, buried and forgotten. Is there really nothing Lord Clavertye can do?'

'Oh, there is a great deal that he *can* do. He could order a separate investigation into the possibility that Blunt is taking bribes. He could investigate the coroner and whether the inquest had been conducted properly; or whether the jury had been tampered with. What did you make of the jury?'

'They appeared to be thoroughly domesticated. Whether they were paid or not is hard to say. But the coroner as good as directed them to find a verdict of death by misadventure, and they did so without hesitation. Yes, I agree, Lord Clavertye could investigate them.'

'But will he actually do so?' asked the rector. 'Clavertye is a rising star in politics. If he orders an investigation without cause, and someone important complains to London, his shining reputation will be tarnished. We will have to present Clavertye with the evidence, complete, wrapped and tied up with ribbon, before he will act.'

'Then, what shall we do?'

The rector glanced over at the corner of the churchyard, where a plain wooden cross marked the last resting place of the young Frenchman. He sighed. 'Let us review what we do have,' he said, running his hand through his hair. 'It is Friday night. A party of smugglers lands at St Mary's Bay.'

'Are they, or are they not, the Twelve Apostles?'

'For the moment, let us assume they are. Let us also assume that Blunt has been tipped off about their arrival. He has requested additional men from Deal, and he is waiting near St Mary's Bay with these and his own men, including the unfortunate Miller. But why? If the smugglers are paying him off, why does he pick a fight with the Twelve Apostles?'

She mulled this over. 'Perhaps there was a falling out among thieves. Perhaps they are not paying him enough.' Then she opened her eyes. 'If Mr Miller was part of Blunt's gang, he might have known that Blunt is corrupt. Or – heavens! He might have been corrupt himself. Perhaps *he* was receiving money from the Twelve Apostles.'

'That is pure conjecture,' he reproved her gently. 'But I think we must consider the possibility that Miller was not on the side of the angels. But we have still to resolve the question of why Blunt was waiting for the Apostles, and that brings us back again to the question of who they are. We have assumed they are smugglers, but what if they are something more?'

'Such as?'

The rector turned his head and looked east towards France. 'The dead man was French. Is that a coincidence?'

'You think the Twelve Apostles might be French spies? Now look who is engaging in conjecture.'

He bowed to her. 'Quite so. Let us return to what we know. Meanwhile, in another part of the Marsh, the Frenchman has been captured, subdued after a struggle, and locked in the back room at the looker's hut. His possessions have been taken from him.'

'But he knows that the Apostles are due to make their run,' she said, 'so he is desperate to escape.'

'And somehow, we do not yet know how, he effects that escape and runs eastward to meet the Apostles. To warn them? That is what his last words would seem to mean. "Tell Peter and Mark there is treason." Someone had betrayed them to Blunt. But his escape is discovered too soon, and he is pursued and killed before he can reach his destination.'

'Meanwhile,' said Mrs Chaytor, 'the Apostles collide with Blunt's men in the dark. The Customs men are routed, they run away. But before they do so, someone shoots Mr Miller.'

'Next, the rifleman who killed the Frenchman hears the shooting. Perhaps he mistakes how far away the firing is, and decides that discretion is the better part of valour. He goes back to the looker's hut, where hastily he collects the dead man's belongings and his own kit. He is in great haste, perhaps even in something of a panic.'

'Why do you say that?'

'He overlooks the gold watch, which somehow ended up in the corner of the room, invisible in the darkness. Perhaps he drops the watch as he hurries out of the hut, or perhaps it had been knocked there earlier during a fight; it doesn't matter. The killer retreats over the fields and is not seen again.'

Mrs Chaytor nodded. 'At around the same time,' she said, 'Blunt returns to the scene of the action. He finds Miller lying dead, and drags his body away until he rejoins his own men. Together, they carry the body to New Romney and Blunt sends for Dr Morley. What do you think?'

'I think it is an admirable summary of what we know – and has a number of gaping holes that remind us of what we *don't* know.'

She laughed. 'What we need to establish now is the connection between Blunt and the man or men who kidnapped and killed the Frenchman.'

They paused for a very long time, while the clouds continued to build on the western horizon. 'Can you think of one?' she asked.

'No.' He shook his head. 'And even the picture of events that we have just painted rests on so many assumptions and guesses that it is hardly sustainable. I fear it is coming on to rain, and we have looked at the church roof for long enough.'

As they walked back through the churchyard, she turned her head to look at him. Her eyelashes were very fine, he decided. Her blue eyes were also very serious.

'I said that earlier that if you continue to investigate you will displease the dean, and if you do nothing, you will displease Lord Clavertye,' she said. 'But that is not the end of it.'

'Oh, quite. What Lord Clavertye has asked me to do is to spy on my neighbours, my parishioners. Oh, I know that is not what it is, but that is how it will be seen. And if they find out – *when* they find out what

I am doing, they may turn against me. As I said to young Turner, the free-traders can be dangerous if crossed. And if the French are somehow involved too . . .'

'But you will go on. As will I.'

'Mrs Chaytor, I greatly value your ideas and your perceptive nature. But it would not be right for me to encourage you to continue; especially not when, as you have pointed out, there is danger ahead.'

'You cannot prevent me, you know,' she said gently.

They had reached the lychgate. 'Why?' he asked. 'Why carry on?'

She paused, looking out across the Marsh with her eyes far away. 'I think of them,' she said at last. 'I think of the last moments of their lives. I think of Miller, shot by his own folk without even the chance to defend himself, dying in agony, his blood pouring out onto the ground; dying all alone, far from his home in Deal. Did he have a family, I wonder? And the French boy, running and running across the Marsh in darkness, probably able to hear the man following him, knowing that the moment of his death was approaching. How terrified he must have been in those final minutes!'

She shivered and looked back at Hardcastle. 'I cannot bear it. I don't care whether they were French or English, law officers or smugglers or spies; it does not matter. I cannot live with myself knowing that two men died in pain and terror and I did nothing to learn the truth. And, I fancy, that is why you intend to carry on as well.'

He made no answer, but opened the lychgate and ushered her through, then closed it behind them both. In the road outside the rectory gate, he turned to her and said, 'Thank you. I need your help, that much is plain. I will do what I can to shield you from risk.'

'Do not concern yourself,' she said softly. 'For the past three years, I have been dead among the living. For the first time since my husband died, I begin to feel alive.'

He bowed to her, and she saw the ghost of the courtliness and grace that he must once have possessed.

'Good day, Reverend,' she said gently, and she turned and walked away down the road towards the village, and her home.

7

The Twelve Apostles

It rained all day Thursday, and most of Friday too. On Friday morning the rector went out to visit two of his parishioners, the widow of a fisherman whose husband had drowned in a storm the previous winter, and a young sailor who had been discharged from the navy after losing a leg at the Glorious First of June. Both lived in considerable poverty, and the rector did what he could to give them spiritual comfort, leaving discreet purses of money behind when he departed.

He arrived home, soaking wet and needing a drink, to find a letter waiting for him.

WADSCOMBE HALL, TENTERDEN.
12th of May, 1796.

My dear Hardcastle

I have now returned from London, and will be in the country for next week or more. If you have any news for me, please send word to me here by fastest post. It is imperative that this matter be set to rest as soon as possible. Do whatever is necessary. I shall of course defray any expenses you incur.

Yr very obedient servant

CLAVERTYE

PS have you and Cornewall fallen out again? I have had a damned impertinent letter from him, complaining of your conduct. I simply haven't time to deal with his nonsense. Try to keep him quiet, will you?

'Do whatever is necessary,' growled Hardcastle to himself. 'Like what, pray tell?' He damned His Lordship's eyes, but was inwardly relieved that

Clavertye had made no reference to the events of the inquest. He wondered what to do about Cornewall and whether to seek him out at the Star but then Mrs Kemp, just returned from the Friday market in the village. remarked that Mr Cornewall had departed for Canterbury. She then scolded the rector for not changing into dry clothes, and went away to prepare dinner. The rector decided the Dean of Canterbury could go hang, and went to change his clothes as ordered.

That evening, a week since the murders, he drank more than his regulation two bottles of port and fell asleep in his study chair. He dreamed that once again someone was knocking at the door. He rose in near panic, stumbled to the door, opened it and looked out, but there was no one. Then he heard the creaking of a tree in the wind, and realised that this was the noise he had heard in his sleep. Muttering, he blew out the lamp and went upstairs to his bed.

He woke early on Saturday morning with a headache and a raging thirst. The rain had stopped. He dressed and put on his hat and coat and went out to walk for three miles over the Marsh. He came back blowing but feeling better, and sat down to a breakfast of ham, eggs, boiled cod and coffee. Finishing this, he went into his study, where he took up pen and paper and began to work on tomorrow's sermon, but he could not concentrate on this for long. Taking a fresh piece of paper, he drew a sketch map of the surrounding Marsh, west to east from Ivychurch to St Mary's Bay and south to north from Old Romney to a point some way south of Dymchurch. He drew lines on the map indicating the likely courses followed by the various parties: the Frenchman, the rifleman, Blunt's Customs officers and the smuggling crew, who for the time being he was still assuming to be the Twelve Apostles.

He pored over the map for several hours, giving himself another headache but coming no closer to the truth.

When the bell rang for luncheon he rose and went to the fire and burned the map before going into the dining room. He ate absently, consuming cold lamb cutlets without really tasting them and downing a pint of claret, and then returned to the study. Concentrating hard, he barely heard the knock at the front door, or Mrs Kemp going to answer it. He looked up only when the housekeeper entered the room and said, 'Mrs Chaytor to see you, Reverend.'

'Show her in. And bring us some tea, if you please.'

He rose when Mrs Chaytor entered the room. She was slim and quietly but beautifully dressed, and she smelled like spring. Conscious of the fact that he had been wearing the same suit for several days and that the desk was a mess of papers and books, he bowed. 'I fear that I rarely receive ladies.'

'Never mind. I like a room that is lived in.'

The door opened and Mrs Kemp arrived with tea and a plate of ginger-bread. Mrs Chaytor bit into one of these, and smiled at the housekeeper. 'These are delicious, Mrs Kemp. I have had gingerbread from Gunter's, but I declare these are finer.'

'You are very kind, ma'am.' The housekeeper's face did not change, but the rector thought he detected a slight softening beneath her vinegary exterior. She was proud of her skills in the kitchen, and if one praised her cooking she would forgive most transgressions. Eventually.

Mrs Kemp curtseyed and withdrew. 'I came to tell you,' said Mrs Chaytor, 'that I wrote to the Customs post at Deal after we last spoke.'

His headache stabbed him, and he closed his eyes for a moment. Opening them again, he saw her looking at him with concern. 'Are you all right, Reverend Hardcastle?'

'I do apologise,' he said. 'I fear I am a little tired.'

'I see.' Her voice went quiet and again the faint drawl died away. 'Claret-tired?'

He met her eye. 'Yes.'

'This is harming you, you know. You should stop.'

'My dear,' he said, his own voice gentle, 'I really have no reason to stop.'

After a pause of several seconds she said in her normal light voice, 'I wrote to Deal two days ago, seeking information about the late Mr Miller. This morning I received a reply from a Mr Steadman, Collector of the Customs there. He has been most cooperative.'

'Has he? Heavens, how unlike a Customs man.'

'It would seem that I have the gift of persuasion. Curtius Miller was thirty-one years old. He had been in the Customs service for two years; before that he had been in another government service, but Mr Steadman does not say which one. He was dedicated to his work and Mr Steadman regarded him as one of his most reliable agents. He had undertaken a number of posts on detached service. I assume this means some sort of field investigation?'

It meant, spying. 'Yes. What else does Mr Steadman say?'

She raised her eyes to his. 'That he had a wife named Annie and three children. He has kindly given me their address in Deal. I mean to go and visit them.'

After another pause he said, 'I think that is a very good idea.'

'I don't know if I can offer any consolation; probably not. But I just might learn something about Mr Miller that will help us to understand why he died. And, to understand who he was.'

'You still think he might be a wrong 'un?'

'One cannot discount the possibility,' she said in her light drawl. 'But as I said, it doesn't greatly matter. He was murdered.'

He thought it did matter to her, a great deal. He had already recognised that her sympathies were more strongly engaged where Miller was concerned, whereas he still thought primarily of the Frenchman. That was understandable; she had stood over the spot where Miller had died. 'When will you go?'

'I thought I would drive up on Monday.'

'You will take care,' he said.

'Of course.'

The following day was Sunday, 15th May. He rose early, went for a walk, breakfasted on ham and eggs and kidneys with a tankard of beer, and then had a glass of port to lubricate his throat before matins. He had once known a clergyman who beat a raw egg into a glass of port and drank it before preaching, but the rector regarded this as a desecration of good port.

Feeling suddenly more cheerful, he walked out into a fresh damp morning as the bells began to toll and crossed the road to the church. In the nave he turned and nodded to the bell-ringers, pulling on their long ropes, and then went into the vestry and robed himself. He took a quick gulp from the flask of brandy that he kept in the vestry cupboard, and then strode out into the church. The bells had stopped ringing, and the church door closed with a quiet slam as the bell-ringers departed. Bellringers, in the rector's experience, were the greatest atheists of all;

he had yet to preach in any church where the bell-ringers stayed to hear the service.

'In the name of the Father, and of the Son, and of the Holy Ghost,' he intoned. The words came easily to his lips and rolled in his deep rich voice down the nave of the church. There was something infinitely comforting, he thought, about the services in the Book of Common Prayer, laid down by Cranmer more than two centuries ago and surviving all the vicissitudes of time. War might rage, violence might threaten, storms might break, but the church and its rituals went on; nothing could harm them, or change them. This was a rock of permanence to which he could cling, when all else around was threatening to drown him.

The congregation was the usual one: three elderly women (two spinsters, one widow), one old man from Brenzett (perpetually malodorous), one octogenarian verger (deaf), one churchwarden (asleep) and himself. At Christmas and at Easter, a few more might trickle in. Otherwise, as Mrs Chaytor had said, the church filled on only three occasions: baptisms, marriages and funerals. It was the same everywhere in the country, of course, there was nothing special about St Mary in the Marsh; all across the land, vicars complained to their bishops that their churches were empty. The rector did not mind; his parishioners (or most of them) paid their tithes, and after that it was up them. If they wanted pastoral care they could have it, through home visits or in the common room of the Star. If they wished to come to church on Sunday they could do so; he would be there always, regardless of whether they came, rapt in the glory of the service and its musical words.

At the end of the service he stood in the church porch to speak with his congregation as they withdrew. The old man from Brenzett shook his hand as always, and as always the rector smiled and thanked him for coming, trying not to look as if he was edging away from the smell. The two spinsters, Miss Roper and Miss Godfrey, came smiling to greet him; they wore flowers in their ancient bonnets, as they did every spring.

'We do hope you are feeling much better, Reverend.' Both had been at the inquest, blast them. He bowed. 'I am entirely recovered, ladies, and I thank you for asking.'

'It was a most *fascinating* event,' said Miss Godfrey, who had attended every inquest ever held in the parish and always said the same thing after each one. 'We were particularly taken by young Mr Turner's testimony.'

'Were you? And why was that?'

'Well,' said Miss Roper, 'it is the strangest thing. But when he said that he had seen the young man who was so sadly taken outside your house, and described him, both Rosie and I realised that we had seen him too.'

'Really?' said the rector, keeping his voice calm. 'That *is* fascinating.'

'We had no idea that he was French,' said Miss Godfrey.

'What would a Frenchman be doing here?' Miss Roper wondered. 'Do you think it is the beginning of the invasion, Reverend?'

'I think that unlikely, ma'am, but it is curious all the same. I am interested to know more about this man, if you can help me? I feel . . . well, responsible, you know.'

'Come to tea,' said Miss Godfrey, leaping at the chance of a good gossip, 'and we will tell you *all* about it. Tuesday at five?'

He bowed. 'I should be delighted.' When they had gone he returned to the vestry and removed his robes and then walked back to the house, wondering how long the Frenchman had been walking around the parish in broad daylight, and how many other people had seen him and not yet remembered.

The rector lunched briefly on cold roast beef and claret, firmly pushing Mrs Chaytor's words to the back of his mind, and then retired to his study with a bottle of port. For the first time in a long time, a very long time, he took down a leather-bound volume of Cicero from the bookshelf, blew off the dust, settled into the room's single, rather shabby armchair and began to read, sipping his port from time to time. He remembered how reading used to bring him so much peace and pleasure, and resolved to do more of it. Settling back into the armchair after dinner, he even thought drowsily of the book he had once planned to write himself, a biography of his great hero, Cranmer. Then his eyelids drooped, and closed.

When next he stirred, it was after dark. The bottle was empty and the fire was burning low. The book lay on the floor beside the chair where it had fallen from his hand. He rose sleepily, covered the fire and went to shoot the bolts on the front door. He could hear Mrs Kemp moving about in the kitchen, called a vague goodnight to her, then stumbled upstairs.

Here he cast off his clothes, strewing them around the dressing room, and dragged on his nightshirt. Putting out the candle, he climbed into bed and fell at once into a deep and very sound sleep.

The rector woke suddenly. The candle was lit and he could not understand that, for he distinctly remembered snuffing it before he went to bed. Then he saw the shadows, huge, wavering shadows, black and terrifying, climbing the walls to the ceiling; shadows, of the masked and hooded men who stood all around the bed, looking down at him. The light of the candle glinted dully off the steel they held in their hands.

He had faced death before; he knew its appearance. He knew also how to meet it.

He sat up in the bed, looking around at the men. There were six of them. 'Who the devil are you?' he demanded.

'We ask the questions,' said one of the men. He, like all the others, was dressed from head to toe in black including the mask that covered most of his face; only his mouth and his square chin were visible, his eyes lost in shadow. He was tall and thickset with the beginnings of a paunch. He held a pistol in his hand, covering the rector, its muzzle a black pit amid the golden glow of the candle. The rector stared at him, then looked around at the others. He could sense their determination and their ferocity of purpose, even though their masked faces were blank and inscrutable.

He thought, *I should have listened to that ass Cornewall, and stayed out of this.*

'The Twelve Apostles,' he said softly. 'Where are the rest of you?'

'Outside on watch,' said the big man.

Sudden anger swept over the rector. 'Where is my housekeeper?' he demanded.

'In the kitchen, tied to a chair. You can set her free when we have gone.'

'By God! If you scoundrels have so much as hurt a hair on her head, I will see you swing, every damned last one of you!'

The other men stirred, menacingly, and their shadows shivered, more menacing still, but the big man smiled below his mask. 'You are a plucky one, I'll give you that. Just answer our questions, Reverend Hardcastle, and then we will go. Cooperate with us, and you'll not be harmed.'

The rector folded his arms across his chest, still angry at the thought of what had happened to Mrs Kemp. 'What do you want to know?'

'We want to know what you know,' said the big man, 'and what you did not tell the inquest.'

'I told the inquest everything.'

'Beat it out of him,' said a man standing at the foot of the bed. He was hooded and masked like the others, but a stray lock of hair, copper red in the candlelight, had escaped from his hood and fell across his forehead. 'It's the only way.'

'Not yet.' The big man moved closer to the bed, and his shadow ran up the wall behind him and crawled across the ceiling, spreading black wings above the rector's head. 'Now listen, my fine gamecock. One of our informers was present at the inquest. She heard you, and saw you. You pretended to be drunk, or made yourself drunk, so that no one would take you seriously or ask you questions. That means you are hiding something. *What is it?* What were you so anxious not to tell the inquest?'

There was a pause, while the rector realised bitterly that his subterfuge had failed. The shadows hovered tensely on the wall, waiting to spring at him and tear at his flesh. 'I have been kind to you so far,' said the big man, his voice beginning to growl, 'but my patience is limited.'

'Beat it out of him!' insisted the red-haired man again.

'Very well,' said the rector, looking at the masked face of the big man. 'What I was anxious not to say out loud is that Blunt, the customs officer, is corrupt. He takes bribes from the smugglers. In return, he does not interfere with their runs.'

'Everyone on the fucking coast knows that,' said another man sharply. 'You'll have to do better than that, Reverend.'

'Blunt also lied about the death of Curtius Miller. Was he one of yours?'

'We know all about Miller. We're not interested in him. The man who was killed here. What do you know about *him*?'

'Not a damned thing!' said the rector angrily. 'I have no idea who he is or why he came to my door. Nothing!'

'No,' said the big man, and he moved closer still, the gaping black hole of the pistol's muzzle growing larger and larger, a huge black eye staring at the rector. 'That won't do. Tell me. *What do you know?*'

In the silence he felt his heart beating, very fast and hard. 'I will tell you,' said the rector suddenly, 'on one condition. That you tell me who he was.'

'Go on!' said the man with the red hair. '*Hurt* the old bastard!'

The big man bent over Hardcastle, every line of his body full of menace. Hardcastle could see beads of sweat on his neck below his mask. 'I *will* hurt you,' he said, his voice venomous. 'Unless you tell me. Now.'

The rector did not flinch. 'Anything,' he said. 'Tell me anything at all. His name, for God's sake! He must have had a name!'

There was a pause of about five seconds. 'His name was Paul,' said the big man. 'That is all you will get,' and the shadows flickered and then poised, ready.

'He spoke just before he died,' said the rector. 'That is what I did not tell the inquest. I heard his last words. He said, *Tell Peter . . . Mark*. And then in French he said, *trahison*. Treason.'

The six men in the room stood still, watching him intently. Then the big man turned his head and looked at the red-haired man. He made a small gesture with his hand, and two of the others came and stood behind the latter, one reaching out to relieve him of his sword and pistol.

'For God's sake!' said the red-haired man contemptuously. 'Do you believe any of this crap?'

'I don't know. We'll find out the truth very soon.' The big man turned back to the rector. 'You're a damned plucky one,' he repeated. 'But go carefully in future. There is a time to be plucky, and a time to yield to main force. You may cross the line between them one day, and regret it.'

'Thank you for the advice,' said the rector stonily. 'Now, get out of my house.'

The other man bowed. 'We'll be on our way. Your housekeeper has been gagged to avoid her giving the alarm, but you'll find her quite unharmed. No,' he said mockingly. 'Don't get up. We'll see ourselves out. Goodnight, Reverend.'

He found the housekeeper in the kitchen, tied to a chair and gagged but, as promised, otherwise unharmed. She sobbed as the rector removed the gag. 'Oh, Reverend! What is the world coming to, when decent folk are assaulted in their own homes by highwaymen!'

'Be easy, Mrs Kemp.' The rector brought her glass of brandy, which she normally never touched but now took gratefully, and almost as an afterthought poured a glass for himself. 'We must be thankful that we are unharmed.'

'But the silver! Your strongbox!'

'I think we will find that they are untouched. These were no ordinary robbers, Mrs Kemp.'

'Oh?' Her tears stopped and she looked at him, her small eyes bright with suspicion. 'Was this to do with the boy who was killed?'

'Yes.' He took a handkerchief out of the pocket of his dressing gown and handed it to her. She blew her nose with a honking sound.

'Then I will say this to you, Reverend,' she said wiping her eyes. 'Get on and find out quickly who killed him, so that we can go back to living in peace and quiet!'

He convinced the housekeeper to retire, and then went to his own bed but did not sleep. At first light he dressed and went outside, brandishing his heavy walking stick for reassurance as much as protection. He searched the rectory grounds from side to side, but found nothing, not even a footprint. It was uncanny; they had entered the house and left again without so much as a mark to show their passage, and a part of his mind began to wonder if he had dreamed the entire affair, Mrs Kemp's distress included. Then he crossed the road to the churchyard.

The red-haired man lay sprawled on his side, draped across the newly dug earth of the grave of the Frenchman, Paul. His clothes were dirty and torn. His hands were tied behind his back. His hood and mask had been removed and he had been beaten very savagely about the head and face.

Bending over the body, the rector saw at once that his neck was broken. He was quite dead.

8

The Widow's Tale

Amelia Chaytor pulled her gig to a halt outside the front door of the rectory, so swiftly that her groom, travelling with her, had to cling to her seat to avoid falling off. She engaged the brake, jumped down and knocked rapidly at the door. The housekeeper answered, drying her hands on her apron, her lined face betraying not a trace of the ordeal last night.

'Mrs Kemp,' said Mrs Chaytor, 'forgive me for calling unannounced, but I was just about to depart for Deal when I heard the news. It is true? Another body has been found?'

'In the churchyard, heaven help us,' said the housekeeper. 'The rector is there now. I ask you, Mrs Chaytor, what is the world coming to?'

'A bad end, I expect,' said Mrs Chaytor without thinking. 'Please, forgive me for disturbing you.'

She crossed the road to the churchyard, the tower of St Mary the Virgin standing dark against the clouds. Letting herself in through the lychgate, she saw the rector and Dr Morley bending over something on the ground. The doctor looked up and saw her and then stood up, calling out in alarm that she should come no closer. The rector rose too, laid a hand on the doctor's arm and crossed the grass towards her.

'It is good of you to wish to spare my feelings,' she said astringently. Then she saw the lines of exhaustion in the rector's face and said, 'Are you unwell?'

'A little tired. Genuinely, this time.' He drew her back towards the lychgate, out of earshot of Morley, who had resumed examining the body. 'But at least this time we know who the dead man is. It is one of the Apostles. That, my dear, is Mark.'

Her eyes opened wide. 'How do you know?'

'Because the Apostles came calling last night,' he said. He told her the story quickly, without detail, and her hand flew up to her mouth. 'Oh, dear Lord!' said Mrs Chaytor softly. 'Did they harm you? Or Mrs Kemp?'

'They tied poor Mrs Kemp to a chair, but did her no harm. They did not lay a finger on me. But,' he said heavily, 'I told them our secret. It seems that Mark was the traitor. They left the house, and brought him here to receive his punishment. So, you see, it is thanks to me that he was killed. I should have kept my peace.'

'In which case *you* would have been killed,' she said strongly, 'and probably Mrs Kemp as well.' She took his limp hand in her gloved one. 'Reverend Hardcastle, go home. Go and rest. Let Dr Morley and Mr Fanscombe do what needs to be done.'

'Lord Clavertye must be informed.'

'They will inform him. Go home, my dear.'

'I cannot leave yet. I must wait until the doctor has finished.'

She nodded reluctantly, and turned and recrossed the road to the rectory. Stepping up into the seat of her gig, she shook the reins and drove away to the north, her mind a whirl.

The rector was right about one thing, she thought. Their investigations into this affair had suddenly taken a deadly turn. It was difficult to know whether one should mourn the man, Mark; he was a member of a particularly ruthless gang of smugglers who had betrayed his comrades. The Frenchman, Paul – at least they had a name for him now! – must be a smuggler too. But then, of course, so were many of the people she knew, and as she herself was perfectly happy to buy smuggled lace and run scent, she supposed she was also complicit in the free trade. It was difficult in these times to know where one's loyalties really lay.

Loyalties! Heavens, it seemed that everyone involved in this affair was loyal only to themselves. The smugglers, bent on enriching themselves. Blunt, taking bribes from the smugglers and casually betraying his men. The coroner, lining his own pockets. The Twelve Apostles, terrorising people in their homes in order to further their own purposes; whatever those were. Cornwall, the dean, ready to do anything to avoid scandal. Even Lord Clavertye, she suspected, took an interest in this business mainly in order to further his own reputation.

Only the rector, bless his heart, was acting entirely without self-interest. That poor man, she thought. He has little self-interest left to preserve . . .

And herself? What or whom was she loyal to? There was one bond of loyalty that she would never break; beyond that, she really did not know. She knew that something unpleasant awaited her in Deal, but she could face that. At least she had an excuse to do something, to breathe fresh air, to use the brains she had been given to some purpose, rather than simply sitting at home alone, waiting for nothing.

From Dymchurch to Hythe the road was straight and smooth; she shook the reins and the little horse responded willingly. The gig flew down the road, the wind whipping at her bonnet and her hair. She laughed with exhilaration, ignoring the petrified look on the groom's face. Her late husband had loved to race, and he had taught her to drive so that she could share that love with him. Both were known to their friends as demon drivers, and it was widely prophesied that both would die of broken necks. But in the end it was a simple, mundane illness that had taken him from her.

She sighed and reined in a little. Thinking about John would not get her any closer to solving the mystery, or mysteries, that swirled around St Mary in the Marsh.

It was late afternoon when she reached Deal. She pulled the gig to a halt outside the King's Head and went inside to ask for a room, adding casually that she had come to call on the widow of Mr Miller and offer her condolences. The landlady of the King's Head, who had strong views about single women travelling and been about to show her the door, relented at this and gave her a room. Mrs Chaytor thanked her kindly, and asked if it would be possible to send a message to Mrs Miller, announcing her arrival.

'Certainly,' said the landlady, still not quite beyond suspicion. 'Mind you, don't go mentioning Mr Miller's name too loudly around these parts.'

'Why not?'

'He was a Customs man, wasn't he? They're not well liked round here. Me, I've nothing against them, they're just trying to do a job. But there was folk dancing for joy in my common room, the night the news came through that he was dead.'

'How horrible,' said Mrs Chaytor directly. Inwardly she felt a great sense of relief; Miller must have been an honest man, for the smugglers to have hated him so much. 'Thank you, I will write that letter now.'

She called at the Millers' little cottage the following morning, pulling the gig up outside the door. Leaving the groom to look after the rig, she knocked at the door. A dark-haired woman opened it and looked at her with suspicious eyes. 'Mrs Miller is not at home.'

'I am the lady who wrote yesterday,' said Mrs Chaytor quietly. 'I have driven up from the Marsh to see Mrs Miller. This concerns her husband.'

There was a long pause. 'Then you had better come in,' said the woman.

She was shown into a tiny parlour, where a small, slightly plump woman with red eyes rose to greet her, determinedly polite. Three children peeped around the door for a sight of the stranger, and were quickly shooed away by the dark woman. 'My sister,' explained Mrs Miller. 'She has come to stay with me until . . . until . . .'

She broke down, sobbing helplessly into her hands. Amelia Chaytor, heart wrung, watched her for a moment, then crossed the room to the other woman and put an arm around her shoulders. She soothed her as one might soothe a child, and slowly the woman's sobbing ceased.

'Thank you,' Mrs Miller whispered. 'You are ever so kind.'

'My dear, I know – I *know* – what a terrible time this is for you. You see, I lost my own husband three years ago.'

'Oh!' Mrs Miller looked up in surprise and then her eyes filled again. 'I am sorry,' she whispered, and for a few more minutes the two women clung to each other in silence. Then Mrs Miller remembered herself and urged her guest to sit, taking a seat herself; Amelia perched on the edge of a chair, hands folded in her lap, a tight pain beating in the middle of her chest.

'I am glad you came,' said the other woman. 'You understand.'

I understand what it is like to lose a husband, Amelia thought. But I did not have three children, nor did I live in a town where people were willing to dance on my husband's grave.

'Does it grow easier?' Mrs Miller asked. 'The pain?'

'Yes, and no,' said Amelia. 'Someone once observed that time is a great healer, and in my experience that is true. The pain fades. The emptiness that replaces it, however, is equally horrid.'

'How did you . . . What did you do?'

'I gave up the house where we lived, and moved away to make a fresh start. That has helped, a little.'

'It is something I should consider,' said the other woman slowly. She roused a little. 'Mrs Chaytor, I am so sorry. May I offer you some refreshment, some coffee perhaps?'

'Thank you, no. I will not intrude on you for long.'

The other woman's dark eyes searched her face. 'Your letter said that you had something to tell me about my husband.'

Amelia had spent much of the drive to Deal yesterday thinking about the words she would use.

'Yes. You will know of course that the inquest returned a verdict of death by misadventure. It was said that your husband was injured fatally by an accidental discharge of his pistol. What I have come to tell you, in confidence between ourselves, is that there is doubt over this.'

Mrs Miller's mouth opened and she stared for a moment. Then she closed her mouth and lowered her eyes, looking down at her hands.

'You did not believe the verdict either,' said Amelia quietly.

'No,' said the woman flatly. She was calm now, her grief under control, and Amelia knew that she was watching and listening very closely. 'Curtius was very careful, very precise about everything he did. He did not *have* accidents. Mrs Chaytor, you said also in your letter that you had some questions for me. Ask, and I will answer if I can.'

'Thank you . . . Mr Steadman of the Customs here in Deal says that your husband had formerly worked for another government service. Which one, pray?'

'The Treasury. No, not the Excise; he was employed direct by the Treasury in London, though he was always posted down here. I'm sorry; he never told me about his work. He said it was safer for me not to know.'

'Did he travel? Was he away often?'

'Oh, yes, sometimes for weeks. When he joined the Customs I thought, now I'll have him at home for a bit. But he kept right on travelling. He was away most of last month. He had only been home for a week before he went down to Dymchurch . . . He had been in France.'

'France!' Amelia's blue eyes opened wide. 'Whatever for?'

'I fear I do not know. There was something important, though, some game afoot, for he went off with hardly a moment's notice and little but the clothes on his back, and I did not hear from him the whole time he was away. He only told me it was France when he got back, and then gave me a bottle of scent, and laughed and said not to worry, for it wasn't run.'

Something told Amelia Chaytor that this was not true, that Mrs Miller knew precisely why Miller had been in France, and that no power on Earth would make her divulge her dead husband's last secret. She sympathised, and did not press the issue. 'Why did he join the Customs? Was he not well suited at the Treasury?'

'Oh, no. He had a good job there. People thought the world of him.' Now Amelia saw plain the calculation in the other woman's face; she knew Amelia knew something, and was prepared to barter a little of what she herself knew in exchange. 'He was a fine man, and I know they were sorry to let him go . . . He did once say that there was something he wanted to do in the Customs, but he didn't plan to stay there for ever. And, I'm pretty much certain that he kept in touch with his old friends at the Treasury.'

'I am glad to hear it,' said Amelia. 'Those old friends, Mrs Miller, will they look after you?'

The red-rimmed eyes filled again. 'Everyone has been most kind.'

'I am glad . . . Did your husband have any particular friends, in the Treasury or in the Customs?'

'It is hard to pick out anyone in particular. There was one man, called George. I never knew his surname. He called yesterday, though, to see that I had all I needed.'

'Could you describe George for me?'

'He's a gentleman,' said the widow, somewhat unhelpfully. 'Always very well dressed. What can I say? He was younger than Curtius, perhaps twenty-five or twenty-six, though I'm not good at guessing these things. A little . . . portly, but he holds himself well. I think he is perhaps a little too fond of high living.'

That doesn't narrow it down a great deal, thought Amelia. But perhaps that was the intention . . .

There was a little silence, and then the other woman said directly, 'Mrs Chaytor, may I ask a question of my own? Why do you want to know these things?'

'Because something happened that night,' said Mrs Chaytor, 'something that is very wrong. You are right not to believe the verdict of the coroner's inquest. Your husband was with the Dymchurch Customs officers when they came under fire from a gang of smugglers, and he was killed some time during that exchange of fire. But it was not his own pistol that caused his fatal wound. Someone else killed him.'

'The smugglers,' said the woman slowly.

'That is one explanation,' said Mrs Chaytor.

There was a long pause, during which they understood each other perfectly. 'That makes it better,' said the other woman. 'It gives me hope. There might be justice for him, now.'

'There *will* be justice,' said Mrs Chaytor gently. She rose to her feet. 'Thank you, Mrs Miller, you have been most kind.'

With a mask of steely gallantry covering her pain and loneliness, Mrs Miller escorted Amelia to the door. On the step the latter turned, pressing a visiting card into the other woman's hand. 'This is my address in St Mary. If I can ever do anything, anything at all . . .'

'Find out why Curtius died and who killed him,' said Mrs Miller. 'It won't bring him back, but it will give me and my children some ease. Find out the truth for me, Mrs Chaytor.'

'I will do what I can.' She stepped up onto the seat of her gig, drew on her driving gloves and released the brake. Neither woman noticed the heavyset young man standing in a shadowy doorway further down the street, watching them both. 'Goodbye, Mrs Miller.'

'Goodbye, Mrs Chaytor. Remember me.'

On the way home Amelia Chaytor whipped up the reins again until the gig raced at reckless speed along the road from Deal to Dover. I will remember you, Annie Miller, she thought, you may depend upon it. And as for you that killed him: damn you, damn your dark corrupt soul to everlasting hell. I may not yet have the evidence to convict you of the murder of Curtius Miller, but I will find it. And then, I will take great delight in watching you swing.

A very special kind of evil, the rector had said. She did not name the killer yet, not even to herself; but in her mind, she was certain that she knew who it was.

9

The Gentleman from France

On the afternoon of Tuesday 17th May, while Mrs Chaytor was still driving back from Deal, the rector strolled into the village. He had lunched, resisting the temptation to have a second pint of claret with his cold beef, and he smiled cheerfully at his parishioners as he passed down the street. Joshua Stemp looked up from his own doorway, where he sat mending a net.

'It's turning out fine, Reverend.' The clouds were breaking up and the afternoon sun poured in warm shafts down onto the village and its surrounding fields.

'It'll stay fine tonight,' replied the rector. 'A good night for fishing?'

'Only if the cloud comes back. It's nearly the full moon.' The fisherman winked. 'Moonlight scares the fish away.'

And gives the Preventive men a good sight of your boats coming ashore, thought the rector as he walked on. He reached Rightways, the last cottage on the eastern side of the high street, and knocked at the door.

'Enter!' called a voice from within. The rector pushed the door open and followed the sound of the voice into a parlour, reeling faintly as he entered the room. Even though the window was open, the reek of paints and solvents filled the air and made his eyes water.

'Oh, it's you,' said Turner in his usual curt way. 'I've been expecting you. Do you want a drink? I only have gin.'

'No,' wheezed the rector, 'no, thank you.' He made his way to the window, where he drew several deep breaths of fresh air and then turned to face the painter again. Turner had a nearly finished canvas up on an easel and was applying the final touches to it, occasional brushstrokes followed by long periods of contemplation of the result.

'You want to ask me about the Frenchman,' said Turner.

'Indeed I do.' The rector sat down on the window seat, hoping he was not sitting on any fresh paint. 'If you would be so kind, that is.'

'Ask away, sir. I'm not sure how helpful I can be, but I will try.'

'First of all, what made you think he was the man killed at the rectory? I'm not aware that anyone described him, or what he was wearing.'

'Oh, I didn't know. I took a guess. If when I described him, and your man had been older, or wearing different clothes, I daresay someone would have corrected me. But when no one did, I knew I was right.'

'You said you saw him on Wednesday, the fourth. What time of day was it?'

'Getting on for evening.' Turner thought. 'About six, at a guess.'

'Did you see him again after that?'

Turner shook his head, concentrating on a brushstroke. The rector waited and then said, 'Where did you see him?'

'Down the road. Just by the gates to New Hall.'

'You said he was walking past the entrance.'

'Yes. Although ...' Turner paused and turned to face him. 'That is what I thought at the time, but looking back now, I am not so certain. He *might* have come down the drive from New Hall and turned into the road. And I recall thinking, when I first saw him and realised he was French, I thought he was perhaps some relative of Mrs Fanscombe. I can't imagine any other reason for a Frenchman to be in St Mary, can you?'

'It seems an obvious conclusion,' said the rector, nodding slowly. 'Did you see where he went?'

'He walked down the road a little way, then turned and made off across the fields to the west.'

'Anything else? Did he look around to see if anyone was watching him? Did he seem agitated, or nervous?'

'Quite the contrary, and he did not look around. He did not see me, for example, or at least I am pretty certain of it. He looked like a gentleman out for an evening constitutional in the country. And I thought no more of it until I heard all the news, and then I began to think, hullo. I wonder if that is the same fellow? And it turns out it was.'

The rector rose to his feet. 'Thank you, Mr Turner. You have been most helpful.'

'Glad to be of service. What is this about?'

'I do not yet know,' said the rector slowly.

'Oh, come, sir. All three of these murders are linked, aren't they? And that Customs man never shot himself. Anyone who believes that verdict is an imbecile.'

'Perhaps so. But at the moment there is no evidence to support any other view.'

He looked hard at the painter. He had told no one except Mrs Chaytor about the visit of the Twelve Apostles to his bedroom. Now he said, 'Something is happening here that goes beyond mere smuggling, I think. I gave you a warning once, and I will repeat it. Be careful what you do, and what you say and to whom, and where you go, especially after dark. And don't tell anyone else what you have told me, especially about the connection with Fanscombe.'

On that other occasion Turner had scowled, a feckless young man rejecting the advice of a cautious older one. This time he did not scowl. 'You don't need to tell me, sir,' he said soberly. 'But thank you for the thought, all the same.'

He came, with unusual courtesy, to show the rector out. At the door he said, 'I saw two other people around the same time. I don't see a connection, but you might.'

The rector nodded. 'The first was Dr Morley,' said Turner. 'Now he *had* been at the Fanscombes'. He turned right out of the drive and walked up the road into the village. I remember it because I called good evening as he passed, and he cut me dead. It's never happened before; he has always been quite cheerful. He has even been complimentary about my pictures, which is more than most people in this aesthetic desert can manage. But this time he walked right past me without a word.'

Hardcastle thought about this. 'And the other?'

'Another stranger. This one was passing through. He was mounted on a big roan. I must say, that fellow could ride. He came through the village on an easy canter, and even though he was a bit on the heavy side he looked like he was glued to the saddle.'

'Heavy side?'

'Well-fed,' said Turner, glancing at the rector's own girth. 'Green riding coat and breeches. I thought at first it was Fanscombe, but this fellow was a far better rider than old Sack-of-Potatoes. He was younger too, perhaps mid-twenties. Fair hair, strong-featured face with a strong jaw and chin. I got the impression that his eyes missed nothing as he rode. As he passed the gates of the Fanscombe place he turned his head and looked up the drive for just a second, then rode on. I thought he was admiring the house; it is a handsome property, after all. Is that helpful?'

'It is,' said the rector slowly. 'Very helpful. Thank you again, Mr Turner.'

The painter watched him, clearly bubbling with curiosity, but he bowed. 'Glad to have been of service. Call again any time, Reverend.'

The rector bowed in his turn and then walked back up the street, deep in thought. The mask of course made things difficult, but everything else tallied. He was quite certain that Turner had just described the leader of the Twelve Apostles, the man who had threatened him in his bedroom two nights ago.

Ivy wreathed the door of the cottage where Miss Godfrey and Miss Roper lived, and crawled artistically up the walls. Eventually it would crumble the walls and grow into the roof where it would tear down the thatch, but Miss Godfrey and Miss Roper were not bothered; they were already in their sixties, and by the time the cottage fell down they would both be in their graves. They welcomed him in with great cheer and offered him tea in their little drawing room, served with sandwiches and a hard, inedible cake that made him long for Mrs Kemp's gingerbread.

Miss Godfrey poured out the tea. 'Would you like a little something to go with it, Reverend?' asked Miss Roper, holding a flask in her hand.

'You are a queen among women, Miss Roper.'

'Oh, Reverend Hardcastle, you do say some odd things,' she said, giggling archly and pouring brandy from her flask into his tea. She added a liberal dose to Miss Godfrey's cup and her own, and then sat down and raised her cup. 'Your very good health, Reverend.'

'And yours, ladies.' They drank, and he felt a faint shiver as the hot brandy ran down his epiglottis and into his stomach. His hostesses had lived here together in St Mary in the Marsh for many years, and were the subject of a certain amount of local gossip; some said that they were sapphic lovers, others opined that they were witches. The rector thought the first was quite likely, the second doubtful, but did not really care either way. They were among his most loyal parishioners; indeed, in terms of church attendance, they were about his *only* loyal parishioners.

'Now, dear Miss Godfrey, dear Miss Roper,' he said after the teacups had been refilled, this time with the ratio of tea to brandy a punishing half and half, 'you had something to tell me about the Frenchman.'

'Oh, yes!' said Miss Godfrey. 'We saw him twice, didn't we, my dear? The second time was the evening of the Wednesday; that is what struck us about Mr Turner's testimony, for we must have seen him at about the same time.' Questioned gently, they corroborated what Turner had said. The young man had walked out through the gates of New Hall and then west across the fields looking quite nonchalant; 'almost *too* cool, wouldn't you say, my dear?' asked Miss Godfrey of Miss Roper. 'I thought he was putting on an act, trying to pretend to be insouciant. So different from when we first saw him, wouldn't you say?'

'Oh, my word, yes!' said Miss Roper. 'He was quite a sight then!'

'And when was this?' prompted the rector.

'Why, it was several days earlier, Reverend. It was very early one morning, wasn't it, dear? We often rise early, especially in fine weather, before the sun and go for a walk; it is so glorious to see the sun rise and listen to the larks. One feels so especially alive at that hour, don't you think?'

'And it was at that hour,' said the rector gently, 'that you saw the young man?'

'Oh, yes,' said Miss Godfrey. 'We were walking towards the sea, down the path to St Mary's Bay, and we met him coming towards us. Soaked from head to foot, he was, and breathing as if he had just run a race. We did not know him, but we stopped to ask if he was in need of assistance. He said no, his boat had overset, and now he was going back to New Hall to put on dry clothes. He was staying there, he said, as a guest of Mr and Mrs Fanscombe.'

Had Miss Godfrey lit the fuse of a grenade and then thrown it into the room, she could not have caused greater astonishment to the rector. 'Are you certain it was the same man?' he said cautiously. 'When he spoke, did you detect an accent? French perhaps?'

'No,' said Miss Godfrey, thinking hard. 'He was well-spoken, but I don't recall that he had an accent.'

'Oh, *I* do,' said Miss Roper. The tea had run out, so she simply filled their cups with neat brandy. 'I remember distinctly, dear. He had ever so strong a French accent, and I thought to myself, he has just landed in a boat from France! It must be the beginning of the invasion.'

'Clara, dear,' said Miss Godfrey severely, 'you thought nothing of the kind. You invented that much later, once you heard that he was French.'

'Oh, yes, so I did! Oh, Reverend Hardcastle, do forgive me. My wits are not what they once were.' And she giggled merrily. 'But, I have just remembered something else – oh, dear, at least I think have! There was that other Frenchman who came to New Hall. Do you remember him, Rosie?'

'Indeed I do,' said Miss Godfrey. 'It was such a surprise, was it not, to see him again? It has been several months since he last called. Reverend, do you remember Mrs Fanscombe's brother? Monsieur de . . . Monsieur de . . . Oh, dear.'

'Monsieur de Foucarmont,' said Miss Roper, enunciating with great rigour. 'One must be so careful when pronouncing these foreign names,' and she giggled again.

The rector recalled meeting Monsieur de Foucarmont on a couple of occasions in the past, and hearing him introduced as Mrs Fanscombe's brother. Miss Godfrey and Miss Roper eagerly filled in the details. Foucarmont was an emigré, one of the French gentry who had been forced to flee France in fear of their lives after the Revolution broke out. Mr Fanscombe was not particularly fond of him; there were rumours that the two men had quarrelled, and some time last autumn Foucarmont had ceased to pay visits. All of this information, it seemed, came from the gossipy servants at New Hall.

'And now you say this man is back?'

'Oh, we are quite sure it is him,' said Miss Godfrey. 'It was on one of our early morning walks again, wasn't it, dear? It was really only just light when we went out for our ramble. And there he was, riding up from the south all wrapped up in a cloak, quite muffled up, but we were positive it was him. He rode very well, with a fine seat in the saddle. Clara and I have always admired a fine seat in the saddle.'

'And when was this, pray?'

'Why, it was Wednesday morning. The same day that we saw the young man for the second time.'

'Two Frenchman in one day!' giggled Miss Roper. 'It really must be an invasion, don't you think?'

The rector decided to make his excuses while he could still stand upright, and began to take his leave. Just before the front door he turned to his two hostesses. 'Ladies, forgive me, but just one more question. Does Dr Morley often call at New Hall?'

They looked at each other. 'Yes,' said Miss Godfrey, beginning to giggle. 'But only when Mr Fanscombe is absent.'

'Oh? Why is that?'

'Because he is tupping Mrs Fanscombe,' said Miss Roper, who then shrieked with laughter. 'Clara, really!' said Miss Godfrey. 'Reverend, I do apologise. I fear my friend is a little tipsy.'

'Think nothing of it,' said the rector, bowing. 'Ladies, thank you for a delightful tea.'

Outside in the street he took a few deep breaths in attempt to sober up. The sun was dipping down into the west, and a mellow evening light streamed through the village. The bleating of sheep came from nearby fields. A crow cawed somewhere in the distance.

He turned towards the rectory, but he had only taken a few steps when he halted again.

Paul had been staying at New Hall. Fanscombe must have known him, Mrs Fanscombe too. Yet neither seemed to recognise him from Turner's description at the inquest. Or . . . He remembered the sudden flicker of Eugénie Fanscombe's eyes. They know something about this, he thought; and perhaps her brother does too.

He had promised Clavertye that he would be discreet. So far, discretion had got them a little information, but not enough. It was time, perhaps, to take a few risks.

Turning, he walked south through the village past Turner's cottage and on down the New Romney road until he came to a handsome stone gateway on the east side of the road. The gates stood open. The rector walked up the drive past a massive chestnut tree in flower, its white candles glowing in the evening light. Beyond was a fine brick building with an elegant white-trimmed facade, the roofs of outbuildings visible behind it. More trees lined the park, effectively separating the house from the village, although when he glanced around he realised that a gap in the trees gave a view of the rear elevation of Rightways, Turner's cottage.

The rector walked to the front door and rang the bell. A footman opened it, bowing and ushering him into the hall and taking his coat. 'I wish to see Mr Fanscombe, if he is at home,' said the rector.

The footman bowed again and withdrew, and presently Mrs Fanscombe came into the hall, dressed in a rather décolleté rose-pink gown that offset her black hair and sharp black eyes and long nose. Put a whippet in a pink gown, thought the rector irreverently, and it would look exactly like Eugénie Fanscombe. She and Morley! Good heavens, the things that happened under one's very nose. I wonder how I had not heard about this before?

'What brings you here, Reverend Hardcastle?' Her voice was sharp, overriding the natural softness of her French accent. 'Why do you wish to see my husband?'

'Oh, it was nothing of great importance,' said the rector hastily, bowing. 'I was merely passing, and thought of a question I wished to ask him. It concerns the inquest for that poor man who was found in the churchyard, that is all.'

He waited for a reaction. There was none; either she knew nothing, or she was an excellent actress. Reluctantly, Mrs Fanscombe signalled to the footman, who bowed and left the hall. He was back in a moment, bowing again. 'Mr Fanscombe will see you now, Reverend.'

With Eugénie Fanscombe still watching him, he followed the footman across the hall and into Fanscombe's study. The contrast between this study and the rector's own bookroom could not have been greater; the room was bright and tidy and there was not a single book in sight. Most of the walls were covered with pictures of hunting scenes and dead animals.

Fanscombe, still in his blue riding coat, stood up sharply behind his desk as they entered. 'Shall I bring refreshments, sir?' asked the footman, bowing again.

'No. Get out.' The footman closed the door behind him, and the justice of the peace looked sharply at Hardcastle, every trace of his usual bonhomie quite vanished. 'What do you want, sir?' he asked brusquely.

'Forgive me for calling without notice,' said the rector, sticking briskly to the civilities. He repeated his line that he had been passing by and dropped in on the spur of the moment; well, it was true in a way. 'Has a date been set for the inquest of the man found in the churchyard?'

'Monday. You will receive your summons tomorrow.'

'Thank you, that sets my mind at ease. I don't suppose it has been possible to identify him?'

'No,' said Fanscombe. His manner changed; he sat down suddenly, slumping behind his desk. 'Not yet.'

The rector sighed. 'Two murders of unidentified men in two weeks, and both near the church and rectory. What is the world coming to?' He lowered his voice, conspiratorially. 'I say. You don't suppose the two deaths were related in some way? Might there be a connection?'

'How should I know?' The fact that, as justice of the peace, he was supposed to be investigating exactly that question seemed to have passed Fanscombe by.

'But it is curious,' the rector persisted. 'And another thing is curious too. All sorts of people now remember seeing the first fellow, the Frenchman, around the village. I don't suppose *you* saw him, by any chance?'

Fanscombe raised his head again, and the rector saw now the beads of sweat on his face and neck. 'Oh, for pity's sake, Hardcastle! Why are you asking? Didn't the dean specifically tell you to stay out of this matter and not bring scandal down on the Church?'

So Cornewall and Fanscombe had talked; hardly surprising, given that they were both important local landowners. 'It is a trifle difficult to stay out of the matter when people keep dumping bodies on my doorstep,' said Hardcastle mildly. 'Believe me, sir, I have no intention of becoming any more involved than I am already. Do you need me to make a statement before the inquest?'

'No,' said Fanscombe waving a hand. 'The man was clearly killed in a brawl, and there is little for the coroner to do. Your evidence on the day will suffice.'

The rector nodded. 'Then I will take my leave,' he said, rising. 'You will have guests, of course, and wish to attend to them.'

'Guests?' said Fanscombe, staring at him. He had started to sweat again.

'A guest,' amended Hardcastle. 'Your brother-in-law is staying with you, or so I was told?'

'Oh, for God's sake!' said Fanscombe, slamming his hand down on his desk. 'Is there anything that we say or do that is *not* subject to village gossip? Is *nothing* private?'

'My dear sir,' said Hardcastle in alarm. 'Please believe that my remark was entirely innocent. I had no intention of giving offence. I had thought that the reunion of your wife with her dear brother would be a matter for rejoicing.'

'And so it is,' said a voice from the doorway.

Hardcastle turned, and bowed. The man in the doorway was tall, slender and rather graceful, beautifully dressed in fashionable silk coat and waistcoat with a snow-white cravat sporting a diamond pin. The buckles on his shoes glittered. 'M. de Foucarmont,' he said.

'Reverend Hardcastle, is it not?' The man's voice was as elegant as his clothes; he spoke accented but beautifully fluent English. 'We met last summer, when I was a regular visitor to this house. It is a pleasure to meet you again, monsieur.'

'And you also,' said Hardcastle, bowing again. 'I'll take my leave now, Fanscombe. Please don't bother, I will show myself out.'

As he left the study he heard the Frenchman say, 'Charles, I have just been out to the stable to see your new Arabian mare. She is an absolute beauty. I am minded to buy her, if you can bear to part with her.' Then the study door closed. The murmur of voices continued, and the rector was just wondering whether he dared to tiptoe back and listen at the door when someone else came into the hall. It was Fanscombe's fair-haired daughter, also dressed for riding; she held a leather riding crop in her gloved hand.

'Miss Fanscombe,' he said gravely, abandoning his earlier design and bowing.

'Reverend Hardcastle,' she said, throwing gloves and crop onto a side table. 'What brings you out of your lair at the rectory?'

'I was passing by,' he said, 'and thought I would call in. You must be delighted to see your uncle once again.'

She went rigid for a moment, as if a spasm had passed through her body. 'Delighted,' she echoed. 'Are you on your way? I'll have the man fetch your coat.' She snapped her fingers at the footman, who scurried away.

'Thank you,' said the rector. 'I expect you must also be terribly sorry about your other guest.'

'*What?*'

'The one who arrived by boat,' said the rector. 'They are saying in the village that he is none other than the poor young man who was shot a few days later. A very sad affair, and very puzzling too.'

The girl looked at the riding crop as if she was considering using it on him. 'I do not listen to alehouse gossip,' she said coldly, 'and neither should you, sir. There is no connection whatever between our guest and *that* man. The man who was our guest has returned to London, from whence he came. Good evening to you, sir.' With that, she tilted her chin and stalked out of the hall.

And that, thought the rector, taking his coat and stepping out into the sunset light, was a young woman repeating something that someone else has told her to say; or I have never heard the like.

Gloaming was descending on the Marsh. He saw lights in the windows of Sandy House, Mrs Chaytor's residence, and knocked at the door. Her housekeeper admitted him at once and Amelia Chaytor herself came out into the hall to greet him. 'I will not stay,' he said, 'I merely wanted to see if you were well, and hear the results of your visit to Deal.'

'It was awful,' she said briefly, passing a hand over her forehead. There were fine lines of exhaustion around her pretty eyes. Small wonder, the rector thought; by his calculation she had driven about sixty miles in the last two days, and conducted a harrowing interview into the bargain. 'But I learned something that may be important. Miller worked for the Treasury before joining the Customs. He was involved in investigative work, and it seems clear that he was still in contact with his old Treasury friends. Mrs Miller remembered one in particular, called George. She said George had been to see her since Miller died; I don't know if that is important. She also said that her husband was often away from home on his investigations.'

'He was a government confidential agent,' said the rector slowly. 'I wonder . . . Go on.'

'He was recently away for a month, and returned only a week before he was killed. He was in France.'

'France!'

'I know. Was he spying, do you think?'

'Very likely. He may have been trying to ferret out the French connections of the smugglers in order to learn more about when and where
they would make their next runs. Or he *may* have been doing something
altogether different. But what was he doing on Romney Marsh facing the
Twelve Apostles?'

'Indeed,' she said. 'Indeed. Every answer brings more questions. And
none of the answers get us any closer to finding evidence of who killed
him, or why. What have you learned?'

He told her that Paul had been staying at New Hall, but that Fanscombe
and his family denied this was so. 'I cannot pursue this line without antag-
onising the Fanscombes, which I am not ready to do.' Not yet, he thought.

She nodded, and then swayed a little. 'My dear, you must rest,' said the
rector.

'I shall. My maid is heating water for a bath. I shall soak in that and go
straight to bed.'

'Good. I am departing for Appledore in the morning. I want to have a
word with Captain Shaw.'

'Oh? Why?'

'It has occurred to me that his utter lack of competence at the inquest
was a little unconvincing. I cannot imagine that his militia found *nothing*
on their sweep over the Marsh. Perhaps he or one of his men saw something but did not realise its importance.'

She smiled slightly. 'I think you are clutching at straws.'

'But straws are all we seem to have . . . I may return late, but I hope we
will have an opportunity to talk before the inquest.'

She smiled again. 'I am sure we shall.'

'Goodnight, my dear Mrs Chaytor,' he said softly.

10

The Isle of Ebony

The following morning the rector rose early, forgoing his usual walk and making a quick breakfast of eggs, kidneys and smoked fish. He then went into his study and sat down at his desk, took out a clean sheet of paper, dipped his pen in the inkwell and began to write to Lord Clavertye.

The Rectory, St Mary in the Marsh, Kent.
18th May, 1796.

My lord,

You asked me to keep you informed of developments with respect to the sad affair of Mr Curtius Miller, and also the anonymous man found dead that same night here at the rectory. The latter event remains as mysterious as ever, but some information has come to light about Mr Miller. It appears that he may formerly have been employed as a confidential agent by the Treasury; and that even after joining the Customs service, he continued to have contacts with his old employers. Indeed, I would go so far as to suggest that Miller may have continued to work for the Treasury all along, and that his role as a Customs officer was a disguise, or cover, which he adopted as part of a Treasury investigation.

Would it be possible for Your Lordship to approach the Treasury, in confidence of course, and ask whether Miller still had a connection there? For if my hypothesis is correct, then it is possible that the men Miller was investigating, whoever they may be, learned somehow of his real identity and had him killed. At the very least, there is more evidence to suggest that his death was no accident. Might Your Lordship then consider approaching the coroner and asking whether he considers his present verdict to still be sound?

On another note, my lord, I wonder if I might trouble you on another matter. This concerns M. de Foucarmont, a French emigré who visited Mr Fanscombe last summer, and is at present staying with him again. He purports to be Mrs Fanscombe's brother. If Your Lordship has any information that can establish this man's *bona fides*, I should be most grateful to receive it.

Yr very obedient servant

HARDCASTLE

Outside, the groom was leading his horse up to the door. He rose, sealed the letter and placed it his pocket. 'I'll be off now, Mrs Kemp. I may be late tonight, so do not wait dinner for me. Leave out a cold collation, that will be sufficient.'

The housekeeper gazed at him unblinking. 'And where are you off to?'

'Nothing you need know about, Mrs Kemp. Lock the doors when night comes, but leave the lamps lit, if you please. My pistol is loaded and in my desk, if you feel the need to protect yourself.'

'Lord's sake, Reverend Hardcastle! I wouldn't have a notion of how to use your pistol. A good stout poker from the fire will be good enough to keep those ruffians out of the house.'

The rector smiled. Mrs Kemp was on the mend.

St Mary was too small to have a postmaster; he stopped at New Romney to post his letter to Clavertye and then rode on up the high road to Apple-dore through a fine fair morning. As he rode, he reviewed what he had learned yesterday. First, fascinating but probably of no relevance, there was the fact that Dr Morley was having an affair with Mrs Fanscombe. Second, Mrs Fanscombe's brother had returned to the village after a long absence, arriving on the 4th of May, the same day that Paul was last seen. Coincidence? Possibly . . . Third, Miss Fanscombe was lying about Paul, and not lying particularly well. She knew full well that he was the mur-dered man, and she did not appear especially upset about this. If she knew, then so did the rest of the family. And fourth . . . Blunt was not the only man in the district who was afraid of something. Fanscombe had been half-frantic, his normally bluff exterior crumbling to expose his nerves.

The latter might have been caused by something simple, of course. Fanscombe might have learned of his wife's affair, and confronted her; and in any battle of wills and words between Fanscombe and his wife, the justice of the peace was bound to come off worst. There was the rumour that he and Foucarmont were not on good terms. But what he had seen yesterday evening was not anger or resentment or jealousy. It was pure, stark fear.

He had seen something of the same look on Blunt's face, when the landlord of the Star asked him about the Twelve Apostles. Both men had secrets. Both knew far more than they were telling about what had happened that fatal night. And both were trying desperately to prevent the truth from coming to light.

And what *is* the truth? he wondered for the hundredth time. Whatever it was, it was not a simple matter of smugglers and Customs officers coming to blows. Another game was being played. The news that Curtius Miller had been spying in France had rung an alarm bell in his mind. It was possible that Miller was spying on the smugglers, but the rector did not believe this. He thought about the French army said to be massing around Boulogne, and of how in six hours that same army could be marching over these very fields. Suddenly the sun did not seem so warm.

It was late morning when he arrived at Appledore, a pretty village situated just where the flats of the Marsh rose up into green rolling hills and heathland. The new semaphore station sat silent on its hill above the village, waiting for the day when the French invasion fleet would set sail. The rector called at the Black Lion, where the landlady, Mrs Scrivenor, welcomed him warmly. Fodder and water were provided for his tethered horse, and the lady promised to set aside luncheon for him. He drank a pint of small beer and set off, hobbling a little, to find Captain Shaw.

He found his quarry at the blacksmith's, standing and watching the re-shoeing of his horse. Inside his wrinkled uniform the captain of militia was as skinny and unprepossessing as ever. He looked surprised when the rector walked into the smithy yard.

'Reverend Hardcastle? A pleasure to see you, sir. You're some way from your own patch.'

'It felt like a fine day for a ride,' said the rector smiling. 'Speaking of such things, is this your horse, captain? He's a beauty.' They discussed horses for a few minutes, the rector quickly discovering that the captain knew even less about the subject than himself. The clunking of the blacksmith's hammer punctuated their conversation from time to time.

Gradually the rector steered the conversation around to the most recent killing at St Mary. 'You do seem to have bad luck,' Shaw said. 'Two corpses in less than ten days, one on your doorstep, the other as good as. I hope you have had no trouble yourself, sir.'

'Oh, none whatever,' said the rector, thinking of waking up and seeing the shadows of armed men on the walls of his bedroom. 'The rumour is that the most recent one was a bandit or a smuggler killed by his own men. Is there any truth to that, do you think?'

Shaw, frowning, confessed that he had not heard this. 'I can ask Mr Fanscombe for permission to send another patrol down to look around St Mary, if you are worried.'

'No, no, do not trouble him, or yourself,' said the rector. 'After all, your last patrol found nothing, did they?'

'No,' said Shaw ruefully. 'Then, of course, we were made to look fairly silly when Mr Turner and the lady then found the place where poor Mr Miller had his accident. My men failed to spot a thing. That is quite unforgivable, wouldn't you say?'

'Oh, I don't think anyone blames you, captain. Of course, your fellows didn't arrive until some hours later, did they?'

'Quite so. I received a runner from Mr Blunt at about nine thirty on the morning after the incident, and one from Mr Juddery a few minutes after. Dr Morley's message arrived somewhat later; closer to ten, I would say. But then of course I had to wait for an instruction from Mr Fanscombe before I could move. That finally arrived, and I called my men out at about eleven and sent a party down to the Marsh to search the area; they would have reached St Mary by perhaps two in the afternoon. When they returned to camp in the evening, I dispatched a second patrol to keep an eye out for movements around the village in the night. I continued this for the next three nights until ordered to cease by Mr Fanscombe. During that time, we saw no signs of suspicious movement or activity.'

What a very complete answer, thought the rector. Almost like he was reading a written report. I wonder who else has been asking him this question? Lord Clavertye, perhaps? 'I suppose you had to wait for Fanscombe's consent before you could send out your men,' he said.

'That's right, sir. In a civil matter, such as this is judged to be, only a justice of the peace or the lord-lieutenant can order out the militia, and then only as an aid to the civil power, obviously.'

Obviously. The young man was speaking as if he was regurgitating a law book. The rector swallowed, aware of his parched throat. 'Do your fellows patrol often by night?'

'Not often.' Was it his imagination, or had Shaw's voice changed a little? 'The Preventive men don't usually invite our assistance. They reckon we would take all the glory.' The captain smiled without much humour, shifting his bony frame within his badly fitting uniform. 'I reckon if we *were* let loose, we could clean up the smugglers in no time.'

'I daresay you could,' the rector said. 'But meanwhile, you are holding yourself in readiness for greater things, hey?'

'Yes, indeed, sir. If the Frogs do decide to invade, me and my men are the first line of defence.'

Then God help England, thought the rector. He could think of no more questions that would not arouse Shaw's suspicions. Either Shaw had been telling the truth on the stand at the inquest, or he was playing with a very straight bat indeed . . . And then the captain surprised him with a question of his own.

'What do you think, Reverend? All these deaths so close together. Are they connected in some way? Or is it all just coincidence?'

The rector collected his thoughts, and when he spoke his voice had the ring of absolute truth. 'Captain Shaw,' he said, 'I really don't know what to think.'

Back at the Black Lion, Mrs Scrivenor had been as good as her word. A grilled sole followed by mutton cooked in beer and seasoned with pepper along with two more pints of ale filled the hollow that the rector had felt growing within himself during the interview with Shaw. Mrs Scrivenor looked after him personally. He was not a regular here, but she always remembered him and gave him the best service. Either she liked him, or she had a general weakness for reprobate clergymen.

'A pipe after your meal?' she asked. 'Oh, I forgot, Reverend, you don't smoke.'

'Can't afford tobacco,' he said, winking at her. 'The duty on it is far too high.'

She laughed merrily at the thought of anyone on Romney Marsh smoking tobacco on which duty had been paid. 'And,' he added, 'I imagine all the best stuff gets packed straight off to London.'

'I expect you are right,' she said, giggling still as she cleared the table. 'You should see the pack trains going through here in the middle of the night. A hundred laden beasts there was, after that last run, on their way up to Tenterden and on to London, and not a blessed thing the Preventives could do about it,' and she laughed again. The rector chuckled appreciatively along with her.

'Straight up the high road?' he said. 'Bold devils, aren't they? I'd have assumed they would use the tracks through the woods, up to Ruckinge and Shadoxhurst, maybe. I've been shooting up there, and I'd say there are lots of secret little byways where a pack train would never be noticed.'

'Oh, there's no doubt they're getting bolder,' said the landlady. 'I reckon they think they have the Preventives under their thumb. They think no one can touch them.'

'That might change if the militia were called out to join in.'

'Oh, sir! We can't have the militia called out on a matter like this. With them dispersed all over the countryside hunting free-traders, who would defend us from the Froggies? And anyway, that Captain Shaw. Catch a smuggler? He couldn't catch a cold.'

She nodded to a man in a red coat sidling up to the bar, a sergeant's stripes on his sleeves. 'Isn't that so, Sergeant Haldon?'

Sergeant Haldon ordered a jug of pale ale for himself and some of his men and confirmed sourly that this was so. 'He's as big a blessed fool as ever put on an officer's epaulettes, and that's saying something. Five nights he had us tramping over the blessed Marsh, and not a blessed thing did we see.'

Five? 'I fear I am responsible for your discomfort, sergeant. I am the rector of St Mary in the Marsh. Here, allow me to pay for those drinks for you and your men. No, no, sir, I insist. It was at my behest that you were called out.'

'Thank you, Reverend, you're a gentleman. Well, for certain we were out four nights around St Mary, but not on the first night. We didn't come within two miles of the place.'

'Oh?' said the rector lightly, and held his breath.

'That's right, sir. We went a little way east of Ivychurch and floundered around in the blessed freezing water for several hours. Never did know what it was about. Not a soul in sight but us, and not a building to be seen either except for some blessed old looker's hut. Finally got the recall about three in the morning and came home. It took me all next day to get me blessed boots dry.' He raised a glass. 'Your very good health, Reverend.'

The temptation was to go back and confront Shaw, and demand to know why he was lying. But Shaw of course would protest that he had not lied; he had not told the rector what his men were doing the night before the first two murders, but then, Hardcastle had not asked. And if the rector did start asking questions now, he would risk giving his own game away.

Straight bat, Shaw, he thought. Very well played. But what the devil are you up to? He realised now that while he had been questioning Shaw the captain had also been probing *him*, very delicately and subtly, trying to find out how much he knew. Was Shaw trying to hide something?

Or – and the thought hit him like a bolt from the blue – did Shaw also have his suspicions, and was he too investigating the murders on the Marsh? He mulled this over, and the more he thought about it the more the latter theory began to look distinctly possible. Shaw might even have Lord Clavertye's backing. His Lordship is a subtle and devious bastard, he thought, quite capable of setting two investigations in motion and not telling either party about the other.

All of this needed more thought.

He asked Mrs Scrivenor, once the sergeant had gone, about the pack train the other night. She told him of hearing the clopping hooves and rising from her bed and peeping out through a gap in the curtain to see the train go by, shadowy in the dark night, each horse led by a masked man with a cudgel or a firearm; it was a sight she was used to, of course. 'And then, once they were gone, all was quiet once more?' he asked.

'Not quite. About an hour later, another party came up from the Marsh. They were a smaller group; I couldn't see how many in the dark, but perhaps only ten or a dozen. All of them were mounted, which is unusual; free-traders don't tend to ride. They stopped to water their horses at the pump, just across the road there.' Mrs Scrivenor waved at the village pump and watering trough a few yards away across the street. 'I thought at first they must be Preventives, but then I realised that they were free-traders too. I overheard two of them talking; they said they were going to Ebony.'

If she had heard them talking from her bedroom at the top of the inn, thought the rector, she must have had hearing like a bat; it was much more likely that she had been downstairs with her ear pressed against the keyhole. He pretended to lose interest in the subject, and instead engaged his nearest neighbour in a discussion of the price that wool was expected to fetch later this summer.

He left the inn at about two, well fed and watered, mounted his equally well-fed and watered horse and turned up the Tenterden Road and headed slowly inland. From Mrs Scrivenor's account, he strongly suspected that the second group might well have been the Twelve Apostles. The number of men fit the bill, and he suspected that the big man with the square chin was just the sort of well-organised ruffian who would have horses waiting once they landed. If Ebony was their hiding place, it was just possible that he could discover a few more clues about them.

Mrs Chaytor was right. Every time they answered one question, another question presented itself. What was *Shaw* doing down by the looker's hut with his men? Was he in league with Blunt? Or had he merely been carrying out orders sent by Fanscombe? That could mean that Fanscombe was in league with Blunt. Or Blunt might have deceived them both, persuading Fanscombe to call out the militia in hopes of intercepting the Twelve Apostles. But, no matter which one of these stories – if any – was true, why did it matter so much? Why was it so important that the Twelve Apostles be stopped?

The answer must be staring him in the face; but he could not see it. Once, years ago during a service, he had been about to recite the Creed and had opened his mouth to speak, only to find that his mind had gone blank. He knew the words, knew them as well as he knew his own name, but his mind refused to summon them up. In the end he had to reach around for the prayer book and remind himself, something he never did. The feeling he had now was akin to that. All the clues were staring him in the face, but his mind refused to give up the answer; and this time, there was no handy book to jog his memory.

Long ago, the Isle of Ebony had been a true island in the middle of the River Rother, home to a community of shipwrights who built ships for the nearby port of Smallhythe. Its church, like his own, was dedicated to St Mary the Virgin, the Star of the Sea, and was now about the only relic of its maritime past. Five centuries before, great storms had changed the course of the Rother so that it now ran into the sea at Rye. The old river channel had dried up. All that remained at Ebony now was the church, a few tumbledown cottages and flocks of sheep grazing the sides of a green hill.

Even though the scene was green and peaceful and the only other living things in sight were the sheep, the rector approached cautiously. He was following the trail of the men who had invaded his home and threatened him with violence, who had coldly beaten to death one of their own number whom they suspected of betraying them.

At the foot of the hill he halted, looking for a place where he could conceal his horse. Two decayed cottages stood across the road from the base of the hill, one with its roof fallen in, both clearly long abandoned. The rector dismounted stiffly, groaning a little with effort, and led the horse behind one of the cottages. Hitching the reins to a wooden post over the wellhead, he walked around the cottage, looking through the empty windows. All was dilapidated; there were no signs of any recent occupation or use. He looked up the hill to the church, took a long look around to see if anyone was watching, and then circled slowly around to the far side of the hill until its slope concealed him from the road. Then he started to climb.

He could walk any distance on the flat, it seemed, but these days climbing hills seemed to leave him out of breath. It took him five minutes to climb the hill, and he was red in the face and perspiring heavily when he reached the top. He stood in the church porch for a while, looking at the churchyard overgrown with weeds among the tombstones and listening for any sound of movement inside; all was silent.

Taking a long deep breath, nerves tingling, he tried the door. At first he thought it was locked, but in fact the hinges were simply stiff with rust. He walked cautiously inside, and looked upon a scene of ruin. Half the wooden box pews were missing – carried off by someone for firewood, quite probably – and there were holes in the roof the size of a man's head, through which sunlight poured. Bat droppings lay thick on the floors and, he was sorry to see, on the altar. The church was desolate, and clearly had been for a long time. A non-resident clergyman and no parishioners would leave any church at the mercy of thieves and the weather.

Which made it just the sort of place to appeal to smugglers, he thought. He walked down the nave, stepping where possible around the bat droppings, towards the vestry door, which stood wide open. He looked into the room and saw more decay, a heavy wooden table covered in dust, a broken window, patches of damp on the walls where the plaster was beginning to disintegrate. A tall oak wardrobe stood with its own door ajar.

A noise came faint to his ear, and he froze, straining his hearing to concentrate. Nothing. He had just begun to relax when he heard it again, and again, louder now; the jingle of harness and the quiet clip-clopping of hooves; horses, making their way up the hill towards the church.

He looked at the church door, but the hill was devoid of cover, and he was bound to be spotted as soon as he stepped outside. Heart pounding, he looked around wildly for a place to hide. The wardrobe! The hooves were right outside the church now. Praying silently, the rector hurried to the wardrobe and opened the door. Divine providence was watching over him; the wardrobe was empty. Quickly he stepped inside, pulling the door closed behind him and then he stood silently in the dusty darkness, trying not to make a sound.

The hooves halted, and from outside the church he heard a man's voice. The hair rose on the back of his neck. He had heard that voice three days ago, on Sunday night, when the Twelve Apostles invaded his bedroom.

'There's no one about, but we'll be careful all the same. Take a good look around, then tether the horses out of sight behind the church and join me inside.'

The church door creaked open. Booted footsteps echoed off the stone floor, ringing a little in the silence. In his hiding place the rector heard a low exclamation of disgust, probably at the mess the bats had made. The footsteps receded, going up the nave, then suddenly grew closer, coming back down the church and stopping outside the open vestry door and halting. Inside the wardrobe the rector stood absolutely still, holding his breath.

The other man stood in the vestry doorway for a moment that, to the rector, seem to last for an hour. Then the other man whistled a few bars of 'Rule Britannia' and the footsteps started again, receding and moving back into body of the church. The rector let his breath out very, very slowly.

'All quiet outside, Peter.' More footsteps, a second voice joining the first. 'All well in here?'

'Just as we left it, Matthew. Ghastly place.'

'Suits our purposes,' said the second man. 'Did the cargo reach London?'

'It did, in perfect condition, and London instructs me to convey its satisfaction to all of you. Payment will be made in the usual way.'

'Good.' There was a pause. 'I keep thinking we should do something for poor old Dusty.'

Speaking of dust, thought the rector, the air in here is full of it. He could feel it tickling his nose and the back of his throat, and knew he would sneeze unless he could get some fresh air. He opened the door about an inch and pressed his face against the crack, breathing shallowly, and the ticklish feeling receded. He found too that by putting one eye to the crack he could see through the vestry doorway and out into the church, where the two men stood talking. He saw the big man, dressed in a gentleman's riding coat and breeches now, his head uncovered; he had fair hair, and there was no mistaking that square chin and jaw. A pound to a shilling, thought the rector, remembering Turner's words, that one of the horses outside is a roan. The other man, facing him, was smaller and older with thinner dark hair; he wore rough workmen's clothes, but there was nothing of the workman about his stance, nor his attitude to the other man.

They were still speaking, and he concentrated on what they were saying, feeling sweat run down his forehead and drip from his nose. 'I saw Annie the day before yesterday,' the big man was saying. 'I called at the house in Deal. She was pretty cut up, of course, but she had her sister with her. I waited around for a little to see if anyone was taking a particular interest in her, snooping around and so forth.'

'And?'

'All quiet. She did have one caller, handsome piece in a gig. The widow from St Mary.'

'Oh? What did she want?'

'Come to offer charity, I expect.'

The other man grunted. 'The lads would like to chip in something for him. After all, he was one of ours.'

'Good, I'll throw something in too. Collect the money and I will take it to her. Now, Matthew, tell me what has been happening in St Mary.'

'There's to be an inquest, of course, on that bastard Mark. Our watcher in St Mary will be present at that.'

'Tell her to attend carefully to the details and report anything that might concern us.'

The man called Matthew nodded. 'Once that's over, I hope things will calm down. The worry is that either the Church or the deputy lord-lieutenant will start poking their noses into things.'

'I'll have one of my friends lean on Clavertye. The Church will give us no trouble.'

'I don't mean the dean and chapter, I mean that bloody rector. I don't trust him.'

The big man chuckled. 'I won't have a word said against the rector. He's a splendid chap, with more balls than most of you put together. What about Blunt?'

'Business as usual for old Blunty. Collecting bribes and shouting at people. What the fuck happened, Peter? I know he turned on us last autumn, but we thought we had sorted things out, remember? We thought we had paid him off again. So what does he do? He sets another ambush for us, and poor Dusty and Paul both get killed trying to stop him.' The man called Matthew paused. 'What do you reckon happened to them, Peter?'

'It's easy enough to work out.' Peter, whom the rector guessed was also called George, was sombre. 'Blunt intended to lie low and let us walk past him, then follow us to the looker's hut. There we would run into Shaw's men lying in wait, and Blunt and his lads would then close the trap behind us. We could be caught between two fires. That is what Paul was trying to warn us about when he was killed. Thank God, Dusty Miller worked it out too, and called out a warning as we came over the Marsh, so we could turn the tables on them. But then the bastards killed him.'

The rector's spine tingled. What had Sergeant Haldon said? *A little way east of Ivychurch . . . not a building to be seen except for some old looker's hut.* Matthew was speaking.

'You reckon Blunt did it?'

'Either he or one of his men. Makes no matter, Blunt is responsible.'

'Blunt,' said Matthew viciously. 'Let's settle him, Peter, let's *really* settle him. Dusty and Paul were good men. Let's make sure Blunt doesn't die too quickly, or too painlessly.'

'We settle him one day, but not yet. Right now, Matthew, we need to prepare for the next run. They tell me this one will be even more important than the last.'

'Oh? What is the cargo?'

'Much the same as before; I've no more details yet. Next full moon is the fifth of June, a Sunday. Any word on the local yokels, and what they might be planning?'

'Not certain yet. Our watchers say there is a rumour they might try a run down near Dungeness on the sixth. It's not certain, though.'

'Well, confirm as soon as you can, then leak word to the Preventives. If the free-traders are down at Dungeness, the Preventives will go after them. We'll make our own landing further north, somewhere around Greatstone and then cut up past New Romney. That should take us away from trouble.' He paused. 'Blunt will be looking for us, of course, but we will be harder to find this time.'

'Yes, especially now that bastard Mark won't be squealing to Blunt every time we make a move.'

'Very well, Matthew. We have a little over a fortnight in which to get organised. As ever, I leave everything down here in your capable hands.'

The two men strolled towards the church door. As they reached it, the rector heard Peter say, 'Then, this will be my last run for a while. I'm needed in Italy. But you'll keep the organisation in being, and stand by for further instructions. I'm sure our masters will continue to find employment for you.'

Then they were outside, and the other man's reply could not be heard clearly. The rector realised that he had been holding his breath again. He let it out very slowly, but still he did not move until he heard the horses moving off. Then he stood for another ten minutes, until he was as certain as he could be that the coast was clear, before stepping out of the wardrobe and walking slowly out into the church. Even then, he half expected at every step to hear a voice calling on him to halt, or the sound of a pistol being cocked.

Nothing happened. He reached the church door and looked around cautiously, but the horsemen were gone. There was no one but himself and the sheep.

Then he did run, throwing himself down the hill and running as if the hounds of hell were after him, not stopping until he reached the ruined cottages. His horse remained where he had left it; the two men had not spotted it. Gasping a quick prayer of thanks he untethered the mare and scrambled into the saddle without any pretence of dignity. Then he turned the horse's head and shook the reins and rode hard, back towards the safety of the Marsh.

11

Lord Clavertye's Decision

The rector returned home late in the evening, the sunset glow fading behind him and the moon high in the sky. He snapped at the housekeeper when she scolded him, ate a little cold food and managed only a single glass of claret before falling asleep at the table. Rousing a little later, he dragged himself up to bed and just managed to undress himself and pull on a clean nightshirt before falling asleep.

As a result, he woke the next morning in an unfamiliar position. Having had next to nothing to drink, he found his mind was astonishingly clear. His body, on the other hand, was a single mass of dull, throbbing pain, reminding him that he was an overweight, middle-aged man who had ridden more than thirty miles the previous day. He ordered water for a bath, which helped a little, but dressing was a slow process as each movement of his back and legs sent shooting pains running up his body. Afterwards, sitting at the breakfast table, he could barely summon the energy to eat his ham and eggs.

'You should go back to bed,' said Mrs Kemp, clearing away. 'It was folly for a man in your condition to exert himself so greatly. Anything could have happened to you. And don't tell me I sound like a nagging wife.'

'You don't,' said the rector. 'You sound like a nagging mother.' The atmosphere at the rectory had once again returned to normal.

The post arrived a few minutes later. There were two letters, one bearing the Clavertye crest and the other with the seal of the Dean and Chapter of Canterbury. The rector glared angrily at the second letter, and opened the first.

WADSCOMBE HALL, TENTERDEN.
18th May, 1796.

My dear Hardcastle

I am in receipt of your letter of today's date and am taking the opportunity to reply by return of post. Your deductions concerning Miller seem perfectly sound. I shall institute inquiries at once. Allow me to commend you for what you have achieved so far, and I urge you to carry on.

Yr very obedient servant

CLAVERTYE

'Pompous, patronising buffoon,' muttered the rector. He was in a foul mood even before he opened the second letter.

OFFICE OF THE DEAN, CHRIST CHURCH CATHEDRAL, CANTERBURY. 18th May, 1796.

Reverend Hardcastle

It has come to the understanding of His Grace the Archbishop that another distasteful incident has occurred in your parish. To be more specific, another corpse has been found. He is particularly appalled to hear that the incident took place on consecrated ground, that is, in your churchyard.

Unfortunately, this affair has now become a matter of public knowledge. His Grace is confident that you did all in your power to prevent this from happening . . .

The rector ground his teeth at this point.

. . . but expresses his sorrow that you were unable to do so. However, His Grace takes this opportunity to remind you that it is his wish – his *express* wish – that, above all else, no scandal should attach itself to the Church. You are therefore to leave this affair in the hands of the proper authorities, and not concern yourself with the investigation in any manner whatever, taking only such steps as are necessary to protect the reputation and interests of the Church.

His Grace makes it clear that this is an instruction, and not a request. As an obedient son of the Church, you will doubtless heed his wishes. Should you fail – yet again – to do so, then His Grace will – with great sorrow – find it necessary to institute proceedings against you. There are, as you know, a number of actions which can be taken to compel obedience, and I advise you again that your present position in the Church is not so secure as you believe it to be. I trust I have made myself quite clear.

Yours in Christ

CORNEWALL

Hardcastle tore the letter across and threw the pieces on the fire, and went down into the village in search of Mrs Chaytor. He found her seated in her comfortable drawing room reading a book, and she rose and smiled when he was shown in.

'I hope you are fully recovered?' he asked.

'Perfectly. And you are well? Oh, my dear man, you are limping.'

'It is nothing,' he said.

'It does not look like nothing. Sit down, and put your foot up on a stool. What have you done? Is it gout?'

'No, I went riding,' said Hardcastle. 'The older I grow, the less convinced I am that horses were ever meant to be ridden.'

'Where did you go?'

Hardcastle told her. At the end of the narrative the widow sat with her chin in her hands, regarding him for a while. 'Does this mean what I think it means?' she asks.

'I suspect so. I shall ask Lord Clavertye to try to find out for us. He won't like it, but it is time he did some work on this case, for a change.'

She smiled. 'I have found out a little more about Blunt.'

She told him her story in turn. Undaunted by the fatigues of the previous two days, while he was riding to the Isle of Ebony she had once again harnessed her gig and driven down to New Romney, there to call on Dr Mackay on the pretence that she was suffering from headaches. While he was measuring out her laudanum, she asked him, pretending idle womanly curiosity, about the events of the night of the 6th, and remarked artlessly that she was surprised he had not been called to attend the dead man. Dr Mackay had retorted, acidly, that so was he, but doubtless the Customs service had their own reasons for regarding Dr Morley's skills as superior to his own. To be sure, it took a great deal of skill to examine a corpse and pronounce it dead. He begged Mrs Chaytor's pardon for his intemperate language.

'I then called for refreshment at the Ship,' she said, 'where I was taken into a nice little parlour room and served coffee by the landlord's wife, Mrs Spicer. You know her? Of course you do, the Ship is a public house. Mrs Spicer was abroad early on the morning in question, and chanced to see Blunt talking to his men. She reported him as being worked up into a great passion; which she thought nothing of, for of course one of his own had just been killed. Then a messenger came down from the north bearing a letter, and Blunt read it through and at once went very quiet. The next thing, he called for his horse and rode hard down the Marsh road towards Appledore, leaving his men to clear up.'

'So he was not present when Dr Morley arrived,' reflected the rector. 'That is odd. I gained the impression from his testimony at the inquest that he was.'

'So did I, though thinking back, I do not recall that he ever said so explicitly. Perhaps we made an unwarranted assumption. But the most important thing is this. The Ship, I have learned, is even more of a hotbed of smuggling than our own beloved Star, and my new friend the landlady was quite happy to gossip about the activities of the smugglers. She knew, of course, that Blunt is complicit in smuggling and takes bribes from the gangs. One of the gangs that used to pay him off was the Twelve Apostles.'

The rector sat upright, and then winced as his back twinged. 'Ah, I thought that would get your attention,' smiled Amelia. 'And on the subject of the Twelve Apostles, Mrs Spicer was full of information. She told me the Apostles first appeared on the scene about four years ago, not long before Britain and France went to war. They were a bit unusual, because they aren't from around here, and they kept aloof from the other gangs; but they never caused any trouble, and the local men gradually accepted them. There was a theory that they were involved in one of the specialist trades, like gold smuggling, but no one knew for certain. But my dear Mrs Spicer was positive that Blunt had done well out of them. Then, last autumn, Blunt and the Apostles had a falling out; at least, that is how she described it.'

'Yes,' said the rector slowly, and a few more pieces clicked together in his mind.

'There are two odd things about this,' Mrs Chaytor continued. 'First, Blunt was terrified. He lived in fear for weeks afterwards, rarely showed his face in public, and went everywhere armed with at least two pistols. He had nothing to fear from the other smugglers, who knew he would cause them no trouble so long as they paid him. It was the Twelve Apostles he was frightened of.'

'And he is frightened of them again now,' said the rector, remembering Matthew's threats to 'settle' Blunt and Peter's promise that it would be done, and in his mind's eye he saw again Mark's battered face and broken neck. 'I would say that he has every cause to be fearful. And the second thing?'

'This is most odd. Around the same time, the Twelve Apostles disappeared. Completely. Until two weeks ago, they had never made another run.'

They thought this over. She looked up at him, her blue eyes very bright. 'It was Blunt, wasn't it?' she said. 'He killed Miller himself.'

'I have believed so almost from the beginning. But we have no evidence to support this. And if Blunt killed Miller, someone else must have killed the young man at the rectory. Both deaths occurred almost simultaneously, remember.'

She sighed. 'What do we do next?'

'We carry on. We continue to look for anything that will tie Blunt to Miller, and anything that will explain the behaviour of the Fanscombes. I fear we must accept, too, that Fanscombe is implicated in this affair somehow. It is even possible that his family is involved too.'

She shivered a little. 'How many people do you think are involved in this . . . whatever it is? Blunt, Fanscombe, the coroner. Where does it end, do you think?'

'I don't know,' he said, sharing her disquiet. The sense of threat he had felt at Ebony that had led him to flee the hill in such an undignified fashion had yet to go away. 'My dear, if you want to walk away from this matter and let it lie, then tell me at once. I will understand entirely.'

She raised her chin at this. 'I will not walk away,' she said. 'I intend to carry on. If you had only seen that poor woman . . . I want to see Blunt hang,' she said with sudden passion. 'I will rejoice in that man's death.'

That will make two of you, he thought, remembering the similar passion in Matthew's voice. 'I begin to think that we have gone as far as we can,' he said. 'If we are to build a case against Blunt and his allies, whoever they are, then we shall need assistance. It is becoming clear that we are up against powers far greater than ourselves. I will speak to Lord Clavertye after the inquest.'

'Do you think he will help? You said once that we would have to present him with the evidence, complete, wrapped and tied up with ribbon, before he would act.'

'Yes,' he said heavily. 'I did say that. But things have changed markedly. I shall try to persuade His Lordship that he needs to take action now.'

'If anyone can, you can,' she said. 'You have known him for a long time.'

The rector was silent, remembering. 'What happened to you?' she asked softly.

The silence continued, and she wondered if he would answer, but then he turned his head slowly and gazed out of the window, out at the roses glowing in the garden. 'I was destined for great things,' he said. 'Or so I thought. I had everything. Presence, intellect, wit, the gift of oratory. Men admired me, or envied me, or both. Women . . .' He paused again and said, 'I was the toast of the Town – for a time. I was an ornament to every salon. Everyone with intellectual pretensions wanted to know me. And I gloried in it all. I was arrogant, shockingly so. I aroused envy, I made enemies, but who does not? Heaven help me, I thought that this was the mark of a successful man.'

'You will know a great man by the quality of his foes,' she said.

He smiled a little at this. 'So I thought. I was the chosen one, and my path to the summit of the Church was pre-ordained. The future was mine to grasp.'

'What happened?' she asked again.

'That is the hell of it, my dear. I don't really know . . . No, that is wrong. I know full well. My arrogance was my downfall. I went too far, in every respect, and I turned people against me. Suddenly, I found myself being passed over. Honours which I deserved were awarded to others. Positions which had been promised to me were quietly taken away.' He sighed. 'I offended the Olympian gods. They made my destiny, then they changed it. Then came the scandals; several of them.'

'Women?'

'They were involved indirectly, yes. I fought three duels. Won them all, too, but the fact of winning became another stain on my reputation. People no longer wanted to know me.'

'Duels? A clergyman?'

'Oh, yes. We're just as wicked and sinful as ordinary people, you know. Have you never heard tell of Sir Henry Bate-Dudley, the Fighting Parson? He was a noted duellist in his younger days.'

'I am very pleased to say that I have never heard of him.'

'You disapprove of duelling. You are right to do so. It is a barbaric custom. I was young, and very foolish. I have learned some wisdom; at least, I hope I have.'

'*I* believe you have,' she said, and her voice softened again. 'Have you never thought of . . . of trying to regain what you lost? You could still rise in the Church, with the right patrons, the right friends.'

'No, my dear. Those days are done. Time and port have dulled my ambitions, and the glittering prizes of my youth no longer interest me. As for friends . . .' He paused. 'There are few in the Church of England, or elsewhere, that care to know me, these days. Truly, I am content where I am.'

She reached out quickly, took his hand, squeezed it hard and let it go again. 'And you?' he said gently. 'Are you content where you are?'

'I do not think I shall ever be truly content on this earth.' It was her turn to gaze out of the window now. 'Like you, I had everything, and like you, I lost it. I was married for ten years to the most wonderful man ever born. I loved him from the moment I laid eyes on him. He was my paradise.' She smiled a little, her eyes soft and very far away. 'I loved him so much that I wanted to do everything he did, and, marvellous man, he let me. I was more than just a wife to him; I was also his dearest friend, and we shared all the things he loved, driving, and shooting . . . He was fond of puzzles, too, riddles and equations; anything that taxed his mind. He taught me how to think about problems and find answers.' She turned her head. 'Don't be alarmed at this, but . . . He was a little like you.'

The rector did not know how to respond to this. 'Was he a soldier?' he asked quietly.

'No, he was in diplomatic service. We lived abroad for four years in Paris, two in Rome, the rest in London. He showed me the world, and we lived it in tandem, a perfect harmony of mind and body.' She bit her lip suddenly and said, 'Three weeks. He fell ill, out of nowhere. Three weeks of suffering, and then he was torn away from me.'

'I am so sorry,' he said softly.

'At first, I wanted to die too. My grief was . . . spectacular. Then the grief faded, and the loneliness began.'

'I am a clergyman,' he said. 'I should have words that could comfort you. But I am afraid that you have heard them all already.'

A smile that was both sweet and sorrowful touched her eyes. 'You do not need to comfort me. Indeed, I suspect we might both find it a trifle embarrassing were you to try. Just go on being what you are. That is comfort enough.'

Amelia Chaytor had opened a window onto her soul, and what he saw there saddened and depressed him. He snapped at Mrs Kemp when she served dinner. She snapped back. He retreated to his study, where he sat at his desk drinking steadily, thinking about Blunt and the justice of the peace and wondering, as Mrs Chaytor had wondered, who else might be involved. It did not take too much imagination – especially when one was three parts drunk – to see Blunt and Fanscombe at the centre of a conspiracy spanning half the Marsh.

As he reached to open the evening's second bottle, he glanced down and saw that one of the drawers of his desk was open. Not by much, only a quarter of an inch, but definitely open. Head spinning, the rector tried to remember whether he had left this drawer open this morning. He was positive he had not; he had not looked in that drawer in days.

He opened it and rummaged around inside amid the detritus of old quill pens, bits of string and lumps of sealing wax. Nothing seemed out of place. He opened all the other drawers, and found nothing missing. But his pistol, which normally rested in the centre of the left middle drawer, had been moved, and a few grains of powder had spilled from the priming pan. And careless fingers had left a grimy stain on a sheet of clean paper.

He stood up abruptly. His books had been disturbed; the dust had been dislodged from some of their covers. And one of the pictures, a rather static landscape by an inferior pupil of Gainsborough, was hanging slightly crooked from the picture rail.

'Mrs Kemp!' he shouted. 'Mrs Kemp!'

The housekeeper waited a few minutes in order to punish him for shouting, then shuffled into the room. 'Heavens above, what is the matter now?'

'This room!' said the rector staring about him. 'My books! Have you dusted my books?'

'Have you taken leave of your senses?' countered the housekeeper. 'Of course I would never dust your books! What are you thinking of?'

'And that picture is hanging askew.'

'More likely it is you that is *standing* askew.'

The rector thought it about this, and it seemed to make sense. He tried leaning first left, then right, then standing what he imagined to be straight upright. It all amounted to the same thing.

'The picture is crooked,' he announced. 'Mrs Kemp, have you been in this room at all this morning, since I left?'

'No, Reverend, I have not,' she said in injured voice.

'And there has been no one else in the house today?'

'Certainly not, or I would have told you when you returned. Will that be all?'

'Yes,' he said heavily, 'that will be all.'

Mrs Kemp closed the door behind her with a discreet slam. The rector sat looking around him, then reached decisively for the second port bottle. He needed to not think about anything for a while.

The room had been searched, thoroughly. For the second time in a week, his home had been invaded by strangers.

The next morning was Friday 20th May, two weeks since the first murders. At mid-morning there came the crunch of wheels on the drive and Mrs Kemp came to announce Lord Clavertye. His Lordship was shown into the study a moment later, tall and elegant as ever, and they shook hands. The housekeeper was sent to the kitchen to fetch refreshments, and His Lordship stood for a moment by the fire to warm himself, for there was a raw cold wind coming down off the North Sea and, for the moment at least, it did not feel much like spring.

'I had a word with the coroner as you suggested, Hardcastle. No luck. He won't change his verdict.'

During his time at the bar, Clavertye had a reputation as a forensic barrister able to break down the hardest witness on the stand, and the rector wondered how he had failed to crack the coroner. His feelings must have shown in his face, for Clavertye rubbed his hands over the fire and said briefly, 'He has an interest.'

Politics again, thought the rector. The coroner must have a powerful patron, whom Clavertye could not afford to cross. He wondered who it was, and essayed a shot in the dark. 'Is the source of his interest by any chance the Dean of Canterbury?'

Clavertye did not respond, but his silence told the rector that his guess had been correct. 'Mr Cornewall has written to me,' said Hardcastle, 'reminding me to keep out of this affair and threatening to eject me from this living if I do anything to bring scandal on the Church.'

'Your living is quite secure,' said Clavertye a little impatiently. 'Cornewall's threats are bombast. Ignore him. Ah, here is Mrs Kemp.'

They watched in silence as the housekeeper laid out cups and saucers, poured two cups of coffee and left the room.

'It is not Cornewall's threats that concern me,' said the rector. 'What bothers me is why he is making them at all. Why is he so concerned to keep me out of this affair? And now he is supporting the coroner. He is in short doing everything in his power to keep the entire affair quiet. Why?'

'It is an excellent question,' said Clavertye. 'But so long as Cornewall's highly placed friends in London and Canterbury continue to support *him*, it is unlikely that we shall ever know.' He changed the subject briskly. 'Now, have you any further news for me?'

It was going to be a day for dishonesty, the rector decided. He had already made up his mind as to what he would tell His Lordship, and what he would hold back. He now told Clavertye about Blunt's behaviour the morning after the killings, as witnessed by the landlady at the Ship, and her confirmation that Blunt was receiving bribes from smugglers.

Clavertye listened in silence. 'It adds very little to what we already know,' he said dismissively. 'Blunt is bent, but we have nothing that would stand up in court.'

'Doesn't the fact that Blunt is corrupt give you an excuse to re-open your inquiry into the death of Miller, my lord?'

'That is a matter for the head of the Customs service, which employs – employed – them both. I cannot interfere.'

Or won't, thought the rector. He suspected that 'interests' were once again at stake. The Customs service was jealous of its privileges and territory, and was touchy about interference from outsiders. Aloud he said, 'I understand, my lord. Were you able to learn anything further about Miller?'

'Yes. My friends at the Treasury were grudging, and not a little put out to find that I had guessed who Miller was, but they confirmed what you had suggested. Curtius Miller was a confidential Treasury agent who was used on a number of investigations into corrupt practice. He transferred to the Customs at his own request.'

'And did he remain in contact with his old associates, my lord?'

'That was all that they would tell me. They gave me to understand that they would not answer further questions, and would be displeased if I were to press them. In other words, I was told to mind my own business.'

'And M. de Foucarmont, my lord?'

'Information about Foucarmont was much easier to obtain. There is nothing secret about the man. He is an emigré, formerly an officer in the French army. He is of noble blood, even though he does not have a title, and he judged it prudent to leave France soon after the execution of the king.' His Lordship paused. 'His estates in France were sequestered by the government, but he still seems to have plenty of money. He cuts quite a dash about Town.'

'Yes. He appears able to support a good tailor, at least,' mused the rector. 'What is your interest in him?'

'He is Mrs Fanscombe's brother. He stays at New Hall from time to time, and was there last week. I thought of Turner's testimony, saying that he had seen our murder victim near the house. It struck me that Foucarmont might have known him, perhaps even been involved in the events that led to his death. But if you say he is sound, my lord, then there is an end to it.'

'I had not appreciated the Fanscombe connection. But you are right, if this fellow is Fanscombe's brother-in-law, then he must be sound. Fanscombe can be a bit of an ass at times, but his heart and head are in the right place. He would know if this fellow was up to any tricks.'

'Indeed, my lord.'

The fire popped again. Clavertye watched him intently. 'What else have you to tell me?'

'I have learned a little more about the Twelve Apostles.'

'Ah, yes. The gang whose name no one at the inquest claimed to recognise. I suspected they were a gang of smugglers, but could see no connection between them and this affair. But you have found something?'

'The Twelve Apostles are not just connected with this affair, my lord, they are at its very heart. And they are no ordinary gang of smugglers. They run very special cargoes across the Channel from France, small but highly valuable to the right people. Like the other smugglers along the coast, they paid bribes to Blunt until last autumn, when he broke their agreement. They tried to renew the arrangement recently, but Blunt betrayed them again and set up an ambush for them on the Marsh. It was during that ambush that Curtius Miller was killed.'

'Just a moment,' Clavertye interrupted. 'How the devil do you know all of this?'

'I think Your Lordship would find it more convenient not to know the sources of my information,' Hardcastle said.

The fire crackled in the silence. He could almost see Clavertye's brain at work, weighing up the options. 'Continue,' said His Lordship finally.

'It is my belief, my lord, that the Twelve Apostles are agents working in government service. Curtius Miller, whom his friends called Dusty and who was also a government agent, was working hand in glove with them before he died. The young man who was killed here at the rectory, a Frenchman who went by the name of Paul, was also working with them.

It is my further belief that both were killed because of their association with the Twelve Apostles.'

'And the third man? The one found in the churchyard? Is he connected too?'

'I have no idea,' said the rector, telling his first outright lie of the day. 'Mr Fanscombe is of the opinion that the man died in a brawl, and I am in no position to contradict him. But, my lord, this brings us back to Mr Fanscombe. His heart and head may well, as you say, be in the right place, but if that is so then someone is pulling the wool over his eyes. Paul, the Frenchman, was a guest at New Hall for several days before his death. Several witnesses now recall seeing him. And yet, when I put this to both Fanscombe and his daughter, they denied it.'

Another man would have uttered an oath or an exclamation, and been flummoxed. Clavertye's face remained expressionless while the smooth oiled wheels turned in his barrister's brain. 'Is there any proof that this man was at New Hall?'

'None; yet. But I believe this to be true. And if I am right, it means that Fanscombe was playing host simultaneously to both a prominent French emigré and to an agent of the Twelve Apostles, who is now dead.'

'It may be a coincidence.'

'Neither you nor I, my lord, used to believe in coincidences.'

A brief smile flickered across Clavertye's face. 'True. Very well, but we must proceed with great caution. We cannot make any kind of accusation against Fanscombe or his household, not without direct evidence. As for the Twelve Apostles, I believe your hypothesis about them to be absolutely correct, but again, I do not see how we can prove it. I am certain that the Treasury, if asked about them, would deny all knowledge.'

'My lord, I doubt very much that these men are working directly for the Treasury, or the Customs, or any of the services of which we know. These men are well armed, well organised and very dangerous. They do not hesitate to kill those who interfere with their tasks. This means that the work they do must be very secret indeed. I would venture to suggest, my lord, that the true nature of this work is known only to a few, and among them, the highest in the land.'

There was a long silence while Clavertye digested this.

'This affair has become much more complex than we ever imagined at the outset,' the rector said. 'There are wheels within wheels. I have done as you asked and investigated to the best of my ability. But there is only so much that I can do. We must face the possibility that we are dealing with treason, as well as murder.'

'What are you asking of me?' Clavertye demanded.

'I am asking you to open a formal investigation into this entire affair. Hang what the coroner says, the man was almost certainly bribed to deliver his verdict. Miller and the Frenchman Paul were murdered by enemies of the state. These people must be tracked down.'

He watched Clavertye's face, waiting; and the moment he had been waiting for, arrived. 'We have no real evidence,' said Clavertye. 'Nothing that will stand up in court.'

'No,' said Hardcastle. 'Not yet. But you are the finest barrister to come out of the Inns of Court for twenty years. If there is evidence, you will find it.'

Clavertye smiled, a genuine smile this time, full of warmth, and suddenly Hardcastle was taken back to their youth, to Cambridge and the golden days . . . to a time that he found suddenly painful to think about. 'I can, with your help,' said the deputy lord-lieutenant. 'I'll need you to carry on your good work down here, old fellow. But, by God! If we work together, we can crack this affair wide open. You realise, Hardcastle, that this could bring us both a great deal of credit. People will sit up and take notice. There could be an official post in the offing. And you . . .' He paused, suddenly doubtful.

'Strange though it may seem,' said Hardcastle, 'I am only really interested in seeing justice done.'

'Of course, of course. I shall go at once to London and see what can be done. You'll remain here, of course, and continue to keep me informed.'

'You may rely on me. And what should I do if the dean renews his threats?'

'Send him my compliments, and tell him to go bugger himself.'

Hardcastle was still smiling as he watched Clavertye's coach drive away. The past was past, and would never return; but it was good to have the old Clavertye back, however briefly.

*

That was Friday. The rector passed Saturday lost in thought, barely noticing the passage of time. But on Sunday he conducted his church service as usual, and afterwards contrived without much difficulty to receive another invitation to call on Miss Godfrey and Miss Roper on Tuesday.

Monday morning, the day of the second inquest, dawned. Hardcastle was just finishing breakfast when the letter arrived.

MIDDLE TEMPLE, LONDON.
21st May, 1796.

My dear Hardcastle

I have considered again our conversation when last we spoke. I would again like to express my thanks for your diligence and good work thus far. You have fulfilled all my expectations of you, in exemplary fashion. And I must say, it was a real pleasure to see that fine mind of yours in action once again!

However, reluctant though I am to admit it, the time has come to make an end. We have worked hard, but I think even you will admit that all we have to show for our efforts is a number of fanciful theories, all of them unproven and unprovable. Reviewing the matter in my capacity as an officer of the law, I find that we have almost nothing in the way of tangible evidence; nor do I see any realistic chance of such evidence emerging in the near future.

Thus, I see no merit in our proceeding further. We are both busy men, and have many other duties to fulfil.

I trust you will see the matter as clearly as I do, and will take no further action in this matter.

Yr very obedient servant

CLAVERTYE

Quietly, the rector laid the letter down on his desk and gazed into space. Fresh and clear in his mind was the voice of Peter who was also called George, speaking in the church at Ebony.

I'll have one of my friends lean on Clavertye.

The 'leaning' had happened almost at once; probably, all had been arranged even before Clavertye reached London. Peter's friends must be powerful indeed. Clavertye had been warned: *stay away from this affair of the Twelve Apostles. If you dig any further, it will damage you. Mind your own business.* And he had heard the warning, and heeded it. He would take no further part in this affair.

Dusty Miller and Paul and Mark would lie lonely in their graves, and the truth would never be known.

12

Storm Clouds

The inquest was convened on the morning of Monday 23rd May, at the Star. Lord Clavertye did not attend, it being announced that His Lordship had urgent business in London. Amelia Chaytor was present as an onlooker along with most of the rest of the parish. A few curious sightseers arrived from Dymchurch and New Romney, hoping for a repeat of the excitement of the previous inquest. They were disappointed. Only three witnesses were called, and there were no fireworks.

The sexton, who looked after the church fabric and grounds (though he seldom darkened its door during a regular service, being nearly as much of an atheist as the bell-ringers), gave evidence that he had cut the grass in the churchyard the previous evening. He had seen no signs of a body, nor of a struggle, nor of a trespass of any kind. The rector, impeccably sober, described his finding of the body along with its position and condition. Finally, Dr Morley summarised the medical verdict already given in his written report to the coroner. The man had been badly beaten and then died of a broken neck. There were no marks of identification on the body and he had never seen the man before. The rector, recalled briefly, confirmed that the man was a complete stranger. No one else in the room contradicted this.

A verdict of unlawful killing was rendered. In the absence of the deputy lord-lieutenant, Mr Fanscombe as justice of the peace gave assurances that the matter would be investigated fully. His own opinion was that the man had been killed in a fight, perhaps a falling out between thieves or a disagreement between rival gangs of smugglers. A murmur passed around the room at this last, and as it died away the coroner declared the inquest adjourned.

The rector stepped out of the Star, clapping his hat onto his head, and turned to find Blunt standing and watching him, his face red and his expression ugly. 'Walk with me,' said the Customs man. It was not a request.

They walked north towards the rectory and church until they were out of sight of the other villagers. Then Blunt stopped and turned and faced the rector, his meaty fists clenching and unclenching. 'What the devil do you think you are playing at?'

The rector took his time about answering. 'Whatever do you mean?'

'Snooping around. Prying into things. Asking questions, about Miller and . . . other things. You and that blasted woman.'

'You will leave Mrs Chaytor out of this,' said the rector, his own voice hardening.

'Too late for that now. You dragged her into this business.'

'Oh? And what business is that? Tell me, Blunt, I am keen to know.'

The eyes of a murderer looked out of Blunt's face. 'Don't play games with me, Hardcastle. Stay out of my way. Stay in your rectory, and stick to your books and your booze.'

Books. 'It was you who searched my study,' said the rector suddenly.

'What the devil are you talking about?' He thought Blunt's surprise seemed genuine, and he already knew that the man was not a good actor.

'Never mind. You are mistaken, Blunt. I have express orders from both Dean Cornewall and Lord Clavertye. I am to stay clear of this affair, and not become involved in any way with the official investigation.'

There was no official investigation, as they both knew. Blunt stared at him, sick eyes glaring, face twitching a little. He looks like he has not slept in days, thought the rector. Good heavens, is it possible that his conscience is troubling him? Or more likely, does he fear exposure? Can he feel the hangman's noose already beginning to tighten around his neck?

'Stay away from me,' snarled Blunt. 'Stay out of my business, and tell the woman to stay out too. If you continue to meddle, both of you will suffer.'

'And Fanscombe?' said the rector. 'Should I stay away from him also?'

Blunt snapped. One big fist clenched white, and he drew his arm back and aimed a hard punch at the rector's face. Then he gasped and stepped back, clutching at his arm, for the rector had smashed him hard across the forearm with his walking stick. Hardcastle raised the stick again, pointing it warningly at the other man's throat.

'No, Blunt,' said the rector, his deep voice hard. 'In this, I am your master.'

'Damn you!' snarled Blunt, and he raised his fist again.

'I say!' a young man's voice said sharply. 'What the devil is going on?'

It was Captain Shaw, hair floppy, red uniform untidy on his scrawny frame, but with a rare expression of authority on his undistinguished face. He too had been at the inquest, watching in silence, and now he came hurrying up the street towards them. His eyes were sharp. 'What is this?' he demanded. 'Fisticuffs in the street? You're an officer of the law, Mr Blunt, you should know better than that.'

His eyes raging, Blunt turned to the militia officer and for a moment the rector thought he would strike Shaw instead. The captain held up a hand. 'I think you had better go,' he said sternly. 'Go back to Dymchurch and cool yourself down, Mr Blunt. You've no more business here.'

Slowly Blunt subsided. He gave the rector one last glare, his eyes promising revenge. Then he turned on his heel and walked back towards the village, holding his bruised arm. 'Reverend Hardcastle,' said the captain, full of concern, 'are you injured?'

'Not at all, captain. And I thank you for coming as you did. Your arrival was most timely.'

'Whatever was that about, Reverend? What can have upset old Blunty so? He's a bit of a shouter, if you know what I mean, but it is not like him to raise his hand to anyone, especially to a man of the cloth. I am deeply shocked, I truly am.'

'It was an unfortunate misunderstanding,' said rector. 'I am certain the matter will resolve itself. And thank you again, Captain Shaw.' He changed the subject. 'Do I understand that you were coming to see me?'

Shaw shifted a little. 'Well, yes I was. I wanted to see you, sir, because I have a confession to make.'

The rector pricked up his ears, and waited.

'I apologise most humbly if I misled you when we met in Appledore. The truth is, I wasn't myself at all. I had some bad news that morning.

My mother up in Ashford had been taken ill, and I was anxious to be off to see her, but my horse had thrown a shoe the previous day and that fool of a blacksmith still hadn't re-shod the beast. I was anxious to be away, and did not give you my full mind.'

'My dear captain, there really is no need to apologise. How is your mother?'

'Well, she's still poorly, sir, but the physician up there says she is improving. I don't mind telling you that I am still very worried for her.' The young man's face was indeed anxious, Hardcastle thought.

'Is your mother being cared for? Should you not still be in Ashford yourself?'

'My sisters are both there looking after her, so there's no call for me to hang on, and of course I have my duties here, but . . . Anyway, sir, there's no need for me to burden you with my problems. I'll come to the point. We were discussing the patrols I sent down into the Marsh at the request of Mr Fanscombe, to look for any signs of trouble and also to ensure your safety, Reverend, so far as we could.'

'Yes, that is right. I believe you said you patrolled for four nights. I was, and am, most grateful.'

'Yes, but that's where I may have deceived you, inadvertently, you see. We'd actually been down in the Marsh the night before, too, the night the killings took place. You remember I said at the inquest that I had been out on patrol with my men? But we didn't come near St Mary then, we were only a little east of Ivychurch. That too was part of a request for aid from the civil power from Mr Fanscombe.'

'Oh? What orders did you have on that occasion?'

The young captain rubbed his bristly chin. 'Well, it was never really quite clear, sir. We were to hold a line east of Ivychurch and try to inter-cept any smugglers coming west; that was all I was told. But we never saw anyone. We heard the shooting, of course, but it was a long way to the east and north-east. We just stood there wet and cold, and never saw a thing. Finally about three in the morning I gave it up as a bad job and ordered my men back to Appledore.'

'I see. You didn't say any of this at the inquest.'

'Not when I was on the stand, no. But I'd said all of this in my statement to Mr Fanscombe. And he knew all about it, of course, for it was he who had given the orders in the first place.'

The rector nodded slowly. 'Why are you telling me all of this now, Captain Shaw?'

The young man looked up sharply, and then unexpectedly he smiled. He actually had quite a pleasant smile, the rector thought.

'You're a sharp one, Reverend. I always thought so. Very well, I'll come clean. I obeyed Mr Fanscombe's orders that night, but I wasn't happy about it. The order came late, and there was something peremptory about it, quite unlike his normal manner. Normally he comes to see me in person and tells what he wants done and why. This was just, "Go there, do this."'

'I see. You don't think Mr Fanscombe was his usual self?'

'Well, no, sir, but I think there is more to it than that. There is something about this whole business that makes me uneasy. We were called out and then stuck in the wrong place, or at least that's how I see it. Were we being used for some other purpose? Was Mr Fanscombe himself maybe deceived? There's something wrong, I'm sure of it.'

'And you thought you would fish around and see if I knew anything?'

'There it is,' said the young man, smiling again. 'You have the right of it. It's impertinent of me, to be sure. I'll quite understand if you brush me off.'

'No,' said the rector slowly. 'I share your feelings. I too am concerned that no one seems to know the name or identity of the young man who was killed here, or why he was murdered. I have many questions, Captain Shaw, but answers have so far eluded me. I wish I could help you, but I fear I cannot.'

Shaw nodded. 'You'll understand why I had to ask, though, Reverend. If some game is afoot and whoever is playing it is trying to involve the militia; well, that is a serious business. I want to get to the bottom of this.'

'Then I wish you luck, captain. And if I do hear anything that might be important, I will certainly let you know.'

'I'd be right pleased if you would. Well, then, sir, good afternoon to you.'

*

THE RECTORY, ST MARY IN THE MARSH, KENT.
23rd May, 1796.

My dear Freddie,

I trust this letter finds you in excellent health, and Martha also. I recall she had a bad chest during the winter, and hope that this has entirely cleared. How is young William? Making a name for himself at Cambridge now, I trust.

I write to you to ask a small favour. I believe you have in your parish a widowed lady by the name of Shaw. Her son is currently serving with the militia down here at Appledore, and reported to me recently that his mother is unwell. He seemed most concerned about her. Would you be able to have some report of her condition? I should like to be able to be of some use to him, especially should she take a turn for the worse. This is of course in confidence between us, for I should not like Captain Shaw to think I was prying into his affairs.

Yr friend as always

M.A.H.

Amelia Chaytor presented herself at the rectory after midday, and Mrs Kemp showed her into the study with more civility than she usually offered his guests.

'Another splendid public performance,' she said. 'Even I believed you when you said you had never seen the man before.'

'It was almost true,' replied the rector. 'During our only previous encounter he had been masked and hooded. Technically, I did perjure myself, but given that the man who administered the oath is himself corrupt, I feel no unease on that score.'

'Nor should you.' She looked at him sharply, and at the half-empty bottle beside him. 'What is wrong?'

He described the confrontation with Blunt, and also how his study had been searched. She listened in silence and then said, 'Could they have found anything?'

'I very much doubt it. I have made a few notes and scribbles from time to time, but I have always been careful to burn them. I have to say, I am not at all certain it was Blunt who searched the room. He seemed genuinely puzzled when I mentioned it. Also, searching through my papers might be a bit too subtle for him. As we are learning, he prefers more direct methods.'

'Blunt by name, blunt by nature. He is nevertheless becoming dangerous,' she said thoughtfully. She said it in the same tone that she might have used when discussing the ordering of furniture in a room.

'He is becoming desperate, which does indeed make him dangerous. Make doubly certain that your doors and windows are locked at night.'

'Be assured that I have already done so, but thank you for the advice. Did you speak with Lord Clavertye?'

He told her the gist of Clavertye's letter, and she listened with her hands resting gently in her lap. 'He has cast us adrift,' she said.

'Damn His Lordship for a weak-minded fool,' said the rector bitterly. 'He has put himself and his own ambitions ahead of the truth. He'll make a fine politician, won't he? But it is too late. Blunt and his confederates know that we suspect them.' He did not say it, but it was likely to be her visits to Deal and New Romney that had given the game away. 'They will not believe that we have stopped. We will continue to be in danger, no matter what we do.'

'Then it seems we have no choice but to carry on investigating,' she said. 'We need now to bring this affair to a conclusion, as swiftly as we can.' Her hands remained still in her lap, and yet again the rector marvelled at her composure.

'There is another thing,' he said, and he related his conversation with Captain Shaw. 'I don't know what to make of it. If he is genuinely investigating this matter, then he could be a very useful ally. But I could not bring myself to trust him.'

'Is it possible to check his story? About his mother?'

'I have already written to a friend in Ashford to do so.' He sighed. 'This affair has become so tangled and so complex that I no longer know who is involved. Perhaps everyone is,' he added.

' "I don't trust anyone except me and thee, and between us, I am not too sure about thee." ' She smiled. 'It is a joke. It was one of John's favourite sayings.'

The rector regarded her. He recalled that Peter and Matthew had referred to the Twelve Apostles' informant in St Mary as a woman. Could it be . . . ? No, of course not, it was a ridiculous notion. Ridiculous . . . 'We must keep an eye on Shaw,' he said, wrenching his mind away from the seed of doubt that had been planted there. 'His men think he is a blunderer, but I begin to wonder if he might be deeper than he looks.'

'That would not be hard. In appearance, Captain Shaw is the quintessence of shallowness.'

'True, but that could be a masquerade. What he said about Fanscombe troubles me. It seems clear that, whether he knows it or not, Shaw's men were supposed to be part of the ambush that would trap the Twelve Apostles. And we know now that it was Fanscombe's orders that sent Shaw there.'

'We've long suspected that our justice of the peace is mixed up in this business. It begins to look as if we are right.'

The rector smiled. 'Lord Clavertye says he is a sound man, beyond reproach. "His heart and head are in the right place", says His Lordship.'

'I see. That in itself surely gives us cause for suspicion.'

He laughed aloud. 'My dear Mrs Chaytor, you are nearly as suspicious and cynical as I am myself.'

'I have never thought of myself as cynical,' said Amelia Chaytor thoughtfully. 'Perhaps I am. I tend to think of myself as a realist. I actually quite like Fanscombe, though I prefer him in small doses. His bluff and hearty manner would be irksome, were it not so obviously a front.'

'What do you make of Mrs Fanscombe?'

'I am *frightfully* glad that I am not married to her . . . but in fact, I cannot help liking her too. She is pleasant enough, when she is not with her husband.'

'And Fanscombe's daughter?'

'Eliza? Who knows what goes on inside *her* pretty head? For the last several months she has barely been on speaking terms with her stepmother. My girl had this from the maids at New Hall.' She paused. 'I will play devil's advocate for a moment. There might be innocent explanations for all of Fanscombe's actions. Blunt might have deceived him about the Twelve Apostles; Fanscombe may have thought that he was merely upholding the law and assisting the Customs.'

'And what of Paul, who was a guest under their roof?'

'They simply may not have known his real identity.'

'True. But you will recall that I gave Fanscombe a clear opportunity to tell me the truth about Paul's visit to the house, and he failed to do so. And when I asked Miss Fanscombe a question about Paul, she responded with an outright lie.'

Mrs Chaytor pursed her lips. 'Very well. What is the connection between Fanscombe and Blunt?'

'My feeling is that it is Blunt who pulls the strings. Fanscombe, assuming he is involved, is there to provide cover for Blunt. As justice of the peace, it would be easy for him to conceal evidence and steer official investigations in the wrong direction. For example, Fanscombe may have arranged the bribe for the coroner.'

'But what about Eliza?' she frowned. 'What possible reason could she have for lying?'

They could think of no answer to this. She looked out the window, her gloved hands very still in her lap, and then looked back at him, her blue eyes steady. 'We have pushed Blunt as far as we can, and he has started to strike back. Let us turn our attention now to the Fanscombes. Let us find out who they really are, and what they really know.'

'There is still danger in doing so.'

'My dear man, of course there is. But as I said earlier, we cannot stop. We must see this matter through.'

'What then do you propose?'

'I propose that we shake the tree. I have lived here for more than half a year, and have yet to entertain my neighbours. It is time I remembered my position. Reverend Hardcastle, will you do me the honour of dining with me on Saturday, the twenty-eighth of May?'

'I am delighted to accept.' He was puzzled, not understanding what she meant, but he said nothing further. He had learned by now that it was best to let her do things in her own way.

He showed her out, and then returned to the study and poured another glass of port. Her husband had been in diplomatic service; was that a coincidence? Or did she too have interests in high places? Was her presence in the Marsh simply a matter of chance? Or was she reporting her suspicions and her findings to someone else? Was she the Twelve Apostles' agent in St Mary in the Marsh?

It was ridiculous, of course. If she was hand in glove with Peter, why would she then confide in him? On the other hand . . . what other woman in the Marsh had her coolness, her penetrating intelligence and her courage? He wondered.

13

Secrets at New Hall

On Tuesday morning the rector harnessed his horse to the creaking dog cart and drove carefully down the rutted track to the Cadman farm. Old Cadman was now in a bad way; a combination of marsh fever, rheumatism and gin had sent him to his bed, and Dr Morley, seen the previous day in the village, had remarked that he might not last the week. He found the old man peacefully comatose, his son and daughter-in-law and their children distraught; he offered all the comfort that could be offered in such situations, and then drove back to the village.

It was about eleven on that warm May morning when he reached the ivy-clad crumbling cottage of Miss Godfrey and Miss Roper. They offered him tea and brandy and some pastries created by the fair hand of Miss Roper herself, full of sickly sweet stewed fruit and wrapped in thick, fat-laden cases. He managed to eat two of these with a straight face. They asked him about Mr Cadman's father, discussing his symptoms with a clinical exactitude that would have tested Dr Morley.

'On the subject of Dr Morley,' said the rector, once a fair amount of brandy had been consumed. 'You are certain he is having assignatious with Mrs Fanscombe?'

Delighted by the chance to gossip, they gave him times and places: usually at the doctor's house, once or twice at New Hall when Fanscombe was away, several times at a house said to be somewhere near Rye. The girl who cleaned for them had all of this directly from those ever-flowing fountains of information, the maids at New Hall.

'Goodness me,' said the rector. 'And this has been going on for over a year? Well, well.'

'The morals of that house are simply shocking,' pronounced Miss Godfrey. 'Simply shocking. Mrs Fanscombe is not the only one to transgress either,' and she looked brightly at the rector.

The rector duly took the bait. 'Don't tell me Mr Fanscombe has a lover somewhere?'

'Oh, no, he is quite blameless, poor man.' Miss Roper checked. 'At least, so far as we know. He might have a fancy woman hidden away somewhere, but if he does, he has kept it very quiet. No, my dear Reverend, I mean his daughter. Elizabeth.'

The rector raised his eyebrows and waited. 'They say,' said Miss Godfrey, leaning forward and dropping her voice to a confidential murmur, 'that she has been *compromised* by that Frenchman, F-f-f-. . .'

'Foucarmont,' enunciated Miss Roper. 'That is the typical behaviour of a Frenchman, is it not, Reverend Hardcastle? I daresay that when the invasion comes, all we ladies will be subjected to a great ravishing by *hordes* of Frenchmen. All very hairy and smelling of garlic, no doubt.'

'No, no, it will never come to that,' said the rector absently. 'Lord Clavertye's new semaphore system will protect you . . . Ladies, this cannot be correct, surely? M. de Foucarmont is the girl's uncle, even if only by marriage.'

'Ah, but is he?' Miss Godfrey said in the same low voice. 'The maids at the house *say* that the relationship is a pretence, nothing more. Mr Fou-car-mont and Mrs Fanscombe are in no way related.'

'Then . . . why does he come to stay at New Hall?'

'That is the mystery, is it not?' asked Miss Roper cheerfully. 'Why indeed? Do you suppose he is a French spy, come to prepare the way for the invasion?'

'Clara, dear,' said Miss Godfrey severely, 'you are quite obsessed with this idea of a French invasion.'

The rector reflected that it would be a good thing if a few of their leaders in Whitehall were similarly obsessed. 'M. de Foucarmont is a French royalist of unimpeachable character,' he said, 'and very much on our side. That is the word from Lord Clavertye, who should know.'

'I think the pair of them deserve each other,' said Miss Godfrey. Miss Roper nodded. 'He is rich and handsome, and she is ambitious. There is a certain vulgar expression which fits her admirably.'

The rector knew the expression. 'All teeth and tits,' was how young Bessie Luckhurst at the Star had described Eliza Fanscombe some weeks back, to the delight of the common room. He had reprimanded Bessie gently for her language, but admitted to himself that Eliza was admirably equipped with both assets. 'I don't know the young lady well,' he said cautiously. 'What little I have seen suggests a young woman of spirit, but whose manners could be improved.'

'Oh, she does not lack spirit,' said Miss Godfrey acidly. 'Her behaviour, quite apart from this business with Mr F-f-f-.' She waved an airy hand. 'You know who I mean. Him. Regardless, her behaviour is not that which one would expect from a girl of good family.'

'What do you mean?' asked the rector.

'She is a hoyden,' said Miss Godfrey. 'She goes riding alone, at all hours of the day and night. Who *knows* what she gets up to, or whom she meets? And she is quite out of control at home. She ignores her father entirely, and treats her stepmother quite abominably. They fight like cat and dog, we understand, and do not always disguise their quarrels from the servants.'

'There have been some *dreadful* scenes,' said Miss Roper, nodding. 'That girl is going wild, mark my words. And her parents cannot, or will not, tame her.'

'She goes out at night?' asked the rector, astonished.

'She certainly does. She has been seen, riding alone across the Marsh on nights of the new moon, when the smugglers make their runs. She is gaining a reputation,' said Miss Godfrey solemnly.

'I cannot imagine why she would be so foolish,' mused the rector as Miss Godfrey refilled his cup.

'She is young,' said Miss Roper, with unusual tolerance. 'She is full of spirit. She does not want to live the same narrow, dull life as her parents. I do not entirely blame her. Indeed, on one level I almost envy her.'

'Clara!' said Miss Godfrey, staring at her open-mouthed. 'My dear, you never cease to amaze me!'

He detached himself gently from their company after a while and walked home, his belly uneasily full of brandy and lard. He could eat little of his luncheon, which incurred the displeasure of Mrs Kemp, and afterwards lay down on the settee in his study, listening to his stomach rumble and looking up at the branches of the elms waving in the south-westerly wind.

Today was 24th May. The moon was on the wane. Matthew had said that the next smugglers' run would likely be on 6th June. That was less than two weeks from now. What would Blunt do? He had lost his agent inside the Twelve Apostles, but he was likely to have other sources of information. The rector had no doubt that Blunt would try once again to capture or kill Peter and his men. There would be more violence, more death on the Marsh.

Unless, somehow, he and Mrs Chaytor could prevent it.

They desperately needed allies. Clavertye had abandoned them. Cornewall was already set firm against them. Who else? He thought about approaching Captain Shaw, and wondered whether the young man really would continue to investigate. There was little that the captain could do officially without sanction from above; he could not call out his men, for example. But he might have another perspective and other, better sources of information. He was, it was now clear, cleverer than he looked, and he might spot something that the rector himself had missed. The same was true of Turner, the painter, with his famous eye for detail and detachment from local affairs.

Then, there was Dr Morley.

He disliked the doctor as cordially as ever, but even he had to admit that Morley worked hard and was dedicated to his profession. Furthermore, he was intelligent and perceptive and in a position to hear gossip and acquire useful information. The affair with Eugénie Fanscombe need not necessarily be held against him. Morley had been as closely involved in this affair as he himself. Should he perhaps now sound out in the doctor? Could he help them in any way?

He promised himself that he would think about the matter, and then fell asleep.

On the following morning, Wednesday, the rector rose early and walked down to St Mary's Bay under a cloudy sky. Here he laboured up to the crest of the dunes and stood for a long time, the hem of his overcoat flapping in the fresh wind, looking at the coast of France so perilously near. There was no sign of Turner; perhaps the light was not right for painting.

He wondered what was happening on that far shore. The armies of revolutionary France were large and powerful; for four years they had defied the rest of Europe. There had been hopes that a royalist uprising the previous autumn would overthrow the republic, but that uprising had been suppressed and the new revolutionary government, the Directory, appeared stronger than ever.

There was every chance that one day the Directory would launch its armies across the thirty miles of windswept water that lay between France and England. And when that day comes, the rector thought darkly, there are not a few Englishmen who will welcome them with open arms. Men full of revolutionary zeal, men to whom loyalty to their king means nothing. Men who, driven by political beliefs or greed, would betray their country.

Miss Roper might not be so hazy-witted as she seemed. What if this whole affair really was the prelude to an invasion? What if Blunt and his confederates, whoever they might be, were part of a plot to deliver England to her enemies? He thought about this for a long time, staring out at the coast of France as if he expected to see the invasion barges sailing across the water at any moment. But nothing stirred on the rolling steel-grey sea except for a few fishing boats.

He drew a long breath of sea air, and his mind began to work more clearly. Things which had been obscure started to make sense. He had never understood why Blunt had been prepared to betray the Twelve Apostles. He had seen the man's terror and desperation at first hand. Bullies like Blunt never stood up to men stronger and more dangerous than they, unless . . .

Unless someone more powerful still was calling the shots. Blunt must be taking orders from someone, and that someone must know the Twelve Apostles were not just a smuggling gang. He must know exactly who the Apostles were, and what their business was. So, Blunt probably knew as well.

That meant that Blunt was not just a murderer; he was also a traitor.

And where did that leave Fanscombe and his family, and Foucarmont? Miss Godfrey and Miss Roper had told him a few of the secrets of New Hall, but he was certain that the Fanscombes' domestic troubles were not at the heart of the matter. Something was very wrong in that household. Distasteful thought it might be to contemplate, it was likely that either Fanscombe or Foucarmont was involved – even if unwittingly – in Blunt's treason.

Could he take this knowledge to Clavertye, and ask him to rethink his position? But once again, he told himself, to quote His Lordship, I have no evidence, only a fanciful theory, unproven and unprovable.

Eventually his stomach reminded him that it was past time for breakfast, and he turned and walked back to the village. He passed the rest of the day engaged almost absent-mindedly in pastoral duties, thinking hard but coming to no conclusions.

On the following day, Thursday 26th, a letter arrived.

THE RECTORY, ST MARY THE VIRGIN, ASHFORD.
25th May, 1796.

My dear Marcus,

How perfectly splendid it is to hear from you, old fellow. Thank you very kindly for asking about Martha; yes, she is entirely recovered from her chill. Even as I write, I can hear her outside berating the gardener; from which you may deduce that she is in fine fettle! How are things in your sleepy old Marsh? By the way, thanks most sincerely for the fine bottle of brandy you sent at Christmas. I trust there is plenty more from the same source!

I know Mrs Shaw, of course. She was quite poorly for some time before anyone knew of it; she is, I fear, the sort of lady who prefers to suffer in silence, rather than risk being a burden to others. When I learned she was ill, I sent at once for her family. I recall Captain Shaw visiting her; he called on me afterwards, and I gained the impression of a very devoted son. His sisters, Mrs Shaw's daughters, are here and nursing the old lady, who is now very much on the mend. But I will certainly inform you if her malady takes a turn for the worse.

William is tearing up Trinity College, and we wait daily for news of his expulsion. Young dog! Ha-ha!

In friendship and in Christ

FREDDIE

So, thought the rector, reading the letter in his study after breakfast, Shaw's story was true. He seems genuine . . . Indeed, he has never given me any reason whatever to distrust him. I have been prejudiced against him because he is a gangling, scrawny, untidy young man whose mannerisms irritate me. I wrote him off at the beginning as the nearest thing to a halfwit. Perhaps it is time I revised my opinion of him.

He pondered this, drumming his fingers on the table and wondering once more whether to take Shaw into his confidence. Then he came to a sudden decision. Not yet, he told himself, not until I know more; and I will discuss it with Mrs Chaytor too. We may yet need Shaw; but let us keep quiet until we know for sure.

There was a knock at the front door, and he heard Mrs Kemp go to answer it. He had thought it would be Mrs Chaytor, but instead he heard a man's voice in the hall, and then Mrs Kemp appeared in the doorway with the usual expression of disapproval on her lined face. 'Mr Turner to see you, Reverend.'

Turner was shown in, and Mrs Kemp was dispatched for coffee. 'Does she always look like that?' the painter asked.

'She disapproves of you. You are a foreigner; that is, you do not come from the Marsh. Also, like many of the older women here, she suspects you of interfering with the virgins of St Mary.'

'A virgin, in St Mary? You'd sooner find a buffalo in Bond Street.' Turner suddenly recalled that he was talking to a clergyman, and coughed. Mrs Kemp returned with coffee, served it, and slammed the study door as she departed.

'What may I do for you, Mr Turner?' the rector asked.

Turner coughed again, still embarrassed. 'This is a bit delicate,' he said. 'But . . . I think that there is something odd going on at New Hall.'

The rector's ears began to tingle. 'Go on,' he said gently.

'For one thing, the place is like Piccadilly. People come and go all the time. Dr Morley calls three times a week, though to my knowledge no one there is ill. Blunt has been there twice in recent days, slipping through the grounds like a burglar and looking over his shoulder before he reaches the door. There've been half a dozen others, too, some coming openly by day, others at night. And then there is Mad Eliza, galloping out yesterday at ten in the evening, if you like, and not coming back until nearly dawn.'

'Why do you call her Mad Eliza?'

'Because she's . . . Mad is too harsh a word, perhaps, but I think she is ten pence in the shilling.' Turner tapped his head. 'She is, what, eighteen? But she behaves like a spoiled child.'

The rector sipped his coffee, and waited. 'I should make it clear that I don't spy on them,' said Turner. 'The back windows of Rightways look out over the gardens and the front of New Hall, and it is difficult not to notice these things. No one else in the village would see, because none of the other houses overlooks the gardens or the drive.'

'I understand,' said the rector. 'Does Mr Fanscombe go out often? Or M. de Foucarmont, who I assume is still there?'

Turner looked at the rector for a full half-minute, his eyes searching the older man's face. 'You also think something is wrong,' he said finally.

'I do. But I am not yet certain what it is.'

'I should have known you would be aware of this,' said Turner half to himself. 'To answer your question, I have not laid eyes on Foucarmont, but I have seen his valet. So I assume Foucarmont is still there, but lying low. Fanscombe rode out yesterday and was gone for most of the day. Dr Morley called while he was absent. I assume Dr Morley's . . . business, was with Mrs Fanscombe.'

'It seems likely. You must have a very low opinion of the morals of this parish, Mr Turner.'

Turner smiled. 'On the contrary, I quite like it here. But Blunt is an unpleasant sort of cove, and I cannot work out what he is doing hanging around. Surely *he* isn't . . .'

'No. He needs to see Fanscombe on official business, of course.'

Again Turner gave him a long searching look. 'And what else?' he asked.

'Again, I fear, I do not know.' At all costs, he had to prevent Turner from following up his suspicions on his own; any interference by him might spoil the rector's own inquiry, and could also be dangerous for Turner himself. 'I fear we are looking at the beginnings of a domestic tragedy at New Hall,' he said quietly. 'There are secrets under that roof, I am quite certain, but they are secrets that concern the Fanscombe family only. We must allow them their privacy.'

He was lying, and Turner knew it. The painter gave him another long look, and then nodded. 'You are warning me off,' he said. 'Doubtless you have your reasons. I know you well enough by now to trust you. But if I learn anything else of importance, then I will come to you again; and next time, I will insist on an explanation.'

'Next time,' said the rector, 'you shall have it.'

Now the rector was worried. When he called on Amelia Chaytor later that morning her servants told him that she was away; she had driven down to stay with a friend near Rye and would not return until Saturday morning, the day of her dinner party. He was surprised that she had gone without telling him, and once more he contemplated where her true loyalties lay.

That evening he visited the Star, and sat down in the common room with Joshua Stemp and Jack Hoad, fishermen and veterans of the free-trade. He found them as gloomy as himself, for different reasons. Rumours of invasion were spreading along the coast again. Stemp and Hoad feared mostly for their boats; these were their main livelihood, licit and illicit, and they worried that in event of war the boats might be damaged or, worse, confiscated. There was a persistent rumour that in the event of an invasion, the Royal Navy would burn or sink every fishing boat along the coast to prevent the French using them to bring men and supplies across the Channel. 'You're a clever man, Reverend,' said Stemp, 'so you'll know the answer to this. Why don't the government do something to prevent the Frenchies gettin' ashore? Way it is now, I reckon they could land any-where they liked, and be marchin' through London in a week.'

The rector stirred a little. 'Be careful what you wish for, Joshua. If the government sends troops and builds forts along this shore, that could be the end of the free trade.'

They muttered at this. It was late, and the three of them sat alone in the common room, the fishermen drinking gin and the rector nursing a tankard of beer; behind the bar, Bessie Luckhurst was yawning openly.

'I reckon I'd rather lose the free trade than be taken over by them fuckin' Frogs,' said Hoad, who tended to say what he thought, without embellishment.

'Might not come to that,' argued Stemp. 'I don't see how a few redcoats is goin' to stop the free trade. It's been around since my granddad's day. It ain't goin' away.'

'Not so long as the smugglers keep paying the Customs to look the other way when they make their runs,' observed the rector.

The others nodded at this, straight-faced, and agreed that corruption was a terrible thing, much to be deplored. 'Blunty's a greedy bastard,' said Hoad, which seemed to sum up his entire feelings on the affair.

'He is an unpleasant man, to be sure. Do you suppose it is only the smugglers who are paying him off?'

Hoad finished his gin, and the rector signalled to Bessie for another round. He was chancing his arm here, hoping that the fishermen might have heard something, even if only a rumour. Now Stemp rubbed his chin and looked thoughtful. 'There's something odd about him, that's for certain. Take this business of the Twelve Apostles, now. They were payin' him off sweet and regular, just like the rest of the gangs. Then suddenly he stitches them up, takes their money and then tries to kill them. What's that all about?'

The rector knew exactly what it was about, but did not say so. Instead, he lowered his voice. 'Gentlemen; what do you think of this business of the officer who was killed? Miller, his name was. Blunt insisted that his death was an accident.'

There was a long pause. 'Well,' said Stemp, the smallpox pits on his cheek full of shadow in the lamplight. 'It *might* have been an accident. And then, it might not.'

'What have you heard?' asked the rector quietly.

Hoad shifted on his wooden bench and stared hard at the rector. 'Why do you want to know, Reverend?'

'Jack. Do I ask your business when you go out to sea at night? Take my word for it, this has nothing do with the free trade.'

Stemp nodded and lowered his voice still further to a bare murmur. 'There's a rumour, only a rumour, mind, that Blunty killed Miller. They had a quarrel earlier in the day, so 'tis said. And some say, when the Twelve Apostles came over the Marsh, Miller called out to them. That's when Blunty shot him. Then he came back and tidied things so it would look like an accident. That's what they say.'

'Who says, Joshua?' In the silence that followed, the rector added, 'I repeat, this has nothing to do with the free trade. Reassure your associates that I am not interested in them.'

Stemp and Hoad looked at each other, and the latter nodded. 'There's a fellow called Snathurst,' said Stemp. 'He's one of Blunty's men at Dymchurch. He's bent, like the rest of that crew.' The fisherman looked around, and then leaned forward and whispered, 'He knows something about that business. He let it be known that he'd sell what he knew, if anyone was interested in payin' his price.'

The rector controlled his sudden excitement. 'He wants money?'

'He's known as Five-Guineas Snathurst. People reckon that for five guineas, he'd cut his own grandmother's throat.'

'And do you know how I could get a message, in private, to this Five-Guineas?'

'I reckon it could be done.' Stemp came to a decision. 'In fact, leave it to me. But, you be careful, Reverend. Don't go askin' too many questions. You don't want to upset the wrong people.'

'Don't worry, Joshua,' said the rector, draining his pot. 'I can handle myself. I've spent most of my life upsetting the *right* people.'

He walked slowly home, feeling the wind at his back. He did not see the shadows in the rectory garden, but in the morning he found footprints in the soft, rain-dampened soil around the roses. He realised, sombrely, that his every move was now being watched.

14

Shaking the Tree

On the early evening of Saturday 28th May, reasonably sober and tidily dressed, the rector presented himself at Sandy House. A butler, a quiet elderly man who the rector had not seen before and whom he guessed was hired in from the agency in Rye, admitted him with grave courtesy. Amelia herself came out to greet him, smiling, looking very fetching in a pale green high-waisted gown. 'Prepare yourself for a little shock,' she said taking his arm. 'I have invited Dr Morley.'

He stared at her. 'I thought you disliked the man.'

'I find him odious. But have faith. There is method in my madness.'

She escorted him into the drawing room, where the other guests were already gathered, and presented him to a pretty young woman in an elegant silk gown. 'This is my friend Mrs Merriwether,' said Amelia. 'She and her husband live at Merriwether Hall, down near Rye. I was staying with her, and I have carried her back with me for dinner.'

'Enchanted,' said the rector bowing. He knew Merriwether Hall, a tumbledown country house just on the border of Kent and Sussex; Lord Merriwether, its owner, was an old man renowned for his tight purse and terrible temper. This lady must be his daughter-in-law.

'I recall meeting you in Rye two years ago, Reverend,' she said cheerfully. 'It was the reception for the Warden of the Cinque Ports, do you recall? It was quite a splendid occasion. The Duke of Dorset was there, and so many other grand names. I declare that as a little country mouse, I felt quite overwhelmed.' She prattled happily, he smiling and nodding his head and pretending to listen while he looked at the other occupants of the room. Turner the painter, drinking sherry and gazing morosely out of the window, clearly wishing he was back at his easel with a brush in hand. Miss Godfrey and Miss Roper, both already a little bit merry. Captain Shaw, slightly less untidy than usual, attempting to make small talk with Eliza Fanscombe, who was barely responding to him. Her father, for once not in riding dress but wearing instead a plum-coloured coat and highly vulgar waistcoat, standing and talking in his most hearty voice to Dr Morley, the man who was cuckolding him, while his wife watched him with her pointed nose drawn back a little, her eyes full of dislike. Another man, elegant in dark blue silk, turned and caught the rector's eye, and bowed a little; Foucarmont.

He took a glass of sherry and let Mrs Merriwether run on until Amelia came and fetched her away to talk to Turner. The rector turned then, and found Foucarmont beside him.

'It is a pleasure to see you once again, Monsieur Hardcastle,' the Frenchman said in his perfect, faintly accented English. 'I trust that you are well?'

'I am very well, sir. I did not expect to find you here. I had not seen you about for some days, and assumed you had returned to London.'

'Not yet, though I shall return very soon. I must say, I do enjoy this charming village. The vistas and the sea air are so restful, after the bustle of London. Tell me, in the autumn, is there much shooting in these parts?'

Something tingled down the rector's spine. 'There is wildfowling,' he said. 'Are you a sportsman, sir?'

'I enjoy shooting, when time permits. I have never taken to your English sport of fox-hunting; I confess that it puzzles me. It is the most inefficient method of killing foxes that one could imagine.'

'Killing foxes is not the true object of the sport,' said the rector drily. 'It is more of a side-effect,' and the Frenchman laughed. They talked for a while longer; the rector found him pleasant company.

They went in to dinner, he escorting Mrs Merriwether, seating her and then bowing to Miss Fanscombe as she took her seat on his other side. She too was wearing a high-waisted gown, with a décolletage that might have been appropriate for a London ballroom but was somewhat out of place on Romney Marsh. If she drops a spoon down there, he thought, averting his eyes from her cleavage, it will fall all the way to the floor . . . Turner was staring at her; so was Miss Roper, her eyes bright with sherry and mischief. The rector realised that this evening was unlikely to turn out well.

In fact, everything went very well at first. Bessie from the Star, neat and bright as a new-minted pin, had come in to help Mrs Chaytor's maids serve and clear away; she and Turner ignored each other studiously throughout the meal. The food was excellent, the wine also, and the rector drank enough to make himself go red in the face and laugh a little more loudly than usual, but not enough to dull his perceptions. Fanscombe drank heavily; Morley barely touched a drop, and he glanced pointedly at the rector's glass from time to time.

Amelia Chaytor guided the conversation dextrously. She drew Turner out of himself and coaxed him to talk about painting and those artists that he most admired. Captain Shaw, surprisingly, turned out to be very interested in painting and confessed with a mild blush that he dabbled a little in oils himself; but only as a hobby, he hastened to add, he was not a serious painter. Turner looked relieved. Fanscombe and Foucarmont talked about horses, and then just when some of the rest of the party were beginning to grow bored, their hostess steered the conversation skilfully away to Paris, where she had lived for several years after her marriage. Miss Roper and Miss Godfrey were familiar with Paris too, and Mrs Fanscombe suddenly came out of her shell and talked with lively animation of the city where she had been born. From Paris they turned to music, and Mrs Merriwether said smiling, 'Our dear friend is quite a skilful musician in her own right, did you not know? Amelia, my dear, you must play for us after dinner.'

At the end of the meal they rose and the ladies withdrew, leaving the rector, Fanscombe, Morley, Turner, Foucarmont and Captain Shaw with the port decanter. It was, thought the rector, quite the most uncomfortable gathering he had attended for a long time. They talked about horses again, or rather Fanscombe did; under his bluff surface he was as nervous as he had been the day Hardcastle had called on him, and the port did nothing to steady him. Morley sat and listened, a faint sneer on his face. Foucarmont talked calmly of London society, which made Captain Shaw fidget for he had never been to London and knew nothing about society. Turner said nothing, studying them all. The rector drank two glasses of port, and the conversation withered and died.

With relief they joined the ladies in the drawing room, where Mrs Merriwether was playing the harpsichord. They applauded as she finished, and she rose and curtseyed smiling. 'Amelia, dear,' she said, 'it is time you showed off your talents.' Amelia rose with what the rector thought was genuine reluctance, and took her place at the instrument. She played Bach, and the rector thought that Mrs Merriwether had not exaggerated; her playing was both skilful and beautiful.

At the end she turned, smiling and inclining her head as they applauded her. 'You are far too kind to my poor talents,' she said. 'Reverend Hardcastle, would you be so kind as to ring the bell for tea?' The maids appeared and began setting out tea. 'I am so glad to have you all here,' said Mrs Chaytor, still sitting on the bench by the harpsichord. 'While you gentlemen were talking over your port, we had a small discussion here in the drawing room. I, or rather we, would like to ask a favour of you.'

Despite the port, the rector felt his spine tingle again. Foucarmont inclined his head gallantly. 'Whatever you wish, madame.'

'It is this. Do you recall poor Mr Miller of the Customs who came to an untimely end on the Marsh three weeks ago? His widow lives in Deal; she has three small children, and little means. I would like to get up a fund to support her.'

'Why, of course,' said the Frenchman. 'It would be a pleasure to contribute. After all, this poor man died while doing his duty. Do I understand correctly? He was killed by accident, by his own weapon?'

'Well,' said Mrs Chaytor, 'that of course is another story.'

There was a little silence. 'Lucy, Bessie, that is all,' said Mrs Chaytor gently. The two maids departed, both extremely unwillingly, and closed the door behind them.

'What do you mean, another story?' asked Shaw, genuinely puzzled. 'Surely the evidence at the inquest was clear.'

'Oh, captain, don't tell me you believed that charade. Everything about that evidence was wrong, and I am quite convinced that the coroner was bribed to render a verdict of misadventure.'

'Bribed!' said Fanscombe. He too was red in the face, and sweating heavily. 'By whom, pray?'

'Goodness, Mr Fanscombe, truthfully I have no idea.'

'But what are you suggesting, Amelia?' exclaimed Mrs Merriwether, and Mrs Fanscombe said levelly, 'Yes. I think you should make it clear what exactly you do mean.'

The rector sat immobile, holding his cup of tea and watching the rest of the room out of the corners of his eyes. No one was looking at him; every eye was fixed on Mrs Chaytor.

'I said I had an eye for detail,' said Amelia. 'I noticed at once an inconsistency in the testimony given. It was said that Mr Miller carried a pistol through his belt, and that the accidental discharge of this pistol caused his wound.' She stood up. 'But I ask you if this is possible. His pistol would have been here,' and she picked up the sugar tongs and held them against her own waist, 'pointing downwards and away from his belly. Had the pistol discharged, the ball would surely have hit him in the leg, not the belly. Am I not right, Dr Morley?'

'You are, ma'am,' said Morley.

'Now, just hold on a moment,' said Fanscombe, leaping to the conclusion which the rest of the room had already arrived at. 'If you are right and the man didn't shoot himself, then someone else must have shot him.'

'What do you say, doctor?' asked the rector.

Morley stirred where he sat on the settee beside Miss Godfrey. 'I think it entirely likely that Mrs Chaytor is right,' he said unexpectedly. 'I too had my doubts about that verdict.'

'Great heavens,' exclaimed Captain Shaw, 'then why did you not say something at the time?'

'Because I was not asked,' said Morley. 'My testimony concerned only the actual cause of death, which was a gunshot wound. It was for others to determine how that wound was inflicted. But, in my opinion, Mrs Chaytor is quite correct. The wound Mr Miller received could only have been caused by a pistol pointed directly at his belly and fired from very close range.'

'Meaning that someone else must have fired the pistol,' said the rector.

Morley shook his head. 'Any view by me as to *how* that pistol came to be fired would be pure speculation on my part.'

'Well, then,' said Turner, 'by all means let us speculate. We have concluded that Miller did not shoot himself. That leaves us with two possibilities. Either he was shot by a smuggler, or he was shot by one of his own men.'

'We went over this at the inquest,' said Shaw, still looking puzzled. 'According to Mr Blunt's testimony, the nearest smugglers were fifty yards away.'

'But,' said Mrs Merriwether, equally puzzled, 'that would mean that someone from his own side – oh, how dreadful!'

'Oh, yes,' said Foucarmont gravely. 'It is possible that this man Miller may have been killed by someone from his own side. Such things happen, sadly. Men lose their heads and fire their weapons at random. I can recall many instances of soldiers being killed by their own side in the heat of battle. And things grow worse, of course, when it is very dark. But such an incident would still count as an accident.'

'Yes,' said Mrs Chaytor. 'You are right. It *could* have been an accident.'

Eliza Fanscombe was sitting on the window seat and the rector could sense she was growing irritable; probably because she was not the centre of attention. 'Why does it matter?' she asked crossly. 'He was only a Customs officer, for heaven's sake.'

'But my dear, he was still a man,' said Miss Godfrey gently.

'He was a rat!' said Miss Fanscombe. 'A creeping, crawling rat, sneaking around in the dark where he had no right to be.'

'Eliza!' said Mrs Fanscombe sharply.

'Oh, fiddlesticks, Eugénie. All the Gentlemen are trying to do is make a living, and those horrid Preventives creep around trying to stop them, shooting at them and even hanging them when they catch them. It isn't right! They should let them alone!'

'*Eliza!*'

Miss Fanscombe kicked her heels petulantly, but fell silent. The rector watched her out of the corner of his eyes, thinking about the midnight rides and her disappearances from the house during the smuggling runs. Heavens, he thought, I have overlooked her entirely. I have concentrated on Fanscombe and Foucarmont; but what if she too is involved?

He needed time to think about this. Turner was frowning. 'What do you make of all this, Reverend?' he asked. 'What do you think?'

The rector frowned also. 'I too was puzzled at the inquest,' he said, affecting not to see the smiles that flitted across the faces of some of the others. 'I was interested in the questions that were asked, but even more by the questions that were *not* asked. For example: Dr Morley, why were you summoned down to New Romney to examine Mr Miller when there is already a physician and coroner's deputy in that town?'

'Search me,' said Morley. 'I assumed at the time that Dr Mackay was out on another call. I was as surprised as anyone to learn later that he was at home all the time. And yes, I would have expected that question at the inquest.' He paused. 'I am also surprised that you remember, Hardcastle. You were a little under the weather at the time.'

This time some of the smiles were open. 'I found later that I could recall a great deal,' said Hardcastle smoothly. 'Do you agree that the coroner might have been bribed, as Mrs Chaytor suggests?'

'Oh, that is certainly possible. But there were others present who also could have asked more searching questions about Miller's death. Lord Clavertye, for example.'

'Great heavens!' said Miss Godfrey. 'Are you suggesting that Lord Clavertye bribed the coroner? Whatever reason could he have?'

'I am suggesting no such thing, ma'am. I agree that His Lordship would appear to have little reason to take such a course of action,' said Morley, and he glanced at the rector. The latter nodded and said, 'Indeed not. I have known His Lordship for many years, and he is a man of the highest probity.'

'But he has been very quick to wash his hands of this affair,' said Mrs Fanscombe, looking hard at her husband and then around the room.

'Has the investigation has been abandoned?' asked Miss Roper. One could see the disappointment in her face; endless opportunities for gossip would be lost.

'No, no,' said Fanscombe hastily, 'not in the least. Only, His Lordship has asked me to, er, well. Take no extraordinary measures. Those were his words. And then there is the dean, of course.'

He shut his mouth suddenly, with the air of a man who realises he has said too much. Morley shot him a look of mild disgust. 'Of course, we must not over-exert ourselves to find the truth,' he said. 'Two unknown men have died of violent causes, a public official may have been bribed, a second may have died accidentally but equally may have been murdered. It is hardly a matter for serious concern.'

'Heavens!' exclaimed Mrs Merriwether. When you put it that way, how dreadful it all sounds.'

'It is dreadful, ma'am, for the families of those involved and for all the people hereabouts,' said Morley quietly. 'I for one am quite moved by Mrs Chaytor's account of the distressing position of the widowed Mrs Miller, and shall dig deep into my pocket to help her. I trust you will do the same, Fanscombe; it is the least you can do.'

Suddenly, shockingly, Fanscombe slammed to his feet and stood glaring down at the doctor. 'What are you insinuating, Morley?'

'I am insinuating nothing. I merely hope that you will see fit to make a suitable contribution to the fund for Mrs Miller.' Fanscombe remained standing, and the doctor added sharply, 'Sit down, man, you are embarrassing our hostess.'

'Oh, I am tired of hearing about Miller!' declared Fanscombe's daughter, her highly visible bosom heaving as she too rose to her feet. 'All we hear is how sad it is that he died, and oh, his poor widow! What of all the free-traders, good and gallant men who have died over the years, hunted down by craven men like Miller?'

Turner was right, thought the rector. The body of a woman, but the mind of a child. Before anyone else could speak, he said, 'My dear Miss Fanscombe, we are not speaking here of ordinary free-traders. The men that Mr Blunt and Mr Miller were hunting on the Marsh that night were a gang known as the Twelve Apostles.'

They all stared at him. 'The Twelve Apostles!' said Turner sharply. 'Lord Clavertye mentioned that name several times, at the inquest.'

'Indeed he did.'

'How do you know about them?' asked Shaw, his face more puzzled than ever.

'Indeed,' said Foucarmont. 'I too should like to know the answer to that question, monsieur.'

'I keep my eyes and ears open,' said the rector simply. 'There is plenty of gossip about these men, if you know where to listen for it.'

They continued to stare at him. Eliza Fanscombe, so furious at being ignored that she quite forgot her manners, stamped her foot. 'This is nonsense! The free-traders are gentlemen, like brave knights of old, or

Robin Hood and his men! If they are outside the law, it is because the law is wrong! And if the Preventives come after them, then they deserve everything they get!'

'Eliza,' said Fanscombe heavily, 'you are making a spectacle of yourself. Sit down.'

'Do as your father says,' commanded his wife. 'Mrs Chaytor, I do apologise.'

'Don't you dare apologise for me, Eugénie! Don't you dare criticise my conduct, not you, not of all people!'

Mrs Fanscombe stood up. 'Eliza, I do not care a fig for your behaviour towards me. But you are embarrassing your father.'

'*I* am embarrassing him? Oh, that is rich. You can say that to me, when you carry on under his very nose with *that* man?' And she flung out one arm, her accusing finger pointing directly at Dr Morley.

The room froze. Everyone sat or stood, staring at the young woman. She looked wildly around, then burst into tears and fled the room; they heard the front door slam a moment later. Within the drawing room, attention now transferred to Mrs Fanscombe. She looked around at the others, calmly meeting their eyes, her little whippet's face sharp and determined.

'Mrs Chaytor,' she said calmly. 'Thank you very much for your hospitality. I hope to see you at New Hall very soon.' She made an elegant little curtsey and departed with a swish of skirts.

'You should go after her,' said the rector to Fanscombe, and the latter, standing like a man in a trance, shook himself, remembered to make a sketchy bow to Mrs Chaytor, gave one glance of agonised fury at Morley, and departed in haste. Dr Morley rose unhurriedly to his feet and bowed too. 'I think the time has come for me to take my leave also,' he said drily. 'Thank you, Mrs Chaytor, for a most fascinating evening. Mrs Merriwether, it was a pleasure to meet you. Ladies.' He walked to the door, turning once to glance keenly at the rector, and then he too was gone.

Slowly, the atmosphere in the drawing room relaxed. 'Goodness,' said Mrs Merriwether, 'what exciting lives you lead in St Mary. Did no one know they were having an affair?'

'Oh, everyone knew,' said Miss Roper, 'except poor Mr Fanscombe, of course. Now that he knows, the affair will probably end. What a pity.'

'Yes,' said Turner sourly. 'Now you will have to find someone else to gossip about.'

When all the others had gone, all save Mrs Merriwether who was staying the night, the rector faced Amelia Chaytor in the empty drawing room. 'Well?' he prompted gently.

'Well, we have certainly set the Fanscombe family at each others' throats. I advised M. de Foucarmont, as I showed him out, that if life becomes too difficult at New Hall there are excellent rooms at the Star. What did *you* think?'

'Fanscombe looked bluff and bewildered, but he began to perspire heavily when you raised the notion that there might have been corruption at the inquest. He was generally unconvincing, but gave up no secrets.'

'Certainly not enough to put a noose around his neck,' she said, 'or Blunt's. What did you make of the mysterious M. de Foucarmont?'

'He behaved impeccably. He listened very intently but did not make a judgement, and only volunteered an opinion when he thought it might be helpful. Although he was keen to know how I knew about the Twelve Apostles.'

'Yes, his manners are quite beautiful. He apologised profusely for the behaviour of the Fanscombes, even though he had no reason to do so. That in itself is interesting.'

'The main thing that puzzles me is the behaviour of Eliza.'

'Does it? I am not puzzled at all. She is young, not overly intelligent, thoroughly spoiled, and bored. She has never forgiven her father for re-marrying. She is in the mood for rebellion. She envies the smugglers, for they are rebels too in their own fashion. What do you think?' she asked. 'Did we do well?'

'We did well. I thought perhaps I had overplayed my hand when I mentioned the Apostles.'

'Not at all. I thought that was a master-stroke. Now they know that we know about the deeper plot.' She smiled, a little wearily. 'Whoever *they* are, and whatever the deeper plot is.'

He was sure of her now, and he was relieved; the thought of not being able to trust her had caused him an almost physical pain.

'We must watch the Fanscombes,' he said. 'When people fly into a fit of passion they are likely to make mistakes, as I know only too well . . . As for the rest, I think we made our position clear without giving away too much of what we really know. We told them our suspicions about Miller's death and hinted at murder, and we let them know that we know about the Twelve Apostles. They know too that we are still investigating, and do not intend to stop. Now, we must wait and see how they react.' He smiled a little. 'We have shaken the tree, my dear. Now we must see what falls from it.'

15

The Fire is Kindled

The rector walked home quietly in the evening light. Behind him, he knew, Mrs Chaytor was locking her doors and windows and shutters. She had told him, when he asked, that she had a pistol and knew how to use it. He was not surprised. He had long since given up being surprised by Amelia Chaytor.

He let himself in through the rectory gate and looked around. He saw no shadows; when he walked around the house there were no more boot-prints in the grass. But he knew, beyond any doubt, that the house was still under watch. That night he too shut the doors and windows securely, drank a single glass of brandy in thoughtful silence by the fire, and went to bed nearly sober.

The following day was Sunday 29th May, just over a week before the next run was due to take place. He conducted matins to a nearly empty church, and afterwards in the church porch shook the grimy hand of the old man from Brenzett and greeted Miss Godfrey and Miss Roper. 'Is there any news from the Hall?' he asked.

'Oh, *my*,' said Miss Godfrey, lowering her voice dramatically. 'The word is that Mr Fanscombe became raving drunk, produced a pistol and threatened to blow out his brains in the drawing room unless Mrs Fanscombe ended her affair with the doctor. And she said, as calm as anything, that he could do whatever he liked. And then M. de F-f-f . . . the French gentleman took the pistol away from Mr Fanscombe and made him go to bed. And then young Miss Fanscombe became hysterical and accused her stepmother of being, well . . . you know. No better than she ought to be.'

Thoughtfully, Hardcastle walked back to the rectory. He ate his cold luncheon as usual in solitary silence, thinking about unseen watchers outside, the rumours among the fishermen, the malevolence of Blunt in the street after the second inquest, the Twelve Apostles in the shadows preparing for their run. He thought of the Fanscombe household and, with no particular remorse, the implosion of the family. He spent some time considering Foucarmont, urbane, precise, careful; the French emigré who was fond of shooting and wildfowling.

If you think of the devil, you will presently find him at your elbow. He had just risen from the table when there came a knock at the front door, and Mrs Kemp appeared in the study doorway with a card. 'A French gentleman to see you, Reverend,' she said, her lip curling with distaste. Mrs Kemp disliked all French people on general principle.

A moment later Foucarmont walked into the study, smiling and bowing. 'What a splendid collection of books,' he said, looking around. 'I perceive that you are more than just an ordinary clergyman, monsieur. You are a man of letters.'

'I had pretensions in that area, once upon a time,' said the rector, unlocking the cabinet and pouring two glasses of brandy. He passed one to Foucarmont, who raised it in toast. 'Your very good health, monsieur.'

'And yours also, sir. Is this a social call?'

'Of course, you know already that it is not. I came in part to apologise for the Fanscombes. Their behaviour was quite unacceptable. I am sure Mrs Chaytor is much distressed.'

'It takes rather more than a spoiled young woman's temper tantrum to distress Mrs Chaytor, sir. But I do not understand. Why should you wish to make their apologies? It is not, after all, as if you are kin to any of them.'

A slow smile spread over Foucarmont's face. 'You are perceptive, sir. No, I am not Madame Fanscombe's brother; thank God,' he added thoughtfully.

'Forgive me for being inquisitive, sir, but what then brings you to the Marsh?'

'A love of sea air? A chance to gaze out over the water at my homeland, which I miss so terribly? No, it is none of those things.' Foucarmont shook his head. 'I think you have guessed a great deal about me. Allow me to fill in the blank spaces for you.'

The rector waited while Foucarmont sipped his brandy. The Frenchman then set down his glass and leaned forward a little. 'What I am about to tell you must not leave this room,' he said. 'Even the ever-watchful Mrs Chaytor, who I see is your friend, must not be told. You are in enough danger already, and she too.'

'I am honoured that you should choose to confide in me. May I ask why?'

'Because I hope to persuade you to step back from this affair and take no further risks. Monsieur Hardcastle, I must reveal myself. I am an agent in the service of the British government. My visits to Romney Marsh are part of an investigation into a very serious and very dangerous affair. You are now caught up in that affair. I hope to detach you from it. I do so with the aim of ensuring that both you and Mrs Chaytor remain safe.'

'That is very good of you,' said Hardcastle.

Foucarmont bowed. 'My mission,' he said, 'is to seek out the gang of men you know as the Twelve Apostles. I intend to capture them if possible, to kill them if not.'

'I see,' said Hardcastle slowly. 'And who are these men, sir?'

'They are traitors to their king and country,' said Foucarmont quietly. 'They are employed by the Directory in Paris. Their smuggling operation is a masquerade, which covers their real activities and real purpose. The cargoes they run into England from France are small and of little value. What is important is what they carry *out* of England. They have sources of information in very high places. Will you believe me, monsieur, if I tell you that even the most secret decisions made in Mr Pitt's Cabinet are known to Monsieur Barras and his minions in Paris within a week? And the Twelve Apostles are the men who carry those secrets.'

He paused, watching the rector for reaction. 'Go on,' the latter said.

'I first became aware of these men and their activities last year. I set several traps for them, which they eluded; they are very skilful. I then changed my own tactics, and with some difficulty I inserted an agent of my own into this group. This man reported every move the gang made to me. Last October, we set another trap for them and this time we very nearly caught them. They escaped by chance, but now they were aware that they had been exposed. They disappeared from sight, and I thought for a time I had succeeded in, as the English would say, putting them out of business.'

The rector opened his mouth, then closed it again. 'Yes?' said Foucarmont inquiringly.

He had been about to ask if the agent's name was Mark, but in the nick of time thought better of it. 'Nothing,' he said. 'Do go on, sir.'

'In April, my agent informed me that the gang had reassembled and was preparing another operation. He gave me details of the time and place. I used my authority to bring in the Customs service and also reinforcements from the militia. Unfortunately, once again things went wrong. The trap was sprung too early and the Apostles escaped. Sadly, very shortly thereafter, my agent's true identity became known.' Foucarmont leaned forward a little further. 'I can tell you in confidence, monsieur, that it was his body that was found in your churchyard. Now, do you need any further evidence of the ruthlessness of these men?'

Hardcastle shook his head. 'What happens next?'

Foucarmont nodded. 'The loss of my agent is a blow, but not an irreparable one. I have made new plans, and gathered my forces. This time, I am certain that there will be no mistake.'

The rector thought of 6th June. 'Are Mr Blunt and Captain Shaw in your confidence? And Mr Fanscombe?'

'Fanscombe to a very limited degree. He transmits my orders to Mr Blunt and Captain Shaw as if they were his own. As far as they know, they are working for the justice of the peace and, through him, the lord-lieutenant.'

'And the lord-lieutenant? What does he know?'

'He has been kept in the dark. This affair is entirely secret, and the fewer people who know of my real role, the better. Believe me, sir, only the urgency of the situation compels me to reveal my identity to you now. I hope that, as you are a clergyman, I can trust in your entire discretion.'

Hardcastle inclined his head. 'And you sit behind the scenes,' he asked, 'pulling the strings?'

Foucarmont spread his hands. 'That is how we work in my world, I fear.'

'And the other man? The young man who was staying at New Hall the week before the two deaths? Was he also working for you?'

'He was, and I hear that you believe him to be the same man as was killed here at the rectory. I fear you are labouring under a misapprehension. The man staying at the Hall did work for me, and still does. He is a courier and watcher. On the Wednesday evening before the events you have been investigating, he took a message to Appledore. On my orders, he then proceeded to London to wait for me there. He is still very much alive and well. About the man whose body you found, I fear have no idea.'

'And the name of your courier?'

'His name is Jacques Morel. He is, like myself, a French emigré. I have known his family for many years. Of course, in my service he goes by an alias; indeed, several of them. And now, I think that I have told you all that it safe for you to know. Please understand, monsieur, that I am thinking primarily of your own safety.'

'Your concern for my well-being does you great credit, sir. And in gratitude, I wish to tell you something in return.'

'Go on.'

'Curtius Miller was murdered on the Marsh on the night of Friday 6th May. His own superior officer, Henry Blunt, is responsible for his death. I intend to find the evidence which will convict Blunt of this murder, and I will not stop until I have done so. I shall leave the Twelve Apostles to you. But Blunt is mine. Do I make myself clear, sir?'

After a long moment, Foucarmont nodded slowly. 'You want to see justice done. I understand. For the moment, I need Blunt. I need his men to help me stop the Twelve Apostles. But when task has been accomplished . . .'

'I may proceed with my investigation of Mr Blunt?'

'My friend, if what you say is true, I myself will help you gather the evidence.'

Old Mr Cadman died that night. Word reached the rectory on the morning of Monday 30th. The rector looked at the weather; it was pouring with rain, and the track to the Cadman farm would by now be just a muddy ooze across the Marsh, impassible for the dog cart. Putting on a waterproof cape and hat, he walked the mile and a half from the village to Cadman's farm.

Dr Morley was there, just packing his bag; they exchanged a few remarks about the disposal of the body and then the doctor departed. The rector remained for another two hours, helping the family to make arrangements for the funeral next day and offering comfort, which was gratefully received. Curious, the rector thought, how quickly people return to their forgotten faith in times of sorrow. He had never seen the old man in church, yet the family accepted the rector's assurance that their father and grandfather had gone to a better place, and seemed comforted by it.

By the time he took his leave the rain had eased off a little, but a steady drizzle was still falling. He walked through the rain towards the village misty in the distance, keeping up a steady pace. The flat wet fields of the Marsh were empty; wind rustled in the grass and hissed in the hedgerows; yet, as he walked, he felt that eyes were boring into his back. So strong was the feeling that twice he turned sharply and looked behind him, only to see nothing there. But the sense of threat remained, and grew.

He crossed a plank bridge over a sewer, one of the many drainage ditches that ran across the Marsh, next to a ford where cattle and wagons crossed. A low bank of earth ran along the far side of the sewer. As he reached the near end of the bridge he heard a sharp noise behind him, and whirled around. Once again there was nothing there.

He drew a sharp breath, steadied himself and turned around again, facing the village – and froze. A moment ago the bridge had been empty; now a man stood at its opposite end ten feet away, cloaked and masked with rain dripping from the brim of his hat. He held a pistol aimed steadily at the rector's heart.

Hardcastle looked around for aid, but he looked in vain. The bleak fields were empty and there was not another soul in sight; the nearest house was half a mile away. Accepting the inevitable, he gazed calmly at the other man's masked face.

'I am a clergyman,' he said. 'There is very little money in my purse, but you are welcome to what is there. My watch is of some value. You may take them freely; I ask only that you offer me no violence.'

'Oh, for God's sake,' the other man said irritably. 'I'm not a bloody footpad. If I were, I would ply my trade somewhere more profitable. I only want a word with you, somewhere out of sight of witnesses. I pulled the pistol in case you did anything stupid, like shouting for help.'

Then Hardcastle recognised the voice, and saw the jut of the chin below the mask. He allowed himself to relax, just a little. 'Peter,' he said quietly. 'How very good it is to see you again.'

'How do you know that name?' demanded the other, staring through the eyeholes of his mask.

'I heard one of your associates mention it,' the rector said, staring back. 'You said you wanted a word with me. What is it?'

'Foucarmont came to see you yesterday. What did he want?'

'Are yours the people watching my house?'

'Some of them. What did Foucarmont want?'

'He wanted to tell me the truth about himself, and you.' The rector summarised in a few sentences what Foucarmont had said. The other man nodded slowly. 'So. We are a gang of traitors smuggling secrets from England to France, and he is a government agent out to stop us. When he mentioned Mark's death, did you tell him that we had also invaded your house and threatened to harm you?'

'No.'

'How curious. Why not?'

The rector drew breath. 'Because,' he said, 'I do not believe a single word of Monsieur de Foucarmont's story.'

Silence fell. In it the wind hissed, spitting a fresh gust of rain at them. Hardcastle mopped his face.

'Why not? The story seems sound enough.'

'Indeed. And I might have believed him,' said the rector, 'had I not been at Ebony the day you met Matthew, and overheard your entire conversation. I think you might lower that pistol now.'

After a moment the other man gave a brief laugh. He did lower the pistol, though he still held it firm in his hand. 'What in hell's name were you doing at Ebony?'

The rector told him. When he described his hiding place, Peter snorted and cursed himself for an incompetent fool. 'That will teach me to make a *complete* search next time. All right. You think we are on the side of the angels. In fact we are working for His Majesty's government, which is not quite the same thing, but close enough given the circumstances.'

'And Foucarmont?'

'From what you say, it seems fairly clear that he is working for the French. He is a clever bastard, I'll give him that. We knew someone was running an operation against us, but we thought Blunt was the ringleader.

We only started having our suspicions of Foucarmont last month. Well, Reverend. It looks like I owe you one.'

'What will you do now?'

'Carry on. Foucarmont is right about one thing. You need to stay out of this business. If you do not, you might get hurt.'

'And what about Blunt?'

'Never mind Blunt. We will deal with him in our own way. Foucarmont too, if need be.'

'No,' said the rector strongly. 'There will be no more murders. If these men have committed crimes, let them be brought to justice.'

The masked man laughed. 'Justice? How the hell would you get them before a court? There is no evidence against either of them.'

'Not yet. I intend to find it.'

'Then you're a damned fool. This affair is bigger than you can imagine.' The big man touched the brim of his dripping hat. 'Keep your head down, Reverend. Stay out of trouble.' And with that he turned and climbed up over the bank and down into the field beyond, and walked away through the gathering mist.

Tuesday, the last day of May, dawned grey and cloudy once more, the air full of mist. The rector ate his usual hearty breakfast and then crossed the road to the church as the bells begin to toll for the funeral. In the church he nodded to the bell-ringers as usual and then went into the vestry to robe. By the time he walked back out to the churchyard a crowd had gathered, all sombrely dressed and talking in quiet tones, occasionally looking skyward and hoping it would not rain. The rector smiled softly. Old Cadman had been popular; it was good to see his neighbours turning out to send him on his way. He realised that Amelia Chaytor was among them, a black bonnet half hiding her face.

A cart drew up slowly behind the lychgate, followed by a little knot of mourners. The coffin was unloaded and carried solemnly to the gate. The rector raised his hand.

'I am the resurrection and the life, saith the Lord,' he intoned slowly in his deep voice as he entered the church, the coffin and its bearers following. 'He that believeth in me, though he were dead, yet shall he live; and whosoever liveth and believeth in me, shall never die.'

The casket was laid before the altar, and he stepped up to the pulpit. Looking out over the congregation, who sat and watched him with pale earnest faces, he read the service; and when he came to the magnificent end of St Paul's epistle, his voice rang in the rafters.

'Oh death, where is thy sting? Oh grave, where is thy victory? The sting of death is sin, and the strength of sin is the law. But thanks be to God, which gives us the victory through Our Lord Jesus Christ. Therefore, my beloved brethren, be ye steadfast, unmoveable, always abounding in the work of the Lord, forasmuch as ye know that your labour is not in vain in the Lord.'

Midway through the service Mrs Cadman, who had been weeping copiously when she arrived at the church, dried her eyes and sat up straight. The coffin was borne out again to the grave in the churchyard, where the sexton waited, leaning on his shovel, and the body was committed. The mourners departed, talking in low voices, most of them on their way to the public house to drink to their neighbour's passing. Some stopped to thank the rector and shake his hand. Amelia Chaytor stood silently and watched them.

'Very impressive,' she said in her light voice, once they were alone. 'This is the first time I have seen you perform your duties.'

'Thank you.' Standing before her in his robes, he felt strangely self-conscious. 'This is of course only a small part of what I do.'

'Yes, I am sure. It is odd. I watched them, rather than you, when you spoke. "The sting of death is sin." It is nonsense, of course, the sting of death is *death*, itself. Yet, they were comforted. I wonder why.'

'My dear self-doubting agnostic, you must not take every word in the Bible literally, or the Book of Common Prayer either. Think what is meant by that passage, not the few words you quoted, but the whole of it.'

She thought. 'That if we do things that are right and good, we will not have lived our lives in vain.'

'That is good enough for me,' he said smiling.

'Yes,' she said, reluctance in her voice. 'Actually, it was another passage that keeps running in my mind.

"*I held my tongue and spake nothing; I kept silence, yea, even from good words, but it was pain and grief to me.*

My heart was hot within me, and while I was thus musing the fire kindled; and at the last I spake with my tongue." '

The words were from Psalm 39. He waited and she said, 'I felt as if someone else had put into words what I feel about this case. I could have held my tongue and said nothing. But something kindled a fire in me, a fire in ashes that I thought had gone cold. I had to do something. So maybe that is what it comes down to. Doing good things gives our life purpose; or restores purpose, when it has been lost.'

'He was quite a good student of character, old St Paul,' he said. He offered his arm and they turned away from the grave, where the sexton continued to shovel stolidly, and walked back to the church. 'Why did you come?' he asked.

'In hopes of having a quiet word with you. I fear our shaking of the tree has not produced much fruit.'

They were out of earshot of the sexton. 'That is not entirely true,' he said gently, and he told her in quick succession of his meeting with Foucarmont and his encounter with Peter. 'We have smoked Foucarmont out into the open. He made a mistake there, for I was in two minds as to whether to suspect his involvement in this plot. Now I know for certain.'

'That is curious. For my part, I thought he was a wrong 'un from the start.'

'Women's intitution?' he asked, tongue in cheek, and she looked up and smiled for a moment, then grew serious again. 'There is someone else whom we have overlooked,' she said. 'Someone who certainly knows the truth about Fanscombe and Foucarmont, but is concealing it. I mean, of course, Eugénie Fanscombe.'

'I know.'

'Do you wish to approach her?'

'She is already suffering, I think. I do not wish to add to her pain. If possible, we should find another way to do this.'

'But time is running out,' she said quietly, and she looked around to see that there was no one else within earshot. 'Today is Wednesday. The next run is on Monday night. We must do something.'

'We could pursue our case against Blunt. This man Five-Guineas may know something.'

'I know, and I have always said that my main ambition is to see Blunt hang. But things have changed. This has gone beyond simple murder now. And if we don't stop these people, who will?'

He was silent at this. 'Leave Eugénie Fanscombe to me,' she said, and smiled quickly and turned and walked away through the mist.

Later he went to the Star to drink a few mugs of beer with the mourners, and Cadman came and thanked him again for the service. Bessie Luckhurst, who had been there too, smiled at him as she poured his beer. 'Funny old life for you, Reverend. You only get busy when there is a funeral.'

He waved around the crowded common room, where her father was serving out jugs of ale. 'Much the same for you, my dear.'

Back at home he ate some bread and cold chicken to soak up the beer, and then drank a bottle of port and fell asleep in his study. He woke hazy-headed to find the evening grey and damp. He wondered how many peo-ple were outside watching the rectory. He was getting used to the feeling of being watched, now, and no longer felt so menaced. Mrs Kemp, so far as he could tell, had not noticed the watchers at all, and would probably not care so long as they did not enter the house again.

As the light began to fail, Turner called. The housekeeper, her face more sour than ever, showed him into the study. 'I will not stay long,' said the painter. 'But I said I would tell you if I had news. An hour ago a horseman arrived, coming up the New Romney road and galloping like the devil himself was after him. Judging by his stiffness, and the amount of mud on his cloak and boots, I would say he had ridden post for a long way. Perhaps even from London.'

The rector pressed his hand to his forehead. 'Where did this horse-man go?'

'New Hall, of course,' said Turner impatiently. 'He is a courier on urgent business, or I have never seen one. You promised me an explanation.'

Hardcastle nodded and pointed Turner to a seat, and rose and unlocked the cabinet and poured two glasses of brandy. He drank one down, feeling his head spin and then clear, filled it again and passed the second glass to the painter.

'You will have gathered,' he said, resuming his seat carefully, 'that we believe Curtius Miller was murdered. It seems entirely likely that he was killed by Blunt, or by someone acting for Blunt, but we cannot prove this. If we could . . .'

'But why, in God's name?'

The rector paused, thinking carefully about how much to say. 'There is a conspiracy,' he said, 'in which at least one member of the Fanscombe household is involved. At the moment, I do not know which one. This conspiracy goes beyond mere murder. The safety of the realm is involved.' He looked up at the painter and said, 'Once again, I can prove none of this.'

'What about Lord Clavertye?'

'His hands are tied. Without proof, he can do nothing.'

'Then tell me how I can help,' said Turner simply.

'Do what you are doing. Continue to watch, but do it carefully. Do nothing to alert them or make them suspicious.'

'You can count on me,' said Turner. He drained his glass and took his leave, and the rector sat staring out into the dark evening until Mrs Kemp came in and drew the drapes. Well, they had an ally after all; though how much real good the young painter could do remained to be seen.

Another knock at the door; but it was only the evening post from New Romney. There were two letters.

OFFICE OF THE DEAN, CHRIST CHURCH CATHEDRAL, CANTERBURY.
30th May, 1796.

Reverend Hardcastle

This is to inform you that I shall arrive in St Mary in the Marsh on Thursday 2nd June. I shall stay as usual at the Star, but I expect to call on you upon my arrival, about midday. There is an urgent matter that I wish to discuss with you. I will say no more at this point, but will explain more fully when I arrive.

Yours in Christ

CORNEWALL

Ah, thought the rector, his lips curling in a sneer. Another run is planned, and the dean is coming down to protect his investment. This reminded him that the run was due to take place in just six days. And still there was nothing he could do to stop Blunt and his men from ambushing the Twelve Apostles. He opened the second letter.

Meet F-G at the bay, tomorrow early. Bring money.

The latter was undated and unsigned. But he guessed that the spidery, laboured handwriting was that of Joshua Stemp.

In the morning the rain had cleared, and a fresh west wind was slowly blowing the clouds away. Booted and cloaked, the rector walked to St Mary's Bay. He was not followed; in fact it would have been difficult on a clear day to follow a man unnoticed over those flat treeless fields and marshes. Never mind; the watchers would be waiting when he returned.

On the beach he found an upturned boat, fishing nets strewn on the sand beside it. A man in smock and rough breeches and hose with a battered hat sat on the boat, smoking a pipe. He watched the rector approach without moving. The coast of France lay low in the distance, dark with menace.

'John Snathurst?' said the rector, halting a few feet away.

'That's right.'

'You're with the Dymchurch Customs. One of Blunt's men.'

'That's right.'

'And you have something to tell me.'

'That's right,' the man said again. 'If you've the money.'

'I was told five guineas was the going rate.'

'Let's see it first.'

The rector drew a small weighted bag from the pocket of his cloak and tossed it across. He waited while the man opened the bag and counted out the five guineas, testing one on his teeth. The man nodded, put the purse away, then finished his pipe and tapped it on the side of his boot to empty it.

'Let's get one thing squared away from the start,' he said. 'I'm talking to you here privately. I'll not repeat this in public. If you try to put me on a witness stand, I'll deny everything.'

'You and all the Dymchurch Customs men are being paid by the smugglers to look the other way,' said the rector. 'Blunt organises it, and you all get a percentage. And you would rather the world did not know about this.'

'That's right.'

'Mr Snathurst, I have no interest whatever in your financial arrangements with the free-traders. I am interested only in the murder of Curtius Miller. What can you tell me about that?'

'Murder's a strong word.' The other man stood up abruptly. The rector tensed, half expecting an assault, but the other man stood still, hands hanging down at his sides. Slowly the rector relaxed again.

'I'll tell you what I saw,' said Snathurst, 'and that's all. On the evening of the sixth of May, the fellows from Deal came down and joined us. Almost at once, Mr Blunt was there ordering us to arm and get ready to march.'

'Just a moment. Was there any friction between Miller and Blunt? Did they quarrel?'

'Not that I know of. I never heard of nothing between them. In any case, there was no time for a quarrel, for we were on the move almost at once. We came down the beach as far as St Mary's Bay and saw all was clear there. Mr Blunt ordered us to fall back from the beach, about half a mile or so. Then he halted us and said we was to wait, watch for any sign of movement, but if we saw anyone we was to keep quiet, let them go past and then follow them.'

'Did you know this gang you were facing was the Twelve Apostles?'

'We knew. We weren't much happy about it. Last autumn, Mr Blunt told them he wasn't taking money from them any more. They got mad as hell, and threatened all of us. They're a hard crew, much harder than the ordinary free-trader.'

The rector nodded. 'Go on.'

'Just about midnight, near enough, we heard a few gunshots from up north. I thought, hell, that's the ones we're looking for. But Mr Blunt told us to hold our ground and wait. Then a few minutes later we saw the shadows moving. There were men coming towards our position, through the dark. Mr Blunt whispered and we fell back a little to the south, keeping low and moving quiet. I was on the left of the line, last man to the west. Then Miller came up past me, almost on my shoulder, and then bore away beyond me, further away to the west; I could see him about twenty yards away, just at the edge of the sewer. I'd lost sight of Mr Blunt and most of the others.'

'What happened next?'

'Well, next thing is, Miller shouts at the top of his lungs, "Turn back! Turn back!" Then he turns and runs away from us. But he only gets a few steps when there is someone in front of him. "Damn you!" cries Miller, and then the other man shoots him, full in the guts. Miller goes down kicking and thrashing like a wounded horse, and the other man makes off, splashing in the sewer.

'Next thing, shit is falling on us from a great height. The other lot were shooting at us from every direction, musket balls going every which way. We got the hell out as fast as we could, not stopping 'til we was halfway to New Romney. Then Mr Blunt came up, swearing like anything and demanding to know what had happened to Miller. And that's it.'

'Did you see the man who shot Miller?'

'It was pretty dark.'

'But you could see clearly enough to know that it was Blunt.'

The man nodded. 'That's right,' he said. 'I don't know why he done it, and I don't much care. But I know he done it.'

16

Eugénie

The Rectory, St Mary in the Marsh, Kent.
1st June, 1796.

My lord,

In your last letter, you instructed me to stop pursuing our investigation into the deaths of Curtius Miller and the unknown Frenchman. However, an important item of information has come to light, and it would be remiss of me not to inform you.

In brief, my lord, a witness has been found, a member of the Customs service who saw Blunt shoot Miller in very much the manner we have hypothesised. I spoke to the witness myself and heard his story, and am convinced he is telling the truth. The witness insisted that he was speaking to me in confidence, and would not testify in court. However, I believe this witness to be involved in a great many corrupt practices. If he were promised immunity from prosecution, or at least a lenient sentence, I feel certain he could be prevailed upon to change his mind.

My lord, I believe this is sufficient cause to re-open the investigation, into both the death of Miller and the behaviour of the coroner during the original inquest. I leave this matter in your hands, and hope to receive further instructions from you soon.

Yr very obedient servant

HARDCASTLE

That same afternoon, Wednesday 1st June, Eugénie Fanscombe knocked at the door of Sandy House and was quickly received and drawn inside.

Lucy the maid brought tea and was dismissed. 'Thank you for coming,' said Mrs Chaytor.

'I nearly did not come. I am surprised that you should want to see me again.'

Amelia smiled. 'I thought you might be in need of a friendly face,' she said, 'and a consoling cup of tea. I confess I was concerned about you.'

The sharp face stared at her. 'Why should you concern yourself with me?'

'Because I sense that you are alone,' said Amelia quietly. 'And I know a great deal about loneliness.'

Silence fell. They sipped their tea. She saw how Eugénie's eyes were rimmed with red, her cheeks a little hollow. Her heart sank. This was going to be difficult, even cruel, but it had to be done.

'Are you safe?' she asked directly.

'What?' The other woman stared at her. 'Oh, yes, I suppose so. Charles would never dare . . .' She fell silent again.

'Is there somewhere that you can go?' Amelia asked. 'Have you money?'

'Everything is in my husband's name.'

'Oh . . . Would Dr Morley help you? Lend you some money, on the quiet, of course?

'Morley?' Eugénie made a small choking sound and set down her cup of tea. 'He has made it clear that he no longer wishes to have anything to do with me. He said, and these are his exact words, that he no longer found me amusing.'

'*Amusing?*' Amelia set down her own cup, so hard that it rattled the saucer. 'Is that all we women are? Toys, to amuse the men?'

'So it would seem,' said the Frenchwoman bitterly. 'He seduced me because deceiving my husband gave him pleasure. Once Charles knew the truth, the fun went out of the game. I was nothing. Just as you say, a toy.'

Morley, thought Amelia Chaytor, I was right to scorn you. You are even more of a snake in the grass than I suspected. 'I am so sorry,' she said. 'But I think you must leave the house. I think you may be in danger. I will lend you money, and you can repay me whenever you are able.'

Eugénie Fanscombe's lip trembled. 'I cannot leave Eliza.'

'From where I sit, my dear, you owe your stepdaughter very little.'

'Oh, but it has not always been like this!' said Mrs Fanscombe with a sudden wail. 'We were so close, once! Eliza was a child still when I married Charles, but she was so good to me! There is only ten years between us, we have been more like sisters than mother and daughter. Then about a year ago, she changed. She became what you see now, spoiled, wilful, full of rebellion and spite. I cannot bear it. I am losing her, and it breaks my heart.'

'What changed her, my dear?'

'*He* came.' She spat the words out in sudden anger, and Amelia felt her sorrow for this small, unhappy woman increase. 'Foucarmont. He corrupted Eliza. Curse him, damn him, he has corrupted us all. *Il est un démon, un diable.*'

Her lapse into French was a sign of her distress. 'He is not your brother,' Amelia said quietly.

'No. That is the story that I was forced to tell.'

'And you know what he truly is?'

'He is an agent of the French government. He has been sent here to work with a network of spies already operating in England. I do not know who any of the others are.'

'None of them? What about Henry Blunt?'

'Blunt is a tool; that is how Foucarmont describes him. He is a mercenary, I think, who serves for money.'

'And your husband?'

'He too is a tool. No; believe me. He hates the French; more than ever, now. He is not a willing member of this conspiracy.'

'Then why does he take part?'

'Foucarmont knows too much about him. If he were to talk, my husband would go to prison. I would be ruined, and so would Eliza.' She swallowed suddenly, painfully. 'I think he seduced Eliza ... in part, because that is what men do, and in part to gain a greater hold over us, to ensure our loyalty; mine in particular. He knows I would never leave Eliza in danger.'

'And your husband connives at the smuggling?'

'He has for years, both he and Blunt. Foucarmont found out about this, and is using this knowledge to manipulate them both. They must do as he says, or he will expose them.'

'Did your husband bribe the coroner at the inquest?'

'I don't know.'

'How often does Blunt come to New Hall?'

'Usually about once a month, but recently more often. The three of them, my husband, Blunt and Foucarmont, meet in secrecy in the study; no one is allowed near. Eliza tried once to listen at the door, and they caught her. Foucarmont did not lay a hand on her, but he reduced her to wreckage with a few words. He can be so cruel,' she added, her eyes dark as she remembered.

'And the young Frenchman who came to stay here, the man they call Jacques Morel. Did you know him?'

'I met him once only before. He called two months ago, asking for a contribution to a fund that supports destitute emigrés, those of my own people who left all their money when they fled France and have nothing to live on. He asked if I knew many of the emigrés. He mentioned Foucarmont's name then.'

'And later?'

'He appeared early one morning, very wet and dishevelled. He said he had gone out sailing from Rye, but his boat had overturned. He was full of apology, but asked if he might stay a day or two in order to salvage his boat. Foucarmont was here as well. He took a great interest in the young man.'

'Eugénie . . . I am so sorry to tell you this. M. Morel is the man who was found dead outside the rectory.'

The woman nodded, her face a picture of misery. 'I knew it,' she whispered. 'I knew it from the moment I heard about the rifle bullet.'

'Oh?'

'Foucarmont has a rifle. It is one of his prized possessions. He sometimes goes out shooting when he comes to stay. Or at least, he says he does.'

My God, thought Amelia, *we have hit the gold*. She kept her face still and said, her voice gentle, 'Eugénie, thank you. It was very brave of you to come here. But I hope that, very soon now, you will be relieved of M. de Foucarmont for ever.'

Hope softened the sharp face. 'I would give anything for that to be so. Now, I have answered your questions. Will you please answer some of mine? Who are you, Mrs Chaytor, and why are you asking these questions?'

*

Evening was drawing on when the knocker at the front door of the rectory sounded loud, and a few moments later Mrs Chaytor was shown into the study. She looked tense; she too was well aware of the watchers outside his house, and hers.

'I hope I have done the right thing,' she said, after recounting the conversation with Mrs Fanscombe. 'I had to tell her some of what we are doing. She has been lied to so often by so many people; she deserved a little of the truth, at least.'

'I understand. But now that she knows, she is not safe in that house.'

'She will not leave without Eliza. But also, once she learned of our intentions, she begged to be allowed to help us. She wants revenge . . . She intends to spy out whatever she can about Foucarmont's plot, and pass it on to us.'

'Heavens! Then she really will be in danger.'

'She will have it no other way, and I could not persuade her.' She looked at him. 'I am sorry. If anything happens to her, I will never forgive myself.'

'I shall write again to Lord Clavertye,' said the rector, coming to a decision. 'He must involve himself in this business once more. We have strong circumstantial evidence against this crew now, strong enough to warrant an investigation at least.'

'Eugénie cannot give evidence against her husband.'

'Indeed. But she *can* give evidence against Foucarmont.'

'And the run? The Twelve Apostles?'

'Whatever Foucarmont is planning must be stopped. We need Clavertye. He *must* involve himself.'

Dawn on Thursday morning found Romney Marsh covered by a thick, heavy sea fog. The rector came back from his morning walk with his coat and hat damp with clinging moisture. His mood was as damp as the weather, for he was bitterly worried about Eugénie Fanscombe; and also, the dean was due to arrive today. He ate his breakfast and then did some necessary correspondence in his study, writing absently with only half his mind engaged.

The Rectory, St Mary in the Marsh, Kent.
2nd June, 1796.

My lord,

I apologise for troubling you again, so soon after my last letter. However, information of a very serious and sensitive nature has reached my ears. There is reason to believe that the French officer M. de Foucarmont, who we believe to be a royalist emigré, is in fact a secret agent of the Directory, acting on orders from Paris. He is hatching a plot to capture or kill the Twelve Apostles and prevent their bringing information out of France. Blunt and Fanscombe are both implicated.

Your Lordship will know better than I the extreme seriousness of this situation. So far the evidence is only circumstantial, but I believe that a full investigation will expose the entire plot and forestall the attack on the Twelve Apostles. However, the authorities must move quickly. The next smuggling run is on Monday, in four days' time. There is, literally, not a moment to lose.

I hope to receive further instructions from you very soon.

Yr very obedient servant

HARDCASTLE

It was just on midday, fog still hanging heavy in the branches of the elms, when the dean's carriage rolled up the drive, and Mrs Kemp with a face bleak as a winter night showed Cornewall into the rector's study. They made no attempt to shake hands. 'I shall stay only for a few minutes,' said the dean, his face longer and more horse-like than ever. 'I wish to discuss with you, briefly and in a civilised fashion, I hope, this unfortunate business and its consequences.'

'By unfortunate business, do you mean the murders of three men in this parish?'

'Murders—' Cornewall checked. 'Mr Miller's death was determined to be an accident. You were present at the inquest; though of course,' added the dean with a sneer, 'your faculties were somewhat impaired that day.'

'Blithering nonsense,' the rector snapped. 'Miller was murdered, and the coroner was bribed to cover it up.'

'Hardcastle,' said the dean raising his hands helplessly and letting them fall again. 'I am running out of patience, and so is His Grace. You were given a direct order not to involve yourself in this business, but what have you done? You have defied us, and carried on.' He raised a hand to forestall any possible interruption. 'We know very well what you have been doing these past few weeks, Hardcastle. You have been gallivanting around the Marsh, you and that *woman*, both of you meddling in matters that are quite beyond you.'

The rector stood up behind his desk. 'Gallivanting!'

'Sit down!' said the dean sharply. 'Control yourself, man!'

Reluctantly, the rector sat. 'Now, hear me out,' said the dean. 'I have reminded you on several occasions of the need to avoid a scandal that would implicate the Church. Now I learn that you have been keeping close company with a woman, and that she is even some sort of assistant to you, travelling without a chaperone, asking questions on your behalf. Good God, man! What were you thinking of? Involving a woman, and a young widow at that? What will people think of you? What will people think of *her*?'

When the rector spoke again, his voice was deep and dangerous. 'Damn your eyes, Cornewall. If you are suggesting that there is anything improper about my relations with Mrs Chaytor—'

'Good God, Hardcastle, are you witless? It doesn't matter what *I* think! It matters what everyone else thinks! You *must* cease and desist in this affair, and you certainly must break off your connection with the woman.' A sneer crept into the dean's voice. 'Of course, that may be difficult for you. Perhaps the relationship is not as innocent as you protest? I recall you once had quite a weakness for demi-mondaines.'

'Of course,' the rector echoed. 'Speaking of which, how is the fair Mrs Cornewall?'

The dean's long horse-face went white. When he spoke again it was with barely controlled fury. 'We – that is, His Grace the archbishop and the archdeacon and I – have a very generous proposition to offer you.

His Grace knows of a vacant living in the West of England. Its patron is willing to offer it to you.'

'The West!'

'Yes. Herefordshire, to be precise.'

'Herefordshire! *Herefordshire!*'

'You will be perfectly comfortable there. Nothing ever happens in Herefordshire, and there will be no opportunities for you to become involved in mischief.'

That really was the limit, the rector thought. 'There have been three murders here, Dean. Three men are dead. And you call it *mischief*? If you truly believe that, then I wonder about the soundness of your mind. And by God, sir! If you ever say another word against Mrs Chaytor, or suggest that her reputation is anything other than entirely spotless, then I will call you out! Damn me if I don't!'

'Don't be a fool!' said Cornewall, raising his own voice. 'Even if you do not care about your own reputation, Hardcastle, think of that of the Church! That is more important than you, than me, than any of us. We must protect the Church!'

'Against what?' said the rector. Both had risen to their feet now. 'No one has yet uttered a word to suggest that the Church has any involvement whatever in this business. Are you trying to tell me that it does?'

'You made that accusation once before,' said Cornewall sharply. 'I warn you not to repeat it. If you so much as utter a word to slander His Grace –'

'Damn your eyes, Cornewall, I am not slandering His Grace, I am slandering *you*! Do you take me for a blathering idiot? Don't you think I can smell your foul stench all over this affair? Was it you who bribed the coroner, Cornewall? Are you tied up somehow with Blunt? Or do your interests lie with the smugglers? Come on, out with it!'

'You drunken, ignorant sot! You know *nothing* of the affairs in which you meddle!'

'Then explain them to me, you dunghill rat!' Both were now angry beyond reason; they raged at each other, calling each other names of ever greater colour and originality, until finally the dean cracked. He turned and stamped out of the house, climbed into his coach, slammed the door and drove away; five minutes later the coachman, red in the face, knocked on the door and apologised profusely, explaining that the dean had been in such haste that he had forgotten his hat and coat.

Still seething, the rector stormed out of his own house and marched down the fogbound high street to the Star, where he forgot his usual custom and demanded a pint of strong ale. Bessie Luckhurst, who served him, regarded him with ill favour. 'Have you had another quarrel with the dean, Reverend?'

'I fear I have.'

'It's all very well, but then he comes down here and takes it out on us. He swore at father and demanded a different room from the one we gave him, with such a tone in his voice! You would think he was the Emperor of China, or something.'

'He is staying here?'

'Yes, he asked for a room for several days. Until next Monday.'

Monday 6th June. The day the run was set to take place. A finger of doubt ran down the rector's spine. He had not been serious when he accused the dean of having a hand in the conspiracy. Now he was not so certain.

He returned home to find Amelia Chaytor waiting for him in the drawing room, still wearing her overcoat and gloves. She had refused refreshment. Her face was taut.

'Eugénie Fanscombe has sent me a message.'

'How?' The rector sat down, watching her.

'She gave an envelope to one her maids, swearing her to secrecy. The girl gave it to her friend who works for Miss Godfrey and Miss Roper, who passed it to Miss Godfrey, who in turn delivered it to me. I made sure the seal had not been tampered with.'

'It is still dangerous.'

'I know . . . The message was that Blunt called again at New Hall this morning. He spent two hours closeted with Fanscombe and Foucarmont.' With a courage born of anger and despair, Mrs Fanscombe had listened at the door. She had been able to stay only for a few minutes, but what she had heard was enough to implicate all three men fully in the attack on the

Twelve Apostles. She also confirmed what the rector had assumed, that despite the loss of Mark they still had sources of intelligence and knew that the Apostles were planning another run. Blunt was preparing a new ambush, and had been warned by Foucarmont in no uncertain terms that this time he must not fail.

'She adds that as soon as the meeting finished, Fanscombe departed, giving out that he was going down to Rye on business,' she said. 'He took a bag with him. I wonder what that means.'

'He has a specific role in this new plot, and is moving into position.'

'Yes. I wonder what that role is. I also wonder if *on business* is a euphemism.'

'You think he might have a lady friend? And that she is there in part to provide him with an alibi, should things go wrong?'

'Toys, for amusement,' Amelia said wrathfully. 'I will ask Mrs Merriwether to find out. If Fanscombe has a mistress in Rye, the ladies' gossip society there will surely know about it.' She gazed at Hardcastle. 'What do we do about Eugénie?'

'Get her out of that house,' said Hardcastle grimly. 'Foucarmont is clever and subtle. He will guess, sooner or later, that he has been betrayed. We *must* get Mrs Fanscombe away. Could you persuade her to come and stay with you for a few days, while her husband is away?'

'And leave her stepdaughter unchaperoned with Foucarmont?'

'Frankly, I am more concerned about Eugénie Fanscombe's life and health than I am about Eliza's reputation.'

She nodded. 'I shall go now, and persuade Eugénie to leave with me.'

The fog lingered on through the afternoon. In the early evening he walked into the village and knocked at the door of Sandy House, and Mrs Chaytor came out to meet him. He saw at once the relief in her face.

'She is here. She was reluctant to leave Eliza, but in fact the girl has barely been home since this affair blew up. Eugénie knows about her visits to the smugglers, and is terrified that she is about to do something stupid.'

If there was something stupid to be done, Miss Fanscombe would undoubtedly do it. 'Never mind Eliza for the moment. Take good care of Mrs Fanscombe, and keep your doors and windows locked.'

'I shall. Oh, I feel so sorry for her. She feels utterly alone in the world; even that rat Morley has deserted her. I feel as if I am her only friend.'

'I suspect you may be,' the rector said gently.

Her eyes searched his face. 'It is about to happen, isn't it? Whatever "it" is.'

'I fear so. That is why I must urge you again to take great care.'

'I shall. And while you are at it, you might take some of your own advice. Did you write to Clavertye?'

'This very morning. The letter should reach him tomorrow, assuming he is in the country and not in London. That gives us three days. That should give him just enough time to take action.'

'Yes,' she said quietly. 'Just enough time. Marcus, I am growing afraid. Not for myself, but for what might happen.'

No one had called him Marcus since his university days. He detested the name, but he decided that perhaps in her voice it sounded a little better. Then he remembered Cornewall's accusation, and anger stirred in his mind. Not trusting himself to speak, he raised her hand to his lips and kissed it gently, then bowed and withdrew.

Walking back up the street towards the Star, he was surprised to encounter two giggling young women, both cloaked and hatted against the damp. 'Miss Fanscombe,' he said bowing gravely, 'Miss Luckhurst. It is a damp, unpleasant day to be abroad.'

'We don't mind,' said Bessie cheerfully. 'We're off to New Romney.'

'And what do you do in New Romney, young ladies?'

'Whatever we please,' said Eliza archly. Two years older than Bessie, she acted much the younger.

'We are calling on a friend of mine,' said Bessie. 'I have told Eliza she needs to get to know more people in the Marsh, not just her father's snooty friends. After all, she will inherit the Hall one day. She needs to make herself known.'

They disappeared down the street, their laughter still audible even after the fog had swallowed them. Puzzled, the rector walked home. Two weeks ago, Bessie had roundly abused Miss Fanscombe in the common room at the Star; now here they were, apparently bosom friends. The young, he thought, are so fickle in their likes and dislikes; give it another week and they will be at each other's throats ... And there was Eliza, giggly and giddy; listening to her, one would never know of the storm that had broken around her, or that her father and stepmother had both moved out of the family home. What was going on in that head of hers?

The inconsistency of the young was a theme of conversation over the bar at the Star later that evening. Bessie had not yet returned from New Romney, and her father the landlord was glum. 'She's of an age,' he explained to the rector and Stemp, 'when I tell her what wants doing, and she listens meek and mild and nods her head – and then goes off and does exactly the opposite.'

'Aye,' nodded Stemp, 'they're like that. You need to take a firm hand, Tim. Show her who is the master.'

'Oh, yes, that is easily done. You wait 'til your young ones are grown, Josh Stemp, and you'll see just how easy it is.'

'Got a few years to wait yet,' said Stemp, whose eldest was nine. 'Same again, Reverend?'

'Thank you, Joshua, you are a gentleman, but I think I shall wend my way home.'

'It's not above ten,' said Stemp in surprise.

'I shall surprise Mrs Kemp by making an early night of it.' In truth, he was weary; he rarely slept well, but lately his dreams had been wild ones in which hordes of armed men emerged from the darkness to attack the rectory from all sides. He shrugged on his overcoat, put on his hat, took up his stick and made his laborious way out into the street.

The night was inky black. The fog was heavier than ever, and no trace of starlight penetrated it. The lights from the windows of the Star gave him visibility for about thirty yards; after that he was lost in the swirling fog. He shuffled forward, using his stick like a blind man to feel the ground in front of him. Feeling a damp chill around his neck, he turned up the collar of his greatcoat. That action saved his life.

He felt rather than heard the movement in the fog. Then something struck his arm a painful blow and his stick went spinning. Before he could react, someone seized him from behind. He felt the man's body hard and strong against his back, breath hissing angrily in his ear, and the rector had just time to register a sweet and rather sickly smell; then his head was pulled roughly back and a rigid forearm crashed across his throat and stayed there, pressing hard, choking him.

Gasping, too winded to shout for help, the rector clawed at the man's arm. It remained immovable, hard as a bar of iron. The thick collar of his greatcoat provided his neck with some protection, but he could feel the pressure increasing steadily, and his own strength was failing. The man behind him swore and shifted his stance, pressing his arm still harder against the rector's throat. *'Damn you, you old bastard,'* an angry voice hissed in his ear. *'Hurry up and die, will you?'*

Indeed, the rector was dying. He gagged horribly as his epiglottis closed, and stars began to explode in front of his eyes. Consciousness departed.

And then, unexpectedly, returned. He found himself on his hands and knees, his breath whining and whistling as his lungs sucked in air. Beside him, above him, two men were fighting, and dimly he heard the gasps and grunts and the sound of blows hitting home. Then one of the men broke off and ran, his footsteps pounding and then fading. The other bent over the rector, a wraith shape in the dark fog. He too was breathing hard.

'Are you all right, Reverend?'

'I will be soon.' The other man gave him a hand and helped him to his feet. 'You saved my life, my friend,' the rector said, still gasping. 'To whom do I owe thanks?'

'Call it a little gift from Peter,' the other man said, handing him his stick. 'Goodnight, Reverend. Go carefully.'

17

New Moon

The next morning, Friday, found the fog still hanging thickly over the Marsh. The rector, more shaken than he cared to admit, forwent his morning walk and ate his breakfast quietly. His throat hurt, and he wore his neckcloth higher than usual so as to conceal the bruises on his neck.

THE RECTORY, ST MARY IN THE MARSH, KENT.
3rd June, 1796.

My lord,

There have been two further developments. First, Blunt has had a meeting with Foucarmont and Fanscombe. That all three are implicated in this affair cannot be doubted. We have extricated our prime witness from the Fanscombe household, but it is essential that she be taken as soon as possible to a place of greater safety.

Lest you think I exaggerate the danger to her, I must inform you that last night a murderous assault was committed upon my person. I am safe and well apart from a few bruises, but I believe that the attack on me is connected with this affair, and that more such assaults may be committed in future.

I await further word from you,

Yr very obedient servant

HARDCASTLE

After signing and sealing this and marking the envelope EXPRESS, he took his pistol out of his desk and loaded it, then went into the hall and put on his hat and coat. He was just about to call the groom to harness the horse to the dog cart when there was a knock at the door. He opened it himself and found Mrs Chaytor in a hat and long dark cloak, wearing her driving gloves. The gig stood behind her, dim in the gloom. Beyond, lurking invisible in the fog, were the watchers.

He let her in and closed the door quickly. 'How is Mrs Fanscombe?'

'The laudanum Dr Mackay gave me came in useful. She was drugged, but at least she slept. She is full of terrors.' Her eyes searched his. 'Were you going out?'

'To New Romney, to post a letter to Lord Clavertye.'

'I am just off there myself. I will happily post it for you. Another letter? What has happened?'

He told her about the attack last night. She went pale, but remained resolute. 'My heart was hot within me, and while I was thus musing the fire kindled,' she said softly.

'The fire has certainly been kindled, and it nearly scorched me. The man who attacked me did so without warning and his intention, I am quite certain, was to kill. Someone thinks we are getting too close to the truth. If you insist on driving to New Romney, take your pistol with you.'

'It is here,' she said, patting the pocket of her cloak. She remained pale but there was defiance in her pretty eyes. 'You are right. We must be getting close to the truth, and they are starting to panic. If they make mistakes, we shall catch them.'

Assuming we live long enough, the rector thought to himself. He let her out, watched until she had driven away down the high street, then locked himself and Mrs Kemp inside, and instructed the housekeeper not to open the doors to anyone. Surprised and alarmed, she obeyed.

Just before midday there came a rapid knocking at the front door. The rector rose cautiously and went to the door, opening it a few inches until he saw Mrs Chaytor on the doorstep. Once again he ushered her in quickly, closing and locking the door behind her.

'I have just returned from New Romney,' said Mrs Chaytor. 'I had a feeling, a woman's intuition, if you must. I saw Eliza Fanscombe and Bessie Luckhurst going off arm in arm yesterday evening, and something about their attitude struck me as . . . unlikely. These two have never had any time for each other. What were they doing thick as thieves yesterday? And they were very late back; Lucy says they did not return until nearly midnight.'

That would have been well after he himself was attacked, the rector thought. The thought of the two girls abroad in a dark night full of armed men chilled him. 'So, I thought I would try to find out whether they were up to mischief,' said Amelia, 'and if so, whether their mischief had anything to do with our business. And I was right.'

She shivered. The rector ushered her into the study and then unlocked the cabinet and poured her a small glass of brandy to ward off the chill; she did not refuse it. 'No one I talked to saw Bessie at all,' said Amelia. 'Where she went and what she did are a matter for conjecture, though I suppose the most logical answer is that she has a lover. But my friend Mrs Spicer the landlady at the Ship certainly saw Eliza. She had a rendezvous with two gentlemen in one of the parlour rooms that lasted for about two hours. The girl had brought a letter, and there was a map that all three discussed, tracing routes from the coast inland. They seemed to be discussing which route would be used.'

'Let me guess,' the rector said gently. 'One of the gentlemen was Blunt.'

'Yes.' Mrs Chaytor drew breath. 'The other was Folliott Cornewall.'

The rector slapped his hand down hard on his desk. 'I *knew* it! I knew that infernal scoundrel had to be involved somehow. By God, this time I will have him!'

'This time?' she asked, the corners of her mouth twitching a little.

'It's . . . a long story. I'll tell it to you another time.'

'Give me the short version of it, then.'

He threw up his hands. 'It involves a lady of a certain . . . disposition. I was aware of this disposition. Cornewall was not.'

Unexpectedly, she began to giggle. 'You took her from Cornewall.'

'In fact, it was the other way around. But Cornewall discovered, while courting her, that she was also connected to me. He spread a rumour which did my reputation no end of harm, so subtly that I did not realise for some time that he was at the back of it. My name ended up in the mud, and the lady married Cornewall. No doubt she has had plenty of time to repent of this.'

'And you have spent many years waiting for an opportunity for revenge. But remember, we have more serious matters to deal with. It seems clear that Eliza Fanscombe is acting as courier between Foucarmont and Blunt.'

'Little fool!' He pounded one fist into his palm, his own pains forgotten, Cornwall forgotten too. 'A pound to a shilling says she has no idea of the danger she is in.'

'We must get her away from him,' said Amelia. 'I shall go to New Hall at once.'

'I will go with you.' They drove her gig down the high street, slowly in the fog, and if she heard the tapping footsteps behind them she did not let on. They pulled up outside New Hall, dark and shrouded in the gloom, and she engaged the brake and jumped nimbly down and rang the door-bell. A frightened servant showed them into a drawing room, and Eliza Fanscombe joined them a few moments later. She wore a plain wool gown with a shawl arranged around her neck. At first they could see nothing wrong with her, but when she turned her head they saw the bruise on her cheek and a swelling black eye.

'Oh, my,' said Amelia Chaytor, moving swiftly to her. 'Sit down, dear, sit down. Have you sent for the doctor?'

'No,' said Miss Fanscombe, bursting into tears.

The rector gripped his stick hard, rage welling up inside him. 'Where is Foucarmont? By God, I will teach that filthy French brute to lay a hand on a woman!'

'He is gone!' wailed Miss Fanscombe. 'He is gone!'

'What happened, dear?' asked Amelia quietly.

'I only asked him if I could help. I wanted to help, I truly did! I said that I loved him, and I wanted to be at his side, but he refused, he made me wait here. I said that if he departed I would follow him, and he struck me! He knocked me down, and then while I lay there . . . he kicked me, just as one would kick a dog! Oh, how I *hate* him!'

'I think we had better send for Dr Morley,' said Amelia to the rector. He yanked furiously at the bell rope and sent the frightened servant scuttling out to fetch Dr Morley. 'Do you truly hate him?' asked Amelia gently.

'I despise him! He is cruel and wicked, and I hate the ground he walks upon!'

Mrs Chaytor glanced at the rector. 'Then, will you help me?'

'What do you want from me?' sniffed the girl.

'Tell me what you were doing in New Romney yesterday,' said Mrs Chaytor. 'Do it, and I promise you will have your revenge on Foucarmont.'

She told them everything, adding what she knew about Foucarmont's departure and where he might be going. They listened in silence. Morley arrived just as she finished, Turner close behind him; he had seen the rector and Mrs Chaytor arrive and then the doctor, and had put two and two together. Morley examined her, gently and professionally, and pronounced no bones broken and gave her a liniment for her bruises. 'I do not advise that she stays here alone,' he said.

'I will take her home with me,' said Amelia. 'Come, my dear. The servants can fetch your things later.'

'Is *she* there?'

'She is. Now then, Eliza, do not be foolish. This is for your own safety.' Mrs Chaytor rose and looked down at the girl and in a voice both soft and steely said, 'You will come with me, my dear. Now.'

'What can I do?' asked Turner.

The rector turned to him. 'Have you a pistol, Mr Turner? Good. Can you keep watch at Sandy House tonight? I fear that both Miss Fanscombe and Mrs Fanscombe may be in danger.'

Turner sketched a bow. 'I am happy to serve.'

Much later, when Morley had gone and Eliza was asleep in bed, and Eugénie Fanscombe sat white and cold as marble before the drawing-room fireplace, staring into the flames, Amelia walked the rector to the front door.

'We have them,' he said. 'We know where and when and how they have planned the ambush. There is enough now for Clavertye to arrest all three of them when he arrives. It is almost over.'

'Almost, but not quite. I still want to know what Fanscombe is doing in Rye. I am going down there tomorrow. Do not worry, I will be quite safe; I shall stay with Mrs Merriwether.' She added, 'I hope that leaving them alone with each other for a few days will give them time to talk. They may be able to find some peace for themselves, and each other.'

He was uneasy about this, but he was uneasy about everything these days. 'I will look in on them when I can. For heaven's sake,' he said quietly, 'be careful.'

'You are the one in greater danger, I fear. I am only a woman, they will not take me seriously. You, on the other hand, are a threat to them. Don't go out in the evenings.'

'I will not unless I must.' He bowed and walked to the door, aware that her eyes were troubled as they followed him.

Saturday morning, 4th June, dawned quietly. A wind had risen in the night and swept the fog away out to sea, but it still hung heavy over the Channel, obscuring the coast of France. The rector walked on the beach at St Mary's Bay, regarded the fog gloomily, and then returned home for breakfast.

MIDDLE TEMPLE, LONDON.
3rd June, 1796.

My dear Hardcastle

I am in receipt of your letter of 1st June, which was forwarded to me here. Your discovery of course puts a different complexion on the matter. I have urgent business to attend to here in London, but will come to St Mary once that is concluded. I will travel down to Wadscombe on Sunday and expect to be with you by three of the clock on Monday afternoon. We can discuss how best to take this matter forward.

I might have known that you would disobey my instructions! But I am very glad that you did. I am greatly pleased with your conduct in this matter, and will remember it.

Yr very obedient servant

CLAVERTYE

The rector's heart sank. This letter had been written yesterday morning, at which time Clavertye had only seen the first of his recent missives. His Lordship did not at that point know about Eugénie Fanscombe's revelations, nor the additional news provided by Eliza, or the attack upon himself. He cursed himself briefly for a fool; he had written to Clavertye at his house in Kent, but of course the letters then had to be forwarded on to London, and that took an extra day. He had no doubt that Clavertye would act swiftly once he knew the full story; but would he – could he – act in time?

He called at Mrs Chaytor's house after breakfast. Turner was nowhere in sight; his night vigil over, he had presumably gone home to get some sleep. He found Eugénie Fanscombe once again sitting motionless before the fire; her stepdaughter was keeping to her room, even taking her meals there. 'She will not speak to me,' said the older woman, and the rector saw how her small-featured face was a mask of pain.

'If it is of any help, she has abandoned her romantic attachment to Foucarmont. She was all too ready to tell us everything she knew about him.'

'I fear that has made her more rebellious than ever. She has another plan. She continues to see the smugglers as romantic figures, modern equivalents of your famous Robin Hood. Foucarmont did nothing to discourage her fascination with them; it is only the Twelve Apostles who are his enemies.' Eugénie's shoulders slumped. 'Now that he has spurned her, she is threatening to run away and join the smugglers.'

The thought of an eighteen-year-old girl getting caught up in the midst of a smuggling gang made him almost physically sick. He knew that decent men like Stemp and Hoad would never touch her, but plenty of others would. 'Do what you can to keep her indoors, just for the next few days. Until that time, both she and you are in danger. Try to make her see that.'

She nodded. 'I shall try. What do you think will happen?'

'Lord Clavertye arrives on Monday morning; in the nick of time, but it should be enough. Once I have laid the full case before him he will be persuaded, I hope, to use main force, calling out the militia if need be, to apprehend Blunt. What happens after that is in God's hands, but I hope we shall succeed in laying this conspiracy bare.'

He went home feeling more depressed still, drank a bottle of port and fell asleep in front of the fire in his study. He woke with an aching head to find evening drawing in, dusk coming early under the blanket of low cloud. The wind had dropped and there were patches of mist here and there.

There came another knock at the door.

He opened it to find Eugénie Fanscombe, breathless and wide-eyed. 'She has gone.'

'What? How?'

'She climbed out of the window of her room. It must have happened some time this afternoon. I went at once to New Hall, and found that one of the grooms had seen her come in. Her horse is missing too, and she has taken one of my husband's pistols.' The woman was shivering. 'She has gone to join them. I know it.'

The thought crossed his mind that she had gone to track down Foucarmont, and then perhaps use the pistol. He prayed that she would be unsuccessful in her quest. 'Help me,' Eugénie pleaded. 'I do not know what to do.'

'Go back to Mrs Chaytor's house and wait.' He escorted her back through the gathering fog to Sandy House and went to knock on the doors of several cottages, rousing Joshua Stemp and Jack Hoad and three other men, all locals; he considered Turner, but the painter did not know the area and in any case he was needed to guard Eugénie. Together they went out and searched the fields around New Hall. They found the tracks of Eliza Fanscombe's horse quickly enough, heading southeast and then south towards New Romney, but after about a mile and a half they came to a shallow sewer. There they lost the trail; the girl had clearly used the old smuggler's trick of riding up the ditch and letting the water erase the tracks of her horse. They cast about on both banks for an hour, finding nothing. Darkness was settling, and patches of fog came drifting in off the sea.

'Not much more we can do tonight, Reverend,' said one of the men.

The rector looked at the others, now dim figures in the gloom, and sighed. 'I fear not. Gentlemen, thank you. It was good of you to give up your time to assist me.'

The lights of New Romney gleamed yellow in the middle distance. 'Ah, well,' said Hoad. 'We were coming down to the Ship tonight anyway, weren't we, lads? Why don't we go over now and wet our whistles. Care to join us, rector?'

He was worried sick, but he was also tired and thirsty. More to the point, while at the Ship he could ask around and learn whether anyone had seen Eliza. 'Lead the way, Jack,' he said.

The common room of the Ship was full of noise and tobacco smoke and people; the rector had never seen it so full. Fifty men, perhaps sixty were crammed into the room drinking and talking, all seemingly at once; the noise was like a solid wall. They pushed gently through the press to the bar, exchanging jovial greetings with the local men, and asked Mrs Spicer for beer. The rector paid. 'And have you seen Miss Fanscombe from New Hall in the town today, or perhaps on the roads nearby?'

'Why no, Reverend. I haven't seen the lass for two or three days now.' The look she gave him was full of strange sympathy, which he could not understand.

He found a seat by the window and drank his beer; when it was finished, someone brought him another one. He listened to the conversation flowing around him. There was an air of celebration about the gathering in the Ship, and the rector wondered why. Then, suddenly and unexpectedly, he heard a man's voice murmur the name of Cornewall, the Dean of Canterbury. He stared into the middle distance, affecting not to hear but in fact paying very close attention indeed. After that conversation had finished, he sat for a while with a thoughtful air.

He asked the nearest of the New Romney men about Miss Fanscombe. 'Haven't seen the lass. Oh, I know who you mean right enough, but she's not been around today.'

'Strange,' said another man, grinning. 'Not like her to be shy when there is a run on. She's normally prowling around, sniffing the air, so to speak.'

'Sniffing something,' said a third, a big portly man known as the Clubber, and some rather throaty chuckles followed. 'She's a hanger-on,' one of the others explained to the rector. 'She finds it all exciting. She likes to watch the runs come ashore. Fancies herself a smuggler, I reckon. Another drink, Reverend?'

'She'll get herself a smuggler too, if she carries on,' said the first man.

'Aye, she will,' the others agreed, and the man who was getting the drinks in came back to the table and quipped, 'Fine by me. She could smuggle me anywhere between them tits of hers!' The others roared and slapped their thighs, then remembered the rector and apologised. He accepted graciously. 'You said there was a run on. That's not until Monday.'

'Nah. Been brought forward, don't ask me why. Run's tonight. We're just waiting for Yorkshire Tom to give us the signal to move.'

There was a cheer at this and the men banged their mugs together. The rector sat smiling, his mind working furiously. He had assumed he still had forty-eight hours; in fact, he had perhaps two hours, no more. Lord Clavertye was not here. He was on his own.

If the local smugglers were making their run tonight, the chances were that the Twelve Apostles knew of it and were also coming tonight.

Did Blunt and Foucarmont know? Yes, they must. That was why Foucarmont had sent Eliza to find Blunt here in New Romney; to tell him about the change of plan. Great God! *Eliza* must know. She had told them everything about the plan to intercept the Twelve Apostles; everything except the changed date. The little fool had kept that to herself. She wanted to watch the run, to see the excitement, and she had lied to make sure that no one interfered with the smugglers.

Except that Blunt would be out there on the Marsh. He was already out there, now, laying his ambush.

What was about to happen would be mayhem, death and betrayal. His head began to spin at the thought, and he felt sick.

He sat upright, but the sick feeling persisted. He opened his mouth to speak to Jack Hoad, and found that his tongue was so swollen that it would not answer his commands. My God, he thought, how much beer have I had? Not enough to feel like this, surely. A sudden suspicion struck him and he raised the pot of beer to his nose and sniffed. The tang of raw spirits cut through the smell of hops and assailed his nostrils.

He wondered, through the gathering haze, who had doctored his drink. It could have been anyone, behind or in front of the bar. Whoever they were, they had poured the spirits with a generous hand. He tried to stand up, but found his legs had turned to jelly. On the third attempt he managed it. The others were watching him with some concern. 'Are you all right, Reverend?' asked Hoad.

'Outside. Need to go outside.' He stumbled through the press, aware that men were laughing at him; there goes the old rector again, their eyes said, drunk as a lord. Same old story. He felt anger at this, a flash of red haze, for he knew he should not have been drunk. Someone had done this to him . . .

He staggered out into the street. Noise and laughter from the inn followed him. Stumbling, he managed to make his way along the street to a dim alley beside the inn and there he bent over and vomited profusely. It took several heaves to clear his stomach, but when he stood up again, although his head whirled, he could think a little more clearly.

He stumbled back along the alley, a new urgency pounding in his brain. The run. The run was about to happen. Look for the signal. Wait for Yorkshire Tom. Must join the run.

Must get to Blunt. Must stop Blunt. Must stop Blunt before he kills Amelia . . . His head spun again and he stopped, gasping, his hands resting on the wall of the nearest house.

Something circled out of the dark and struck him across the back of the head, and he fell senseless to the ground.

18

The Run

Very slowly and somewhat painfully, the rector came to his senses. He smelled horseflesh, and felt the hair of a horse's coat under his hands, and heard the jingle of a bridle. He heard too the noise of other horses around him, and men, many men moving swiftly over the flat fields. He heard the distant rush and roar of the sea.

He opened his eyes. He was on the back of a horse, slumped forward over its neck. All was dark, but he could make out the figures of walking men, including two leading the horse by the reins. All of the men were masked, and most carried heavy wooden cudgels in their hands. Some had pistols or fowling pieces.

He groaned, and tried to sit up. One of the masked men at the horse's head turned. 'You're awake then, Reverend. Sit still now, you took a nasty knock.'

He recognised the voice as that of Stemp. He moistened his lips; his tongue still felt thick, and he realised the alcohol was still heavy in his veins. 'Where am I?' he said, his voice slurring.

'With the Gentlemen,' chuckled Hoad, the other masked man. 'You'll have something to dine out on now, Reverend. You're about to see a smuggler's run at first hand.'

'Wha . . . What happened?'

'You'd had too much to drink. You went outside, and there some cut-purse clouted you over the head. When Josh and I came out of the Ship he was standing over you. We shouted, and he turned and ran off. We reckoned we'd better bring you along with us for safe-keeping. You're in no condition to go home on your own.'

That much was certainly true; his head throbbed as never before. He sank back on the horse's neck, every stride the beast took jolting through his body and causing blurry waves of pain to radiate from his head. He felt sick again, but this time managed to hold his stomach down.

They were passing through the dunes. They were at the edge of the sea. Torches burned here, rows of them thrust into the ground; there was no attempt at concealment. A dozen big boats had been run up onto the shore, and men splashed bare-legged in the surf, carrying boxes and casks ashore. Pack horses were already being laden for the journey inland. The rector tumbled off his horse and lay for a while on the sand at the foot of the dunes, watching the men move to and fro in the lamplight. They laughed and shouted and sang as they carried their burdens. Their fee for this run would be a tiny portion of the value of the cargo they carried, but it would still be enough to keep them and their families in comfort for some time.

To and fro the smugglers passed, shouting to each other, taking their burdens from the boats and dumping them on the sand. Some of the brandy had already been opened and bottles were passed around as they worked. Down the beach went other men, masked too but with inventories rather than weapons in their hands, checking that all the cargo had landed and no items were missing. 'Come on, lads!' called one of these. 'Shift yourselves. We've half an hour before the boats must be away.'

'Ah, keep your wig on, Clubber!' They laughed again, and shouted and sang and drank and carried their loads through the blazing dark. Against his will, the rector felt their mood seeping into him. There was something wild about the scene; the running figures seemed to dance in the flickering torchlight, and their songs roared in the air. He sat up, feeling his own pulse pounding, and looked around.

Where were they? The coast looked the same as the rest of the shoreline of the Marsh, flat beach backed by a line of dunes tufted with coarse grass. He remembered the sound of the sea as he had lain on the back of the horse; it had come from the left for most of the way, and then from straight ahead. That meant that they had travelled south from New Romney, skirting the lagoons that lay inland of Greatstone, and then turned east towards the coast. They must now be east of Lydd, a mile or more south of Greatstone.

Greatstone was where the Twelve Apostles had planned to land; and somewhere between there and the Isle of Ebony, Blunt was lying in wait. He wondered if he could slip away, and whether he could get to Greatstone in time.

'All right, lads, that's the last of it ashore! Get them horses loaded! Porters, see to your own loads! Sorry, Reverend, you'll have to walk this time. We need the horses.'

'Go on without me,' protested the rector. 'I'll make my own way.'

The masked and hooded head shook with mock severity. 'It's dark out there, Reverend, and there are salt marshes and bogs so deep that if you fell in them you'd still be sinking in a hundred years. You stay with us, sir. We'll look after you.'

The boats pushed off and vanished out to sea. The men formed up in a column, packhorses at the head and masked porters carrying their loads slung over their shoulders following behind. As he stood up, the rector saw that there were scores of men, perhaps two hundred in all. No wonder they felt invulnerable.

The column began to wind its way back through the dunes. The rector found himself among the porters, burly men with kerchiefs around their heads and masks on their faces. He stumbled among them, feeling sick again, and they jeered at him; by their accents they were men from Lydd, not his own people. He fell back through the press of men, hoping to find them. The column had crossed the dunes and now their boots splashed in shallow water. Around him voices roared, singing out of tune, hilarious with drink and excitement.

Here's to the maiden of bashful fifteen,
Here's to the widow of fifty!
Here's to the flaunting extravagant quean,
Here's to the housewife that's thrifty.
Let the toast pass! Drink to the lass!
I'll warrant she'll prove an excuse for a glass!

Fog drifted across the Marsh in patches; the column went from clear starlight into dense fog that dampened clothes and draped itself in clammy skeins around their faces.

Let her be clumsy or let her be slim
Young or ancient, I care not a feather.

So fill up a bumper, nay, full to the brim!
And let us all toast them together.
Let the toast pass! Drink to the lass!
I'll warrant she'll prove an excuse for a glass!

Then the fog parted again and in the distance more torches sprang into light and a faraway voice cried, 'Halt! In the name of the King!' In response the column around Hardcastle exploded into laughter. 'Why, it's Juddery! Brave old Juddery! Come and have a crack at us, you Excise pimps!' Further along the column there were flashes and bangs as fowling pieces were discharged; distant flashes showed that Juddery's men were firing back, but at this range it would be an extraordinary fluke if anyone hit a target. Deep in the rector's fuddled brain an idea emerged, and crawled to the surface. *Juddery. Must get to Juddery.*

First, he had to get away from the column without being spotted; he didn't want any of the smugglers to get the idea that he was trying to aid Juddery against them. He stumbled again, this time by design, and fell back further still. The porters, still jeering and yelling at the Excise men, ignored him. He staggered again, and this time contrived to trip and lie still. The column passed on, and the last of the chanting, yelling men vanished into the darkness ahead of him. He lay still for a few minutes in case there were any outliers, and then rose cautiously to his feet.

A horse came up out of the darkness and nearly knocked him over. He managed to jump aside and the horse whinnied and reared up; the rider cursed it and him, bringing the animal down onto four legs again. He realised dimly that it was a woman's voice. 'Clumsy oaf! You had better get moving. Your column is heading off without you!'

His head rang and he stared up at the woman on horseback, cloaked and masked in black, a phantom against the starlight.

'*Miss Fanscombe?*'

She gasped, and steadied the horse. 'Reverend Hardcastle! Whatever are you doing out here?'

'I could ask you the same thing,' he said severely, his voice still slurring.

'I came to watch the fun,' she said breathlessly. 'Oh look! They are shooting again! Oh, it is exciting! Go on, brave Gentlemen!' she shouted.

'Push the Excise back! Ah, see, they are running with their tails between their legs!'

'Miss Fanscombe,' he said, struggling to control his voice, 'I need your help. I need to get to Mr Juddery. And . . . I am having some trouble walking.'

'You mean, you are drunk,' she said with scorn in her voice. 'I can smell it from here. You can crawl to Juddery, I'm not going near him. I am following the Gentlemen.'

'Miss Fanscombe,' the rector said desperately, 'do you recall the story you told us after Foucarmont had abused you? What he and Blunt were planning? Well, that plan is about to be carried into effect. Even as we speak, Blunt and Foucarmont are laying an ambush for the Twelve Apostles. The only force that can stop them now is Mr Juddery's Excise men. Will you help me?' And he added, 'It would be a fitting revenge on Foucarmont.'

The girl made up her mind in a split second. 'Climb up behind me. Quickly. Now, hold on.'

He scrambled somehow across the back of the horse and managed to sit upright, and rather gingerly put an arm around her waist. He felt the butt of the pistol she carried in a saddle holster, and then she shook the reins and the horse lurched into motion, nearly pitching him back over its tail. He clung desperately to the girl as the horse cantered away across the marshland, splashed through a ditch and then careered on through the darkness. He could not see where they were going, and could only hope that Eliza Fanscombe had truly decided to help him and was not carrying him straight to Blunt.

He had his answer soon enough. He heard shouts ahead. 'Who's that coming? Hi, there! Halt, in the name of the King!'

He slid off the horse to the ground and fell over. By the time he had staggered upright, Juddery was there, shadowy in the starlight with a pistol in each hand. 'What is this? Who are you?'

'It is Hardcastle,' the rector gasped.

'Reverend Hardcastle! What are you doing here? My God, man, you're drunk!'

'No. I mean, yes. No, I mean— Blast it all, Juddery, I'll explain later. Look here! Somewhere up north of us, a group of men in government service are landing on the coast. They are bringing some vital secret into the country – vital, I tell you! It could concern the French invashion. Invasion. Blunt is working with a French spy, and he is up there with at least forty men, ready to ambush them and prevent the secret getting through. I tell you, we must get up there and stop Blunt.'

'Blunt, you say!' In the starlight, he fancied Juddery's eyes had narrowed. He wondered how much of the rest of his narrative had even been heard. Around him the Excise men growled with pleasure. 'We've only twenty men,' said Juddery.

'Never mind that,' snarled a voice. 'Any Excise man is worth ten of those scaly bastards from Customs. Let's get at 'em.'

There was a roar of assent. 'All right,' said Juddery. 'Go quietly, lads. We'll get the drop on them, likely enough. Where do you reckon they'll be, Rector?'

'Inland from Greatstone. About half a mile.' He reeled again as he spoke, but his head was beginning to clear at last.

'They'll have to get around the lagoon,' said Juddery. 'They'll probably go north about, to avoid running into us. If we circle around and come in from the west, we can push Blunt straight into the lagoon. All right, lads, move, and remember – quietly!'

They moved, spreading out into a skirmish line with Juddery roughly in the centre, loping through the starlight and the rector panting and stumbling after him. After a few minutes he realised that Eliza Fanscombe was following, trotting her horse some distance behind and keeping them in sight. He cursed, hoping her horse and its noise did not give the game away. When they plunged into another fog bank he thought they might lose her, but no; she followed them out of the fog into more starlight. A few lights glowed dimly to the north, and he realised that this was New Romney; New Romney, where someone had half-poisoned him by someone putting raw spirit into his beer, and then knocked him over the head. How long ago had that been? He had lost all track of time.

The stars glimmered faintly in the misty sky overhead. Gasping and wheezing, he collided with Juddery, who had halted.

'Blunt's men are up ahead, hidden in the grass or in the sewer that runs into the lagoon,' Juddery was whispering fiercely to his men. 'Silcock, take half the men and get out to the right to cut them off. I'll take the rest straight in and hit them from behind.'

'Take them alive,' gasped the rector. 'Most of the Customs men don't know about the plot; it's Blunt that we want. Don't shoot unless you must.'

'That depends on Blunt's men, Reverend. If they shoot, we'll shoot back. All right, lads. Ready—'

From somewhere up ahead there was a hissing noise, like a snake preparing to strike. Suddenly light exploded across the Marsh, an eerie, shivering, unearthly blue light that showed the scene before them in garish contrast. The light glowed off a column of men making their way silently across the Marsh, masked and hooded men with weapons cradled in their arms. Nearer at hand, other men crouched in the grass and the ditch, their own weapons levelled.

'What the hell is that?' gasped Juddery.

'False fire,' said the rector. 'Oh, dear God. We are too late.'

Gunfire erupted like a thunderstorm. From their hidden positions on three sides, Blunt's men poured fire on the column of men. The latter dived for cover, and Hardcastle could see some of them wriggling across the ground, others coolly returning fire, but some were lying very still. He could hear Blunt yelling at his men, urging them to complete the encirclement and then close in. Another flare erupted, its evil blue light glaring across the Marsh.

Rage roared in the rector's mind. The alcohol swimming in his blood caught light and burned blue as the false fire. He clenched his fists, bellowing his fury, and then to the astonishment of the Excise men he charged across the fields towards Blunt's men, still roaring incoherently. 'After him!' screamed Juddery, and the Excise men charged too, and even as the bewildered Customs officers turned to see what the commotion was, furious shapes wielding cudgels raced out of the dark and fell on them. A Customs man sprang to his feet; Hardcastle felled him with one furious blow of his fist, then grabbed the pistol the man had dropped and reversed it to use as a club. When the pistol was knocked from his hand he picked up a cudgel someone had dropped and laid about him, lashing out indiscriminately at anyone who came near him, blundering on through the fray with no thought at all in his mind except to hit and hit and hit again.

Gunfire crashed and boomed, pistols fired at point-blank range. The Twelve Apostles had gathered themselves and charged into the melee too, seeking to break out of the trap. Pistol balls whizzed around Hardcastle, clubs lashed at him, but nothing touched him. He felled two men with his own cudgel, not knowing or caring which side they were on. He turned as a someone shrieked a warning behind him and saw a Customs man kneeling and aiming a pistol straight at him, his face a rictus of rage and fear, but before the other man could fire a dark phantom rode out of the night into the shivering blue flame and the rider lashed the weapon from the Customs man's hand with her riding crop. Dropping the whip as the man spun away clutching at his arm, she drew her own pistol and fired it blindly into the air, screaming again like a banshee as she rode on through the press.

The rector roared in response. He ran towards the nearest knot of struggling men, aiming to join in the fray, but then tripped over something lying before him. He fell heavily, the ground coming up to slam against his chin. Lights flashed in front of his eyes, and then darkness enveloped him once more.

19

Peter Removes His Mask

Consciousness returned gradually. The first sensations came from his own body; his head throbbed like a steam engine, and his body seemed to be a single mass of pain. His mouth was dry and felt as if it was full of ash. Then, as his mind cleared a little more, he became aware of the world around him. All was quiet nearby, though from the west he could hear distant shouts and the occasional shot echoing across the fields. The false fires had gone out, and the Marsh lay dim and shadowy under the stars.

Suddenly he felt sick again. He lay still while the sickness passed, and then became aware that part of the pain in his body came from something beneath him, an object with sharp protrusions that were digging into his belly. He dragged himself slowly to his hands and knees, and then scrabbled in the darkness until he found the object again. It was a leather satchel with a folding cover, and the protrusions he had felt were the heavy buckles of the straps that kept the cover closed.

He remembered then that he had tripped over something, and turned to look. It was a body, a hooded and masked man in black lying sprawled face down in the mud. He reached out and touched the man's arm. His skin was still warm, but there was no heartbeat. One of the Twelve Apostles had made his last run.

The rector staggered to his feet, clutching the leather satchel. Away to the west, silence had fallen. He wondered how many of the other Apostles had been killed. Sickness washed over him once more as he realised that he had failed. The ambush had been sprung. Blunt and Foucarmont had won.

Well. Perhaps not entirely. Juddery's men had distracted Blunt, at the very least, and it was possible that some of the Apostles had escaped in the confusion. At that very moment more gunfire broke out again, far away now, and he heard a distant confused shouting and yelling as men joined battle once more. The rector felt suddenly cold, and knew that he had to get away, get to his home. Then he heard more voices, very close at hand.

'Search the area. Quickly. We got at least two of the bastards, and one of them might have been carrying it.'

The voice was Blunt's. Another voice said, 'It is dark. We'll need to light a lantern.'

'Do it. The others are far away now.'

The rector sank quickly to the ground and lay down once more on top of the dispatch case, face down. Fifty yards away a lantern hissed into life. From the corner of his eye he saw two men moving slowly towards him.

'What are we looking for, Mr Blunt?'

'A bag or case. Anything that might be used for carrying papers. God damn Juddery! We had them pinned down. We had them right where we wanted them, and then that maniac showed up.'

'What was the fool doing? Could he not tell who we were?'

'God knows. He's an Excise man, they haven't a brain between them. He's gone too far this time, though. I'll settle him for good . . . Oh, for God's sake! Here comes the fog again.'

White vapour drifted over the scene, blotting out the men from the rector's vision. 'I can't see my hand in front of my face,' said the man with the lantern.

'All right, all right. We'll leave it for now, but we're coming back at first light.'

The voices receded. Breathing a silent prayer to the merciful God who had sent the fog, the rector struggled to his feet again and set off across the Marsh, north towards St Mary.

The cocks were crowing and the eastern horizon was pale with light when he reached the rectory. The front door had been bolted and he had to knock hard, several times, to wake the housekeeper. Finally he heard her trembling voice behind the door and called reassuringly, 'It is only me, Mrs Kemp. Kindly let me in.'

He heard the bolts being drawn, and the door opened. The house-keeper took one look at the spectre that stood before her, dripping with water and mud, dried blood streaking one side of his face, his hat gone and his hair standing on end, and screamed.

'Heaven help us, Reverend Hardcastle! Is it you, dead and come back as a ghost?'

'I assure you, Mrs Kemp, that I am very much alive. I apologise for the inconvenience at this hour, but will you kindly heat some water for a bath? And coffee would be very welcome.'

'Oh, Lord save us!' Clearly not entirely convinced that he was not a spectre, she went off to the kitchen. Hardcastle struggled upstairs and slowly peeled off his ruined clothes. His head ached, and he winced when he touched his scalp where he had been clubbed in New Romney, half a lifetime ago. He scrubbed away some of the blood and mud and slowly drew on his nightshirt and dressing gown.

Then, while he waited for his bathwater, he went down to the study carrying the leather satchel. He unlocked the cabinet and poured a brimming glass of cognac, drank it down and filled another, and then hobbled stiffly to the desk to look down at his prize.

The satchel was bound, as he had guessed in the dark, by two leather straps held by heavy buckles. It was further secured by a third strap attached to the first two below the buckles, and on this were two locks. To open the first two straps the third would have to be removed, and to do this required a key for the locks.

He did not have the key. He rang the bell and asked Mrs Kemp to bring him a very sharp knife. She returned with this a moment later, along with a steaming pot of coffee and a cup. She was bursting with questions, but he shooed her out of the room and closed the door behind her. Then he slit the bottom of the satchel, a task which took some time and effort as the leather was quite thick. Finally he drew out the contents, a slim packet of sheets of paper covered with neat writing.

Seated quietly at his desk, the rector read the papers. They were written in French, and he understood at once why Blunt had been searching for them, and why the Twelve Apostles had been prepared to kill, and die, to get these papers safely through to London. There were about forty pages in all, closely written with a great many facts and figures and numbers. At the end was the signature of a man whose name the rector knew from the newspapers; Lazare Carnot, a member of the Directory and also the French Minister of War.

'Well, well,' he said quietly, staring at the wall. 'Blunt hasn't won after all.'

Sunday morning, the day after the run, dawned silently and peacefully. The rising sun dispersed the Marsh mists and with them the skeins of powder smoke that still hung in the air. The combatants had long since departed, and the bodies had been taken away; the white-faced sheep could graze once again in peace.

The rector woke from a short sleep riddled with bad dreams, his head and body shuddering with pain. He washed and dressed slowly, instructed the housekeeper to keep breakfast for him and went out and hobbled down the street to Mrs Chaytor's house. The housekeeper, looking frightened, admitted him. He found Eugénie Fanscombe in the drawing room. She did not look as if she had slept at all.

'I beg your pardon for intruding at such an early hour. I wished to know whether your stepdaughter had returned.'

The small woman shook her head. 'Not yet. Did you find any trace of her?'

'I did more than that,' said the rector. 'I saw her last night. She had followed the smugglers.'

'Oh, my God,' said Eugénie Fanscombe, and she collapsed into a chair, her face a picture of misery. 'I must ask you,' said the rector. 'Has she done this before?'

'No. She has talked of it sometimes, but I do not think she had ever dared to actually go out.'

The rector doubted this, very much, but he was hardly going to add to the poor woman's misery now. She looked up at him, her dark eyes wet and her face softened by sorrow.

'Oh, Reverend Hardcastle, please bring her back to me.' The voice was a moan of despair, ending in a choked-off sob. He considered all of the things he had to do within the next few hours; but this was a mission of mercy that he could not refuse.

'I will do what I can,' he said gently. 'It will not be easy for you to effect a reconciliation with her. You know that.'

'I will do anything. Anything. I love her, Reverend Hardcastle. And I have nothing else to love. My marriage of fifteen years is at an end. I had two children of my own after I was married, but both were stillborn. Eliza is all that I have.'

How terribly we misunderstand other people, the rector thought as he let himself out, and how woefully I in particular have misunderstood the tortured life that went on under the Fanscombe roof . . . He limped up the drive to New Hall, the big house standing quiet in the still, silent morning; when he knocked at the door he fancied the noise could be heard all over the village.

'I am here to see Miss Fanscombe.'

'She is asleep, sir,' said the maidservant who answered, looking more frightened than ever.

'Then wake her, and send her down to me at once. I will not accept no for an answer.'

Ten minutes later Eliza Fanscombe descended the stairs, dressed in an ordinary gown but looking white and drawn. The bruises on her cheek and around her eye were almost black against the pallor of her skin. But her chin was up, and she attempted bravado.

'What is it?'

'Fetch your coat and bonnet, and come with me. I am returning you to Mrs Chaytor's house.'

'No! I do not wish to go!'

'Miss Fanscombe,' he said, not caring that the servants were listening, 'you have two choices. You can suffer arrest for aiding and abetting smugglers, see your reputation ruined for ever, and go to prison. Or you can come with me, now.'

He had not lost the power of command. She did as he bid, mute, and he turned to the servants. 'You will not see the master of this house again. Lock the door and keep all within secure. The king's men will arrive within the next few days. When they do, you are to admit them without delay.'

They bowed or curtseyed, more frightened than ever. He took the girl's arm and half-dragged her out of the house and down the drive. 'You little fool!' he said. 'You are already in this business up to your neck. What did you think you were doing last night? If you had been caught out there on the Marsh, it would be all over for you.'

'I have done nothing wrong! Let me go! You cannot prove anything against me.'

'I do not have to,' he said brutally. 'I mentioned two choices. There is a third. I will tell Foucarmont that you betrayed the plot to Juddery's men, and even joined him in breaking up the ambush on the Marsh. What do you think he will do to your pretty face then?'

She stared at him in silent horror. When he took her arm again she was unresisting. 'You are not a witless child,' he said. 'You are a grown woman. It is time you began to act as one.'

They halted at the door of Mrs Chaytor's house, and by this time the enormity of what she had done was sinking in. Her spirit was broken. 'In a day or two,' he said, 'a king's officer will come and ask you questions. You will tell him everything about your connection with Foucarmont and the messages you carried for him. You need not tell the officer that Foucarmont was your lover, and you need not tell him about your visits to the Marsh during the runs; these things have nothing to do with the case. But you will tell everything else. I shall be present during the inquiry, to ensure that you *do* tell the truth. Do you understand?'

'I understand,' she said in a small voice.

'Good. Now, go inside and find your stepmother, and make your peace with her. She is, if only you realised it, your best friend. The two of you will need each other very greatly, Eliza, and very soon.'

The rector rushed home to a hasty ham and eggs, closing his ears while the housekeeper scolded him for eating too quickly, and then hurried across the road to the church and into the vestry to robe. He preached as well as usual, though Miss Godfrey did remark to Miss Roper that the reverend seemed a little distracted this morning, and wasn't his throat a bit scratchy? It was to be hoped that the poor man was not coming down with a cold. In fact, the rector performed much of the service by rote, barely hearing his own words. His mind was still full of wavering blue light, in which shadowy figures wrestled and clubbed and hacked and shot at each other, shouting and screaming.

At the end of the service he stood in the church porch and thanked his parishioners with a warm smile as they departed. Returning to the vestry he hung up his robe and came out into the fair, warm late morning sun and, still stiff and sore, walked down the quiet village street to the Star. He was in search of medication for his pains, but he also had another purpose in mind. Over the past couple of weeks the rector had devoted part of his time to considering the identity of the female informer who kept watch for the Twelve Apostles in St Mary in the Marsh. He had had his suspicions all along, but over the past few days the suspicions had hardened into certainty.

He reached the Star and stepped under the low doorway into the common room. It was still early, and he was the only one there. Bessie Luckhurst came out from the back, wiping her hands on her apron and looking bright and neat as usual. 'What will you have, Reverend?'

'A mug of strong, Bessie, there's a good lass.' She filled a tankard and passed it across to him. He drained it a single draught, feeling the warmth spreading from his belly through his body. In his imagination, the pain was already easing. He lowered the empty tankard and sighed with pleasure.

'Another, Reverend?' she said laughing.

'If you please. And Bessie; when you've filled it, there's something else you may do for me.'

She nodded brightly, setting the foaming tankard in front of him. He slid a coin across the counter, and looked her straight in the eye and said quietly, 'Tell Peter I need to see him. As soon as possible, if you please.'

When he had finished his beer he asked the somewhat subdued Bessie for directions to Cornewall's room, and climbed stiffly up the stairs and knocked at the door. A sharp voice said that the occupant did not wish to be disturbed. Hardcastle opened the door anyway and passed inside, closing the door and locking it behind him.

Cornewall had been writing letters at a desk before the window, but now he stood up. 'You! How dare you come here and interrupt me? What is the meaning of this?'

'I wanted a quiet word,' said Hardcastle equably. 'I should sit down if I were you, Dean. I have some nasty shocks for you.'

Slowly, suspiciously, Cornewall sat. Hardcastle remained standing, leaning on the doorframe. 'I have just had a very interesting night,' said the rector. 'I participated, quite unwillingly, in a smuggler's run. It was fascinating. But nothing on the run was quite so fascinating as what I learned beforehand. You'll recall that, when last we spoke, I accused you of being involved in smuggling yourself. I admit to you now that I didn't make the accusation with any serious intent. We were both angry, and I was looking for mud to throw at you.'

'Good. Then you have come to offer an apology,' the dean said stiffly. 'Once I have heard it, I will consider whether to accept it.'

'Oh, don't get your hopes up, my dear Dean. You see, after our meeting I gave the matter more thought. It struck me as curious how you, like a carrion bird, arrived on the scene in St Mary so quickly after the first bodies were found. And thereafter, whenever we reached a point of crisis, such as the third killing or the news that another run was about to take place, you again appeared promptly on the scene. Your explanation, of course, was that you were safeguarding the interests of the Church, but that never rang true. What interest can the Church possibly have in any of this?'

'You will not drag the Church into this!' shouted the outraged clergyman.

'No, I will not. In fact, the Church has no interest at all. You, on the other hand, do. According to a deeply interesting conversation that I overheard last night, quite a lot of the cargo run in by the men from New Romney and St Mary was destined for various church buildings around the Marsh and upcountry. The goods would be stored there, no questions asked, until transported to London. And you, Dean, would receive a handsome fee for making these buildings available.'

A better liar would have had a story ready. The dean simply gabbled incoherently until the rector silenced him. 'Enough. When this affair is over, Dean, I strongly advise you to leave Canterbury. Go into the West Country. Herefordshire, perhaps,' he added with malice. 'Nothing ever happens there.'

There was a final attempt at bluster. 'Or else? What will you do?'

'Lay a dossier detailing your activities before Lord Clavertye,' said Hardcastle. 'He arrives tomorrow, to begin a detailed inquiry into a case of murder, conspiracy and treason. You have associations with men who are deeply involved in this case. If you truly care about the reputation of the Church, Cornewall, then there is only one choice open to you. Depart for Canterbury within the hour and, once there, draft a letter asking His Grace asking his permission to lay down your office and retire to another part of the kindgom.'

The dean sat silent, and Hardcastle saw in his face that he was broken. Quietly, without any sense of triumph, he let himself out and limped back downstairs.

The Rectory, St Mary in the Marsh, Kent.
5th June, 1796.

Mr Blunt,

It is urgent that I speak with you as soon as possible. I have information of great importance to convey to you, concerning the attack made upon you by Mr Juddery and the Excise men last night. You will doubtless be seeking an explanation for his behaviour; I can provide it.

It is also possible that I may be able to help you in your search for the object you were seeking out on the Marsh.

Please meet me in the church of St Mary the Virgin at three of the clock in the afternoon, tomorrow, the 6th of June.

Yr very obedient servant

HARDCASTLE

The Rectory, St Mary in the Marsh, Kent.
5th June, 1796.

My dear Fanscombe,

I understand that you are away from home at the moment, but I hope your servants will be able to forward this letter without delay. As you will doubtless have heard, there was another affray on the Marsh last night, between smugglers and Preventive men. The Twelve Apostles, the group I mentioned earlier, were also involved.

I am sorry also to report that your daughter was present both during the run and the subsequent affray. I am able to assure you that Eliza has been foolish, but no more; but it is clear that she was seen by many people, and tongues will soon begin to wag. I would like to assist you and your family, but we must act quickly if we are to prevent a scandal that will engulf you all.

Will you please meet me in the church of St Mary the Virgin at three of the clock in the afternoon, tomorrow, 6th June? We can be assured of privacy there.

Yr very obedient servant

HARDCASTLE

THE RECTORY, ST MARY IN THE MARSH, KENT.
5th June, 1796.

M. de Foucarmont,

I need to speak to you most urgently about the Twelve Apostles. I believe your men tried to apprehend these traitors on the Marsh last night, and did not succeed. However, information has come into my possession that will allow you to lay them by the heels.

We need to meet, preferrably somewhere quiet and private. I suggest you meet me in the church of St Mary the Virgin at three of the clock in the afternoon, tomorrow, 6th June.

Yr very obedient servant

HARDCASTLE

THE RECTORY, ST MARY IN THE MARSH, KENT.
5th June, 1796.

My dear Dr Morley,

You will doubtless have heard the news of the violent affray last night on the Marsh. The smuggling gang known as the Twelve Apostles were ambushed by Blunt's men east of Lydd, and there was a great fight between them. This affair grows very serious, and I believe it is time that it was dealt with, once and for all.

I have invited a number of those involved in this matter to meet with me at St Mary the Virgin tomorrow, 6th June, at three in the afternoon. You have been involved in this matter to some extent, and will be able to provide testimony. Also, it would be very useful to have you present as a witness.

I do hope you will be able to join us,

Yr very obedient servant

HARDCASTLE

THE RECTORY, ST MARY IN THE MARSH, KENT.
5th June, 1796.

My dear Turner,

Matters have come to a head, slightly sooner than expected. I promised you a full explanation. If you come to St Mary the Virgin at three of the clock tomorrow afternoon, you shall receive one. I would also be very grateful for your presence as a witness.

Yr very obedient servant

HARDCASTLE

THE RECTORY, ST MARY IN THE MARSH, KENT.
5th June, 1796.

My dear Captain Shaw,

You will have heard of last night's affray on the Marsh. I assume also that your suspicions will have quickened, and you are wondering if this affair and the events of last month are connected. You are absolutely right; they are. The smuggling gang known as the Twelve Apostles were ambushed by Blunt and his men, who were seeking to find a certain dispatch case full of secret papers from France. They failed in their quest, but they will shortly be aware that I know of their plot, and where the dispatch case is.

I have invited the chief conspirators to meet me at the church of St Mary the Virgin at three of the clock in the afternoon tomorrow. I would be grateful if you would join us. Your assistance in apprehending these men will be greatly appreciated; by myself and, no doubt, by Lord Clavertye.

Yr very obedient servant

HARDCASTLE

Evening, with the sun low over the line of hills to the west. Doves cooed in the churchyard trees, and he could hear sheep bleating in the distance. The rector sat in one of the box pews and stared at the altar, gleaming dimly among the shadows in the chancel, and waited.

Behind him, the door opened quietly and then closed. Soft footsteps sounded and then a man was standing beside him, a big man, strong and heavily built with fair hair and a hard face with a square chin and jaw. He could have been a prizefighter. He could easily also, the rector thought a little sadly, have been myself in my younger days.

'Sit down,' Hardcastle said quietly.

The other man opened the door of the pew and sat, and the rector studied him for a few moments. It was the first time he had seen the other man's face full-on and unmasked; at Ebony, he had seen only his profile, from a distance.

'You sent for me,' said Peter who was also called George.

'Yes. I wanted you to have something. I am sorry for the urgent summons, but it is only a matter of time before Blunt and his confederates work out what has happened and come to search my house again. You will agree, I think, that this is worth the risk of my calling you out here.'

He handed over the leather satchel. The other man frowned, then reached through the slit leather and took out the papers. He glanced through them, turning the pages quickly and in silence. Then he looked up.

'I take it you have read these yourself.'

'I have.'

'And you know what they are?'

'They are papers from the French War Office,' said the rector, 'written over the hand of Lazare Carnot, the Minister of War. They are instructions to General Moreau of the Army of the Rhine and General Bonaparte of the Army of Italy, laying out plans for the invasion of south Germany and northern Italy, and the destruction of the Austrian field armies. The aim is to knock Austria out of the war by the end of the year.'

He paused. 'It means that French attention has turned east. There will be no invasion of Britain, at least not this year.'

'No. And we will pass these plans to the Austrians, and then help them halt the French and throw them back. If we are successful, there may not be any invasion, ever. If the French armies fail in the field, that could be the blow that brings down the Republic.' Peter looked at the rector, his eyes searching. 'I must ask how you came by these papers.'

'I was there, last night.' The rector told the story, from the time someone tried to kill him in New Romney to Juddery's attack on Blunt and his own part in that. 'I collapsed on top of the dispatch bag by pure chance. I fear the body may have been one of your own men.'

'Philip.' The other man's face was sombre. 'He was carrying the dispatch bag. I lost two good men last night, Philip and Bartholomew, and three more hurt.'

He stopped, and the rector said, 'When did you realise the bag was missing?'

'Not for a couple of hours. Those of us still on our feet got out of the melee any way we could and made our way individually to the rendez-vous point. I was the last one in; I found the others waiting at Ebony, but no sign of Philip or the dispatches. You can imagine our feelings pretty well, I think.'

'It was a terrible blow to your hopes.'

'That puts it mildly. We did not know what was in the papers, of course, but we had been warned that they were important. We knew too that the French were aware the papers had been stolen – another of our men died getting them out of Paris – and were hot on the trail, but we thought we had given them the slip in France. Once we landed in England, we thought we were almost home. Then came the ambush, and the ship-wreck of our hopes.'

He put the papers back in the case, and looked up. 'But thanks to you, my friend, we have won through after all. I am very grateful to you, Reverend.' His face was suddenly rueful. 'And I am afraid that this is probably all the thanks you will ever get. As you can imagine, this whole matter is under the rose. Officially, it never happened.'

The rector nodded. 'I understand. If you want to thank me, then answer a question for me. Who are you?'

The other man paused for a long time, looking at the evening light shining in long shafts through the church windows. 'I reckon you deserve to know,' he said finally. 'My name is George Maskelyne, and I'm a gentleman, of sorts. I am leader of the Twelve Apostles, of course, but I also work with another group in government service. The chief of that group reports directly to the prime minister.'

'I had guessed that much.'

Maskelyne nodded. 'I won't tell you about the others,' he said, 'for it is best that you do not know. I'll tell you a little about the Twelve Apostles, in case you run across their track again.' He talked for several minutes, the rector listening intently. 'So,' said Maskelyne at the end, 'we follow the paths of darkness, but we are on the side of the light. As least, we try to be.'

'I understand,' said the rector again. 'What will you do now?'

'Rejoin my men, and then get these papers to London with all speed. After that, you may not see me for quite a while, if ever. I'm needed out in Italy. I should be there already, but I stayed to look after this affair.'

They rose to their feet, and Maskelyne said, 'Out of curiosity, how did you identify our fair informer here in St Mary?'

'It was not so difficult, once I had overheard you and knew that the informer was a woman. From there it was a process of deduction. Only a limited number of women are in a position to see and hear everything that goes on in the village, and of those only two had the boldness and wit that would be needed by anyone working with you. One was easily eliminated; the other therefore had to be your informer. Bessie is a good girl. Be careful how you use her.'

'Bessie is one of the best. When she is older, I'll take her into the service, if she still wants it.' Maskelyne chuckled. 'You're a perceptive man, Reverend. Perhaps you should join us too. I reckon you'd make a fine codebreaker.'

'I shall take that as a compliment. Thank you, but no. My present calling gives me all that I need.'

The door of the pew opened and closed; the other man's footsteps faded in the nave; then the outer door too opened and closed. The rector sat on for a while, gazing at the altar until the shadows deepened, and then he rose and walked slowly across the road to the rectory.

20

Stella Maris

It was Monday, the sixth day of June; a month to the day since the man called Jacques Morel died in the hallway of the rectory, and Curtius Miller met his end out on the Marsh.

The rector woke after a long sleep and went out for his morning walk. The weather was fine; the wind sweeping over the fields and salt marshes had a chilly tang to it, but the air was clear. The line of low hills beyond Appledore seemed to be so close that one could reach out and touch them. The sea rolled and hissed on the beach at St Mary's Bay. The white cliffs of France shimmered in the sea spray; but this morning, thanks to what he now knew, they seemed less menacing. Breathing deeply, his lungs full of clean air, he returned home to breakfast.

He spent the morning in his study, reading Cicero and wondering how many and which of the seven would show up at the church this afternoon. His letters were a dangerous and complex double-bluff, hinting that he knew more than he said while concealing how much he really knew. Blunt must be aware by now that he was under suspicion; to Foucarmont and Fanscombe he had pretended ignorance of their own roles. It was to be expected that all three would compare notes, but the promise of information about the Twelve Apostles and the whereabouts of the dispatch bag would lure them to the church. They would come full of suspicion; but they would come.

He ate his luncheon absent-mindedly, rehearsing what he would say. He felt a pang of guilt about not inviting Amelia Chaytor, but there was a chance that this meeting could become dangerous, and she had risked enough already. She would be angry with him when she found out; but not, he hoped, for very long.

At a quarter to three, well-groomed, alert and sober, the rector let himself quietly out of the house and walked through the afternoon sun across the road to the church. Captain Shaw was waiting at the lychgate, in civilian clothes rather than his usual uniform. The change was not an improvement; his brown breeches were baggy at the knees and his black coat was wrinkled; the cravat around his neck had the merest gesture of a knot. There was an ungainly lump in his coat pocket which Hardcastle guessed was a pistol. This was probably a wise precaution. The rector had, after some debate, left his own weapon at home. He was a man of God in the house of God; it was not for him to spill blood there.

'Thank you for coming, Captain Shaw. I appreciate you taking the time from your duties to join us.'

'I'm delighted to be of assistance, Reverend. I thought it best to leave my uniform behind; if these fellows think I am here on official business, then they might take fright.'

'A sensible precaution,' said the rector approvingly.

'What do you need from me, sir?'

'First of all, I need you as a witness. I've invited several others, but the more the better. Then, you will need to apprehend these men. Lord Clavertye is joining us, and he will no doubt give you further instructions.'

'Lord Clavertye will be here?' Shaw rubbed his hands together, looking eager. Performing his duties well in front of Lord Clavertye would bring him to the deputy lord-lieutenant's attention; and having Lord Clavertye's favour would mean much to a young man like himself. There was a chance of patronage now, perhaps promotion to a better post where he could make a name for himself. They walked up the path to the church to the porch, and the rector opened the door and ushered Shaw inside.

The nave was quiet, filled with afternoon sunlight pouring through the tall windows. The rector walked towards the font at the rear of the church and turned to face the door. From here he could see the entire church; more importantly, none of the others could get behind him. He stood, clasping his hands behind his back, and Shaw took up a position too, standing silently a little closer to the door.

The door opened, and two men came in quietly; Turner, stocky and faintly pugnacious, and Dr Morley, elegant and quiet as ever. The latter nodded to Shaw and then turned to the rector. 'Well? Will they come?'

'They will come,' said the rector tranquilly. Morley nodded and stood to one side, lounging against the back of the nearest pew; Turner stood a few paces away, arms crossed over his chest.

Two minutes passed and then they heard huffing and puffing outside and Fanscombe strode in, dressed as ever in his riding coat. He stopped dead when he saw Morley. 'You!'

It struck the rector that Fanscombe sounded surprised rather than angry. 'Come in, please, Mr Fanscombe,' he said. 'Dr Morley has been invited here today for a purpose, as have you. I beg you to put aside your personal differences for the moment.' And as the justice of the peace hesitated, the rector said quietly, 'Upon my honour, Mr Fanscombe, this is vitally important. I would not have summoned you otherwise.'

They heard Blunt striding up the flagstone path and then the Customs man stood in the doorway, his beefy face hard with suspicion. 'What is this, Hardcastle? I thought this was going to be a private meeting, just you and I.'

'My apologies for the deception,' said the rector, bowing a little. 'My purpose will, I hope, become clear in time. Now, we are waiting only for His Lordship. I left word at the rectory that he was to join us here . . . and here, I fancy, he is.'

Lord Clavertye strode into the church and looked at the others. 'Hardcastle. It seems that you got your dates wrong.'

'I fear so, my lord. The smugglers chose to make their run two days early. However, all ended well.' Foucarmont was not there, but he had not really expected the Frenchman to show himself. The others were enough. 'Thank you all very much for coming,' he said gravely.

'You are most welcome,' said the doctor, 'but I think it might help if we knew why we were all really here. Your letter was a touch mysterious.'

'I said that it was time to deal with this matter for once and all,' said the rector. 'That is the truth, though I freely confess it is not the whole of the truth. We will come to the whole truth shortly, but first I have a story to tell you. You will find this story fascinating, I think, though each of you will find it so for different reasons. Are you all comfortable?'

No one spoke. 'Then I shall begin,' said the rector.

Just before New Romney Amelia Chaytor's horse threw a shoe. She would have to stop; she still had some distance to go, and could not risk the horse going lame. She drove the gig at a walking pace into the town and pulled up outside the smithy, where she stepped briskly down, unhitched the horse and led him into the yard. 'Can you help me? I need to get to St Mary, quickly.'

'Be with you in a minute, ma'am.' The blacksmith raised his head and looked at the lathered horse. 'Aye, you are in a hurry.'

She had been pushing hard all the way up from Rye, rushing to get to St Mary with her news. The blacksmith ambled slowly over to look at the horse, and she fought down the urge to scream at him to hurry. The man looked at the animal's hoof, then strolled back into the workshop and begin rummaging in a wooden box beside the forge. He pulled out a shoe, held it up to the light and squinted at it.

'Please,' said Amelia a little desperately, 'I really am in a frightful hurry. I'll pay you well.'

'Now, now, ma'am. These things have to be done right. More haste, less speed, as they say.' He picked up a bellows and puffed the forge into glowing light, then turned and began rummaging again. 'Now, where did I put my nippers?'

'Allow me to take you back four years ago, to the year 1792,' the rector said. 'The year we went to war with France. That same year, a new gang of smugglers appeared on the Channel coast. It was quite a small gang, originally twelve men, though the numbers have fluctuated over the years.'

'The Twelve Apostles,' said Morley.

The rector nodded. 'To all intents and purposes they were just another gang, smuggling small quantities of brandy and tobacco and lace from France. In fact, the cargoes carried by the Apostles were merely a ruse. What they really smuggled was secrets. M. de Foucarmont tried very hard to persuade me that they were French agents carrying important information out of England into France, and I allowed him to think that I believed him. In fact, I already knew the truth.'

'Which is?' asked Turner.

'The truth is that the Twelve Apostles are British agents. They smuggle secrets from France to England, not vice versa. They are confidential agents employed by our government, at the very highest level.'

The men in the church shifted, looking at each other. The rector watched their faces. 'Last October, the Apostles were attacked shortly after they landed in Kent,' he said. 'They realised that their enemies must have known they were coming, that information about their movements and activities was leaking out. They launched an investigation of their own, hoping to plug the leak. Their leader, who went by the name of Peter, had a connection with a former Treasury agent now working with the Customs service at Deal. His name was Curtius Miller.'

Turner let out a little sigh. Lord Clavertye nodded slowly. Morley watched the rector closely, eyes never leaving his face. Blunt had begun to perspire.

'Miller agreed to help the Twelve Apostles. In April he went to France, presumably in disguise, where he worked with another agent connected with the Apostles, a young man named Jacques Morel, code-named Paul. Morel was a French emigré who had fled the excesses of the Revolution, and been recruited by Peter to work as a runner and watcher.

'The Apostles were summoned to make a run in early May. At the eleventh hour, Miller and Paul learned that once again the secret of the run had been betrayed, that the Apostles were to be ambushed while crossing the Marsh. Miller hurried back across the Channel to rejoin the Customs, with a view to warning the Apostles once they landed.

'A day or so later, Morel learned an even more horrifying truth. One of the Apostles, who went by the name of Mark, had turned traitor and was feeding information to the French. Desperate to get this news to his comrades, he stole a small boat and sailed single-handed across the Channel on the night of 3rd May. He attempted to reach Dymchurch, where he knew Miller would be, but the currents took him off course and brought him to St Mary's Bay around dawn. The swells near the English coast were rough and he overset his boat, but managed to swim ashore. Two ladies from the village saw him soon after landing, and testified that he was soaking wet. And Mrs Chaytor said there were traces of corrosion in his watch, as if it had been immersed in salt water.'

He watched the others closely now. 'Morel made his way to St Mary in the Marsh and, needing shelter, knocked at the door of New Hall. Did he tell you who he really was, Mr Fanscombe?'

'No,' said Fanscombe. He looked watchful, but not concerned. 'I recognised him when he came to the house, we had met before. But I knew him only as an emigré gentleman. All the rest of this is news to me.'

'What story did he tell you?' asked Clavertye.

'He said he was down from London on a holiday, my lord, and had been out sailing and overturned his boat. We took him in, of course, gave him dry clothes and a bed; it's what one does. Then he said he wanted to try to recover his boat. He was a pleasant young chap and we got on well, so I told him to stay on until his affairs were in order. He stayed for a couple of days, then went off to London.'

'No, Mr Fanscombe. That is not true. Jacques Morel did not go to London.'

Turner was tense; he had guessed the truth. 'How do you know?' asked Morley.

'Because I saw him,' said the rector tersely. 'So did you.'

'What happened?' asked Captain Shaw, his brow furrowed.

'M. de Foucarmont was also staying with the Fanscombes at the time. I invited him to join us today, but it would appear that he has declined the invitation. A pity, as I am sure he could shed much light on what happened next. However, since he is not here, I shall tell you what I know about him. To begin with, Foucarmont is not Mrs Fanscombe's brother.'

There was a hiss of indrawn breath from someone; that was Turner, suddenly putting two and two together. 'Fanscombe?' said Lord Clavertye sharply. 'Is this true?'

The justice of the peace held up his hands. 'Upon my honour, my lord, I cannot credit what I am hearing! Not my wife's brother? Are you suggesting she would deceive me . . .'

His eyes fell on Dr Morley, who gave a little cough of embarrassment. 'Hardcastle, I think that once again you must explain. How do you know he is not Mrs Fanscombe's brother?'

'I know he is not Mrs Fanscombe's brother because he told me so,' said the rector impatiently. 'Morley, if you are going to interrupt me every minute to ask how I know things, we shall be here until midnight. When I say that I know something, believe me: I *know* it.'

Morley made a dismissive gesture with his hand. Fanscombe, still staring at the doctor, swallowed suddenly. He too had begun to perspire.

'Foucarmont is a French spy,' the rector said quietly. And into the chill silence that fell over the church, he added, 'He is also a ruthless killer. It was his rifle that ended the life of Jacques Morel, the man who was shot on the doorstep of the rectory. That is what I meant, doctor, when I said that you had seen him.'

He had their full attention now; Morley's eyes remained riveted on his face. 'What I do *not* yet know is how Foucarmont discovered who Morel was. Perhaps Morel himself said or did something that gave the game away. At all events, Foucarmont set a trap for him. I suspect that a false message arrived from the Twelve Apostles, asking Morel to meet them at the looker's hut. Morel went there, all trusting. He was met instead by Foucarmont and his confederates. Morel was beaten, and his pockets were emptied and searched for clues. When he refused to tell what he knew, he was locked in the back room of the hut.'

'Why?' asked Clavertye. 'What did they want from him? The timing and location of the run?'

'No, my lord, thanks to the traitor Mark they knew that already. They wanted to interrogate Morel more thoroughly, find out how he had learned about them and what else he knew. But time was running out; the Twelve Apostles were coming. Morel was locked in the hut and left until they could deal with him at greater leisure.'

'Knowing that the Apostles had been betrayed and desperate to give warning, Morel broke free of his bonds and kicked down the door. Foucarmont had left the building, for whatever reason; we may hypothesise that he had gone to help with arrangements for the ambush, but it is of no importance. Morel began to run across country to the east, hoping to find the Apostles and warn them. But Foucarmont returned, found he was missing, and began to hunt him down.'

The rector sighed. 'Poor Morel never had a chance. Among other things, Mrs Fanscombe told me that Foucarmont is a very keen huntsman and a superb tracker. Even in the darkness and the wind, he tracked his man over the Marsh like an avenging fury. One of his proudest possessions, which he had brought to England with him, was a German hunting rifle. When he caught up with Morel, the young man was knocking at my door. I think Morel must have heard something behind him, something that caused him to turn around. Foucarmont was standing in my garden by the elm trees, and he raised his rifle and shot Morel through the chest.'

'He did not die immediately,' said Morley quietly.

'No. I deceived you on that score, doctor, and you also, my lord. Morel lived long enough to breathe his last words in my ear. I did not understand his words, not at first, but they were enough to convince me that this was no ordinary murder.'

'What did he say? And why did you not tell me?' demanded Clavertye.

'Those words were a dying man's confession, my lord. What passed there was between us alone, and God.' There were some things about the case that not everyone needed to know. Clavertye subsided, a little huffily.

'Meanwhile,' the rector continued, 'a little way to the east of St Mary, the second half of the tragedy was played out. Curtius Miller was with Blunt's men waiting in ambush on the Marsh. When the Apostles came close, he called out to warn them. Another man from the Customs shot him through the belly, and he died. But, he did not die in vain. The Apostles heard the warning, and made their escape.'

'Rubbish!' shouted Blunt. 'He shot himself! It was an accident, for Christ's sake!'

'It was not. Dr Morley has confirmed that the wound could not have been self-inflicted. And in any case, we have a witness who saw another man shoot Miller in the belly.'

Blunt, glaring at Morley, jerked his head around at this. 'Who?'

The rector ignored him. 'I shall skip over many of the remaining details, for I am sure that you know them already, or have guessed. The Twelve Apostles learned the identity of Mark and killed him; his was the third body, the one found in the churchyard. Meanwhile, Foucarmont received fresh orders from France, insisting that the Twelve Apostles must be stopped. The loss of Mark was a blow, but Foucarmont's chief, who I will come to in a moment, undoubtedly has many sources of information up and down the coast, and these sources collected rumours and fed them back to him. Foucarmont and his allies laid their plans.

'Then the local smugglers moved their run from the sixth of June to the fourth, and the Twelve Apostles followed suit. When Foucarmont learned of this, he sent a messenger to warn Blunt.'

'Damn you, he never did!' said Blunt sharply.

'Oh, yes, he did. Eliza Fanscombe was the messenger. Dean Cornewall was present at the meeting too, and I am sure he will swear to the matter. Dean Cornewall is rather anxious for some credit with the authorities, just at the moment.'

Ignoring Clavertye's stare, the rector went on. 'So we come to the night of the fourth of June. Juddery attacked you, Blunt, because I told him to.'

Blunt stared at him. 'Have you taken leave of your fucking senses?'

'Not in the slightest. You see, Blunt, by then I knew the truth. I knew you were more than just Foucarmont's unwitting tool; you were in on the entire plot. That is why *you*, Blunt, slaughtered Curtius Miller in cold blood; not just to stop him from warning the Twelve Apostles, but because he knew or had guessed that you were a traitor. And so, on Saturday night I saw you were about to ambush the Twelve Apostles, and I told Juddery to stop you. He believed that he was acting in the name of the king. Lord Clavertye will judge whether I acted correctly.'

Clavertye looked at the Customs man, his barrister's face firmly in place. 'Well, Blunt? What have you to say? Why did you turn traitor?'

'This is shit,' said Blunt contemptuously. 'This old fool doesn't know what the hell he is talking about. He's so drunk that half the time he doesn't know what day it is. Has anyone smelled his breath now?'

'If Mr Blunt won't answer, then I will,' said the rector. 'For years now, Blunt has been taking bribes from the smuggling gangs all along the coast to allow them free passage. Foucarmont learned of this, and blackmailed him into assisting the plot. The Twelve Apostles used to pay him too, but Foucarmont forced him to betray them. That is one of the reasons why Blunt is so frightened of the Apostles; they have threatened several times to kill him.'

Blunt heard him out, suddenly and surprisingly calm. In fact he even grinned, disquietingly, pulling back his fleshy lips over yellow teeth. 'You'll never prove a single damned word of this,' he said, glancing around the group. 'Never.'

'We will,' said the rector calmly. 'We have evidence, Blunt, witnesses who will testify that you took bribes, and as I said, we also have a witness to the killing of Miller. Most damning of all, though, will be the evidence given against you by your confederates in this plot.'

'And who might those be?' asked Clavertye.

'The Dean of Canterbury, who though not a traitor himself, knows enough to implicate you. And then of course there is Foucarmont, when he is caught.'

'That assumes Foucarmont *will* be caught,' Morley observed.

'He will, said Clavertye stonily, and then added, 'but it may take some time. Who else do you have, Hardcastle?'

'Who else? Well, I am sure you must have known we would come to you eventually, Mr Fanscombe.'

She was tired when she returned to St Mary in the Marsh, but she drove past her own house and went directly to the rectory. As she turned into the drive, she noticed the lychgate of the church standing open.

Stepping down from the seat of the gig, she knocked at the rectory door. Mrs Kemp opened it a few moments later, gazing in surprise at a tall woman with flushed face and hair coming down from under her bonnet. 'Good afternoon, Mrs Chaytor,' she said curtseying. 'I fear Reverend Hardcastle is not at home. Was he expecting you?'

'No,' said Mrs Chaytor, 'Do you know when he will return?'

'No, ma'am. He went over to the church, and gave orders that he and the others were not to be disturbed.'

Alarm bells began to tingle at the back of her mind. What had the daft man done now? 'What others, Mrs Kemp?'

'Why, His Lordship and Dr Morley, and Mr Blunt and Mr Fanscombe, and that Turner fellow. And Captain Shaw.'

'Oh, dear God,' said Amelia Chaytor, and she felt herself turning white. 'Oh, dear God, dear God.'

'Mrs Chaytor! Whatever is the matter?'

'Go inside, Mrs Kemp, and lock the doors and windows. Do not let anyone in, except for the rector or myself.'

'Oh, Mrs Chaytor! Where are you going?'

'To prevent another murder,' said Mrs Chaytor.

Fanscombe was flushed with fear and anger. 'I swear to you, Foucarmont deceived me. I knew nothing of his true purpose.'

'That is a lie, Fanscombe. Yes, he used you; yes, he blackmailed you; but you acted in full knowledge of who he was and what he did. You are in this up to your neck. It was you who bribed the coroner. It was you who passed on messages to Blunt; using your own daughter as messenger, for heaven's sake! It was you who gave orders to Captain Shaw. Most of all, you provided Foucarmont with cover. Your house was the base for Foucarmont's operations against the Twelve Apostles over the past year. You harboured an enemy spy under your roof, and you knew full well that you were doing so. As a result, you have ruined not only yourself but very probably your wife and daughter as well.'

'Leave my family out of this!'

'Leave them out? Why not? It is a simple enough matter. Make a full confession and sign it, and they will not be troubled again. Miss Fanscombe's role need never be made public. Otherwise, I very much fear that Lord Clavertye's officers will drag her reputation through the mud. A pity about Eliza. A young girl, with so much promise. So much life ahead of her, and now all wasted.'

'My God,' said Morley, disgusted. '*Now* who is the blackmailer?'

'Young, with so much promise,' repeated the rector, iron in his voice. 'Just like Jacques Morel. He was about the same age as your daughter, wouldn't you say, Fanscombe? The man to whom you gave hospitality, and then helped to murder? When Foucarmont captured Morel and locked him up, he was not acting alone.'

'Damn you!' said Fanscombe venomously.

Strangely enough, it was Blunt who intervened. 'Oh, let him talk. Once again, he can prove nothing. This is all just hot air.'

'It is true that the principal witnesses against you are your wife and daughter,' said the rector, 'and of course, neither can be compelled to testify against you in court. But they *can* help to convict others, and those

others, in order to save their own necks, will be only too happy to implicate you, Fanscombe.'

Fanscombe made to speak, but Blunt stopped him with a gesture.
'Others?' said Dr Morley. 'How many others? How widespread is this
conspiracy?'

'As of yet, we do not know. Investigating the full extent of it is likely to
keep Lord Clavertye and his officers busy for months. But we do know the
name of one other man who was part of the conspiracy. Indeed, he was
the man at its very heart.'

'Foucarmont,' said Turner, puzzled.

'No, not Foucarmont. He was the man of action, the killer brought in
to ensure the swift dispatch of the Twelve Apostles and any others who
stood in his way. But Foucarmont had a master, the man who first summoned him down to the Marsh and then gave him direction. It was this
man who identified early on that Blunt and Fanscombe were corrupt and
could be bought or blackmailed. It was this man who collected information and learned where the Apostles would make their next run, and told
Foucarmont when and where they would come. It is this man who is
most dangerous of all.'

'And do you know who he is?' asked Clavertye.

'I know. I have had my suspicions for some time, but now I know. You
played the game well, sir, but you have reached the end of the road. Surely
now, Dr Morley, the gallows awaits you.'

Late afternoon in St Mary in the Marsh. The sun was warm, despite the
keen edge to the breeze. Sheep bleated in the nearby fields. Nearer at
hand, bees hummed around banks of flowers outside the neat cottages.

In the common room of the Star, men sat drinking quietly. They knew
something was in the wind; the arrival in the village of Blunt and Lord
Clavertye had not passed unnoticed. They sat over their tankards and
discussed recent events in low and ominous tones.

The door of the common room opened hard, bouncing off the wall
with a bang. Startled, the men looked up to see a tall, white-faced woman
in dusty clothes, a cloak slung off one shoulder, gloves on her hands and

boots on her feet. In one hand she held a long-barrelled pistol, pointed at the floor.

'Answer me this,' said Amelia Chaytor, her voice rasping with strain and anger. 'Which one of you is Yorkshire Tom?'

Morley uncrossed his legs and stood up a little straighter. 'I am inclined to think Blunt may be right,' he said drily. 'Hardcastle, the drink has affected your wits. I have warned you to cut down.'

'You have played your part well,' said the rector steadily. 'Very, very well. You are an astonishing actor. You deceived me completely for a long time. The evidence of your involvement was there all along, and yet I was so taken in by your performance that I overlooked it.'

'What evidence?' asked Turner, puzzled. Morley turned and gave him a look of disgust.

'You were called down to New Romney to examine Miller's body,' the rector continued. 'I did wonder why, but never really pursued the matter. But of course, Blunt called you because he needed someone to corroborate the story that Miller had died by accident.'

'You are forgetting,' said Morley, 'that when you and Mrs Chaytor advanced the theory that Miller had in fact been murdered, I supported you.'

'I am not forgetting, doctor. You saw that we had worked out the truth, and realised that it would be foolish to pretend. And of course, your evidence did not incriminate anyone. Your confederates remained in the clear.'

'This is ridiculous.'

'And, of course,' said the rector, 'I should also have worked out the truth once I learned the details of your affair with Mrs Fanscombe. You should have been more careful there. Miss Godfrey and Miss Roper have eyes like hawks, and memories of infinite capacity. They thought it perfectly ordinary that you should visit New Hall for your assignations when Fanscombe was absent, but more than a little odd that you should do while he was at home; which you did, frequently. They assumed that Fanscombe was complaisant. Of course, he was not.'

'I damned well was not,' said Fanscombe bitterly.

'Your frequent visits, therefore, had nothing to do with your affair. You went there to meet with Foucarmont, and also to ensure that Fanscombe and Blunt carried out their orders.'

'This is ridiculous. I am a doctor. The Fanscombes are patients of mine. Of course I call at their house, as any doctor would.'

'Eugénie Fanscombe will also testify against you. Yes, I know; a woman wronged. Who will believe her? But if the servants at New Hall corroborate her story, well then; it would be a different matter. But let us move on. You fancy yourself as a ladies' man, don't you, doctor?'

'I will not even dignify that with a response.'

'You like to make yourself attractive to women. Among other things, you use pastilles to sweeten your breath. Liquorice-flavoured pastilles, yes?'

'What are you driving at?' demanded Clavertye.

'Last week, someone tried to kill me outside the Star. A man seized me from behind and began to throttle me. The assailant's face was close beside my head, and I could smell his breath. The killer used breath pastilles, the same ones that Dr Morley uses.'

'Oh, for God's sake!' said the doctor. 'Many people use breath pastilles. This is nonsense!'

'You were interrupted – obviously – before you could complete the task. But you were also in New Romney the night of the run. You mingled with the crowd at the Ship, and you spiked my beer with neat spirit to render me incapable so that you could finish me off later. Then, when I went outside, you tried to kill me once again. I don't *know* that it was you that clubbed me over the head, but I do have a witness who will put you at the Ship that night, and saw you go outside after I departed.'

This last was a bluff. If Morley called it, demanded to know who the witness was, then he doubted he could sustain the lie. He held Morley's gaze steadily; and it was the doctor who cracked.

'My dear reverend,' he murmured. 'You seem to have an answer for everything, don't you?' And from his pocket he produced a pistol, which he cocked and aimed directly at Hardcastle's heart.

No one moved or spoke for a moment. Then Clavertye said sharply, 'Morley! Drop that pistol!'

'No,' said Morley. 'I don't think I shall.'

Clavertye took a fast step forward, hand reaching into his coat pocket and pulling out his own pistol to cover Morley, but he halted as he saw the doctor's finger tighten on the trigger. Now Blunt had a pistol in his hand too. 'If any of you make a move towards me, I shall shoot the rector,' said Morley.

Everyone else stood still. 'Blunt, Fanscombe, you can do whatever you want,' said the doctor, 'but I am not staying here to face the music. I've a boat ready and waiting at St Mary's Bay. On this wind, I shall be in France in a few hours. Do you care to join me?'

Blunt nodded at once; Fanscombe looked irresolute, but then nodded too.

'One question before you go,' said the rector. 'Why, Morley?'

The doctor paused, pistol still levelled at Hardcastle. 'Conviction,' he said finally. 'Fanscombe and Blunt were lured into this business by money, but I have always believed. I am what they call an English Jacobin. I am one of many hundreds of such; I have correspondents and sympathisers all over the country. I believe in liberty, equality and the brotherhood of man. I want to see a Tree of Liberty in Parliament Square. I want to see the guillotine lop off the heads of King George and his ghastly brood. I want to see England become a republic. And I will see it,' he added. 'It will just take a little longer, now.'

'No,' said the rector. 'Even if, God forbid, that day does come, you will not live to see it. My lord?'

Clavertye nodded, his pistol still pointed at Morley. 'Captain Shaw, if you please. Arrest these men.'

Silence fell for half a dozen heartbeats, and then Shaw smiled. 'Sorry, my lord,' he said. 'I'm afraid I cannot comply.' And he raised his pistol too, and while Morley continued to cover the rector, the captain aimed the weapon at Lord Clavertye, still standing with his own pistol in hand pointed at the doctor.

How long they stood in that little tableau the rector never knew; afterward he realised it was probably no more than two or three seconds, but at the time it seemed like eternity.

'Shaw,' he said quietly. 'Why did I not guess?'

The young captain laughed. 'I reckon I gulled you pretty thoroughly, Reverend Hardcastle. The only time I slipped up was when you came to Appledore. When I found out you had talked to my sergeant, I thought I was undone. But once I came down and saw you, and you accepted my explanation so easy, well; then I knew I was home.'

'Then why betray yourself now?' asked Turner, puzzled.

'Well, I'm backed into a corner, aren't I? If I arrest my friends, they will of course implicate me. If I let them go, people will ask why, and then start looking hard at me, and there'll be some things they might find that wouldn't do me any good. Nothing serious, a few bits of money and army supplies that have gone missing here and there, but enough to get me into pretty hot water. So, doctor, I'm all finished. I hope there is room for one more in that boat of yours.'

'Welcome aboard, Mr Shaw. Now, gentlemen. What do we do with these three? If we are to make the boat safely, we need a head start. We cannot risk them getting loose and raising the alarm. So what do you reckon we should do?'

'Easy,' said Blunt. 'We shoot them.'

'I say,' said Fanscombe, alarmed. 'Do we need to do that? Can't we just lock them in the vestry?'

All of the others stood with their backs to the church door. Only the rector could see that the door was opening, very, very slowly.

'Too risky,' said Morley. 'If they manage to get free and sound the alarm before we get to the coast, we could still be caught. I think you're right, Blunt.'

The church door was open about a foot now, still swinging slowly. 'Are you mad?' demanded Clavertye. 'Do you know who I am? You cannot kill a peer of the realm and expect to get away with it!'

'Oh, we can,' said Morley, 'given that we will be in France by the time your bodies are discovered. All right, Shaw, Blunt. Ready?'

'Ready. Let's kill them,' said Blunt, and he grinned again and raised his pistol and pointed it at Clavertye.

'No one is killing anyone,' said a light steely voice from the door.

*

Slowly they turned, and saw the cloaked and booted woman standing just inside the church door with a pistol level and rock steady in her hands, pointed at Shaw. The heavy oak door hid her from the rest of the church, but the men around the font could all see her clearly. Involuntarily, the rector found himself glancing at the altar. St Mary, Star of the Sea; Stella Maris, who comes to the rescue of those without hope. Oh, God, we give thanks.

It was not yet over.

Shaw shifted, and then froze as the woman's pistol levelled at his head. 'Do not move,' said Mrs Chaytor. 'I may be a weak and feeble woman, but I can shoot the eye out of an ace of spaces at twenty yards. Lay your weapons on the floor and step back from them.'

'No,' said Morley, and he smiled and spun lightly to cover the woman with his own weapon. 'You cannot stop us, Mrs Chaytor. I am sorry about this. I don't like the idea of killing a woman, but needs must.'

'You would not dare.'

'I would dare a great many things in the name of liberty, Mrs Chaytor. And now—'

He never finished the sentence. In the confusion, everyone had forgotten about Turner, and now he sprang, leaping like a tiger onto Morley's back and dragging down his gun arm. The pistol fired with a crash that reverberated in the rafters, the ball smashing into the floor and ricocheting harmlessly into the plaster wall. A haze of smoke filled the lower end of the nave; through it, Turner and Morley could be seen wrestling on the floor.

Another crash; Blunt turned to confront Mrs Chaytor and in that instant she fired a precise shot that smashed the pistol from his hand and sent it spinning wrecked across the floor. Shaw turned towards her too, and then a third pistol barked as the Deputy Lord-Lieutenant of Kent spun on one heel and shot the captain through the upper arm. Shaw screamed and dropped his weapon, staggering to his knees with his arm spouting blood. Fanscombe panicked and ran for the door; Mrs Chaytor blocked his way and in another two strides Clavertye was behind the justice of the peace, grasping his shoulder with a grip of iron and hurling him to the floor. In the midst of the smoke Blunt stood stunned, disarmed. Then his

nerves shattered; he too fell to his knees, clutching at his hand, face twitching and body shivering.

As the smoke cleared, Turner dragged Morley to his feet. The doctor was
strong, but the painter was stronger still; Morley struggled for a moment
longer and then stood, arms pinned painfully behind his back.

'There it is,' he gasped. 'Outwitted at last, by a woman and a clergyman.
The shame of it . . . Still, I don't think I shall be going to the gallows any
time very soon.'

'You seem very sure of yourself,' grated Clavertye.

'Oh, I am, my lord, I am. I have plenty to offer in exchange for my
liberty. I told you, I have correspondents and connections with the
Jacobin movement all over England. Including some in some surprisingly high places.'

'And you would sell them out to secure your own freedom?' asked
Turner incredulously. 'What happened to belief? To liberty, equality and
fraternity?'

'They're all very well,' said the doctor, 'but, they are of little use if I do
not live to see them. Bring a clerk, my lord, and a pen and plenty of paper.
You'll find my confession most interesting, I am sure.'

The rector looked back to the altar. He was just in time to see a flicker
of movement, and then a rifle spoke death. Smoke flared around the altar.
Dr Morley staggered as the bullet struck him in the side just below his
right arm. Shot through the heart, he fell to his knees and then face forward onto the floor.

A man ran from behind the altar. He flung himself through the vestry
door before anyone could move, and seconds later there came the sound
of shattering glass. That was the vestry window, the rector knew; once
through it, Foucarmont could make his escape through open country.
But then from outside there came a sound of scuffling, an oath and a cry
of despair. Footsteps could be heard running all around the church; and
then men came pouring through the church door, masked men carrying
heavy wooden cudgels. Their leader bowed to Mrs Chaytor.

'All secure and shipshape, ma'am. We have the building surrounded.
We caught the Frenchy trying to slip out of the vestry window and we
have him safe. Who do we take in here?'

'Him, him and him,' said Amelia, pointing at Blunt, Fanscombe and Shaw. 'Yorkshire Tom, do you realise that this is the first time in history that a smuggler has arrested a Customs officer in the name of the law?'

'We live in strange times, ma'am,' said the smuggler, sweeping off his hood and mask to reveal the pockmarked features of Joshua Stemp.

21

The Return to Mundanity

'I should scold you,' said Mrs Chaytor. 'Very severely.'

They stood by the churchyard wall, looking out through the late sun-light towards Appledore and the distant hills. Behind them, the shadows in the churchyard grew longer.

It was over. Morley's body had been carried away and Shaw's wound attended to; then he, Foucarmont, Blunt and Fanscombe had been bound hand and foot, loaded into a hastily summoned cart and taken away to Ashford. A heavy guard of armed smugglers led by Yorkshire Tom and the painter Mr Turner, all temporarily sworn in as constables, had accompanied them.

Clavertye had briskly taken over the investigation, thanked the rector for his good services, thanked Mrs Chaytor too in a manner that was half courtly and half embarrassed, and departed to continue his inquiries at New Hall and Morley's house. The two of them stood alone in the evening peace, side by side. In the middle distance, a few rooks cawed.

'You should indeed scold me,' acknowledged the rector. 'And I should have sent word to you and told you of my plans. On the other hand, my dear, it was rather useful having you turn up unexpectedly and rescue us.'

'I was nearly too late.'

'But you weren't. In fact, you were right on time.'

'That does not disguise the fact that you were a damned fool.' There was a tenderness in her voice that belied her words. He wondered how to thank her, and then looked at her face and realised he did not need to. She understood.

'How did you know that I might be in danger?' he asked.

'I discovered in Rye that both Morley and Shaw were in on the plot. You will recall that I went down to Merriwether Hall to see what I could learn about Fanscombe, and whether he had a mistress in Rye. My friend Mrs Merriwether checked with the ladies' gossip society, and no one had any recollection of him having a lover there. So I was just about to give it up as a bad job and return home, when I remembered that Miss Godfrey and Miss Roper said that Dr Morley used to take Eugénie to a house near the town.'

'And you found the house?'

'Mrs Merriwether did. Under that cheerful exterior, she has the instincts of a bloodhound. We located the house, more of a fisherman's cottage in truth, and learned that it was owned by a Mr Darby, which is I assume is an alias for Morley himself.'

'We'll find out when Clavertye goes through Morley's papers.'

'We also discovered that Fanscombe was staying there, alone. We paid a couple of boys to keep watch on the cottage, and this morning they reported that a boat had come up to the beach nearby in the small hours, and that Fanscombe had gone out to meet it. They couldn't see much, for it was very dark, but they heard a good deal of shouting, most of it in a language they assumed to be French. They thought also that they heard Fanscombe pleading with someone. Then he ran back up the beach and locked himself in the cottage, and the boat pushed off and was gone.'

'So that's it,' the rector mused. 'That was how they were in contact with France. Boats landing in secret on a dark night. Morley must have used the house for meetings with his French masters. Presumably the plan was to take the papers from the Twelve Apostles and hand them over to the men in the boat, who would take them back to France. The shouting began when Fanscombe had to confess he did not have the papers. I wonder why Morley sent Fanscombe instead of going himself?'

'You will recall that Morley was quite busy just then, trying to kill you. He preferred to do that job himself, rather than trusting Fanscombe or Foucarmont.'

'I never did like him,' said the rector in an injured tone.

'Nor he you, it would seem. Then, just as I was packing up and preparing to leave, one of the boys brought another message. A man had ridden down to the cottage and spent a long time talking with Fanscombe. From the description they gave, it was very easy to recognise Captain Shaw.'

'Once met, never forgotten.'

'It was clear that, if he knew about the house, Shaw might also be involved in the plot. You had begun to trust Shaw and I knew, instinctively I suppose, that you might now be in danger.'

'Women's intuition?' he offered.

'If you use that phrase again, I really shall scold you. I drove back as quickly as I could. You can imagine my feelings when Mrs Kemp told me what you had done. In desperation, I turned to the only people I could think of. The smugglers.'

'I don't how you persuaded Joshua Stemp to give up his beer and come to help me.'

'He is fond of you. Also, I had a pistol. While he was rounding up his mates, I decided to come on ahead and see if you had managed to get into trouble yet. Which, of course, you had.'

'I have a habit of getting into trouble, my dear. You must have realised that.'

'If I didn't before, I do now,' she said with gentle asperity. 'Two things still elude me. Why was Foucarmont hiding behind the altar? And why did he shoot the doctor, of all people, and not one of us?'

'Ironically, I suspect that it was Morley who ordered him to hide there with his rifle. He and the others were armed, of course, but he wanted a card up his sleeve, someone to cover their retreat if trouble developed. So Foucarmont entered the church in advance of us all, and hid there and waited ready to pull Morley's fat out of the fire if necessary. My dear, it is a good thing that you remained standing in the doorway and did not walk out into the room. If you had moved out from behind the protection of that oak door, I suspect Foucarmont would have shot you.'

She nodded. 'Yes,' she said without flinching. 'I expect he would have done so without hesitation. Then the melee developed, and for a while there was too much smoke to see down the nave. But once the smoke cleared he could have shot anyone: you, Clavertye. Me.'

'But by then, who was the most dangerous person in the room? Morley himself. He had just offered to betray the English Jacobins to the authorities. That would also mean the end of the French espionage network in Britain. It would take months, even years to rebuild that network. Foucarmont had one shot, and he used it to silence Morley before he could destroy everything. Then he tried to escape, and would have succeeded had you not had the resource to call in Yorkshire Tom and his friends.'

The sun was setting beyond Appledore. She sighed. 'So it is over. A month of madness ends, and peace descends. I suppose that now we go back to our mundane little lives.'

'There is a great deal to be said for mundanity,' he said, and they both smiled.

Afterword

We can only apologise to the residents of St Mary in the Marsh, whose village we have rearranged and re-developed without so much as a by-your-leave from them. The church of St Mary the Virgin and the Star Inn exist, though we have rearranged their details a little; the present-day church has no vestry in the east end or near the altar, and the door opens in the opposite direction. Some of the details have been borrowed from other churches. We have located the Star further south than it is in the real village. The sewer, or drainage ditch, that runs through the centre of St Mary today does not appear in our story.

The rectory, New Hall, Sandy House, Rightways and other private homes are entirely figments of our imagination. We have at least been relatively faithful in our description of the surroundings. The coastline of Romney Marsh was a little different in 1796 from today; St Mary's Bay was a slight indentation in the coastline, and there was also a large shallow bay extending inland between Greatstone and Littlestone.

There was an invasion scare in Kent in the winter of 1795–6 when it was suggested that the Directory in Paris, having cemented its power by putting down a royalist coup d'état in October 1795, would proceed to invade Britain, which had partly backed the coup. In fact the British government – provided with intelligence through sources such as the Twelve Apostles – had already realised that the main French offensive in 1796 would be directed at Austria and took no further steps to defend the Kentish coast. Not until Napoleon's army was camped on the coast around Boulogne in 1803–4 did the government begin to construct defences such as the Dymchurch Martello towers and the Royal Military Canal.

Blunt, Fanscombe and Shaw were all convicted of treason in the summer of 1796, and hanged. Foucarmont was tried on charges of espionage, but despite overwhelming evidence against him, the jury brought in a verdict of not guilty and he walked from the court a free man. Very shortly after, he disappeared from view.

Mrs Fanscombe cleared her possessions out of New Hall and departed from the Marsh, taking Eliza with her.

Lord Clavertye had hoped to receive the thanks of Parliament for his role in personally closing down an important French spy operation, but in this he was disappointed. On orders from A Very High Place, the entire affair was declared to be a secret never to be spoken of. His Lordship did however receive an invitation to 10 Downing Street, where the prime minister personally shook him by the hand.

Joseph Mallord William Turner went on to become one of Britain's greatest artists. His paintings of north Kent and the Thames Estuary are well known, but strangely, none of his pictures of Romney Marsh have ever been exhibited.

The Very Reverend Folliott Cornewall resigned as Dean of Canterbury and moved to the West Country. He went on to become Bishop of Hereford.

The rector and Mrs Chaytor will return.

Acknowledgements

Truly it is said that no one writes a book alone, and never has that truth been more clearly demonstrated than in the case of this book. We would not be here without our splendid agents, Heather Adams and Mike Bryan from HMA Literary Agency, who put us in touch with Zaffre and guided us into the – to us – brave new world of fiction publishing. Their comments on early drafts have been invaluable; but much, much more that, they provided a steady flow of encouragement, advice and reassurance that we nervous debutant novelists badly needed. Thanks, both of you; and it has been fun working with another husband-and-wife team, too.

Our thanks also to everyone at Zaffre and at Bonnier, who took our text files and turned them into a book we are rather proud of. Particular thanks must go to Mark Smith and Jane Harris, who believed in this project and were willing to take us on, and further to Jane for treating us to a delicious lunch soon after signing – publishing lunches still exist; who knew? – to Kate Parkin for helping us get our house in order in advance of publishing and, again, for a tremendous amount of encouragement and support; to the unfailingly helpful Kate Ballard for coming in and taking us smoothly through to the launch; and especially to Joel Richardson for being there on the other end of the email and patiently answering even the most naïve of questions. Partway through the publishing process, Joel grew a beard. We acknowledge that we may be partly responsible for this. Seriously, Joel; you were terrific and it's been a pleasure working with you. Thanks also to David Watson for his careful editing of the text, and to Claire Johnson-Creek, Annabel Wright and Charlotte Norman for their hard work in production and proofreading.

Thanks must go to the many people in Romney Marsh who helped us and gave us information and advice. Especially we would like to thank Liz Grant at the Kent Wildlife Trust visitor centre, which happens to be almost on the route of Hardcastle's walks from St Mary in the Marsh to the sea; the very kind owner of Mary's Tea Room in Dungeness; and the man who was out walking his dog while we examined the bridge over the New Sewer between St Mary and New Romney. We're so sorry we never got your name, sir, but you were a mine of information.

Rachel Richards at Chameleon Studies has done us proud with her website design, and she, Siobhan Williams and Ian and Jane Colbourne kindly offered their views on the cover design. Many thanks to Gary Beaumont for turning our scribbles on paper into a map. Thanks must go also to Jim, Katharine, Jane and Alex, who looked at some of the early chapters and gave us very helpful comments, and to Thomas Wood, who gave up a large portion of his weekend to read the proofs (well, it was raining). Many thanks as well to Dartmoor National Park for providing the splendid surroundings for some of our editing sessions.

Finally, thanks to all our family and friends who encouraged us and cheered us on. As the Reverend Hardcastle might have put it, just before reaching for another glass of port: bless you all, for your kindness and friendship have made our labours worthwhile.

West Devon, 2016